DEADLY DÉCISIONS

It is a beautiful spring day and in the quiet woods of the FBI's headquarters at Quantico, forensic anthropologist, Dr Temperance Brennan, is teaching a body recovery course when she is urgently called back to Quebec. A gruesome duty awaits her: a biker war is raging and two of the foot soldiers have blown themselves up. The only person qualified to make sense of what remains is Tempe. The body of a nine-year-old girl is wheeled into the morgue, slain in biker crossfire. Fired with anger and a sense of injustice, Tempe vows to lend her skills to fight the clubs. She enters the dark underworld of the bikers—*les motards*—where, pitted against dangerous outlaws and organised crime, she becomes increasingly vulnerable. Will she make a wrong decision—a deadly decision?

DEADLY DÉCISIONS

Kathy Reichs

CHIVERS PRESS
BATH

First published 2000
by
William Heinemann
This Large Print edition published by
Chivers Press
by arrangement with
Random House Group Ltd
2000

ISBN 0 7540 1464 9

British Library Cataloguing in Publication Data available

Printed and bound in Great Britain by
REDWOOD BOOKS, Trowbridge, Wiltshire

Dedicated with love
to the Carolina Beach Bunch

ACKNOWLEDGMENTS

Many people helped me in writing *Deadly Décisions*. Particularly patient were my colleagues in forensic science and law enforcement. I owe heartfelt thanks to Sergeant Guy Ouelette, Division of Organized Crime Unit, Sûreté du Québec, and to Captain Steven Chabot, Sergent Yves Trudel, Caporal Jacques Morin, and Constable Jean Ratté at Opération Carcajou in Montreal.

Among the Communauté Urbaine de Montréal Police, Lieutenant-détective Jean-François Martin, Division des Crimes Majeurs; Sergent-détective Johanne Bérubé, Division Agressions Sexuelles; and Commandant André Bouchard, Moralité, Alcool, et Stupéfiant, Centre Opérational Sud, patiently answered my questions and explained the functioning of police units. Special thanks must go to Sergent-détective Stephen Rudman, Superviseur, Analyse et Liaison, Centre Opérational Sud, who answered many questions, provided maps, and took me through the jail.

Of my colleagues at the Laboratoire de Sciences Judiciaires et de Médecine Légale I must thank Dr. Claude Pothel for comments on pathology, and François Julien, Section de Biologie, for his demonstration of blood-spatter patterning. Pat Laturnus, Bloodstain Pattern Analyst at the Canadian Police College in Ottawa, also helped with this expertise, and provided photos for cover design.

In North Carolina, I would like to thank Captain Terry Sult of the Charlotte-Mecklenburg Police Department Intelligence Unit; Roger Thompson, Director of the Charlotte-Mecklenburg Police Department Crime Laboratory; Pam Stephenson, Senior Analyst, Intelligence and Technical Services, North Carolina State Bureau of Investigation; Gretchen C. F. Shappert, United States Attorney General's Office; and Dr. Norman J. Kramer, Mecklenburg Medical Group.

Others who gave of their time and knowledge include Dr. G. Clark Davenport, Geophysicist with NecroSearch International; Dr. Wayne Lord, National Center for the Analysis of Violent Crime, FBI Academy, Quantico, Virginia; and Victor Svoboda, Director of Communication for the Montreal Neurological Institute and the Montreal Neurological Hospital. Dr. David Taub was my Harley-Davidson guru.

I am indebted to Yves St. Marie, Directeur, Laboratoire de Sciences Judiciaires et de Médecine Légale; Dr. André Lauzon, Responsable, Laboratoire de Médecine Légale; and to Dr. James Woodward, Chancellor of the University of North Carolina at Charlotte for their continued support.

Special thanks go to Paul Reichs for his valuable comments on the manuscript.

As always I want to thank my extraordinary editors, Susanne Kirk at Scribner, and Lynne Drew at Random House, and my slam-dunk agent, Jennifer Rudolph Walsh.

Though I benefited greatly from the advice of experts, any errors in *Deadly Décisions* are strictly of my making.

CHAPTER ONE

Her name was Emily Anne. She was nine years old, with black ringlets, long lashes, and caramel-colored skin. Her ears were pierced with tiny gold loops. Her forehead was pierced by two slugs from a Cobra 9-mm semiautomatic.

*   *   *

It was a Saturday, and I was working by special request of my boss, Pierre LaManche. I'd been at the lab for four hours, sorting badly mangled tissue, when the door to the large autopsy room opened and Sergeant-Detective Luc Claudel came striding in.

Claudel and I had worked together in the past, and though he'd come to tolerate, perhaps even appreciate me, one would not infer that from his brusque manner.

'Where's LaManche?' he demanded, glancing at the gurney in front of me, then quickly away.

I said nothing. When Claudel was in one of his moods, I ignored him.

'Has Dr. LaManche arrived?' The detective avoided looking at my greasy gloves.

'It's Saturday, Monsieur Claudel. He doesn't wo—'

At that moment Michel Charbonneau stuck his head into the room. Through the opening I could hear the whir and clank of the electric door at the back of the building.

'*Le cadavre est arrivé*,' Charbonneau told his

1

partner.

What cadaver? Why were two homicide detectives at the morgue on a Saturday afternoon?

Charbonneau greeted me in English. He was a large man, with spiky hair that resembled a hedgehog's.

'Hey, Doc.'

'What's going on?' I asked, pulling off my gloves and lowering my mask.

Claudel answered, his face tense, his eyes cheerless in the harsh fluorescent light.

'Dr. LaManche will be here shortly. He can explain.'

Already sweat glistened on his forehead, and his mouth was compressed into a thin, tight line. Claudel detested autopsies and avoided the morgue as much as possible. Without another word he pulled the door wide and brushed past his partner. Charbonneau watched him walk down the corridor, then turned back to me.

'This is hard for him. He has kids.'

'Kids?' I felt something cold in my chest.

'The Heathens struck this morning. Ever hear of Richard Marcotte?'

The name was vaguely familiar.

'Maybe you know him as *Araignée*. Spider.' He curled his fingers like a child doing the waterspout rhyme. 'Great guy. And an elected official in the outlaw biker set. Spider is the Vipers sergeant at arms, but he had a real bad day today. When he set out for the gym around eight this morning the Heathens blasted him in a drive-by while his ole lady dove for cover in a lilac bush.'

Charbonneau ran a hand backward through his hair, swallowed.

2

I waited.

'In the process they also killed a child.'

'Oh, God.' My fingers tightened around the gloves.

'A little girl. They took her to the Montréal Children's Hospital, but she didn't make it. They're bringing her here now. Marcotte was DOA. He's out back.'

'LaManche is coming in?'

Charbonneau nodded.

The five pathologists at the lab take turns being on call. Rarely does it happen, but if an off-hours autopsy or visit to a death scene is deemed necessary, someone is always available. Today that was LaManche.

A child. I could feel the familiar surge of emotions and needed to get away.

My watch said twelve-forty. I tore off my plastic apron, balled it together with the mask and latex gloves, and threw everything into a biological waste container. Then I washed my hands and rode the elevator to the twelfth floor.

I don't know how long I sat in my office, staring at the St. Lawrence and ignoring my carton of yogurt. At one point I thought I heard LaManche's door, then the swish of the glass security doors that separate portions of our wing.

Being a forensic anthropologist, I've developed some immunity to violent death. Since the medical examiner turns to me to derive information from the bones of the mutilated, burned, or decomposed, I've seen the worst. My workplaces are the morgue and autopsy room, so I know how a corpse looks and smells, how it feels when handled or cut with a scalpel. I'm accustomed to bloody

3

clothing drying on racks, to the sound of a Stryker saw cutting through bone, to the sight of organs floating in numbered specimen jars.

But I have always been unsettled by the sight of dead children. The shaken baby, the battered toddler, the emaciated child of religious zealots, the preteen victim of a violent pedophile. The violation of young innocents has never failed to agitate and distress me.

Not long ago I had worked a case involving infants, twin boys killed and mutilated. It had been one of the most difficult encounters of my career, and I didn't want to reboard that emotional merry-go-round.

Then again that case had been a source of satisfaction. When the fanatic responsible was locked up and could order no more executions, I felt a genuine sense of having accomplished something good.

I peeled back the cover and stirred the yogurt.

Images of those babies hovered in my mind. I remembered my feelings in the morgue that day, the flashbacks to my infant daughter.

Dear God, why such insanity? The mutilated men I had left downstairs had also died as a result of the current biker war.

Don't get despondent, Brennan. Get angry. Get coldly, resolutely angry. Then apply your science to help nail the bastards.

'Yep,' I agreed with myself aloud.

I finished the yogurt, drained my drink, and headed downstairs.

* * *

Charbonneau was in the anteroom of one of the small autopsy suites, flipping pages in a spiral notebook. His large frame overflowed a vinyl chair opposite the desk. Claudel was nowhere to be seen.

'What's her name?' I asked.

'Emily Anne Toussaint. She was on her way to dance class.'

'Where?'

'Verdun.' He tipped his head toward the adjoining room. 'LaManche has begun the post.'

I slipped past the detective into the autopsy room.

A photographer was taking pictures while the pathologist made notes and shot Polaroid backups.

I watched LaManche grasp a camera by its side handles, then raise and lower it above the body. As the lens moved in and out of focus a small dot blurred then condensed over one of the wounds in the child's forehead. When the perimeter of the dot grew sharp, LaManche depressed the shutter release. A white square slid out and he pulled it free and added it to a collection on the side counter.

Emily Anne's body bore evidence of the intensive effort to save her life. Her head was partly bandaged, but I could see a clear tube protruding from her scalp, inserted to monitor intracranial pressure. An endotracheal tube ran down her throat and into her trachea and esophagus, placed in order to oxygenate the lungs and to block regurgitation from the stomach. Catheters for IV infusion remained in her subclavian, inguinal, and femoral vessels, and the circular white patches for EKG electrodes were still pasted to her chest.

5

Such a frantic intervention, almost like an assault. I closed my eyes and felt tears burn the backs of my lids.

I dragged my eyes back to the small body. Emily Anne wore nothing but a plastic hospital bracelet. Next to her lay a pale green hospital gown, bundled clothing, a pink backpack, and a pair of high-top red sneakers.

The harsh fluorescent light. The shining steel and tile. The cold, sterile surgical instruments. A little girl did not belong here.

When I looked up, LaManche's sad eyes met mine. Though neither of us made reference to what lay on the stainless steel, I knew his thoughts. Another child. Another autopsy in this same room.

Putting a choke hold on my emotions, I described the progress I was making with my own cases, reassembling the corpses of two bikers who'd been blown apart by their own folly, and asked when antemortem medical records would be available. LaManche told me that the files had been requested and should arrive on Monday.

I thanked him and went to resume my own grim task. As I sorted tissue, I remembered my previous day's conversation with LaManche, and wished I were still in the Virginia woods. Was it only yesterday LaManche had called me there? Emily Anne was alive then.

So much can change in twenty-four hours.

CHAPTER TWO

The day before I had been in Quantico teaching a body recovery workshop at the FBI Academy. My team of evidence recovery technicians was unearthing and mapping its skeleton when I looked up to see a special agent approaching through the trees. He reported that a Dr. LaManche urgently wished to speak to me. Feeling uneasy, I left my team and started out of the woods.

As I threaded my way toward the road, I thought about LaManche and the news his call might bring. I began consulting for the Laboratoire de Sciences Judiciaires et de Médecine Légale after going to Montreal in the early nineties as part of a faculty exchange between McGill and my home university in Charlotte. Knowing I was certified by the American Board of Forensic Anthropology, LaManche had been curious as to whether I could be of any use to him.

Quebec Province had a centralized coroner system, with sophisticated crime and medico-legal labs, but no board-certified forensic anthropologist. Then, as now, I served as consultant to the Office of the Chief Medical Examiner in North Carolina, and LaManche wanted me for the LSJML. The ministry funded an anthropology lab, and I enrolled in an immersion course in French. For more than a decade now, the skeletonized, decomposed, mummified, burned, or mutilated cadavers of Quebec Province have come to me for analysis and identification. When a conventional autopsy is of no use, I tease what I can from the bones.

Rarely had LaManche left me a message marked urgent. When he had, it had never been good.

Within minutes I crossed to a van parked on the side of a gravel road. I released my hair and ran my fingers backward across my scalp.

No ticks.

After reclipping the barrette, I dug my pack from the back of the van and fished out my cell phone. The tiny screen told me I had missed three calls. I punched up the list of numbers. All three had come from the lab.

I tried dialing, but the signal cut in and out. That's why I'd left the phone in the van. Damn. Though my French had become fluent over the past ten years, background noise and bad connections often caused me problems. Between the language exchange and the weak signal, I'd never get the message straight on this phone. I had to hike down to headquarters.

I unzipped my Tyvek jumpsuit and threw it in a box in the back of the van. Slinging my pack over my shoulder, I headed downhill.

High above the trees a hawk circled some falconid target. The sky was a brilliant blue, with randomly spaced cotton puff clouds drifting leisurely. The course is usually held in May, and we'd worried that this year's April scheduling might mean rain or cooler temperatures. No problem. The mercury was in the high seventies.

As I walked, I took in the sounds around me. My boots crunching on gravel. Birdsong. The whumping of helicopter blades low overhead. The pop of distant gunfire. The FBI shares Quantico with other federal police agencies and with the

Marine Corps, and the activity is constant and very earnest.

The gravel road met blacktop at Hogan's Alley, just below the simulated town square used by the FBI, DEA, ATF, and others. I skirted far to the left to avoid intruding on a hostage rescue exercise and turned right on Hoover Road downhill to the closest module of a concrete complex of gray and tan with antennae jutting from the highest roofs like new shoots in an old hedge. Crossing a small parking area to the Forensic Science Research and Training Center, I rang a bell at the loading dock.

A side door parted and a man's face appeared in the crack. Though young, he was completely bald, and looked as if he'd been that way for some time.

'Finishing early?'

'No. I need to call my lab.'

'You can use my office.'

'Thanks, Craig. I'll only be a minute.' I hope.

'I'm checking equipment, so take your time.'

The academy is often compared to a hamster cage because of the labyrinth of tunnels and corridors connecting its various buildings. But the upper floors are nothing compared with the maze below.

We wound our way through an area stacked with crates and cardboard boxes, old computer screens, and metal equipment trunks, down one corridor, then along two others to an office barely large enough to hold a desk, chair, filing cabinet, and bookshelf. Craig Beacham worked for the National Center for the Analysis of Violent Crime, NCAVC, one of the major components of the FBI's Critical Incident Response Group, CIRG. For a time the entity had been called the Child Abduction and

9

Serial Killer Unit, CASKU, but had recently reverted to the original name. Since the training of evidence recovery technicians, or ERT's, is one of the functions of NCAVC, it is this unit that organizes the annual course.

When dealing with the FBI, one must be alphabet savvy.

Craig gathered folders from his desk and stacked them on the cabinet.

'At least that will give you some space to take notes. Do you need to close the door?'

'No, thanks. I'm fine.'

My host nodded, then disappeared down the hall.

I took a deep breath, made a mental shift to French, and dialed.

'*Bonjour, Temperance.*' Only LaManche and the priest who baptized me have ever used the formal version. The rest of the world calls me Tempe. '*Comment ça va?*'

I told him I was fine.

'Thank you for calling back. I fear we have a grisly situation up here and I am going to need your help.'

'*Oui?*' Grisly? LaManche was not prone to overstatement.

'*Les motards.* Two more are dead.'

Les motards. Bikers. For more than a decade rival outlaw motorcycle gangs had been battling for control of the drug trade in Quebec. I'd worked on several *motard* cases, gunshot victims who had also been burned beyond recognition.

'*Oui?*'

'So far, this is what the police have reconstructed. Last night three members of the

10

Heathens drove to the Vipers' clubhouse with a powerful homemade bomb. The Viper working the surveillance cameras spotted a pair approaching with a large bundle between them. He took a shot and the bomb exploded.' LaManche paused. 'The driver is in the hospital in critical condition. For the other two, the largest portion of tissue recovered weighs nine pounds.'

Ouch.

'Temperance, I've been trying to get in touch with Constable Martin Quickwater. He's there in Quantico, but he's been in a case-review meeting all day.'

'Quickwater?' It was not a typical québécois name.

'He's Native. Cree, I think.'

'Is he with Carcajou?'

Opération Carcajou is a multijurisdictional task force created to investigate criminal activities among outlaw motorcycle gangs in the province.

'*Oui.*'

'What would you like me to do?'

'Please tell Constable Quickwater what I have told you, and have him contact me. Then I would like you to come here as quickly as possible. We may have difficulty with these identifications.'

'Have they recovered printable digits or dental fragments?'

'No. And it is not likely.'

'DNA?'

'There may be problems with that. The situation is complicated and I would rather not discuss it by phone. Is it possible for you to return earlier than you had planned?'

Following my normal pattern, I'd wrapped up

11

the spring term at UNC-Charlotte in time to teach the FBI course. Now I only had to read the final exams. I'd been looking forward to a brief stay with friends in D.C. before flying to Montreal for the summer. The visit would have to wait.

'I'll be there tomorrow.'

'*Merci.*'

He continued in his very precise French, either sadness or fatigue deepening the timbre of his rich, bass voice.

'This does not look good, Temperance. The Heathens will undoubtedly retaliate. Then the Vipers will draw more blood.' I heard him pull a long breath, then exhale slowly. 'I fear the situation is escalating to full-scale war in which innocents may perish.'

We hung up and I called US Airways to arrange for a morning flight. As I was replacing the receiver Craig Beacham appeared in the doorway. I explained about Quickwater.

'Constable?'

'He's RCMP. Royal Canadian Mounted Police. Or GRC if you prefer French. Gendarmerie royale du Canada.'

'Um. Huh.'

Craig punched in a number and asked about the constable's whereabouts. After a pause he jotted something down and hung up.

'Your guy's in a major case management session in one of the conference rooms down here.' He offered the number he'd written, then gave me directions. 'Just slide in and take a seat. They'll probably break at three.'

I thanked him, and wormed my way through the halls until I'd located the room. Muffled voices

12

came through the closed door.

My watch said two-twenty. I turned the knob and slipped in.

The room was dark save for the beam of a projector and the apricot glow of an illuminated slide. I could make out half a dozen figures seated around a central table. Some heads turned in my direction as I eased into a chair against the side wall. Most eyes stayed fixed on the screen.

For the next thirty minutes I saw LaManche's premonition brought to life in horrifying detail. A bombed-out bungalow, tissue spattered on the walls, body parts strewn across the lawn. A female torso, face a red mass, skull bones mushroomed by a shotgun blast. The blackened chassis of a sports utility vehicle, one charred hand dangling from a rear window.

A man seated to the right of the projector commented about biker gang wars in Chicago as he clicked through the presentation. The voice was vaguely familiar, but I couldn't make out the features.

More shootings. Explosions. Stabbings. Now and then I scanned the silhouettes around the table. Only one had hair that was not closely cropped.

Finally, the screen blazed white. The projector hummed and dust motes floated in its beam. Chairs squeaked as their occupants stretched and reoriented toward one another.

The speaker rose and crossed to the wall. When the overhead lights came on I recognized him as Special Agent Frank Tulio, a graduate of the recovery course from years back. He spotted me, and a smile spread across his face.

'Tempe. How's it hanging?'

13

Everything about Frank was precise, from his razor-cut gray hair, to his compact body, to his immaculate Italian-made shoes. Unlike the rest of us, throughout the bug and body exercises Frank had remained perpetually well groomed.

'Can't complain. Are you still with the Chicago office?'

'Up until last year. I'm here now, assigned to CIRG.'

Every eye was focused on us, and I was suddenly conscious of my current state of cleanliness and coiffure. Frank turned to his colleagues.

'Does everyone know the great bone doctor?'

As Frank made introductions, those around the table smiled and nodded. Some I recognized, others I did not. One or two made jokes about past episodes in which I'd played a role.

Two of those present were not affiliated with the academy. The fuller hair I'd spotted belonged to Kate Brophy, supervisor of the Intelligence Unit of North Carolina's State Bureau of Investigation. Kate had been the SBI's expert on outlaw motorcycle gangs for as long as I could remember. We'd met in the early eighties when the Outlaws and Hells Angels were at war in the Carolinas. I'd identified two of the victims.

At the far end of the table a young woman typed on what looked like a stenotype machine. Next to her Martin Quickwater sat behind a laptop computer. His face was broad, with high cheekbones, and eyebrows that angled up at the ends. His skin was the color of fired brick.

'I'm sure you two foreigners know each other,' said Frank.

'Actually, we don't,' I said. 'But that's why I'm

14

intruding. I need to speak to Constable Quickwater.'

Quickwater graced me with approximately five seconds of attention, then his eyes went back to his computer screen.

'Good timing. We're ready for a break.' Frank looked at his watch, then crossed back to click off the projector. 'Let's get some caffeine and regroup at three-thirty.'

As the agents filed past me one of the members of NCAVC made an exaggerated show of squaring his fingers and peering through, as though focusing on me through a viewfinder. We'd been friends a decade and I knew what was coming.

'Nice do, Brennan. Do you get a deal from your lawn man? Hedges and hair trims, one price?'

'Some of us do real work, Agent Stoneham.'

He moved on, laughing.

When only Quickwater and I were left, I smiled and began a fuller introduction.

'I know who you are,' said Quickwater in softly accented English.

His abruptness surprised me, and I fought back an equally impolite rejoinder. Perhaps being sweaty and uncombed had made me touchy.

When I explained that LaManche had been trying to reach him, Quickwater slipped his pager from his belt, checked the screen, then tapped it hard against his hand. Shaking his head and sighing, he reattached the device to his waistband.

'Batteries,' he said.

The constable watched me intently as I repeated what LaManche had said. His eyes were so deeply brown it was impossible to see a boundary between pupil and iris. When I'd finished, he nodded, then turned and left the room.

I stood a moment, wondering at the man's odd demeanor. Terrific. I not only had two vaporized bikers to piece together, I now had Constable Congenial as an associate.

I picked up my pack and headed back to the woods.

No problem, Mr. Quickwater. I've cracked tougher nuts than you.

CHAPTER THREE

The trip to Montreal was uneventful, except for an overt snub by Martin Quickwater. Though we were on the same flight, he did not speak to me or move to one of the empty seats in my row. We nodded at Washington-Reagan, then again as we waited in the customs line at Montreal's Dorval. His coolness suited me. I really didn't want to deal with the man.

I took a taxi to my condo in Centre-ville, offloaded luggage, and zapped a frozen burrito. My old Mazda turned over after three tries, and I headed to the city's east side.

For years the forensic lab had been located on the fifth floor of a structure known as the SQ building. The provincial police, or Sûreté du Québec, had the rest of the floors, except for my office and a detention center on the twelfth and thirteenth. The morgue and autopsy rooms were in the basement.

The Quebec government had recently spent millions to renovate the building. The jail was relocated, and the medico-legal and crime labs now sprawled throughout the top two floors. It had been months since the move, but I still couldn't believe the change. My new office had a spectacular view of the St. Lawrence River, and my lab was first-rate.

At three-thirty on Friday the normal weekday hustle and bustle were beginning to taper off. One by one doors were closing, and the army of lab-coated scientists and technicians was dwindling.

I unlocked my office and hung my jacket on the wooden hall tree. Three white forms lay on my desk. I selected the one with LaManche's signature.

The *'Demande d'Expertise en Anthropologie'* is often my first introduction to a case. Filled out by the requesting pathologist, it provides data critical to tracking a file.

My eyes drifted down the right-hand column. Lab number. Morgue number. Police incident number. Clinical and efficient. The body is tagged and archived until the wheels of justice have run their course.

I shifted to the left column. Pathologist. Coroner. Investigating officer. Violent death is the final intrusion, and those who investigate it are the ultimate voyeurs. Though I participate, I am never comfortable with the indifference with which the system approaches the deceased and the death investigation. Even though a sense of detachment is a must to maintain emotional equilibrium, I always have the feeling that the victim deserves something more passionate, more personal.

I scanned the summary of known facts. It differed from LaManche's telephone account in only one respect. To date, two hundred and fifteen

17

remnants of flesh and bone had been recovered. The largest weighed eleven pounds.

Ignoring the other forms and a stack of phone messages, I went to find the director.

I'd rarely seen Pierre LaManche in anything but lab-coat white or surgical green. I couldn't imagine him laughing or wearing plaid. He was somber and kind, and strictly tweed. And the best forensic pathologist I knew.

I spotted him through the rectangle of glass beside his office door. His rangy form was hunched over a desk heaped with papers, journals, books, and a stack of files in all the primary colors. When I tapped he looked up and gestured me in.

The office, like its occupant, smelled faintly of pipe tobacco. LaManche had a manner of moving silently, and sometimes the scent was my first clue to his presence.

'Temperance.' He accented the final syllable and made it rhyme with France. 'Thank you so much for returning early. Please, sit down.'

Always the perfect French, with never a contraction or word of slang.

We took places at a small table in front of his desk. On it lay a number of large brown envelopes.

'I know it is too late to begin analysis now, but perhaps you are willing to come in tomorrow?'

The face was army mule long with deep, vertical creases. When he raised his brows in a question, the furrows paralleling his eyes elongated and veered toward the midline.

'Yes. Of course.'

'You might want to begin with the X rays.'

He indicated the envelopes, then swiveled to his desk.

'And here are the scene and autopsy photos.' He handed me a stack of smaller brown envelopes and a videocassette.

'The two bikers carrying the bomb to the Vipers' clubhouse were pulverized, their remains scattered over an enormous area. A lot of what the recovery team is finding is stuck to walls and caught in bushes and tree branches. Amazingly, the largest fragments retrieved so far have come from the clubhouse roof. One chunk of thorax has a partial tattoo that will be useful for establishing identity.'

'What about the driver?'

'He died in the hospital this morning.'

'The shooter?'

'He is in custody, but these people are never helpful. He will go to jail rather than give anything to the police.'

'Even information about a rival gang?'

'If he talks, he is probably a dead man.'

'Are there still no dentals or prints?'

'Nothing.'

LaManche ran a hand over his face, raised and lowered his shoulders, then laced his fingers in his lap.

'I fear we will never get all the tissue sorted out.'

'Can't we use DNA?'

'Have you heard the names Ronald and Donald Vaillancourt?'

I shook my head.

'The Vaillancourt brothers, Le Clic and Le Clac. Both are full patch members of the Heathens. One was implicated a few years back in the execution of Claude 'Le Couteau' Dubé. I don't remember which.'

'The police think the Vaillancourts are the

victims?'

'Yes.'

The melancholy eyes looked into mine.

'Clic and Clac are identical twins.'

*   *   *

By seven that evening I'd examined everything but the video. Using a magnifier I'd gone over scores of photos showing hundreds of bone fragments and bloody masses of varying shapes and sizes. In shot after shot arrows pointed to red and yellow globs lying in grass, entangled in branches, and flattened against cinder blocks, broken glass, tar-paper roofing, and corrugated metal.

The remains had arrived at the morgue in large black plastic bags, each containing a collection of Ziploc bags. Each bag was numbered and held an assortment of body parts, dirt, fabric, metal, and unidentifiable debris. The autopsy photos moved from the unopened bags, to shots of the small plastic sacks grouped on autopsy tables, to views of the contents sorted by categories.

In the final photos the flesh lay in rows, like meat arranged in a butcher's case. I spotted pieces of skull, a fragment of tibia, a femoral head, and a portion of scalp with a complete right ear. Some close-ups revealed the jagged edges of shattered bone, others showed hairs, fibers, and scraps of fabric adhering to the flesh. The tattoo LaManche had mentioned was clearly visible on a flap of skin. It depicted three skulls, bony hands covering eyes, ears, and mouths. The irony was priceless. This guy would be seeing, hearing, and saying nothing.

After examining the prints and X rays I'd come

to agree with LaManche. I could see bone in the photos, and the radiographs revealed the presence of more. That would allow me to determine the anatomical origin of some tissue. But sorting the jumble of flesh into specific brothers was going to be tough.

Separating commingled bodies is always hard, especially if the remains are badly damaged or incomplete. The process is infinitely more difficult when the dead are of the same gender, age, and race. I'd once spent weeks examining the bones and decomposing flesh of seven male prostitutes excavated from a crawl space beneath their killer's home. All were white and in their teens. DNA sequencing had been invaluable in determining who was who.

In this case that might not work. If the victims were monozygous twins they had developed from a single egg. Their DNA would be identical.

LaManche was right. It seemed unlikely I'd be able to divide the fragments into separate bodies and attach a name to each.

A gastric growl suggested it was time to quit. Tired and discouraged, I grabbed my purse, zipped my jacket, and headed out.

*   *   *

Back home, the flashing light told me I had a message. I spread my take-out sushi on the table, popped a Diet Coke, and hit the button.

My nephew Kit was driving from Texas to Vermont with his father. Intent on bonding, they were coming north to fish for whatever it is one hooks in inland waters in the spring. Since my cat

21

prefers the space and comfort of a motor home to the efficiency of air travel, Kit and Howie had promised to pick him up at my home in Charlotte and transport him to Montreal. The message was that they and Birdie would arrive the next day.

I dipped a slice of maki roll and popped it in my mouth. I was going for another when the doorbell sounded. Puzzled, I went to the security screen.

The monitor showed Andrew Ryan leaning against the wall in my hallway. He wore faded blue jeans, running shoes, and a bomber jacket over a black T-shirt. At six foot two, with his blue eyes and angular features, he looked like a cross between Cal Ripkin and Indiana Jones.

I looked like Phyllis Diller before her makeover.

Great.

Sighing, I opened the door.

'Hey, Ryan. What's up?'

'Saw your light and figured you might be back early.'

He gave me an appraising look.

'Rough day?'

'I spent today traveling and sorting flesh,' I said defensively, then tucked my hair behind my ears. 'Coming in?'

'Can't stay.' I noticed he was wearing his pager and gun. 'Just thought I'd inquire as to your dinner plans for tomorrow night.'

'I'll be sorting bomb victims all day tomorrow, so I may be a little zonked.'

'You will have to eat.'

'I will have to eat.'

He placed one hand on my shoulder and twirled a strand of my hair with the other.

'If you're tired we could skip dinner and just

relax,' he said in a low voice.

'Hmm.'

'Broaden our horizons?'

He swept back the hair and brushed his lips across my ear.

Oh yes.

'Sure, Ryan. I'll wear my thong panties.'

'I always encourage that.'

I gave him my 'yeah, right' look.

'Will you spring for Chinese?'

'Chinese is good,' he said, drawing my hair upward and swirling it into a topknot. Then he let it fall and wrapped both arms around my back. Before I could object he pulled me close and kissed me, his tongue teasing the edges of my lips, then gently probing the inside of my mouth.

His lips felt soft, his chest hard against mine. I started to push away, but knew that was not what I wanted to do. Sighing, I relaxed and my body molded to his. The horrors of the day evaporated, and for that moment I was safe from the madness of bombs and murdered children.

Eventually we needed air.

'You're sure you don't want to come in?' I asked, stepping back and holding the door open. My knees felt like Jell-O salad.

Ryan looked at his watch.

'I'm sure a half hour won't matter.'

At that moment his pager sounded. He checked the number.

'Shit.'

Shit.

He rehooked the pager to the waist of his jeans.

'Sorry,' he said, grinning sheepishly. 'You know I'd really rath—'

'Go.' Smiling, I placed two palms on his chest and shoved him gently. 'I'll see you tomorrow night. Seven-thirty.'

'Think about me,' he said, as he turned and headed down the hall.

When he'd gone I went back to the sushi, definitely thinking about Andrew Ryan.

Ryan is SQ, a homicide detective, and occasionally we work the same cases. Though he'd been asking for years, only recently had I started seeing him socially. It had taken some self-persuasion, but I'd come around to his point of view. Technically, we didn't work together, so my 'no office romance rule' didn't apply unless I wanted it to.

Nevertheless, the arrangement made me edgy. After twenty years of marriage, and several as a not-so-swinging single, new relationships just weren't that easy for me. But I enjoyed Ryan's company, so I'd decided to give it a whirl. To 'date' him, as my sister would say.

Oh, God. Dating.

I had to admit that I found Ryan sexy as hell. Most women did. Wherever we went, I'd notice female eyes checking him out. Wondering, no doubt.

I was wondering, too. But at the moment that ship was still in port, the engines stoked and ready to go. The Jell-O knees had just reconfirmed that. Dinner out was definitely a better idea.

The phone rang as I was clearing the table.

'*Mon Dieu*, you're back.' Deep, throaty English with a heavy French accent.

'Hi, Isabelle. What's up?'

Though I'd known Isabelle Caillé only two years,

24

in that time we'd grown quite close. We'd met during a difficult time in my life. In the space of one bleak summer I was targeted by a violent psychopath, my best friend was murdered, and I was finally forced to face the reality of a failed marriage. In a display of self-indulgence, I had booked a single at a Club Med, and flown off to play tennis and overeat.

I'd met Isabelle on the flight to Nassau, and we were later paired for doubles. We won, discovered we were there for similar reasons, and passed an enjoyable week together. We'd been friends ever since.

'I didn't expect you until next week. I was going to leave a message about getting together, but since you are home, what about dinner tomorrow?'

I told her about Ryan.

'That one's a keeper, Tempe. You get tired of that *chevalier*, you send him over and I'll give him something to think about. Why are you back early?'

I explained about the bombing.

'Ah, oui. I read about that in *La Presse.* Is it just terribly gruesome?'

'The victims are not in good shape,' I said.

'Les motards. If you ask me, these outlaw bikers get what they deserve.'

Isabelle never lacked opinions, and was rarely hesitant to share them.

'The police should just let these gangsters blow each other up. Then we wouldn't have to look at their dirty bodies with filthy tattoos anymore.'

'Hm.'

'I mean, it's not like they're murdering babies.'

'No,' I agreed. 'It's not.'

The next morning Emily Anne Toussaint died

25

while walking to her ballet lesson.

CHAPTER FOUR

Howard and Kit had arrived at seven, left Birdie, and continued on their way. Birdie was ignoring me and checking the condo for canine intruders when I left for the lab at eight to resume work on the bomb victims.

Emily Anne had arrived shortly after noon.

Since I needed space, I'd chosen the large autopsy room. I'd rolled the gurneys with the bomb victim remains to the center of the room and was attempting to construct corpses on two tables. Being Saturday, I had the place to myself.

I had identified and sorted all visible bone fragments. Then, using the X rays, I'd pulled the fragments containing bone, and dissected the tissue to search for landmarks. Wherever I found duplicates I divided them between the tables. Two left pubic tubercles, or mastoid processes, or femoral condyles meant two different individuals.

I'd also spotted evidence of a childhood growth problem in some of the long bone fragments. When health is compromised, a child stops growing and skeletal development goes on hold. Such interruptions are usually caused by disease, or by periods of inadequate diet. When things get better, growth resumes, but the stoppages leave permanent markers.

The X rays were showing opaque lines on numerous splinters of arm and leg bones. The narrow bands ran transversely across the shafts and

26

indicated periods of arrested growth. I placed tissue with affected fragments on one table, and tissue with normal bone on the other.

One of the tangles of shattered flesh contained several hand bones. When I teased them out I spotted two metacarpals with irregular shafts. These lumpy areas showed increased density when X-rayed, suggesting one of the victims had broken these fingers at some time in the past. I set that tissue aside.

Tissue without bone was a different matter. With that I studied the adherent fabric, working backward from the sorted tissue, matching threads and fibers from one table or the other to the pieces of tissue remaining on the gurneys. I thought I could make out a woven plaid, khaki of the kind found in work pants, denim, and white cotton. Later, experts from the hair and fiber section would do a full analysis to see if they could corroborate my matches.

Following lunch and my discussion with LaManche, I went back to the bomb victims. By five-fifteen I'd divided approximately two thirds of the tissue. Without DNA I saw no hope of associating the remaining fragments with specific individuals. I'd done what I could do.

I'd also set a goal for myself.

As I'd waded through the Vaillancourt body parts I'd found it hard to empathize with the persons I was reconstructing. In fact, I felt annoyance at having to do it. These men had been blown up while preparing to blow up others. A rough justice had prevailed, and I felt more bafflement than regret.

Not so with little Emily Anne. She was lying on

27

LaManche's autopsy table because she'd been walking to dance class. That reality was not acceptable. The death of an innocent child could not be dismissed as an incidental casualty of maniacal warfare.

Vipers could kill Heathens, and Outlaws murder Bandidos. Or Pagans. Or Hells Angels. But they must not kill the innocent. I pledged to myself that I would apply every forensic skill I could muster, and however many hours I was able, to develop evidence to identify and convict these homicidal sociopaths. Children had a right to walk the streets of the city without being cut down by bullets.

I transferred the sorted remains back to the gurneys, rolled them to refrigerated compartments, scrubbed, and changed to street clothes. Then I rode the elevator to search out my boss.

*   *   *

'I want to work this,' I said, my voice calm and steady. 'I want to nail these bastard child killers.'

The tired old eyes stared at me for what seemed a very long time. We'd been discussing Emily Anne Toussaint. And the other youngster. A boy.

Olivier Fontaine had been on his way to hockey practice when he pedaled too close to a Jeep Cherokee just as the driver turned the key. The bomb exploded with enough force to blast shrapnel into Olivier's body, killing him instantly. It happened on his twelfth birthday.

Until seeing Emily Anne I'd forgotten about the Fontaine murder. That incident had taken place in December of 1995 on the West Island, and involved the Hells Angels and the Rock Machine. Olivier's death had raised a cry of public outrage, which led to the creation of Opération Carcajou, the multiagency task force devoted to the investigation of biker crime.

'Temperance, I can't—'

'I'll do whatever is needed. I'll work on my own time, between cases. If Carcajou is like everyone else they're probably short-handed. I could do data entry or historic case searches. I could liaise among agencies, maybe work links to intelligence units in the U.S. I cou—'

'Temperance, slow down.' He held up a hand. 'This is not something I am in a position to do. I will speak with Monsieur Patineau.'

Stéphane Patineau was director of the LSJML. He made final decisions for the crime and medico-legal labs.

'I will not let any involvement with Carcajou interfere with my normal duties.'

'I know that. I promise I will speak with the director first thing Monday morning. Now go home. *Bonne fin de semaine.*'

I wished him a good weekend, too.

*   *   *

Quebec winters end much differently from those in the Carolina Piedmont. Back home spring slips in gently, and by the end of March and the beginning of April flowers begin to bloom and the air is soft with the warmth of summertime emerging.

Les québécois wait six weeks longer to plant their gardens and window boxes. Much of April is cool and gray, and the streets and sidewalks glisten with melted ice and snow. But when spring appears

29

it does so with breathtaking showmanship. The season explodes, and the populace responds with an enthusiasm unmatched on the planet.

Today that vernal performance was weeks away. It was dark and a light rain was falling. I zipped my jacket, lowered my head, and made a dash for the car. The news came on as I was entering the Ville-Marie Tunnel, the Toussaint murder the lead story. That night Emily Anne was to have received an award in a lower-school writing competition. She'd titled her winning essay: 'Let the Children Live.'

I reached over and turned off the radio.

I thought of my plans for the evening and was glad I'd have someone to buoy my spirits. I vowed not to talk shop with Ryan.

Twenty minutes later I opened my apartment door to the sound of a ringing phone. I glanced at my watch. Six-fifty. Ryan would be here in forty minutes and I wanted time for a shower.

I walked to the living room and threw my jacket on the couch. The machine clicked on and I listened to my voice request a short message. Birdie appeared at the exact moment Isabelle came on.

'Tempe, if you're there, pick up. *C'est important.*' Pause. *'Merde!'*

I really didn't want to talk but something in her voice made me reach for the handset.

'Hello, Isa—'

'Turn on the television. CBC.'

'I know about the Toussaint child. I was at the lab—'

'Now!'

I picked up the remote and clicked on the set.

Then I listened in horror.

30

CHAPTER FIVE

'. . . *Lieutenant-détective Ryan had been under investigation for several months. He has been charged with possession of stolen goods and with trafficking and possession of controlled substances. Ryan surrendered peacefully to CUM officers this afternoon outside his home in the Old Port. He has been suspended from duty without pay pending a full investigation.*

'*And now some other stories that we've been following. In financial news, the proposed merger of—*'

'Tempe!'

Isabelle's bark snapped me back. I raised the receiver to my ear.

'*C'est lui, n'est-ce pas? Andrew Ryan, Crimes contre la Personne, Sûreté du Québec?*'

'It's got to be a mistake.'

As I said the words my eyes flew to the message light. Ryan hadn't called.

'I'd better go. He'll be here soon.'

'Tempe. He's in jail.'

'I've got to go. I'll call you tomorrow.'

I hung up and dialed Ryan's apartment. No answer. I called his pager and entered my number. No response. I looked at Birdie. He had no explanation.

By nine I knew he wasn't coming. I'd called his home seven times. I'd phoned his partner, with the same result. No answer. No response.

31

I tried grading the final exams I'd brought from UNC-Charlotte, but couldn't concentrate. My thoughts kept going back to Ryan. Time would pass and I'd find myself staring at the same essay in the same blue book, my mind absorbing nothing the student had written. Birdie nestled in the crook of my knees, but it was small comfort.

It couldn't be true. I couldn't believe it. *Wouldn't* believe it.

At ten I took a long, hot bubble bath, zapped a carton of frozen spaghetti, and took it to the living room. I chose CDs I hoped would cheer me, and placed them in the player. Then I tried reading. Birdie joined me again.

No good. Same loop. Pat Conroy might as well have been printed in Nahuatl.

I'd seen Ryan's image on the screen, hands cuffed behind his back, uniformed cops on either side. I'd watched them angle his head forward as he bent to slide into the cruiser's backseat. Still, my mind wouldn't accept it.

Andrew Ryan was selling drugs?

How could I have been so wrong about him? Had Ryan been dealing the whole time I'd known him? Was there a side to the man that I'd never seen? Or was it all a terrible mistake?

It had to be a mistake.

The spaghetti cooled on the table. I had no stomach for food. I had no ear for music. Big Bad Voodoo Daddy and the Johnny Favourite band played swing that could make a gulag get up and dance, but it did nothing to brighten my mood.

The rain fell steadily now, drumming the windows with a soft ticking sound. My Carolina spring seemed very far away.

I twirled a forkful of pasta, but the smell made something in my stomach recoil.

Andrew Ryan was a criminal.

Emily Anne Toussaint was dead.

My daughter was somewhere on the Indian Ocean.

I often phone Katy when I'm feeling down, but for the past few months that had been difficult. She was spending her spring on Semester at Sea, circling the world aboard the S.S. *Universe Explorer*. The ship wouldn't return for another five weeks.

I took a glass of milk to my bedroom and cracked the window and stared out, thoughts swirling like five o'clock traffic.

The trees and bushes looked like black shadows through the dark glistening mist. Beyond them I could see headlights and the shimmer of neon from the corner *dépanneur*. Now and then cars swooshed by, or pedestrians hurried past, their heels clicking on the wet sidewalk.

So routine. So normal. Just another rainy night in April.

I let the curtain fall back and crossed to my bed, doubting my world would return to normal for a very long time.

*   *   *

I spent the next day in constant activity. Unpacking. Cleaning. Shopping for food. I avoided radio and television, glanced only briefly at the paper.

The *Gazette* featured the Toussaint murder: SCHOOLGIRL KILLED IN BLOODY SHOOT-OUT. Beside the headline was a blowup of Emily Anne's fourth-grade photo. Her hair was braided and bowed at both ends with large pink ribbons. Her smile showed gaps that adult dentition would never have the chance to fill.

The picture of Emily Anne's mother was equally heartbreaking. The camera had caught a slim black woman with her head thrown back, mouth wide, lips curled inward in a cry of agony. Mrs. Toussaint's knees were buckled, her hands clasped below her chin, and on either side, a large black woman supported her. Unspeakable grief screamed from the grainy image.

The story gave few details. Emily Anne had two younger sisters, Cynthia Louise, age six, and Hannah Rose, age four. Mrs. Toussaint worked in a bakery. Mr. Toussaint had died in an industrial accident three years earlier. Born in Barbados, the couple had immigrated to Montreal, seeking a better life for their daughters.

A funeral Mass would be celebrated Thursday at 8 A.M. at Our Lady of the Angels Catholic Church, followed by burial at the Notre-Dame-des-Neiges Cemetery.

I refused to read or listen to reports about Ryan. I wanted to hear from him. All morning I left messages on his machine, but got no response. Ryan's partner, Jean Bertrand, had also gone incommunicado. I could think of nothing else to do. I was certain no one at the CUM or SQ would talk about the situation, and I knew none of Ryan's family or friends.

After a trip to the gym, I cooked a dinner of chicken breasts with prune sauce, glazed carrots with mushrooms, and saffron rice. My feline companion would no doubt have preferred fish.

34

$$* \qquad * \qquad *$$

Monday morning I rose early, drove to the lab, and went directly to see LaManche. He was in conference with three detectives, but told me to talk with Stéphane Patineau as soon as possible.

Wasting no time, I headed down the corridor containing the offices of the medico-legal staff and the anthropology, odontology, histology, and pathology labs. Passing the Section des Documents on my left and the Section d'Imagerie on my right, I continued to the main reception area and turned left into the wing housing the administrative personnel of the LSJML. The director's office was at the very back.

Patineau was on the phone. He waved me in and I took a chair opposite his desk.

When he finished his call, he leaned back and looked directly at me. His eyes were deep brown, hooded by heavy ridges and thick brows. Stéphane Patineau was a man who would never worry about thinning hair.

'Dr. LaManche tells me you want to get involved with the Toussaint investigation.'

'I think I could be of use to Carcajou. I've worked on several biker cases. Right now I'm sorting out the victims from the Vipers' clubhouse bombing. I'm not new to this stuff. I cou—'

He waved a hand.

'The director of Opération Carcajou has asked if I could assign one of my personnel to act as liaison to his unit. With this war heating up he'd like to be sure the crime lab, the medico-legal staff, and his investigators are all on the same page at the same time.'

I didn't wait to hear more.

'I can do it.'

'It's spring. Once the river thaws and the hikers and campers hit the woods your workload is going to get heavier.'

That was true. The number of floaters and decomps always increased when the weather warmed and the past winter's dead came to light.

'I'll work overtime.'

'I was going to assign Réal Marchand, but you are welcome to give it a try. It's not a full-time job.'

He lifted a paper from his desk and handed it to me.

'There is a meeting at three this afternoon. I'll call to tell them you're coming.'

'Thank you. You won't regret this.'

He rose and walked me to the door.

'Is there a positive on the Vaillancourt brothers?'

'We'll know once their medical records show up. Hopefully today.'

He gave a two-thumbs-up gesture.

'Go get 'em, Tempe,' he said in English.

I returned the gesture and he shrugged, then retreated to his office.

In addition to being a superb administrator, Patineau filled out a shirt more impressively than most bodybuilders.

*   *   *

Mondays are busy for every coroner and medical examiner, and this one was no exception. As LaManche went through the cases I thought the meeting would never end.

A young girl had died in the hospital and the mother admitted only to shaking her. Three years is beyond the age for Shaken Baby Syndrome, and a contusion suggested the child's head had been slammed against a hard surface.

A thirty-two-year-old paranoid schizophrenic was found with his stomach open, innards spewing onto the carpet of his bedroom. The family claimed the wound was self-inflicted.

Two trucks had collided outside St-Hyacinthe. Both drivers were burned beyond recognition.

A twenty-seven-year-old Russian seaman was found in his cabin with no signs of life. He was pronounced dead by the ship's captain, and the body was preserved and brought ashore. Since the death occurred in Canadian waters, an autopsy was required.

A forty-four-year-old woman was beaten to death in her apartment. Her estranged husband was being sought.

Medical files had arrived for Donald and Ronald Vaillancourt. So had an envelope of snapshots.

When the pictures were passed around we knew that at least one twin lay in pieces downstairs. In a splendid Kodak moment Ronald Vaillancourt stood bare-chested, flexing his upper torso. The see-no-evil skull decorated his right chest.

LaManche assigned each of the autopsies to a pathologist, and turned the Vaillancourt documents over to me.

*   *   *

By ten forty-five I knew which twin had broken his fingers. Ronald 'Le Clic' Vaillancourt had fractured

37

his second and third left digits in a barroom brawl in 1993. The hospital X rays showed the injury in the same location as the irregularities I'd spotted on the metacarpals. They also showed that Le Clic's arm bones lacked lines of arrested growth.

A motorcycle accident sent Le Clic back to the emergency room two months later, this time for hip and lower limb trauma. The radiographic picture was similar. Ronald's leg bones were normal. His record also indicated he had been thrown from a car in '95, stabbed in a street fight later that year, and beaten by a rival gang in '97. His X-ray file was two inches thick.

I also knew who had not been a healthy kid. Donald 'Le Clac' Vaillancourt was hospitalized several times during his childhood. As a toddler he experienced prolonged periods of nausea and vomiting, the cause of which was never diagnosed. At the age of six, scarlet fever nearly killed him. At eleven it was gastroenteritis.

Le Clac had also taken his lumps. His dossier, like his brother's, contained a large packet of X rays reflecting many visits to the trauma center. A broken nose and cheek. A knife wound to the chest. A blow to the head with a bottle.

As I closed the dossier I smiled at the irony. The turbulent life of the brothers would provide a diagram for sorting their bodies. Their many misadventures had left a skeletal map.

Armed with the medical files, I returned to the lower level and took up the parts identification process. I began with the tattooed segment of thorax and the fragments I'd associated with it. That was Ronald. He also got the fractured hand and all tissue containing normal long bones.

38

Limb bones with lines of arrested growth went to Donald. Limb bones without lines went to his brother.

Next I showed Lisa, one of the autopsy technicians, how to radiograph the remaining fragments with the bones in positions identical to those on the antemortem hospital films. This would allow me to compare details of shape and internal structure.

Since the X-ray unit was in heavy demand, we worked through lunch, finally quitting at one-thirty when the other technicians and pathologists returned. Lisa promised she would finish as the machine became available, and I hurried upstairs to change.

*   *   *

Opération Carcajou was headquartered in a modern three-story structure on the shore of the St. Lawrence River, directly across from Old Montreal. The rest of the complex was occupied by the port police and the administrative offices of the maritime authority.

I parked facing the river. To the left I could see the Jacques Cartier Bridge arching across past Île-Notre-Dame, to the right the smaller Victoria Bridge. Enormous chunks of ice floated and bobbed on the dark gray water.

Farther up along the shore, I noticed Habitat '67, a geometric pile of residential space originally built for Expo and later converted to private condominiums. The sight of the building caused a constriction in my chest. Ryan lived in that network of boxes.

I pushed the thought from my mind, grabbed my jacket, and bolted for the building. The cloud cover was breaking, but the day was still raw and damp. An onshore breeze, carrying with it the smell of oil and icy water, flapped my clothes.

A wide staircase led to Carcajou headquarters on the third floor. Inside glass doors sat a stuffed wolverine, the totem for which the unit is named. Men and women occupied desks in a large central room, their extension numbers in block letters on signs above their heads. Framed clippings decorated every wall, stories of Carcajou investigators and their quarry.

Some looked up, most did not as I crossed to the secretary, a middle-aged woman with overdyed hair and a mole on her cheek the size of a June bug. She dragged her eyes from her filing long enough to direct me to a conference room.

I entered to find a dozen men seated around a rectangular table, several others lounging along the walls. The unit's director, Jacques Roy, rose when he saw me. He was short and muscular, with a florid complexion and graying hair parted in the center, like the subject of an 1890s tintype.

'Dr. Brennan, we are so glad you're doing this for us. It will be a great help to my investigators as well as to the folks at your lab. Please.' He gestured to an empty place at the table.

I hung my jacket over the back of the chair and sat. As others drifted in, Roy explained the purpose of the meeting. Several of those present had recently rotated on to the Carcajou team. Others were old hands, but had requested a refresher session. Roy would give a quick overview of the Quebec biker scene. When Constable Quickwater arrived he would report on the major case management session he'd attended at the FBI Academy.

It felt like a time warp. It was Quantico all over again, only this time the language was French and the carnage being described was in a place I knew and of which I was fond.

The next two hours revealed a world that few will ever know. That glimpse sent a shudder through my body and a chill into my soul.

CHAPTER SIX

'First of all, a little background information.'

Roy spoke from the front of the room. He had notes on the podium, but didn't use them.

'Outlaw motorcycle clubs began on the West Coast of the United States shortly after World War II. Some returning vets couldn't adjust to the social requirements of peace and took to roaming the countryside on Harley-Davidsons, harassing the citizenry and generally making themselves obnoxious. They formed loose groups with names like the Booze Fighters, the Galloping Gooses, Satan's Sinners, the Winos. Right from the start these guys weren't candidates for the College of Cardinals.'

Laughter and muffled comments.

'The group to have the greatest impact was a collection of social misfits calling themselves the Pissed Off Bastards of Bloomington. The P.O.B.O.B. eventually became the Hells Angels, taking the name and the helmeted death's-head symbol from a World War II bomber squadron. From the founding chapter in San Bernardino, California—'

'Yahoo, Berdoo.' A comment from the back.

'Right.'

'From that chapter the Hells Angels spread across North America. Eventually other groups also went national, then international. Today the big four are the Hells Angels, the Outlaws, the Bandidos, and the Pagans. All but the Pagans have chapters outside the States, though none to the extent of the Angels.'

A man sitting across the table raised his hand. He had a large paunch and receding hairline, and looked strikingly like Andy Sipowicz of *NYPD Blue*.

'How big are we talking here?'

'Figures vary, depending on the source, but the best estimate is that the Hells Angels have over sixteen hundred members throughout Europe, Australia, and New Zealand. Most are in the United States and Canada, of course, but, as of today, they have one hundred and thirty-three chapters around the globe.

'The 1998 Criminal Intelligence Service of Canada annual report estimates the Bandidos have sixty-seven chapters and about six hundred members worldwide. Other estimates bump it to eight hundred.'

'Sacrement!'

'What qualifies as an outlaw motorcycle club?' This questioner looked about nineteen.

'Technically the OMC label designates those clubs not registered with the American Motorcycle Association or the Canadian Motorcycle Association, the North American affiliates of the

Fédération Internationale de Motocyclisme, now headquartered in Switzerland. According to the AMA, these nonregistered clubs account for only one percent of all motorcyclists, but it's this deviant fringe that gives biking a bad name. And it's a tag the boys have graciously accepted, by the way. I've seen the one-percenter logo tattooed on some of the ugliest shoulders in the province.'

'Yeah. The little triangle identifies the truly righteous biker.' The investigator to my right wore a ponytail and a silver stud in his ear.

'The truly rat puke, you mean.' Sipowicz. His French sounded exactly as I would expect if *NYPD Blue* had been set in Trois-Rivières.

More laughter.

Roy indicated a stack of notebooks in the center of the table.

'There's information in those about the structure of OMCs. Read it and we'll discuss it later. Today I want to take a look at the local scene.'

He clicked on a projector. The screen filled with the image of a clenched fist, swastika tattooed on the wrist, the letters F.T.W. in red and black rippling across the knuckles.

'The basic philosophy of outlaw bikers can be summed up in one phrase.'

'Fuck the World!' Shouted in unison.

'F.T.W. Fuck the World,' Roy agreed. 'Your colors and brothers come first and demand total loyalty. Nonwhites need not apply.'

Roy clicked to the next slide. The screen showed a black-and-white photo of sixteen men arranged in three ragged rows. All were unshorn and wore sleeveless leather vests accessorized with pins and patches. Their tattoos would have impressed a

43

Maori warrior. So would their scowls.

'At the end of the seventies the Outlaws and the Hells Angels from the States both partied hard with certain Quebec gangs they wanted to take over. In 1977 the Popeyes got asked to the prom and became the first Hells Angels chapter in the province. At that time the Popeyes were the second-largest OMC in Canada, with 250 to 350 members. Unfortunately, only about 25 or 30 of the boys had impressed the Angels enough to wear the colors, so the rest got the boot. You're looking at some of the rejects here. This is the infamous North chapter. Five of these guys were liquidated by their brother Angels and the chapter became extinct.'

'Why?'

'Each club has a code of conduct that applies to every member. Ever since the Hells Angels formed back in the forties their rules have prohibited heroin and the use of needles. This has become even more important in today's business atmosphere. Keep in mind, these are *not* the bikers of old. This is *not* the social rebellion of the fifties, or the subculture of drugs and revolution that danced through the sixties. Today's bikers are engaged in sophisticated organized crime. First and foremost these guys are businessmen. Junkies can cause trouble and cost the club money, and that isn't tolerated.'

Roy gestured at the screen.

'Getting back to the choir here, in 1982 the Montreal chapter passed a drug law and called for death or expulsion of any Angel defying it. But the members of the North chapter were too attached to their coke, and decided to go their own way.

Apparently the blow had affected their math, because they failed to note that they were strongly outnumbered on this question.'

One by one, Roy tapped his pen on five of the men in the photograph.

'In June of 1985 these guys were found taking the cement siesta in the St. Lawrence Seaway. One of the sleeping bags had floated up, the others had to be dredged from the bottom.'

'Taking care of business.' Ponytail.

'Permanently. They were killed in the Hells Angels' clubhouse out in Lennoxville. Apparently the party they'd gone out there to attend turned out not to be the one they'd expected.'

'Kind of contrary to the old righteous brother outlaw doctrine.' Ponytail shook his head.

'Is that what started the present war?' I asked.

'Not really. A year after the Hells Angels adopted the Popeyes, a Montreal group called Satan's Choice became the first Outlaws chapter in Quebec. They've been killing each other ever since.'

Roy indicated a gaunt man squatting in the front row of the photo.

'War was declared when this Hells Angel killed an Outlaw in a drive-by. For several years after that it was open season.'

' "God forgives, the Outlaws don't." That's their slogan.' Sipowicz wrote his name, 'Kuricek,' on a notebook as he spoke. I wondered how many people called him Sipowicz by mistake.

'True. But the Quebec Outlaws have suffered a severe reversal of fortune since then. Five or six are now in jail, and their clubhouse was burned to the ground a few years ago. The present war really involves the Angels and a Canadian group called the Rock Machine, and their puppet clubs.'

'Classy guys,' offered Sipowicz/Kuricek.

'But the Rock Machine also fell on hard times,' Roy continued. 'Until recently.'

He clicked to a slide showing a man in a beret embracing a leather-jacketed comrade. Centered on the embracee's back was a cartoon-like Mexican bandit, knife in one hand, pistol in the other. Red and yellow crescent-shaped banners above and below the figure identified the wearer as the national vice president of the Bandidos MC.

'The Machine was on its last legs, but appears to be undergoing a major resuscitation since members have recently been spotted wearing patches identifying them as tentative Bandidos.'

'Tentative?' I asked.

'The Machine has been granted hang-around status while the Bandidos decide if they're worthy to prospect.'

'I can see the advantage to the Rock Machine, but what's in it for the Bandidos?' I asked.

'For years the Bandidos were satisfied with local meth and narcotics sales, and a few bucks from prostitution. The national organization ran a pretty loose ship. Now power has shifted, and the new leadership recognizes the advantage of expansion and tight control over member chapters.

'Check out the bottom rocker.' Roy pointed to the lower banner on a jacket in the background. 'Quebec has been changed to Canada. That's a pretty clear indicator of where the Bandidos want to go. But it may not be that easy.'

New slide. A formation of bikes on a two-lane highway.

'This was taken in Albuquerque, New Mexico, a few weeks ago. The Bandidos were on their way to a run organized by the Oklahoma chapter. When police pulled over some of the boys for traffic violations, the club's international president was among them, so investigators took the opportunity to query him about all the new faces. He admitted the Bandidos were checking out wannabe clubs around the world, but refused to answer when asked about the Rock Machine.

'Turns out the arrangement is not a done deal. The pres had just come from a meeting of the National Coalition of Motorcyclists where the Bandidos and the Hells Angels tried to hammer out an agreement about the Machine. The Angels are not thrilled about the Bandidos' expansion campaign, and offered to disband a prospect chapter in New Mexico if the Bandidos would drop negotiations with the Quebec club.'

'So the Machine is really hanging out there?' Ponytail.

'Yes. But if they are patched over, a Bandidos presence could shift the balance here.' Roy's voice sounded grim.

'The Rock Machine is relatively new on the scene, *n'est-ce pas?*' asked the young-looking investigator.

'They've been around since 1977,' said Roy. 'But they only added MC to their name in '97. Before that they didn't think of themselves as anything as conventional as a motorcycle club. It was a little surprise on their Christmas cards that year.'

'Christmas cards?' I thought he was joking.

'Yeah. Tradition means a lot to these guys. It was quite the talk of the prison chat room.' Kuricek.

47

Laughter.

'The cards allow members to keep up with each other,' Roy explained. 'The downside is that they also fatten the intelligence files of rival gangs.'

Roy clicked to a map of Montreal.

'Currently the Rock Machine is battling the Hells Angels over control of the province's illegal drug trade. And we're talking big bucks, here. According to the solicitor general, Canada's illicit drug market is worth seven to ten billion a year to organized crime gangs. Quebec represents a big piece of that.'

He indicated two areas of the city.

'The disputed turf involves the north and east sides of Montreal, and parts of Quebec City. Since 1994 there have been hundreds of bombings and arsons, and no less than one hundred and fourteen murders.'

'Counting Marcotte, the Vaillancourt twins, and the Toussaint child?' I asked.

'Good point. One hundred and eighteen. At least a score of others are missing and presumed dead.'

'How many of these asshole warriors are out there in the trenches?' Kuricek.

'The starting lineup is about two hundred sixty-five for the Angels, fifty for the Rock Machine.'

'That's it?' I was astounded so few could wreak so much havoc.

'Don't forget the second-stringers.' Kuricek leaned back and his chair whooshed softly.

'Both sides have puppet clubs that align with them. It's these losers that do all the dirty work for the organizations.' Roy.

'Dirty work?' It all sounded dirty to me.

48

'Distribution and sale of drugs, debt collection, weapons and explosives buys, intimidation, murder. These puppet clubs are the dregs of bikerdom and they'll do anything to prove their balls to the big dogs. That's why it's so hard to nail a patch holder of a major club. The bastards are slippery as hell and always operate at arm's length.'

'Then if you *do* bust them they make bond and use their baboons to terrorize or kill your witnesses.' Kuricek.

I pictured the shattered flesh that had been the Vaillancourt brothers.

'The Heathens are aligned with the Rock Machine?'

'*C'est ça.*'

'And the Vipers with the Hells Angels?'

'*C'est ça.*'

'Who are the others?'

'Let's see. The Rowdy Crew, the Jokers, the Rockers, the Evil Ones, the Death Riders . . .'

At that moment Martin Quickwater appeared in the doorway. He was wearing a navy suit and crisp white shirt, and looked more like a tax lawyer than an organized crime investigator. He nodded at Roy then his eyes swept the room. When he saw me his eyes narrowed, but he said nothing.

'*Ah, bon.* Monsieur Quickwater can give us the FBI perspective.'

But that was not to be. Quickwater had urgent news. The body count was about to go up.

49

CHAPTER SEVEN

By sunrise the next day I was at the Vipers' clubhouse in St-Basile-le-Grand. The building stood alone on an acre of land that was entirely enclosed by an electrified fence. Surveillance cameras dotted the barrier's upper rim, and powerful floods lit the perimeter.

Gates at the highway end of the road were electrically operated and monitored from inside the house. When we arrived they stood open, and no one questioned us via the intercom. Though I could see a remote camera focused on us, I knew no one was watching. The warrant had already been served, and unmarked cars, cruisers, coroner transport vehicles, and the crime scene van were parked along the side of the drive.

Quickwater drove through the gates and pulled in at the end of the row. As he cut the engine he glanced sideways at me, but said nothing. I returned the pleasantry, grabbed my pack, and got out.

In back the grounds were wooded, in front an open field stretched from the house to the highway. The gravel road on which we'd entered bisected the front clearing and ended at a ring of asphalt encircling the building. Waist-high cement cones bordered the asphalt, placed to prevent parking within fifteen feet of any wall. The arrangement reminded me of Northern Ireland in the early seventies. Like the citizens of Belfast, the bikers of Quebec took the threat of car bombs very seriously. A black Ford Explorer was parked at the edge of the asphalt.

Sunlight mottled the horizon, bleeding yellow and pink into the pale purple of early dawn. An hour ago, when Quickwater had picked me up, the sky had been as black as my mood. I didn't want to come here. I didn't want to deal with Mr. Personality. And most of all, I didn't want to unearth more dead bikers.

What Quickwater told us yesterday had caused a weight to settle over me. As I'd listened to his account I knew that what was to have been peripheral involvement on my part, undertaken only to permit me to work on Emily Anne's case, would now become a major task, and the thought of all I'd have to do was pressing me down like a school-yard bully. I reminded myself that a nine-year-old child lay in the morgue, and her shattered family would never be the same. I was there for them.

The Viper shooter who'd obliterated the Vaillancourt brothers had been willing to deal. Facing his third bust and murder-one charges, he'd offered the location of two bodies. The crown had countered with second degree. *Voilà*. Daybreak in St-Basile.

As we trudged up the drive dawn gave way to morning. Though I could see my breath, I knew the day would warm with the sun.

Gravel crunched underfoot, and now and then a pebble dislodged, skittered across the uneven roadbed, and rolled into a side trench. Birds twittered and scolded, announcing their displeasure over our arrival.

Suck eggs, I thought. My morning began before yours.

51

Don't be a baby, Brennan. You're annoyed because Quickwater is a jerk. Ignore him. Do your job.

Just then he spoke.

'I need to find my new partner. He's just been loaned over to Carcajou.'

Though Quickwater didn't offer a name, I felt sympathy for the unlucky cop. I took a deep breath, hiked up my pack, and looked around as I followed his back.

One thing was clear. The Vipers were never going to win Landscaper of the Year. The front of the property was a good example of what nature preservationists in the U.S. Congress had fought to protect. The bottomland that stretched to the highway was a sea of dead vegetation splayed against the reddish-brown spring mud. The scrub forest behind the house had been left to the decorating of its quadrupedal inhabitants.

When we crossed the asphalt and entered the courtyard, however, a design plan was evident. Inspired by the better prisons of America, the enclosure had all the essentials, including twelve-foot brick walls topped with surveillance cameras, motion detectors, and floodlights. Wall-to-wall cement covered the ground, with basketball hoops, a gas barbecue, and a doghouse with chain-link run. Steel doors had replaced the original courtyard gate, and the garage entrance was steel-reinforced and welded shut.

On the trip out, the one time Quickwater had spoken was to give me the basic history of the property. The house was built by a New Yorker who'd made his fortune running booze during the days of the Volstead Act. In the mid-eighties the

52

Vipers bought it from the smuggler's heirs, put four hundred thousand into renovations, and hung up their logo. In addition to the perimeter security system, the boys had installed bulletproof glass in all first-floor windows, and steel plating on every door.

None of that mattered this morning. Like the gate, the clubhouse door stood wide open. Quickwater entered and I followed.

My first reaction was surprise at the lavish outfitting. If these guys needed to make bail or hire an attorney, all they had to do was hold an auction. The electronic equipment alone would have netted them F. Lee Bailey.

The house was built on multiple levels, with a metal staircase twisting up its core. We crossed a black-and-white-tiled hallway and started to climb. To my left I got a glimpse of a game room complete with pool and Foosball tables and a full-length bar. On the wall above the liquor collection a coiled snake with fleshless skull, fangs, and bulging eyeballs grinned down in orange neon. At the far end of the bar, a bank of video monitors provided sixteen views of the property on small black-and-white screens. The room also held a large television and a sound system that looked like a NASA control panel. A patrolman from the St-Basile PD nodded as we passed.

At the second level I noted a gym with at least half a dozen pieces of Nautilus equipment. Two weight benches and an assortment of free weights sat in front of a mirrored wall to the left. The Vipers were into body image.

On level three we crossed a living room done in late-millennium biker bilious. The carpet was deep red plush, and locked horns with the gold on the walls and the blue in the fabric of the oversized couches and love seats. The tables were brass and smoked glass, and held an assortment of snake sculptures. Wood, ceramic, stone, and metal serpents also lined the windowsills, and snarled from the top of the largest TV I'd ever seen.

The walls were decorated with posters, enlargements of snapshots taken at club soirees and runs. In shot after shot members flexed sweaty muscles, straddled cycles, or held up bottles and cans of beer. Most looked like they came from a point on the IQ curve that sloped low and very gently.

We wound our way past five bedrooms, a black marble bath with a sunken Jacuzzi and open glass shower the size of a squash court, and finally into a kitchen. There was a wall phone to my right, with an erasable message board bearing numbers, gibberish in alphabetic code, and the name of a local attorney.

To my left I noticed another staircase.

'What's up there?' I asked Quickwater.

No response.

A second uniform from St-Basile stood on the far side of the room. 'It's another rec room,' he said in English. 'With an outside deck and ten-person spa.'

Two men sat at a wooden table framed by a small bay window, one disheveled, the other pressed and groomed to perfection.

I looked at Quickwater, who nodded. My heart sank.

Luc Claudel was the nameless unfortunate newly partnered with Quickwater. Great. Now I'd have to work with Beavis *and* Butt-Head.

Claudel was speaking, now and then tapping a document that I assumed was the search warrant.

The man he was addressing looked less than pleased with his morning. He had fierce black eyes, a hooked nose that did a sharp left just below the hump, and more hair on his upper lip than a bull walrus. He scowled at his bare feet as he clenched and unclenched the hands that dangled between his knees.

Quickwater nodded at the walrus.

'The Neanderthal is Sylvain Bilodeau. Luc is explaining that we're here to do a little gardening.'

Bilodeau glanced at Quickwater, then at me, his eyes hard and unsmiling, then refocused on opening and closing his fists. A tricolor serpent wound the length of his arm, and appeared to sway as the muscles tensed and eased. I suspected Quickwater's metaphor had done our Paleolithic cousins an injustice.

After a few more words Claudel stopped talking and Bilodeau shot to his feet. Though he couldn't have been over five foot three, he looked like a poster boy for steroids. For a moment he said nothing. Then, 'This is shit, man. You can't just bust the fuck in here and start digging the place up.' His French was so heavily accented with backcountry joual that I missed a lot of the words. But I definitely caught his drift.

Claudel rose and looked Bilodeau in the eye.

'That's exactly what this little piece of paper says we *can* do. And, as I explained, you've got two choices. You can show class and just sit tight like a good little boy, or we can haul you out of here in handcuffs and treat you to free accommodations

55

for an indefinite period of time. It's your choice, Nose.'

Claudel pronounced the nickname in a mocking tone. Good handle, I thought.

'What the fuck am I supposed to do?'

'You're going to reassure your friends that it's in the best interests of their continued good health not to drop by here today. Aside from that, your day is going to be leisurely. You'll do absolutely nothing. And Caporal Berringer is going to stay here to watch you do it.'

'I'm just taking care of business here. Why the fuck do you have to show up this morning?'

Claudel reached out and clapped Nose on the shoulder. 'Life is timing, Nose.'

Bilodeau shrugged free and stomped to the window.

'Fucking son of a bitch.'

Claudel held up his hands in a 'what can I do' gesture. 'Maybe you've got bigger problems than we do, Nose. Guess the brothers won't be thrilled about you sleeping on watch.'

Bilodeau crisscrossed the room, pacing like a caged animal. Then he stopped at the counter and pounded it with both fists.

'Fuck.' His neck muscles bulged with rage and a vein throbbed like a tiny stream in the center of his forehead.

After a moment he turned, scanned from face to face, then pinned me with a look of Charles Manson intensity. He uncurled one fist and pointed a trembling finger in my direction.

'That motherfucking turncoat prick of yours better get it right the first time.' His voice quivered with rage. 'Because he's a walking dead man.'

*   *   *

The turncoat prick in question had been waiting one hundred yards away in the backseat of an unmarked Jeep. As part of his plea bargain he'd agreed to take us to the grave site. However, nothing would persuade him to get out of the car until we were well clear of the house. He would be driven, or the deal was off.

We left the house and went directly to the Jeep. I took the front passenger seat and Claudel climbed in back while Quickwater continued down the road to check with the recovery team. The cigarette smoke was so thick inside the vehicle I found it hard to breathe.

Our informant was a middle-aged man, with celery green eyes and dull red hair pulled into a ponytail at the back of his head. With his white skin, lank hair, and pale reptilian eyes, he looked like something that had evolved in the waters of an underground cave. Viper was an appropriate affiliation. Like Bilodeau, he was short. Unlike Bilodeau he was not interested in a prolonged stay at the clubhouse.

Claudel spoke first.

'This better be good, Rinaldi, or your folks can start planning a funeral. Looks like your approval rating has plummeted among your peers.'

Rinaldi drew smoke into his lungs, held it, then blew two streams through his nose. The borders of his nostrils blanched as they expanded with the effort.

'Who's the broad?' His voice sounded odd, as though it were being scrambled to hide his identity.

57

'Dr. Brennan will be digging up your treasure, Frog. And you're going to help her in every way you can, aren't you?'

'Pffff.' Rinaldi puffed air through his lips. Like his nostrils, their edges paled with the movement.

'And you're going to be as docile as a stiff in the morgue, right?'

'Let's get the fuck on with it.'

'The morgue bit was not a casual comparison, Frog. The simile will have meaning if this turns out to be a con.'

'I'm not making this shit up. There are two guys eating dirt out there. Let's get this fucking show on the road.'

'Let's,' agreed Claudel.

Rinaldi flicked a bony finger, rattling the handcuffs connecting his wrists.

'Circle the house and watch for a dirt track off to the right.'

'That sounds like a sincere start, Frog.'

Frog. Another fitting moniker, I thought, listening to Rinaldi's strange, croaky voice.

Claudel stepped out and gave a thumbs-up to Quickwater, ten yards away at the crime scene van. I turned to look and caught Rinaldi staring at me as if trying to read my genetic code. When our eyes met he held on, refusing to look away. So did I.

'Do you have a problem with me, Mr. Rinaldi?' I asked.

'Odd job for a chick,' he said, never breaking eye contact.

'I'm an odd chick. I once peed in Sonny Barger's pool.' I didn't even know if the former head of the Hells Angels had a pool, but it sounded good. Besides, the Barger reference was probably lost on

58

Frog.

Several seconds passed, then Frog smirked, gave a half shake of the head, and reached to crush his cigarette in the tiny tray between the two front seats. When the handcuffs slipped I saw two lightning bolts tattooed on his forearm, above them the words 'Filthy Few.'

Claudel got back in and Quickwater joined us, taking the wheel but saying nothing. As we circled the house and cut into the woods Rinaldi gazed silently out the window, no doubt preoccupied with his own terrible demons.

Rinaldi's road was little more than two tracks, and the cars and recovery van behind us moved sluggishly through the mud and wet vegetation. At one point Quickwater and Claudel were forced to get out and clear a tree that had fallen onto the path. As they dragged the rotted branches a pair of squirrels were startled and darted out of sight.

Quickwater returned clammy with sweat and muddy from the knees down. Claudel remained pristine and carried himself as if he were wearing a tuxedo. I suspected Claudel could look prim and tidy when walking around in his underwear, but doubted he ever did that.

Claudel loosened his tie a full millimeter and tapped on Rinaldi's window. I opened my door, but Frog was working on another cigarette.

Claudel tapped again and Frog hit the handle. The door popped open and smoke drifted out.

'Put that thing out before we're all on respirators. Are your memory cells still working, Frog? Do you recognize the terrain?' Claudel.

'They're here. If you'll just shut the fuck up and let me get my bearings.'

Rinaldi got out and looked around. Quickwater gave me another of his stony stares as our informant did a visual sweep of the area. I ignored him and did my own inspection.

The spot had once been used as a dump. I could see cans and plastic containers, beer and wine bottles, an old mattress, and a rusted set of box springs. The ground was marked with the delicate tracks of deer, circling, crossing, and disappearing into the surrounding trees.

'I'm getting impatient, Frog,' Claudel urged. 'I'd count to three, as I do with children, but I'm sure I'd lose you with the higher math.'

'Will you just shut the fuck—'

'Easy,' Claudel warned.

'I haven't been out here in years. There was a shed, man. If I can spot the fucking shed I can walk you to them.'

Frog starting making sorties into the woods, probing like a hound scenting a hare. He looked less confident with each passing moment, and I was beginning to share his doubt.

I've been on many informant-led expeditions, and in a lot of cases the trip is a waste of time. Jailhouse tips are notoriously unreliable, either because the herald is lying, or because his memory has simply failed him. LaManche and I went twice in search of a septic tank reported to be the tomb of a murder victim. Two safaris, no tank. The snitch went back to jail, and the taxpayers picked up the bill.

Finally, Rinaldi returned to the Jeep.

'It's farther up.'

'How much farther?'

'What am I, a geographer? Look, I'll know the

spot when I see it. There was a wooden shed.'

'You're repeating yourself, Frog.' Claudel looked pointedly at his watch.

'*Sacré bleu!* If you'll quit riding my ass and drive a bit farther you'll get your stiffs.'

'You'd better be right, Frog. Or you will be at the center of the biggest cluster fuck of the millennium.'

The men climbed back into the Jeep and the procession crept slowly forward. Within twenty yards Rinaldi held up his hands. Then he gripped the seat behind my shoulders and strained forward to peer through the windshield.

'Hold it.'

Quickwater braked.

'There. That's it.'

Rinaldi pointed to the roofless walls of a small wooden structure. Most of the shed had fallen in on itself, and fragments of roofing and rotten wood lay strewn around the ground.

Everyone got out. Rinaldi did a three-sixty, hesitated briefly, then set off into the woods at a forty-degree angle from the shed.

Claudel and I followed, picking our way through last year's vines and creepers, and slapping back branches still weeks from budding. The sun was well above the horizon now, and the trees threw long, spiderweb shadows across the soggy ground.

When we caught up to Rinaldi he was standing at the edge of a clearing, hands dangling in front, shoulders rounded like those of a male chimp about to put on a display. The look on his face was not reassuring.

'This place has changed, man. I don't remember so many trees. We used to come out here to light bonfires and get wasted.'

'I don't care how you and your friends passed your summers, Frog. You're running out of time here. You're going to be doing twenty-five hard ones and we're all going to read about how they found you with a pipe up your ass on the shower room floor.'

I'd never heard Claudel quite so colorful.

Rinaldi's jaw muscles bunched, but he said nothing. Though there had been frost that morning he wore only a black T-shirt and jeans. His arms looked thin and sinewy, and goose bumps puckered the pale flesh.

He turned and walked to the middle of the clearing. On the right the land sloped gently to a small creek. Rinaldi cut through a stand of long-needle pines to the bank, looked in both directions, then headed upstream. Quickwater, Claudel, and I followed. Within twenty yards Rinaldi stopped and waved his scrawny arms at an expanse of bare earth. It lay between the stream and a mound of boulders, and was scattered with branches, plastic containers and cans, and the usual detritus thrown up by seasonal flooding.

'There's your fucking graves.'

I looked at his face. It was composed now, the look of uncertainty once again replaced by cocky insolence.

'If that's all you're offering, Frog, that pipe has your name on it.' Claudel.

'Don't fuck me over, man. It's been more than ten years. If the broad knows her shit, she'll find them.'

As I surveyed the area Rinaldi had indicated, the bully pressed harder on my chest. More than ten years of seasonal flooding. There wouldn't be a single indicator. No depression. No insect activity. No modified vegetation. No stratigraphy. Nothing to hint at an underground cache.

Claudel looked a question at me. Behind him the stream burbled softly. Overhead a crow cawed and another answered.

'If they're here, I'll find them,' I said with more confidence than I felt.

The cawing sounded like laughter.

CHAPTER EIGHT

By noon we'd cleared vegetation and debris from an area approximately fifty yards by fifty yards, based on Frog's hazy recollection of the grave locations. It turned out he'd never actually seen the bodies, but was going on 'reliable information.' According to gang lore the victims had been invited for a lawn party, then marched into the woods and shot in the head. Terrific.

I'd marked off a search grid, then set orange plastic stakes along the boundaries at five-foot intervals. Since bodies are rarely stashed below six feet, I'd requested a ground-penetrating radar unit with a 500 MHz antenna, a frequency effective at those depths. It had arrived within the hour.

Working with the radar operator, I'd dug a test pit outside the search area to allow assessment of density, moisture content, layer changes, and other soil conditions. We had refilled the hole, burying in it a length of metal rebar. The operator had then scanned the pit for control data.

He was completing the final tuning of his equipment when Frog got out of the Jeep and sidled over to me, followed closely by his guard. It was one of several forays he'd made, the sniper-free morning having allayed his anxiety.

'What the fuck *is* that?' he asked, indicating a set of devices that looked like a contraption from *Back to the Future.* Just then Claudel joined us.

'Frog, you could benefit from some new adjectives. Maybe get one of those calendars that shows you a different word every day.'

'Fuck you.'

In a way I appreciated the English expletives. They were like sounds of home in a foreign land.

I looked to see if Frog was merely cracking wise, but the pale green eyes suggested a genuine interest. O.K. Where he was going Frog wouldn't be having a lot of scientifically broadening experiences.

'It's a GPR system.'

He looked blank.

'Ground-penetrating radar.'

I pointed to a terminal plugged into the cigarette lighter of a four-wheel-drive vehicle.

'That's the GPR machine. It evaluates signals sent from an antenna, and produces a pattern on that screen.'

I indicated a sledlike structure with an upright handle and a long, thick cable connecting it to the GPR box. 'That's the antenna.'

'Looks like a lawn mower.'

'Yeah.' I wondered what Frog knew about lawn care. 'When an operator pulls the antenna across the ground it transmits a penetrating signal, then sends data to the GPR machine. The radar

64

machine evaluates the strength and rebound time of the signal.'

He looked as if he was with me. Though pretending disinterest, Claudel was also listening.

'If there is something in the soil, the signal is distorted. Its strength is affected by the size of the underground disturbance, and by the electrical properties at the upper and lower boundaries. The depth of the feature determines how long the signal takes to go down and back.'

'So this thing can tell you where you've got a stiff?'

'Not a body specifically. But it can tell you there's a subsurface disturbance, and it can provide information about its size and location.'

Frog looked blank.

'When you dig a hole and put something in it, the spot is never the same as it was before. The fill may have less density, a different mix, or different electrical properties from the surrounding matrix.'

True. But I doubted that would be the case here. Ten years of water seepage has a way of obliterating soil differences.

'And the thing that's been buried, whether it's a cable, unexploded ordnance, or a human body, will not send the same signal as the soil around it.'

'Ashes to ashes. What if the corpse has oozed into tomorrow's drinking water?'

Good question, Frog.

'The decomposition of flesh can change the chemical composition and electrical properties of dirt, so even bones and putrefied corpses may show up.'

May.

At that moment the radar operator gave a sign

65

indicating he was ready.

'Quickwater, you want to pull the sled?' I shouted.

'I'll do it.' Claudel volunteered.

'O.K. Get one of the Ident guys to follow you to control the cable. It's not complicated. Start where the operator has the antenna set up just outside the cleared area. When you pass the northernmost line of stakes press the remote button twice. It's on the handle. The signal will set the boundary for that transect. Drag the sled at about two-thirds normal walking pace, keeping your sweeps as straight as possible. Each time you pass an east-west stake, press the button once. When you get to the far end give another double signal to indicate the end of the transect. Then we'll haul the thing back and start a second sweep.'

'Why can't we just go back and forth?'

'Because the printouts from adjacent transects won't be comparable if they're done from opposite directions. We'll do the whole area north to south, that's thirty sweeps, then repeat the procedure east to west.'

He nodded.

'I'll stay with the operator and watch the screen. If we note a disturbance I'll holler and your partner can stake the spot.'

*   *   *

An hour later the search was done and everyone was around the van, unwrapping sandwiches and popping sodas. Twelve blue stakes formed three squares inside the survey grid.

The results were better than I'd hoped.

66

Readings from the third and thirteenth north-south transects showed disturbances with lengths and widths roughly equal. But it was the profile from the eleventh sweep that held my attention. I'd asked for hard copy, which I studied as I ate my bologna and cheese.

The printout showed a grid. The horizontal lines indicated depth, based on our calibration with the control pit, with the ground surface at the top. The vertical lines were dotted, and corresponded to the signals sent by Claudel as each grid stake was crossed.

The pattern just below the ground surface was a wavy but generally flat line. But superimposed over gridline 11 North was a series of bell-shaped curves, one inside the next, like ribs on a skeleton. The profile indicated a disturbance at the intersection of north-south line 11 and east-west line 4. It lay at a depth of approximately five feet.

I switched to profiles of the area taken on the east-west sweeps. Comparing perpendicular transects allowed me to estimate the size and shape of the disturbance. What I saw made my heart pick up a beat.

The anomaly was roughly six feet long and three feet wide. Grave size.

At grave depth.

'This will work?' I hadn't heard Claudel approach.

'We're cookin'.'

'Now?'

'Yep.'

I finished my Diet Coke and climbed into the Jeep. The van slogged along behind as Quickwater drove toward the 11 North 4 East coordinates.

We'd decided that I would dig that location while Claudel and Quickwater investigated the other two disturbances. After I laid a simple grid around each site, they would remove the earth in thin slices, screening every shovelful.

I'd instructed the Carcajou investigators on how to watch for differences in soil color and texture. If they spotted any changes they would holler. Each of us would be aided by personnel from the Section d'Identité Judiciaire, or SIJ, and section photographers would shoot and video the entire operation.

And that's what we did.

Claudel supervised as his team worked the disturbance at 13 North 5 East, approximately ten feet from mine. Now and then I'd glance over to see him standing above his crew, gesturing instructions or asking about something in the dirt. He'd yet to remove his sports jacket.

After thirty minutes a shovel chinked loudly in Claudel's pit. My head flew up and my stomach tightened. A blade had struck something hard and unyielding.

As Claudel watched, the technicians and I revealed the contour. The object was rusted and caked with mud, but the shape was unmistakable. Claudel's SIJ screener made the call.

'Tabernac! C'est un Weber.'

'Eh, Monsieur Claudel, you planning a barbecue? Throw on burgers, bring out the lawn chairs, maybe invite girls?'

'Jean-Guy, tell Luc there's an easier way. They've got these things at the Wal-Mart.'

'Yes.' Claudel never cracked a smile. 'You are so hilarious we may need a body bag because I'm

68

going to die laughing. Now keep digging. We still have to haul this thing out and make sure there aren't any surprises underneath.'

Claudel left the grill to his teammates and walked back to 11 North 4 East with me. I resumed troweling at the north end while Claudel stood over my SIJ helper in the south. By two we were down approximately three feet and I'd spotted nothing in the pit or screen to indicate I was nearing a burial.

Then I saw the boot.

It was lying sideways, the heel projecting slightly upward. I used my trowel to clear dirt, widening the area around it. My helper watched briefly, then continued scraping at the far end of the pit. Claudel observed without comment.

Within minutes I'd found the mate. Handful by tedious handful I peeled away dirt until the pair was fully exposed. The leather was wet and badly discolored, the eyelets bent and rusted, but both boots were reasonably intact.

When the footwear was fully exposed I made notes as to level and position, and the photographer captured my find on film. As I pried each boot loose and laid it on a plastic sheet it was obvious that neither contained leg or foot bones.

Not a good sign.

The sky was delft blue, the sun strong. Now and then a breeze teased the branches overhead, tapping them gently against one another. To my right the creek purled softly as it coursed over rocks abandoned by glaciers long ago.

A drop of sweat broke from my hairline and slithered the length of my neck. I pulled my sweatshirt over my head and tossed it on the pine needles bordering our pit. I was uncertain whether

69

my glands had kicked in due to spring warmth or due to the stress I was feeling.

It was always like this at exhumations. The curiosity. The anticipation. The fear of failure. What lies below the next layer? What if it's nothing? What if it's something but I can't get it out undamaged?

I had a desire to grab a spade and tunnel straight down. But strip-mining was not the answer. Tiresome as the process was, I knew proper technique was crucial. Maximum recovery of bones, artifacts, and contextual detail would be important in a case like this, so I plodded on, loosening dirt, then transferring it to buckets for screening. On the edge of my vision I could see the SIJ tech making the same motions, Claudel silent above him. At some point he had removed his jacket.

We saw the white flecks at the same time. Claudel was about to speak when I said, 'Hell-o.'

He looked at me with raised brows, and I nodded.

'Looks like lime. That usually means there's somebody home.'

The flecks gave way to a layer of sticky white ooze, then we found the first skull. It lay faceup, as if the dirt-filled orbits had twisted for one last look at the sky. The photographer shouted the news and the others dropped what they were doing and gathered around our pit.

As the sun moved slowly toward the horizon two skeletons emerged. They lay on their sides, one in a fetal position, the other with arms and legs bent sharply backward. The skulls and the leg and pelvic bones were devoid of flesh and stained the same

70

tea brown as the surrounding soil.

The foot and ankle bones were encased in rotting socks, the torsos covered with shreds of putrefied cloth. The fabric enveloped each arm, clinging to the bones like some scarecrow parody of a human limb. Wire circled the wrists, and I could see zippers and large metal belt buckles nestled among the vertebrae.

By five-thirty my team had fully exposed the remains. Besides the boots, the plastic sheet held a collection of corroded cartridges and isolated teeth recovered during screening. The photographers were shooting stills and videos when Frog talked his guard into another visit.

'Allô. Bonjour,' he said, tipping the brim of an invisible hat to the skeletons in the pit. Then he turned to me. 'Or maybe I should say bone jour, for you, lady.'

I ignored the bilingual pun.

'Holy shit. Why shirts and socks and nothing else?'

I wasn't in the mood for a lecture.

'That's right,' he sniggered, staring into the pit. 'They made them go shoeless and carry their shoes. But where the fuck are their pants?'

'Ashes to ashes, remember?' I said curtly.

'Shit to shit is more like it.' His voice was tense with excitement, as though the scrambler had been ratcheted up.

I found his callousness irritating. Death hurts. It's as simple as that. It hurts those who die, it hurts those who love them, and it hurts those who find them.

'Actually, you've got it backward,' I spat. 'It's the shit that survives longest. Natural fibers, like cotton

71

Levi's, decompose much sooner than synthetics. Your buddies were into polyester.'

'Fuck, do they look gross. Anything else in there with them?' he asked, peering into the grave. His eyes glinted, like those of a rat sitting on a carcass.

'Bad decision about that party, eh?' he snorted.

Yes, I thought. A deadly decision.

I began cleaning the blade of my trowel, using activity to calm myself. Two bodies lay dead at our feet and this little rodent was getting high on it.

I turned to check if the photographers had finished and saw Quickwater walking in my direction.

Great. Make my day, I thought, hoping he was looking for someone else. He wasn't. I watched him approach with as much enthusiasm as I'd have for frostbite.

Quickwater drew close and drilled me with one of his looks, his face rigid as granite. He smelled of male sweat and pine, and I realized he'd worked throughout the afternoon. While others had taken breaks to check the progress at the main burial, Quickwater had stayed at his task. Maybe he just wanted to keep some distance between us. Fine with me.

'There's something you need to see.'

There was a stillness about him I found unnerving. I waited for further explanation, but Quickwater merely turned and walked back toward his site, fully confident that I would follow.

Arrogant prick, I thought.

The trees were casting long shadows, and the temperature was falling by the minute. I looked at my watch. Almost six. The bologna and cheese seemed like prehistory.

This better be good, I thought.

I trudged across the cleared area to coordinates 3 North 9 East, the site of the disturbance to which Quickwater's team had been assigned. I was amazed to see they'd dug my entire grid.

The object of Quickwater's concern lay one meter down, left in place as I'd instructed. The team had excavated the rest of the square to a depth of two meters.

'That's it?'

Quickwater nodded.

'Nothing else?'

His expression did not change.

I looked around. They'd obviously been thorough. The screen still rested on its supports, flanked by cones of soggy earth. It looked as if they'd sifted every particle of dirt in the province. My eyes went back to the earthen pedestal and its macabre exhibit.

What they'd discovered made no sense at all.

CHAPTER NINE

I closed my eyes and listened to cows lowing softly in the distance. Somewhere life was calm, routine, and made sense.

When I raised my lids the bones were still there but made little sense. Dusk was closing in quickly, robbing the landscape of detail, like a slow fade in an old-time movie. We wouldn't finish the recovery that day, so answers would need to wait.

I would not risk destroying evidence by blundering around in the dark. The burials had been here for some time, and they could stay in place a few more hours. We would remove the exposed remains from each grave, but that was all. The site would be secured and work would resume in the morning.

Quickwater was still watching me. I looked around but couldn't see Claudel.

'I need to talk to your partner,' I said, turning back toward my site.

Quickwater held up a finger. Then he pulled a cell phone from his jacket, punched in a number, and handed it to me. Claudel answered almost immediately.

'Where are you?'

'Behind a poplar. Should I have requested a bathroom pass?'

Stupid question, Brennan.

'Your partner didn't think two skeletons were enough so he found us a third.'

'Sacré bleu!'

'Well, it's not exactly a skeleton. From what I can see, bachelor number three consists of a skull and a couple of long bones.'

'Where's the rest?'

'Very perceptive question, Detective Claudel. That's the source of some confusion on my part, as well.'

'What do you want to do?'

'Let's get all the bones out, then shut it down until daylight. St-Basile will have to seal off the property and post a watch at each grave. It shouldn't be too hard to guard the place since it has tighter security than Los Alamos.'

'The homeowners aren't going to be thrilled.'

'Yeah, well, this isn't how I'd planned to spend

my week, either.'

*   *   *

It took less than an hour to bag the bones and dispatch them to the morgue. The grill and other physical evidence were tagged and sent to the crime lab. Then I covered the holes with plastic sheets and left them in the care of the St-Basile PD.

Predictably, Quickwater and I returned to town in silence. At home, I tried Ryan's number, but got no response.

'Why, Andy, why?' I whispered, as if he were there to hear me. 'Please don't let this be true.'

My evening consisted of a bath, a pizza, and early bed.

Dawn found us all reassembled at the Vipers' picnic ground. The creek still gurgled, the birds still griped, and once again I could see my breath on the morning air. Only two things were different.

Claudel had opted to remain in town to pursue other leads.

Overnight, word of the bodies had leaked to the media, and an invasion force greeted us on our arrival. Cars and vans lined the highway, and reporters assaulted us in English and French. Ignoring them in both languages, we rolled past the cameras and mikes, identified ourselves to the officer on guard, and slipped through the gates.

I reopened each grave and began where I'd left off, starting with the double burial. I excavated to a depth of six feet, but found only a few hand bones and another pair of boots.

I did the same with Quickwater's site, growing

75

more baffled with each scoop of dirt. Aside from the skull and leg bones the pit was completely sterile. No jewelry or clothing remnants. No keys or plastic ID cards. Not a trace of hair or soft tissue. Additional GPR scans produced no evidence of other disturbances in the cleared area.

Another thing was eerie. Though the grave with the two skeletons had been rich with insect remnants, the one at 3 North 9 East produced not a single fossilized larva or pupa casing. I could see no explanation for the difference.

By five we'd refilled the holes and loaded my equipment into the crime scene van. I was tired, dirty, and confused, and the smell of death clung to my hair and clothes. All I wanted to do was go home and spend an hour with soap and water.

As Quickwater exited the gates, a TV crew surrounded the Jeep, refusing to allow us to pass. We slowed to a stop and a middle-aged man with lacquered hair and perfect teeth circled to my side and tapped on the glass. Behind him a cameraman trained his lens on my face.

Not in the mood for diplomacy, I lowered the window, leaned out, and told them in graphic terms to clear the way. The camera light went on and the reporter began to pepper me with shotgun questions. I made suggestions as to places for storage of their live-eye equipment, and destinations they might enjoy. Then, rolling my eyes, I retracted my head and hit the button. Quickwater gunned the engine and we shot away. I turned to see the reporter standing in the road, microphone still clutched in his hand, his flawless features wide with surprise.

I settled back and closed my eyes, knowing there

76

would be no conversation from Quickwater. It was just as well. Questions swirled in my brain, twisting and eddying like the waters of a swollen creek.

Who was this third victim? How had he died? Those answers I hoped to find in the lab.

When had the death occurred? How had part of his cadaver ended up in a clandestine grave at the Vipers' clubhouse? Those queries I figured the Vipers should field.

Most perplexing was the question of the absent body parts. Where was the rest of the skeleton? As I'd removed and packaged the bones for transport I'd watched closely for signs of animal damage. Bears, wolves, coyotes, and other predators will cheerfully dine on human corpses if given the opportunity. Ditto for the family dog or cat.

I saw nothing to indicate scavengers had absconded with the missing parts. There were no gnawed joints or shafts, no tooth scratches or puncture wounds. Nor had I seen any saw or knife marks to suggest the body had been dismembered.

So where was the rest of the deceased?

*   *   *

I planned Wednesday night as a modified replay of Tuesday. Bath. Microwave. Pat Conroy. Bed. Except for stage one, that's not how it went.

I'd just toweled off and slipped into a green flannel nightshirt when the phone rang. Birdie trailed me to the living room.

'*Mon Dieu,* your face is becoming better known than mine.'

It was definitely not what I needed to hear. Having done theater and television for more than twenty years, Isabelle was one of the best-loved performers in Quebec. Wherever she went she was recognized.

'I made the six o'clock news,' I guessed.

'An Oscar-winning performance, charged with raw anger and burning with the passion of—'

'How bad was it?'

'Your hair looked good.'

'Did they identify me?'

'Mais oui, Docteur Brennan.'

Damn. When I dropped to the couch Birdie settled into my lap, anticipating a long conversation.

'Was the tape edited?'

'Not a thing. Tempe, I'm pretty good at reading lips. Where did you learn those words?'

I groaned, recalling some of my more colorful suggestions about placement of the cameras and mikes.

'But that's not why I called. I want you to come to supper on Saturday. I'm having a few friends over and I think you need some social therapy, time away from these dreadful bikers and that Ryan thing.'

That Ryan thing.

'Isabelle, I don't think I'd be very good company right now. I—'

'Tempe, I am not taking no for an answer. And I want you to wear pearls and perfume and get all dressed up. It will improve your whole outlook.'

'Isabelle. Tell me you're not trying another fix up.'

For a moment I listened to silence. Then, 'This type of work you do, Tempe, it makes you too suspicious. I told you. It will just be some of my friends. Besides, I have a surprise for you.'

Oh no.

'What?'

'If I tell you it won't be a surprise.'

'Tell me anyway.'

'*Bon.* There's someone I want you to meet. And I know he would love to meet you. Well, actually you've met, but not formally. This man is not the least bit interested in a romantic relationship. Trust me.'

Over the past two years I'd met many of Isabelle's friends, most of whom were involved in the arts. Some were boring, others captivating. Many were gay. All were unique in one way or another. She was right. A night of frivolity would do me good.

'O.K. What can I bring?'

'Nothing. Just wear your pumps and be here at seven.'

After unturbaning and combing my hair, I placed a seafood dinner in the microwave. I was programming the time when my doorbell sounded.

Ryan, I hoped suddenly, walking to the hall. It was all a mistake. But if it wasn't, did I really want to see him? Did I want to know where he'd been, what he'd say?

Yes. Desperately.

The self-examination proved unnecessary since the security monitor showed Jean Bertrand, not his partner, standing in the outer vestibule. I buzzed him into the building, then went to the bedroom for socks and a robe. When he stepped inside the condo, he hesitated, as if trying to compose himself. After an awkward moment he extended his hand. It felt cold when I shook it.

'Hello, Tempe. Sorry to surprise you like this.'

Apparently surprising me was a hot thing these days. I nodded.

His face was drawn, and a dark crescent underscored each eye. Normally an impeccable dresser, he wore faded jeans tonight and a rumpled suede jacket. He started to speak again but I cut him off with a suggestion we move to the living room. He chose the sofa, and I curled into the chair opposite.

Bertrand studied me, his face tense with emotions I couldn't read. In the kitchen the microwave hummed warmth into my whitefish, carrots, and curried rice.

This is your party, I thought, refusing to break the silence. Finally.

'About Ryan.'

'Yes.'

'I got your calls, but I just couldn't talk about it then.'

'What exactly is 'it'?'

'He's out on bail, but he's been charged wi—'

'I know the charges.'

'Don't be angry at me. I had no idea where you stood in all this.'

'For God's sake, Bertrand, how many years have you known me?'

'I knew Ryan a hell of a lot longer!' he snapped. 'Evidently, I'm a lousy judge of character.'

'Neither of us seems to excel in that area.'

I hated myself for being so cold, but Bertrand's failure to call had hurt. When I had needed information important to me he'd blown me off like I was a drunk on the street with his hand out.

'Look, I don't know what to tell you. This thing's

wrapped tighter than a deb with new tits. I hear that when they're finished with Ryan he won't qualify for a paper route.'

'It's that bad?' I watched my fingers work the fringe on a throw pillow.

'They've got enough to nail him into tomorrow.'

'What is it they've got?'

'When they tossed his apartment they found enough methamphetamine to fry a third world nation and over ten thousand dollars' worth of stolen parkas.'

'Parkas?'

'Yeah. Those Kanuk things everyone's pissing their pants to own.'

'And?' I'd twisted the fringe so tightly it sent pain up my hand and into my wrist.

'And witnesses, videos, marked bills, and a trail of stink leading right straight to the center of the dung heap.'

Bertrand's voice betrayed his emotion. He took a deep breath.

'There's more. A shitload more. But I can't talk about it. Please understand, Tempe. Look, I'm sorry I left you hanging. It took me a while to work through this myself. I just didn't believe it, but—'

He broke off, afraid to trust his own voice.

'I guess the guy never quite left his past behind.'

As a college student Ryan had gotten into booze and pills, eventually dropping the academic life for life on the edge. A knife-wielding cokehead had nearly killed him, and the wild child reversed course, became a cop, and rose to the rank of lieutenant-detective. I knew all that. But still . . .

'I learned that someone ratted Ryan out, and for all I knew it could have been you. But it's not important now. The sonovabitch is dirty and he deserves what's coming down.'

For a very long time neither of us spoke. I could feel Bertrand's stare, but refused to meet it or say a word. The microwave beeped, then shut off. Silence. Finally, I asked.

'Do you really think he did it?' My cheeks felt hot and my chest burned below my sternum.

'For the past few days I've done nothing but chase down leads to show that he *didn't* do it. Anything. Anyone. All I wanted was one tiny hint of doubt.'

When he gestured with thumb and index finger, I could see a tiny tremor in his hand.

'It wasn't there, Tempe.' He ran a hand over his face. 'But it doesn't matter anymore.'

'It does matter. It's the only thing that matters.'

'At first I thought, no way. Not Andrew Ryan. Then I learned the case against him.'

He took another deep breath.

'Look, Tempe, I'm sorry. I'm so sorry for this whole goddam mess I'm not sure who I am anymore or where the world's going. And I'm not sure if it's worth the price of a ticket to ride.'

When I looked up Bertrand's face was filled with pain, and I knew exactly what he was feeling. He was trying not to despise his partner for succumbing to the greed, all the while hating him for the deep, cold emptiness his betrayal had created.

Bertrand promised to let me know if he learned anything. When he left I trashed the fish and cried myself to sleep.

CHAPTER TEN

Thursday I put on a dark blue suit and drove to Our Lady of the Angels. The morning was blustery, the sun appearing only infrequently among the heavy clouds scudding across the sky.

I parked and threaded through the usual collection of gawkers, journalists, and cops. No sign of Charbonneau, Claudel, or Quickwater.

Of the trickle of mourners solemnly climbing the steps, most were black. Whites arrived in couples or groups, each with at least one child in tow. Probably Emily Anne's classmates and their families.

Near the entrance, a wind gust tore the hat from the head of an old woman to my right. One gnarled hand flew to her head while the other fought the skirt whipping round her legs.

I darted forward, trapped the hat against the church wall, and handed it to the woman. She clutched it to her bony chest and gave a small smile. Her wrinkled brown face reminded me of the crab- apple dolls crafted by ladies in the Smoky Mountains.

'You be a frien' of Emily Anne?' the old woman asked in a crackly voice.

'Yes, ma'am.' I didn't want to explain my involvement.

'She my gran'chile.'

'I am so sorry for your loss.'

'I got twenty-two gran'children, but that Emily Anne be somet'ing special. That chile do everyt'ing. She writes her letters, she does dance ballet, she does swim, she does skate on ice. I t'inking that girl be even smarter than her mama.'

'She was a beautiful little girl.'

'Maybe that be why God take her up.'

I watched Emily Anne's grandmother totter on, remembering those same words from a long time ago. A slumbering ache stirred in my chest, and I steeled myself for what was to come.

Inside, the church was cool and smelled of incense and wax and wood polish. Light filtered through stained glass, casting a pastel softness over everything.

The pews were packed in front, with a scattering of attendees in the middle. I slipped into a back row, folded my hands, and tried to concentrate on the present. Already my skin itched and my palms felt sweaty. As I looked around, the organist finished one requiem and began another.

A miniature white casket sat below the altar, heaped with flowers and flanked by candles at either end. Balloons bobbed on strings attached to the coffin's handles. The brightly colored spheres looked jarringly out of sync with the scene.

In the front pew I could see two small heads, a larger figure between them. Mrs. Toussaint was bent forward, a handkerchief clutched to her mouth. As I watched, her shoulders began to heave, and a tiny hand rose and gently rubbed her upper arm.

The dormant ache within me awoke fully, and I was back at St. Barnabas parish. Father Morrison was at the pulpit and my little brother lay in his own tiny coffin.

My mother's sobs were terrible, and I reached up to comfort her. She did not acknowledge my touch, just held little Harriet to her chest and cried onto her head. Feeling utterly helpless, I watched my sister's corn-silk hair grow damp with my mother's tears.

If I had been given a box of crayons and asked to draw my world at six, I would have chosen a single color. Black.

I'd been powerless to save Kevin, to stop the leukemia devastating his tiny body. He was my most treasured gift, my Christmas brother, and I adored him. I had prayed and prayed, but I could do nothing to prevent his death. Or to make my mother smile. I had begun to wonder if I were evil, because my prayers were of no effect.

Almost four decades, and the pain of Kevin's death still lingered. The sights and sounds and smells of a funeral Mass never failed to reopen that wound, allowing the buried grief to ooze into my conscious thought.

I moved my eyes from the Toussaint family and scanned the crowd. Charbonneau had concealed himself in the shadow of a confessional booth, but I recognized no one else.

At that moment the priest entered and crossed himself. He looked young, athletic, and nervous. More like a tennis player approaching a match than a priest approaching a funeral service. We all stood.

As I went through the familiar motions, my skin felt flushed, my heart beat faster than it should have. I tried to concentrate, but my mind resisted. Images bled into my brain, taking me back to that time in my childhood.

An enormous woman took the pulpit to the right of the altar. Her skin was the color of mahogany, her hair braided atop her head. The woman's cheeks glistened as she sang 'Amazing Grace.' I remembered her from the newspaper photo.

Then, the priest spoke of childhood innocence. Relatives praised Emily Anne's sunny disposition, her love of family. An uncle mentioned her passion for waffles. Her teacher described an enthusiastic student, and read the essay that had won a prize. A classmate recited an original poem.

More hymns. Communion. The faithful filed up, returned to their seats. Stifled sobs. Incense. The blessing of the coffin. Soft wailing from Mrs. Toussaint.

Finally, the priest turned and asked Emily Anne's sisters and classmates to join him, then seated himself on the altar steps. There was a moment of absolute stillness, followed by whispered commands and parental nudging. One by one children emerged from the pews and walked timidly toward the altar.

What the priest said was not original. Emily Anne is in heaven with God. She has been reunited with her father. One day her mother and sisters will join her, as will everyone present.

What the young priest did next *was* original. He told the children that Emily Anne was happy, and that we should celebrate with her. He signaled his servers, who disappeared into the vestry, and returned with huge bunches of balloons.

'These balloons are filled with helium,' explained the priest. 'That makes them fly. I want you each to take one, and we will all walk out with Emily Anne. We will say a good-bye prayer, then release our balloons to rise to heaven. Emily Anne will see them and know that we love her.'

He looked at the solemn little faces.

'Is that a good idea?'

Every head nodded.

The priest rose, disentangled strings, placed a balloon in each small hand, and led the children down the steps. The organist began Schubert's *Ave Maria.'*

The pallbearers came forward, lifted the casket, and the procession moved toward the door, the pews emptying in its wake. As the line passed, I slipped in at the end.

The mourners followed the coffin outside then circled around, children on the inside, adults forming an outer ring. Mrs. Toussaint stood behind her daughters, supported by the singer.

I held back on the steps. The overcast had broken, leaving a sky filled with tumbling white clouds. As I watched balloons rise toward them, I felt a grief as sharp as anything I'd felt in my life.

I lingered a moment, then descended slowly, wiping tears from my cheeks, and reaffirming the vow I'd made on the day of Emily Anne's death.

I would find these indiscriminate butchers and put them where they could never kill another child. I could not restore the daughter but I would provide this small comfort for the mother.

Leaving Emily Anne to those who loved her, I drove toward Parthenais, in a mood to lose myself in work.

* * *

At the lab, the Carcajou investigators already had names for the skeletons from St-Basile. Félix Martineau, age twenty-seven, and Robert Gately, age thirty-nine, rode with the Tarantulas, a now defunct OMC, but active in Montreal in the seventies and eighties. Gately was a full patch member, Martineau a prospect.

On the evening of August 24, 1987, the two had left Gately's apartment on rue Hochelaga heading for a party. Gately's ole lady did not know the name or address of the host. Neither man was seen again.

I spent the day with the bones from the double burial, sorting them into individuals and determining age, sex, race, and height. Cranial and pelvic shape confirmed both victims were male. The differences in age and height made the task of individuation considerably easier than with the Vaillancourt brothers.

As soon as I'd finished with the skulls and jaws I'd given them to Marc Bergeron for odontological analysis. I figured his job would be easy too, since both men had obvious dental work.

The taller victim had a well-healed fracture of the collarbone. I was photographing the injury when Bergeron entered my lab Friday morning. The dentist was one of the oddest-looking men I'd ever met, with wild, dandelion hair and a daddy-longlegs build. It was impossible to guess his age, and no one at the lab seemed to know.

Bergeron waited until I'd snapped the shot then confirmed the identifications as positive.

'How did you get the records so quickly?'

'Two very cooperative dentists. And, fortunately for me, the deceased had a commitment to oral health. At least Gately did. Bad teeth, lots of restorations. Martineau was less fastidious, but there were some peculiarities that made him a cinch. The big bad biker was walking around with four baby teeth in his mouth. That's pretty rare for someone his age.'

I turned off the lights on the copy stand.

'Have you started on the third victim?' Bergeron asked.

'Not yet, but I can finish this later. Shall we take a look?'

I'd been wanting to look at the third set of bones all morning and Bergeron provided a good excuse.

'You bet.'

I returned the collarbone to the skeleton on the left side of my worktable.

'Who's who?' I asked, gesturing at the bones.

Bergeron went to his tray and checked the digits on each occipital bone, then those on the small cards I'd set beside the skeletons, and positioned the skulls accordingly. He swept a bony arm over the victim with the broken clavicle.

'Monsieur Martineau.'

Then over the gentleman on his right.

'And Mr. Gately.'

'Was Gately an Anglophone?'

'I assume so since his dentist doesn't speak a word of French.'

'Not too many of those among *les motards.*'

'None that I know of,' Bergeron agreed.

'Will you give the good news to Quickwater and Claudel?'

'I've already made the call.'

I went to the storage shelves and pulled the box containing the third St-Basile victim. Since the remains were coated with dirt, I placed a screen in the sink, set them in it, and ran warm water over them.

The long bones cleaned easily, so I laid them on the drainboard and began brushing mud from the outside of the skull. Its weight told me that the cranial interior was packed solid. When the facial features were clear I inverted the skull and let the tap water run over the base. Then I crossed to my desk to fill out a case identification card.

When I returned to the sink Bergeron held the skull in his hands, turning it faceup, then rotating it for a lateral view. He stared at the features a long time then said, 'Oh my.'

When he handed me the cranium I repeated his movements, then echoed his thought.

'Oh my.'

CHAPTER ELEVEN

One look and I knew I'd been wrong. The smooth forehead and occiput, slender cheekbones, and small mastoid processes told me that bachelor number three was clearly of my own gender.

I got my calipers and took a measurement from one of the bones that lay on the drainboard. The femoral head is a ball-like structure that fits into a socket in the pelvis to form the hip joint. This one had a diameter of only thirty-nine millimeters, placing it squarely in the female range.

And the victim had been young. I could see a jagged line across the top of the ball, indicating that fusion of the growth cap was incomplete at the time of death.

I returned to the cranium. Squiggly lines separated all the bones. I rotated the skull for a

90

view of the base. Just in front of the foramen magnum, the hole through which the spinal cord leaves the brain, there was a gap between the sphenoid and occipital bones.

I showed Bergeron the open suture.

'She was just a kid,' I said. 'Probably in her teens.'

He made a comment, but I didn't hear. My attention had been drawn to an irregularity on the right parietal bone. Cautiously, I ran my fingers over it. Yes, there was something there.

Taking care to cause no damage, I held the skull under the faucet and teased away dirt with a soft-bristle toothbrush. Bergeron watched as the defect came into focus. It took only moments.

What I'd spotted was a small round hole, slightly above and behind the ear opening. I estimated its diameter at approximately one centimeter.

'Gunshot wound?' Bergeron suggested.

'Maybe. No. I don't think so.'

Though the proper size for a small-caliber projectile, the perforation didn't look like a bullet entrance. Its border was smooth and rounded, like the inside of a doughnut hole.

'Then what?'

'I'm not sure. Maybe some type of congenital defect. Maybe an abscess. I'll know better when I empty the skull and get a look at the endocranial surface. I'll also need X rays to see what's going on inside the bone.'

Bergeron looked at his watch.

'Let me know when you've finished so I can shoot some bite-wings on this one. I didn't see any restorations, but I might spot something on the X rays. The right canine has an odd alignment which will be useful, but I'd prefer having the lower jaw.'

'I'll work harder next time.'

'Not necessary.' He laughed.

When Bergeron left I set the skull upside down in a rubber ring and adjusted the water so it ran gently into the foramen magnum. Then I went back to photographing Gately and Martineau, documenting skeletal features relevant to their identifications. I also took multiple shots of the bullet holes in the back of each man's head.

Periodically I checked the unknown female's skull, pouring off muck as the water loosened it. Just before noon, as I was draining sediment, something broke free and tapped against the cranial interior. I placed the skull back on the ring and slipped my fingers inside.

The object felt long and thin. I tried to dislodge it, but the thing had a tail of some sort still embedded in the mud. Barely able to contain my curiosity, I adjusted the tap and went back to the Gately report.

By 1 P.M. the object floated free, but the trailer was still firmly cemented. Impatient, I allowed the sink to fill, immersed the skull, and went downstairs to the cafeteria.

When I returned from lunch the soaking had liquefied the last of the dirt, and I was able to pour it off easily. Holding my breath, I inserted my fingers and delicately manipulated the object free.

The device was less than four inches long, and consisted of a length of tubing with a valve at one end. I cleaned it and placed it on a tray. Certain of its importance, but unsure as to what it was, I washed my hands and went in search of a pathologist.

92

According to the duty board, LaManche was at a meeting of the committee on infant mortality. Marcel Morin was at his desk.

He looked up when I tapped on the door.

'Got a minute?'

'But of course.' His French was warm and lyrical, reflecting the Haiti of his boyhood. I entered the office and placed the tray in front of him.

'Ah. A surgical implant.' His eyebrows rose behind rimless glasses. They were graying, like the tightly cropped frizz of hair retreating backward on his scalp.

'I thought so. Can you tell me more about it?'

He lifted both palms. 'Not much. It looks like a ventricular shunt, but I'm not a neurosurgeon. You might want to talk to Carolyn Russell. She's done some neuro consults for us.'

He flipped through his Rolodex, jotted down a number, and handed it to me, saying, 'She's at the MNI.'

I thanked him, went to my office, and dialed the Montreal Neurological Institute. Dr. Russell was in a meeting, so I left a message. I'd just hung up when the phone rang. It was Claudel.

'You've talked to Bergeron?' he asked.

'He just left.'

'So two make the jump from the list of missing to the list of dead.'

I waited for him to go on, but he didn't.

'And?'

A Claudel pause, then, 'We've started making calls, but no one knows a thing. Not surprising, given the fact that more than a decade has passed and these people aren't geographically stable. Of course they wouldn't tell us spit if we'd hauled their

93

grandmothers out of that hole.'

'What about Rinaldi?'

'Frog's sticking to his story. He knew what he knew by word of mouth. According to club lore Gately and Martineau went to a party and walked right in on their own funeral.'

'In stocking feet.'

'Right. These fellows tend to underdress. But Frog wasn't there when the hit went down. It was probably his night for charity work. What about the third guy?'

'The third guy is a girl.'

'A girl.'

'Yes. What does Frog know about her?'

'Not a thing. But Frog would give nothing up if there wasn't a prize in it for him. What can you tell me about her?'

'She was a white female in her mid to late teens.'

'She was that young?'

'Yes.'

I could hear traffic in the background and figured Claudel was calling from the road.

'I'll get a list of missing teenage girls. What time frame?'

'Go back ten years.'

'Why ten years?'

'I'd say the victim's been dead at least two years, but with what we recovered I can't really pinpoint an upper limit. I have a feeling this was a secondary burial.'

'What does that mean?'

'I think she was buried somewhere else, then dug up and moved to the place we found her.'

'Why?'

'Another   perceptive   question,   Detective

94

Claudel.'

I told him about the surgical implant.

'What does *that* mean?'

'When I find out I'll let you know.'

I'd hardly replaced the receiver when the phone rang again. Carolyn Russell could see me at three. I looked at my watch. If the parking gods smiled I could make it.

I wrote the case number on the lid of a plastic specimen container and sealed the implant inside. Pausing only to tell Bergeron that he could have the girl's skull, I hurried to my car and raced across town.

The Royal Victoria Hospital was built before the turn of the century. A sprawling gray stone complex, it lies in the heart of Montreal, looming over the McGill campus like a medieval castle on a Tuscan hillside.

At the Peel end is the Allan Memorial Institute, infamous for CIA drug experiments conducted there in the late fifties. The Montreal Neurological Institute is located to the east of the Royal Vic, across rue Université. Teaching and research units of McGill University, the MNI, the Neurological Hospital, and the new Brain Tumor Research Institute sit haunch to jowl with the football stadium, a testimonial in mortar and brick to the priorities of the modern university.

The Neuro, as the research institute and hospital are known, dates to the thirties, the brainchild of Wilder Penfield. Though a brilliant scientist and neurosurgeon, Dr. Penfield was not a visionary in traffic control. Parking is a nightmare.

Following Dr. Russell's suggestion, I drove onto the grounds of the Royal Vic, forked over ten dollars, and began cruising the lot. I was on my third pass when I spotted brake lights. An Audi pulled out and I shot forward and into the space, thus avoiding the necessity of tuning to FM 88.5 for a parking update. My watch said two fifty-five.

I arrived at Russell's office sweaty and panting from my dash down avenue des Pins and my trek through the hospital. It had begun to mist, and my bangs lay damp and limp across my forehead. When the doctor looked up, an expression of doubt crossed her face.

I introduced myself and she rose and held out a hand. Her hair was gray, cut short and swept to the side. Her face was deeply creased, but her grip was as strong as that of any man. I guessed she was somewhere in her sixties.

'Sorry I'm late. I had a little trouble finding you.' That was an understatement.

'Yes, this building is confusing. Please sit down,' she said in English, gesturing at a chair opposite her desk.

'I had no idea this place was so large,' I said, seating myself.

'Oh yes. The MNI is engaged in an enormous range of activities.'

'I know the institute is world famous for its epilepsy research.' I slipped off my jacket.

'Yes, more epilepsy surgeries are performed at our hospital than at any other center in the world. The surgical technique of cortical resection was pioneered at this institution. Studies in the mapping of cerebral function began with epilepsy patients here more than sixty years ago. It was that work that paved the way for the MRI and PET brain mapping going on today.'

'I'm familiar with Magnetic Resonance Imaging but what is PET?'

'Positron Emission Tomography. Like MRI, it's a technique used to image brain structure and physiology. Our McConnell Brain Imaging Centre is rated as one of the world's leading facilities.'

'What other research do you do?'

'A tremendous amount of groundbreaking work has emanated from the MNI. The development of electroencephalography, the concept of focal and generalized epilepsies, new methods of frameless stereotactic surgery, contributions to postglandin biochemistry in the nervous system, localization of dystrophin skeletal muscle. I could go on and on.'

I was certain she could. Dr. Russell was obviously proud of her employer. I smiled encouragement, though I understood only part of what she had listed.

She leaned back and laughed. 'I'm sure you are not here for a lecture on the Neuro.'

'No, but it's fascinating. I wish I had more time. But I know you're very busy and I don't want to take up any more of your day than necessary.'

I took the container from my purse and handed it to her. She looked at it, then unscrewed the cap and slid the implant onto a piece of paper on the blotter of her desk.

'This is an old one,' she said, turning it over with a pencil. 'I don't think they've made this model for years.'

'What is it?'

'It's a ventriculo-peritoneal shunt. They're implanted for the treatment of hydrocephalus.'

'Hydrocephalus?' I knew the term, but was surprised to hear her say it. What other

97

misfortunes would I learn about this child?

'It's commonly known as "water on the brain," but that's not really accurate, although that's a literal translation from the Greek, *hydro* being water, and *cephalus* being head. Cerebral spinal fluid is constantly produced in spaces in the brain called ventricles. Normally it circulates through the four ventricles, and flows over the brain's surface and down the spinal cord. Eventually the CSF is absorbed into the bloodstream, and the amount of fluid and pressure in the ventricles stays within acceptable limits.

'But if drainage is blocked, fluid will accumulate, causing the ventricles to swell and press on the surrounding tissue.'

'So hydrocephalus refers to an imbalance in the amount of CSF produced and the rate at which it drains from the ventricles.'

'Exactly.'

'And, as the CSF builds up, it causes the ventricles to enlarge and the pressure inside the head to increase.'

'You've got it. Hydrocephalus can be acquired or congenital, which is not to say hereditary. The term simply means the condition is present at birth.'

'I found the shunt in a normal-looking skull. Doesn't hydrocephalus result in increased head size?'

'Only in infants, and only if left untreated. As you know, with older children and adults the bones of the skull are already formed.'

'What causes it?'

'There are lots of reasons for inadequate CSF drainage. Prematurity puts an infant at high risk. And most babies with spina bifida have

98

hydrocephalus.'

'Spina bifida involves a neural tube defect?'

'Yes. The problem occurs during the first four weeks of gestation, often before the mother knows she's pregnant. The embryo's neural tube, which develops into the brain, spinal cord, and vertebral column, fails to form properly, leading to varying degrees of permanent damage.'

'How common is it?'

'Entirely too common. It's estimated that spina bifida affects one in every thousand babies born in the United States, and about one in seven hundred and fifty born in Canada.'

'I recovered no vertebrae, so I have no way to know if my young lady had spina bifida.'

Russell nodded in agreement, then continued her explanation.

'There are many other causes of hydrocephalus besides spina bifida.' She ticked them off on her fingers. 'It can result from brain hemorrhage. The inflammation and debris resulting from brain infections, such as meningitis, can block drainage pathways. Tumors can cause compression and swelling of brain tissues and result in poor drainage. So can certain types of cysts. And hydrocephalus can be familial.'

'It can be inherited?'

'Yes. Though that's rare.'

'So where does the shunt come in?'

'There is no way to cure or prevent hydrocephalus. For the past forty years the most effective treatment has been the surgical insertion of a shunt. The one you've brought is a bit outdated, but it's really pretty typical.

'Most shunts are just flexible tubes placed into

99

the ventricles to divert the flow of CSF. They consist of a system of tubes with a valve to control the rate of drainage and to prevent back flow. The early ones diverted the accumulated CSF into a vein in the neck, then into the right atrium of the heart. Those are called ventriculo-atrial, or VA shunts. Some VA shunts are still used, but there are problems associated with them, including infection, and, though rare, heart failure due to blockage of blood vessels within the lungs by particles of blood clot flaking off the shunt's catheter tip. Most shunts now drain into the peritoneal cavity. They're called VP shunts.'

She indicated the device I'd pulled from the skull.

'This is a VP shunt. In the living patient you would have been able to feel the bottom tube running under the skin that overlies the ribs. That part of the device is missing.'

I waited for her to go on.

'The peritoneal cavity is large and can usually handle any amount of fluid delivered by the shunt. Another advantage of draining into the abdomen is that the rhythmic contractions of the intestinal organs move the tip of the catheter around. That motion prevents its becoming blocked or sequestered in scar tissue.'

'When do these things go in?'

'As soon as hydrocephalus is diagnosed. As much as thirty-six inches of tubing can be placed in the abdomen of a neonate. As the child grows, the tubing unwinds to accommodate the increased length of the torso.'

'I found a small hole in the skull, near the parieto-temporal junction.'

'That's a burr hole. It's drilled during surgery to insert the upper end of the shunt into the brain. They're usually made behind the hairline, either at the top of the head, behind the ear, or in the back.'

Russell's eyes flicked to a round metal clock on her desk, then back to mine. I was anxious to learn what difficulties might be caused by hydrocephaly, but knew the woman's time was limited. That research would be up to me.

I gathered my jacket and she returned the shunt to its jar, curling the paper and allowing the device to slide gently into place. We rose simultaneously and I thanked her for her help.

'Do you have any idea who your young lady is?' she asked.

'Not yet.'

'Would you like me to send you some reading material on hydrocephalus? There are problems associated with the condition that you might find helpful.'

'Yes, very much. Thank you.'

CHAPTER TWELVE

I left the Neuro and went directly to Carcajou headquarters for the second of Roy's review sessions. The meeting was already in progress, so I slipped into a back seat, my brain still processing what I'd learned from Carolyn Russell. Our conversation had raised as many questions as it had answered.

How had the hydrocephaly affected my unknown girl? Had she been sickly? Disabled?

Retarded? How did a teenager with that condition end up buried near a biker headquarters? Was she a willing participant, or another innocent, like Emily Anne Toussaint?

This time Roy was using transparencies, and a bulleted list filled the screen. I forced myself to focus.

'Outlaw motorcycle clubs are characterized by a number of common elements. Most OMCs are organized according to the Hells Angels model. We'll come back and look at that structure in some detail.'

He indicated the second item.

'All clubs have membership which is very selective, and 'prospects' or 'strikers' are required to prove themselves to earn their colors.'

He moved down the list.

'The colors, or club patch, are the member's most valued possession. Not everyone wears colors, however. Individuals who are useful to the gang are allowed to interact as associates without actually joining.

'The primary focus of an OMC is criminal activity. Each club has rules that condone violence to further the interests of the club and its members. Intelligence gathering is intensive, including the monitoring of other gangs and of law enforcement personnel.'

Roy pointed his pen at the last item on the list.

'The clubhouse, which is often strongly fortified and elaborately outfitted, is the meeting place for club activities.'

I thought of the Vipers' house in St-Basile, and wondered what activities could have included a sixteen-year-old girl with hydrocephaly.

Roy removed the transparency and replaced it with another, this one a tree titled 'Political Structure of an OMC: National.'

Roy explained the hierarchy, starting at the bottom.

'The basic element of the OMC structure is the chapter. An independent outlaw motorcycle club becomes part of a larger organization, such as the Hells Angels, only after a charter has been approved by vote of the national membership. This involves a long process that we can discuss later if we have time.

'Each chapter operates in a specific local area and maintains a certain degree of autonomy, but must live by the rules set out by the organization. These rules, either in the form of bylaws or a constitution, define the rights and obligations of the members and the gang.'

Roy slid a new transparency onto the projector. This chart was labeled 'Political Structure of an OMC: Chapter.'

'Each chapter has its own controlling body, or executive, elected by the members. Typically there's a president, vice president, secretary-treasurer, and sergeant at arms. These are the guys responsible for maintaining order within and peace outside the group.'

'Guess none of our local morons will make the Nobel short list this year.' Kuricek was up to form.

Roy waved down the laughter.

'There's also an elected road captain who takes charge of the runs. Then there are the rank-and-file members—'

'And he does mean rank.' Kuricek held his nose.

'—who have a say in matters affecting the group,

103

but the president makes the final decisions. Some of the larger clubs also have a security officer whose duty it is to keep up-to-date information on rival gangs, reporters, lawyers, judges, public officials, witnesses, and, of course, on yours truly.'

Roy swept his arm across the room.

'What kind of information?'

'Personal, financial, family members, girlfriends, boyfriends, phone numbers, birth dates, addresses, vehicle descriptions, license plates, places of employment, daily habits, you name it, these guys get it. Their photo collections make the National Portrait Gallery look sparse. If there's an intended victim, his dossier may include tips on the best places to kill him.'

'*Merde!*'

'*Esti!*'

Roy worked his pen from left to right across three boxes on the next to lowest line of the diagram.

'At the bottom of the chapter hierarchy are the prospects, the hang-arounds, and the women.'

Roy pointed to the box marked 'Probationary Member.'

'The 'prospect' or 'striker' must be nominated by a full patch member. He does all the shitwork around the clubhouse and during runs. Prospects can't vote and they can't attend church.'

'Church?' Today the ponytailed investigator wore a silver skull in his ear.

'The mandatory weekly chapter meeting.'

'How long does it take to get in?'

'The prospect period averages six months to one year. You can spot these guys because they wear only the bottom rocker of the patch.'

104

'Which gives the chapter location.' Ponytail.

'*C'est ça.* There are several pages showing club colors in the manuals I gave you. Some of them are true artistic marvels.'

Roy's pen moved sideways to the box marked 'Associates.'

'A hang-around must also be sponsored by a full patch member. Some go on to prospect, others never do. Hang-arounds do all kinds of menial jobs, and act as a support structure for the club in the community. They are excluded from all club business.'

Two boxes hung from the one at the far right marked 'Female Associates.'

'Women are at the lowest level of the hierarchy and fall into one of two categories. The ole ladies are wives, either common-law or legal, and are off-limits to other gang members, except by invitation. The club 'mamas' or 'sheep' are a different story. How shall I put it?' He raised eyebrows and shoulders. 'They mingle freely.'

'Warm-hearted ladies, all.' Kuricek.

'Very. Mamas are fair game to any color-wearing member. While the ole ladies enjoy a certain degree of protection, have no doubt about it, outlaw motorcycle gangs are male-dominated and highly chauvinistic. Women are bought, sold, and swapped like hardware.'

'The biker's idea of women's lib is to take the cuffs off after he's through. Maybe.' Kuricek.

'That's pretty close. Women are definitely used and abused.' Roy.

'Used how?' I asked.

'Aside from sex, there's what we might call wage sharing. They get the women into exotic dancing,

105

drink hustling, street-level drug trafficking, prostitution, then rake back the earnings. One hooker from Halifax claimed she had to turn over forty percent of her take to the Hells Angel who pimped for her.'

'How do they find these women?' I felt a knot forming in my stomach.

'The usual. They pick them up in bars, hitchhiking, runaways.'

'Wanna ride my Harley, sweet thing?' Kuricek.

I pictured the skull and shunt.

'Amazingly, there's never a shortage,' Roy continued. 'But don't get me wrong. While many are victimized, some held against their wills, a good number of these ladies embrace the lifestyle with gusto. Macho men, drugs, alcohol, guns, round-the-mountain sex. It's a wild ride and they go along gladly.

'The women also make themselves useful in ways not strictly sexual or economic. Often it's the ladies who carry concealed drugs or weapons, and they're very good at ditching when a bust comes down. Some make very effective spies. They hire on with government agencies, the phone company, records offices, any place they might have access to useful information. Some ole ladies have guns or property registered in their names, either because hubby is prohibited, or to protect his assets from seizure by the government.'

Roy glanced at his watch.

'On that note, I think we'll call it a day. Some folks have just joined us from the CUM, so I may hold one more of these sessions.'

CUM. Communauté Urbaine de Montréal Police. I wondered why Claudel had not been

106

present at today's meeting.

'If so, I'll post the date.'

*   *   *

As I drove to the lab my thoughts went back to the teenager from St-Basile, and to Russell's explanation. Could the girl have been a victim of this biker insanity? Something about her resonated in me, and I tried again to piece together what I knew about her.

She died in her teens, no longer a child but not yet a woman. Her bones revealed nothing about how she had died, but they did disclose something of how she had lived. The hydrocephalus might help identify her.

The well-healed burr hole suggested that the shunt had been there awhile. Did she hate the shunt? Did she lie in her bed at night and palpate the tube running under her skin? Was she plagued by other physical problems? Did her peers torment her? Was she an honor student? A dropout? Would we find medical records associated with a missing girl that would help identify this skull?

Unlike many of my nameless dead, I had no sense of who she was. The Girl. That's how I'd come to think of her. The Girl in the Viper pit.

And why was she buried at the biker clubhouse? Was her death linked to the murders of Gately and Martineau, or was she just another victim in the grim tradition of biker violence against women? Was her life interrupted for a premeditated reason, or had she merely been in the wrong place at the wrong time, like little Emily Anne Toussaint?

As I wound my way through rush hour traffic I

again felt pain and anger. Pain over a life only partly lived, anger at the callousness of those who had taken it.

And I considered Andrew Ryan, with his sky blue eyes and burning intensity. Even the smell of him used to make me happy. How could I have missed his other side, his double life? Could it really be so? My brain told me yes. Bertrand swore it was true. Why did my heart refuse to budge?

My thoughts ran in useless circles. My neck hurt and I could feel a pounding behind my left eye.

I turned onto Parthenais and pulled into an empty spot. Then I leaned back and called a time-out. I needed a respite.

I would tell Claudel what I'd learned, then there would be no bones or thoughts of Ryan for an entire weekend. I would do nothing more serious than peruse Roy's biker manual. I would read, shop, and go to Isabelle's party. But come Monday, I would make a second vow. I would continue my search for Emily Anne's killers and I would also find a name for The Girl in the Viper pit.

CHAPTER THIRTEEN

It was after seven when I got home.

At the lab I'd secured the bones and shunt, then phoned Claudel to pass along what I'd learned from Russell. We decided that I'd research all cases from the past ten years involving partial skeletons. He'd continue with his list of missing girls. If neither of us had a hit by the end of the day on Monday, we'd enter the case into CPIC. That failing, we'd send it south into the NCIC system.

That sounded like a plan.

Following a change of clothes and a brief conversation with Birdie, I walked to McKay, climbed to the gym on the top floor, and worked out for an hour. Afterward I bought a rotisserie chicken from the butcher, and loaded up on veggies and fruit.

Back home I microwaved green beans and split the chicken, stashing half in the refrigerator for Saturday lunch. Then I got out my bottle of Maurice's Piggy Park barbecue sauce.

Montreal is a veritable smorgasbord, home to many of the world's finest restaurants. Chinese. German. Thai. Mexican. Lebanese. No ethnic group is unrepresented. For a fast-food lunch or a lingering gourmet supper the city is unsurpassed. Its one failing lies in the art of barbecue.

In Quebec what poses as barbecue sauce is a brown gravy, as tasteless and odorless as carbon monoxide. A diligent seeker can find the tomato-based Texas variety, but the vinegar-and-mustard concoction of the eastern Carolinas is a delicacy I am forced to import. Montreal friends eyeing the golden potion are skeptical. One taste and they're hooked.

I poured Maurice's sauce into a small bowl, carried everything to the living room, and dined in front of the tube. By 9 P.M. the weekend was still going well. The hardest decision up to that point involved sports allegiance. Though the Cubs were taking on the Braves, I opted for the NBA play-offs, and cheered the Hornets to a 102–87 victory over the Knicks.

Bird was torn, attracted by the smell of chicken,

109

but alarmed by the outbursts and arm waving. He spent the night across the room, chin on his paws, eyes flying open every time I yelled. At eleven he followed me to bed, where he circled twice before settling behind my knees. We were both asleep in minutes.

*   *   *

I was awakened by the sound of the doorbell. Door chirp would be more correct. When a visitor buzzes for entry to my building, the system twitters like a sparrow with hiccups.

The window shade was a pale gray, and the digits on the clock glowed eight-fifteen. Bird was no longer pressed to my legs. I threw back the covers and grabbed a robe.

When I stumbled into the hall I was greeted by an enormous green eye. My hands flew to my chest and I took an involuntary step back from the security monitor.

Chirrrrrrrup.

The eye withdrew and was replaced by my nephew's face. He mugged at the camera, tipping his head from side to side and stretching the corners of his mouth with his fingers.

I pressed the button to allow him in. Birdie brushed my legs, then looked up with round yellow eyes.

'Don't ask me, Bird.'

Kit rounded the corner with a duffel bag in one hand, a brown paper sack in the other, and a backpack slung from each shoulder. He wore a multicolored knit hat that looked as though it would be big in Guatemala.

110

'Auntie T,' he boomed in his rowdy Texas drawl.

'Shhh.' I held a finger to my lips. 'It's Saturday morning.'

I stepped back and held the door wide. As he brushed past I could smell wood smoke and mildew and something like mushrooms or moss.

He dropped the duffel and packs and gave me a hug. When he released me and pulled off the hat his hair did an Edward Scissorhands impression.

'Nice do, Auntie.'

'You are *not* in a position to talk,' I said, tucking strands behind my ears.

He held out the paper bag.

'A little something from the waters of Vermont.' He spotted Birdie. 'Hey, Bird. How's my bud?'

The cat bolted for the bedroom.

I peered down the empty hallway.

'Is Howard with you?'

'Nope. He headed his heinie south.'

'Oh?' As I closed the door I felt a tickle of apprehension.

'Yessir. Needed to get back to the oil game. But I'm going to hang for a while, if that's cool with you?'

'Sure, Kit. That's great.' Awhile? I eyed the mound of luggage and remembered my last visit from his mother. My sister Harry had come for a five-day conference and ended up staying for weeks.

'But right now I'm bushed. Is it O.K. if I shower and siesta for a few? We broke camp before the sun was even thinking about getting up.'

'Sleep as long as you like. Then I want to hear about your trip.' And definitely bathe, I thought.

I got towels and showed him the guest room.

111

Then I threw on jeans and a sweatshirt and walked to the corner *dépanneur* to buy a *Gazette*. When I returned wet towels lay on the bathroom floor and the bedroom door was shut.

I went to the kitchen and sniffed Kit's package. Definitely fish. Adding an outer wrapper of plastic, I stashed it in the refrigerator pending further instructions. Then I made coffee and settled with the paper at the dining room table.

That's when the weekend went off course.

DEATH TOLL REACHES 120:
BODIES OF TWO MORE BIKERS IDENTIFIED

The story was on the third page of the front section. I'd expected some coverage. What I hadn't expected was the photo. The image was grainy, shot from a distance with a powerful telephoto lens, but the subject was recognizable.

I was kneeling by a grave with skull in hand. As usual the caption identified me as '. . . an American forensic anthropologist working for the Laboratoire de Sciences Judiciaires et de Médecine Légale.'

The shot was so poorly focused I was unsure if it had been snapped at the Vipers' clubhouse, or if it was an old file photo taken at another site. My appearance and equipment vary little from dig to dig, and there was nothing in the frame to identify a specific location.

The article was accompanied by three other photos: the usual head shots of the victims, and a view of the entrance to the Vipers' clubhouse. It described the exhumation of Gately and Martineau, and recounted the story of their

112

disappearance. There was a brief recap of the biker war, and an explanation of the revised body count.

O.K. Those facts might have been released through official channels. What followed was what shocked me.

The text went on to discuss a baffling third victim, accurately describing the partial remains found in the other pit. It concluded by stating that, to date, the young woman's identity remained a mystery.

How the hell had they gotten that?

I felt the beginnings of agitation. While I am not fond of media attention, I am particularly uneasy when it threatens to jeopardize one of my cases. Who would have released the information?

I took a long, deep breath and got up to reheat my coffee.

O.K. Someone leaked information. So what?

So that shouldn't happen, that's what.

I punched the quick-timer button on the microwave.

True. But will it compromise the case?

I thought about that.

The beeper sounded and I removed my mug.

No. In fact, the article could trigger a useful tip. Someone might come forward with a name.

So no harm done. But had there been an official decision to release that information? Probably not or I would have known about it.

Someone had talked to the press and that was unacceptable. Who knew about the girl's bones? Quickwater? Claudel? A member of the Ident section? A lab technician? Dr. Russell?

You're not going to figure it out this weekend.

True again.

Intending to deal with the question on Monday, I circled my mind back to reading, shopping. And Isabelle's party.

Kit.

Oh.

I went to the phone and dialed Isabelle's number.

'*Bonjour.*'

'It's me, Isabelle.'

'Tempe, don't you even think about canceling on me.' I could hear *The Rite of Spring* playing in the background, and knew she must be cooking. Isabelle always cooks to Stravinsky.

'Well, something has come up—'

'The only thing that would excuse you tonight would be a fatal fall from a seven forty-seven. Yours.'

'My nephew showed up this morning and he's going to be staying with me awhile.'

'*Oui?*'

'I don't feel right about leaving him alone on his first day here.'

'But of course not. You will bring this nephew with you tonight.'

'He's nineteen.'

'*Extraordinaire.* I think I was once that age. I believe it was the sixties. I had to go through the sixties to get to the seventies. I remember taking LSD and wearing a great many bad outfits. I will see you and this young man at seven-thirty.'

I agreed and rang off.

Right. Now to convince my nephew to spend Saturday night eating lamb chops and snails with a gaggle of seniors.

As it turned out that wasn't a problem. Kit

emerged around three-fifteen, rumpled and starving. He finished the leftover chicken and asked if he could do some laundry. When I mentioned the supper he readily agreed.

I made a note to call Harry. Kit's conviviality was not what I'd expected based on my daughter Katy's teenage years. But Kit was a stranger in town and probably had nowhere else to hang out.

I spent the next few hours finishing a reference letter for a student, cleaning my bedroom, and explaining detergents and fabric settings to my nephew. Around six I zipped to Le Faubourg for a bottle of wine and a small bouquet.

*   *   *

Isabelle lives on Île-des-Sœurs, a small chunk of land in the St. Lawrence owned for generations by the gray nuns, but recently colonized by an order of Yuppies. A 'mixed use' community, the island's condos, town houses, private homes, and high-rise apartments are tastefully integrated with tennis clubs, strip malls, bicycle paths, and carefully tended green spaces. The island is connected to the south shore via the Champlain Bridge, and to Montreal by two small bridges.

Isabelle's condo is on the top floor of a two-building complex at the far northern tip. Following the failure of her third marriage, she signed divorce papers, sold her home and all its contents, and sallied forth to the clean-slate Île-des-Sœurs. The only belongings she brought along were her treasured CDs and photo albums.

Wanting something in keeping with her new 'what the hell' mind-set, Isabelle had chosen a safari theme. Her decorator had blended natural fabrics that looked like they'd been approved by the World Wildlife Fund with simulated leopard and tiger skin. The walls were hung with animal prints, and a collection of African carvings dotted a glass-topped coffee table, the legs of which resembled elephant feet. The king-sized bed in the master suite was swathed in a canopy of mosquito netting.

Kit was enthralled, or at least appeared to be. As Isabelle gave us a tour he asked question after question about the origin of each of her possessions. I wasn't sure of the depth of his interest, but was pleased at his social acumen.

It was not the decor but the view that captivated me. One guest was still expected, so after Kit and I had been issued drinks and had met the other attendees, I stepped onto the balcony to take it in.

A light rain was falling, and across the river the skyline twinkled in every color imaginable. The mountain loomed over the buildings of Centreville, massive and black. I could see the lights of the cross high up on its flank.

From inside I heard the doorbell sound, then Isabelle called my name. I took one last look and went inside.

The final diner had just arrived and was handing his trench coat to Isabelle. When I saw his face my jaw dropped in surprise.

CHAPTER FOURTEEN

'*Vous!*'

It was not one of my more adroit openers. I shot Isabelle a 'just wait till later' look, which she ignored.

'*Oui*. You are surprised, Tempe?' She beamed. 'I said you two had met in an informal way. Now I will officially introduce you.'

The journalist extended his hand. This time it held no mike, and his look was friendly, not the stunned surprise I remembered from our encounter outside the Vipers' clubhouse.

'Tempe, this is Lyle Crease. I'm sure you've seen him on television.'

I could place the face now. He was an investigative reporter with CTV.

'And, Lyle, I know I don't have to tell you Dr. Brennan's name. We call her Tempe. That's with the long 'e' at the end. People do have trouble with that.'

When I allowed Crease to take my hand, he leaned close and kissed me first on the right cheek, then on the left, in traditional Quebec fashion. I stepped back and mumbled something I hoped he'd interpret as cool but polite.

Isabelle introduced Crease to the others, and he shook hands with the men and kissed the ladies. Then she raised her champagne glass in Kit's direction.

'I think in honor of this handsome young Texan, tonight we should all practice our English.'

Glasses shot up as everyone cheerfully agreed.

Kit looked enormously relieved.

'May I help you with dinner?' I asked in frosty English, eager to get Isabelle alone to share some thoughts with her.

'No, no. Everything is ready. Please, everyone, come to the table. There are little cards beside each plate.'

Shit.

Isabelle retreated to the kitchen while the rest of us gathered around to ascertain the seating arrangement. As I'd suspected, I was next to Crease. Kit was on my right.

There were seven in all. An elderly actor sat on Kit's other side. I'd met him on a previous occasion, but couldn't remember his name and hadn't caught it when introduced. I was unfamiliar with the other two guests. It turned out they were a couple, the wife an antiques dealer, the husband a film producer.

We made small talk as Isabelle shuttled plates from the kitchen. The actor had just finished a run as Polonius in a French production of *Hamlet* at the Théâtre du Rideau Vert. Crease recounted his most recent assignment. The story concerned a sixteen-year-old hacker who had broken into an U.S. Army network, then phoned the RCMP wanting to be caught.

'The kid wanted recognition,' said the actor.

'He could have tried out for football,' my nephew offered.

Not bad, Kit.

'And what have you two been up to?' Isabelle asked the couple as she circled the table pouring wine.

When she came to Kit she paused and looked at

118

me. I nodded. What the hell. He was legal in Quebec and I was driving. Kit accepted with enthusiasm.

The producer's name was Claude-Henri Brault. He'd just returned from a three-month shoot in Ireland. His wife, Marie-Claire, ran a shop in Old Montreal and had spent the time buying antiques in Provence. She rambled on about the kingdom of Arles, the Angevin dynasty, and at least a dozen Louis, describing how each had changed the face of the furniture industry. Between bites of veal I stole peeks at Lyle Crease. His hair and teeth were flawless, his creases as sharp as I remembered. The only imperfection I spotted was a sprinkling of dandruff across his collar.

And Lyle was a good listener. He kept his eyes on Marie-Claire, nodding intermittently, as though the aesthetics of fabric and cabinet design were the only thing that presently mattered.

When Marie-Claire paused for breath Isabelle stepped in, redirecting the conversation like an air-traffic controller with several flights on her screen. Though I had to admire her skill, I didn't appreciate the direction she chose.

'Tempe has been working on these dreadful gang murders. Can you tell us something about them?'

'The bikers?' asked Claude-Henri.

'Yes.' I wanted to glare at Isabelle, but decided it would be rude. I also wanted to strangle her, which would be still ruder.

'Were you involved in the discovery I read about in today's paper?'

'Yes. But as Isabelle knows'—I smiled icicles in her direction—'I can't—'

119

'What are you doing with bikers, Aunt Tempe?'

Kit's interest had wandered during the furniture design lesson, but he perked up at the new topic.

'You know that I work for the provincial medico-legal lab.'

He nodded.

'Last week the director asked me to look at some murder cases.' I mentioned nothing about my role with Opération Carcajou.

'How many?'

'Quite a few.'

'More than the Bee Gees?' he persisted.

'Five.'

'Five people iced in one week?' Kit's eyes were huge. Everyone else at the table had gone quiet.

'Two of them were killed in 1987. We recovered their bodies this week.'

'That's what I read about,' said Claude-Henri, pointing a fork in my direction. '*C'est ça.* That was you in the photograph.'

'Who were the others?' Kit pressed on.

Now I wanted to strangle my nephew.

'Two were bomb victims. One was a little girl accidentally killed during a drive-by shooting.'

'*Mon Dieu,*' said Marie-Claire, abandoning the commitment to English.

I reached for my Perrier, desperately wishing I'd paid attention to her so I could dodge with a question about Renaissance veneers.

'Are you counting the young woman whose bones were found in St-Basile-le-Grand?'

I turned at Crease's question. Though his voice sounded casual, his eyes had a glint I hadn't noticed before. If he had hopes of a story, he wouldn't get it from me.

'No.'

'Have you identified her?' He reached for his wine.

'No.'

'Who are you talking about?' Kit asked.

'Near the grave of two of the bikers we also found some other bones. It's a young woman, but we don't know who she is, or if she's connected with the Vipers. Her burial could predate their ownership of the property.'

'Is that what you think?' Crease.

'I don't know.'

'Who are the Vipers?'

I was fast restructuring my opinion of my nephew's social skills.

'They're a puppet club for the Hells Angels.'

'No way!'

'Yes, way. And they and their brothers in arms are responsible for almost one hundred and twenty deaths in this province over the past five years. God knows how many others have disappeared.'

'The bikers are killing each other?'

'Yes. It's a power struggle for control of the drug trade.'

'Why not just let them?' asked the actor. 'View it as a form of sociopath self-regulation.'

'Because innocents like Emily Anne Toussaint, who was nine years old, get caught in the cross fire.'

'And maybe this other girl?'

'Maybe, Kit.'

'Do you think you'll be able to prove that?' Crease.

'I don't know. Claude-Henri, please tell us about your film.'

As the producer spoke, Crease picked up the

121

Chardonnay and reached for my empty glass. I shook my head, but he continued. When I placed my hand over the rim, he laughed, lifted it off, and filled the goblet.

Seething, I pulled my hand free from his and leaned back in my chair. I cannot tolerate people pressing liquor on those who don't want it.

My nephew's voice brought me back to the conversation. Isabelle had turned her spotlight on Kit.

'Yeah, I went with my daddy. He's in the oil business. We drove up from Texas in a big old Winnebago. Pop's idea. He wanted to do this bonding thing.

'We swung by here to drop off Auntie's cat, then east and into Vermont at Derby Line. Pop had this trip planned better than the invasion of Normandy. That's why I remember all the names.

'Anyway, we camped near this town called Westmore and fished the Willoughby River for salmon. The salmon are landlocked, and when they run in the spring it's a big deal. I guess real fishermen view it like some kind of holy place.

'Then we gunned south to Manchester and fished the Battenkill, and my daddy bought all kinds of crap at the Orvis factory. Casting rods, fly rods, and other stuff. Then he motored on to Texas in the 'Bago, and I dropped in on my aunt the biker buster.' He raised his glass to me, and everyone followed suit.

'It's kind of weird,' Kit continued. 'Because my daddy bought me a motorcycle about a year ago.'

I was dismayed but not surprised. Howard was my sister's second husband, a West Texas oilman with more money than sense, and a defect on the

122

double helix that made him incapable of monogamy. They'd divorced when Kit was six. Howard's approach to fatherhood was to lavish toys and money on his son. At three it was ponies and motorized toy cars. By eighteen it had changed to sailboats and then a Porsche.

'What kind of motorcycle?' asked Isabelle.

'It's a Harley-Davidson. Pop's really into Harleys. My bike is a Road King Classic and he's got an Ultra Classic Electra Glide. Those are both Evos. But Pop's real love is his old knucklehead. They only made those from 1936 to 1947.'

'What do those terms mean?' asked Isabelle.

'They're nicknames that refer to the design of the engine head. The Evolution V2 motor was first produced in the early eighties. Originally it was called a blockhead, but that tag never really stuck. Most folks refer to it as the Evo. A lot of the bikes you see today are shovelheads, made from 1966 to 1984. From 1948 to 1965 it was panheads, before that flatheads, which came out in '29. It's easy to identify the era of production by the design of the engine head.'

Kit's interest in bikers was nothing compared with his ardor for bikes.

'Did you know that all modern Harleys descend from the Silent Gray Fellow, the first bike to roll off the line in Milwaukee back at the turn of the century? The Silent Gray Fellow had a one-cylinder twenty-five-cubic-inch motor capable of three horsepower. No hydraulic tappets, no electric starters, no V-twin engine.' Kit shook his head in disbelief.

'A modern Twin Cam engine displaces upwards of eighty-eight cubic inches. Even an old '71 FLH, at seventy-four cubic inches, has an engine compression ratio of eighty point five to one. And today they're pushing nine to one. Yeah, we've come a long way, but every hog on the road today can trace its bloodline back to that old Silent Gray Fellow.'

'Aren't there other motorcycle manufacturers?' asked the actor.

'Yessir,' Kit agreed, his face and voice showing disdain. 'There are Yamahas, Suzukis, Kawasakis, and Hondas out there. But they're just transportation. The British made some good bikes, Norton, Triumph, BSA, but they've all gone out of business. The German BMWs were impressive machines, but for my pesos Harley is the only show in town.'

'Are they expensive?' Claude-Henri.

Kit shrugged. 'Harley doesn't make low-end cycles. It's not cheap equipment.'

I listened as my nephew talked. He had the same reverence for and knowledge of motorcycles that Marie-Claire had for furniture. Perhaps the timing of his visit was fortunate. He could help me understand this strange world I was entering.

*   *   *

It was almost midnight when we said good-bye and pressed for the elevator. I felt ready for bed, but Kit was still wired, yammering on about engines and critiquing the evening's guests and events. Maybe it was wine, maybe youth. I envied him his stamina.

The rain had stopped, but a strong wind blew off the river, bouncing branches and shrubs, and swirling wet leaves across the ground. When Kit offered to get the car I carefully appraised his condition, then turned over the keys and waited inside the lobby.

In less than a minute he pulled up, then got out and circled to the passenger side. When I'd settled behind the wheel he tossed a brown envelope into my lap.

'What's this?'

'Envelope.'

'I can see that. Where did it come from?'

'It was on the windshield, stuck under a wiper. You must have an admirer.'

I looked at the envelope. It was a padded mailer, stapled at one end, with a pull-tab on the back for easy opening. My name appeared in red Magic Marker.

I stared at the letters, an alarm sounding deep in my brain. Who knew I would be on the island tonight? Who could have recognized my car? Had we been followed? Watched?

Gingerly, I prodded the contents. I could feel the bulge of something hard.

'Well!'

I jumped at the sound of Kit's voice. When I turned his face looked eerily pale, his features dark and distorted in the faint yellow light seeping from the lobby doors.

'Goddammit, Kit, this could be . . .' I stopped, unsure where the thought was going.

'Could be what?' Kit leaned sideways and draped his arm over the back of the seat. 'Go on. Open it,' he needled. 'I'll bet it's a prank. One of your cop friends probably spotted the car and left something stupid to creep you out.'

That was possible. Anyone on the job could have

125

run the plate. And I *had* been the butt of jokes in the past.

'Go on.' Kit reached up and turned on the interior light. 'Maybe it's tickets to the Expos.'

I pulled the tab and reached into the mailer. My fingers closed around a small, glass jar.

When I withdrew the container and held it up to the light I felt bile rise in my throat. The rhythmic contractions under my tongue told me I was about to be sick. I barely heard Kit as I lunged for the door handle.

'Holy shit, Aunt Tempe. Who did you piss off?'

CHAPTER FIFTEEN

The eyeball rested on the bottom of the jar, pupil up, tendrils of flesh floating in the cloudy liquid. The organ was blanched and partially collapsed, and one side appeared to have a jagged tear. Though tightly sealed, the container gave off a familiar scent. A folded paper was stuck to its bottom.

Kit reached over and pulled off the note.

'*On te surveille.*' The French sounded odd with his Texas drawl. 'What does that mean, Aunt Tempe?'

'We're watching you.'

With shaky hands I returned the jar and note to the mailer and placed it on the floor of the backseat. The smell of formaldehyde seemed overwhelming. I knew the odor was in my mind, but that did little to allay my nausea. Fighting to bring my gag reflex back under control, I wiped damp palms on my pants and put the car in gear.

'Think it's a joke?' Kit asked as we turned onto boulevard Île-des-Sœurs.

'I don't know.' My voice sounded high-pitched.

Sensing my mood, he didn't press the point.

Once home, I wrapped the jar in a series of plastic sacks and sealed it in a Tupperware canister. Then I cleaned out the vegetable drawer and placed it in the refrigerator.

Kit watched in silence, a puzzled expression on his face.

'I'll take it to the lab on Monday,' I explained.

'It's a real eye, isn't it?'

'Yes.'

'Think it's a joke?' He repeated his earlier question.

'Probably.' I didn't believe that, but had no desire to alarm him.

'I get the feeling I shouldn't ask, but, if it's a joke, why take it to the lab?'

'Maybe it will give the merry pranksters a little scare,' I said, trying to sound casual, then I hugged him. 'Now, I'm off to bed. Tomorrow we'll find something fun to do.'

'That's cool. Mind if I listen to some music?'

'Be my guest.'

When Kit's door closed I double-checked the locks on the doors and windows, and made sure the security system was functioning. I resisted the urge to check for lurkers in my closet or under the bed.

Kit's musical choice was Black Sabbath. He played it until two-fifteen.

I lay in bed for a long time listening to the thud of heavy metal, wondering if it qualified as music, wondering how many calls I'd receive from the

127

neighbors, and wondering who felt strongly enough about sending me a message to underscore it with a human eye.

Though I'd showered for twenty minutes, the smell of formaldehyde remained lodged in my brain. I fell asleep queasy, with goose bumps still prickling my flesh.

*   *   *

I slept late the next morning. When I woke, still tired from having started awake repeatedly throughout the night, my thoughts turned at once to the thing in my produce crisper. Who? Why? Was it work-related? Was there a sicko in the neighborhood? Who was watching me?

I pushed the questions into the deep background, resolving to address them on Monday. In the meantime, I would be extra-vigilant. I checked my Mace, then the direct-dial buttons on the phones and security box to make sure they were set to 911.

The sun shone brightly and the thermometer on my patio said five degrees Celsius. Forty Fahrenheit at 10 A.M. It was going to be a Canadian scorcher.

Knowing the diurnal rhythm of teenagers I didn't expect to see Kit before noon, so I threw on my gear and hiked to the gym. I walked with more caution than usual, skin prickling with tension, eyes alert for anyone or anything suspicious.

After working out I picked up bagels and cream cheese, and a few goodies to go on top of the cream cheese. I also made an impulse buy at the flower cart. Birdie had largely abandoned me since

Kit's arrival, so I'd lure back his affection with a catnip plant.

Neither the bagels nor the catnip were very effective. My nephew appeared around one-fifteen, the cat trailing languidly behind.

'Utter no sentence that includes the phrase "early bird," or "dawn," said Kit.

'Bagel?'

'Acceptable.'

'Cream cheese, smoked salmon, lemon, onions, capers?'

'Delete capers. Run program.'

Birdie eyed the catnip but said nothing.

As Kit ate, I laid out the options.

'It's a gorgeous day out there. I suggest outdoor activities.'

'Agreed.'

'We can take in the Jardin Botanique, prowl around up on the mountain, or I can scare up some bicycles and we can hit the old port, or pedal the path along the Lachine Canal.'

'Do they allow skates?'

'Skates?'

'Rollerblades. Can we rent some in-lines and do this bike path?'

'I think so.' Oh boy.

'I'll bet you're a popper on Rollerblades. Harry's pretty good.'

'Um. Huh. Why do you call your mom Harry?'

I'd always been curious. Since he first started speaking, Kit had referred to his mother by name.

'I don't know. She's not exactly *Little House on the Prairie.*'

'But you've done it since you were two years old.'

'She wasn't domestic back then. Don't change the subject. Are you up for in-line skating?'

'Sure.'

'You're a can o' corn, Aunt Tempe. Let me grab a shower and we're on our way.'

*   *   *

It was close to a perfect day. I started out rocky but quickly picked up the rhythm, and was soon gliding along as if born on skates. It brought back memories of roller-skating on city sidewalks as a little girl and the several times I had almost hit pedestrians or skated into the paths of cars. The sunshine brought out swarms of jocks, crowding the path with cyclists, skateboarders, and other in-line skaters. Though shaky on turns, I learned to maneuver well enough to avoid collisions. The only skill I didn't master was that of the sudden stop. Drag brakes for skates had not been invented when I was a kid.

By the end of the afternoon I was sailing along smooth as *Black Magic I* in the America's Cup. Or shit through a mallard, as Kit put it. I did insist, however, on wearing enough padding to defend an NHL goal.

It was after five when we turned in the skates and pads and headed to Chez Singapore for an Asian dinner. Then we rented *The Pink Panther* and *A Shot in the Dark* and laughed as Inspector Clouseau demonstrated how one could be both part of the solution and part of the problem. The movies were Kit's choice. He said the French immersion would acclimatize him to Montreal.

Not until I lay in my bed, tired and achy and full

of popcorn, did I even remember the eye. I tossed and turned, trying not to picture the object in my refrigerator and the evil person who put it on my car.

*   *   *

Monday was still warm, but dark clouds had gathered over the city. They hung low, trapping a loose fog close to the ground, and forcing drivers to use headlights.

Arriving at work, I took the jar to the biology section and made a request. I didn't explain the source of the specimen, and they didn't ask. We gave the sample an unregistered number, and the technician said she'd call with results.

I had a suspicion about the eye's origin, which I hoped was wrong. The implications were just too frightening. I held on to the note, pending the analysis.

The morning meeting was relatively brief. The owner of a Volvo dealership was found hanged in his garage, a suicide note pinned to his chest. A single-engine plane had gone down in St-Hubert. A woman had been pushed from the Vendôme métro platform.

Nothing for me.

Back in my office, I logged on to my terminal. Using *anthropologie, squelette, inconnue, femelle,* and *partiel* as my descriptors, I searched the database for cases consisting of unidentified partial female skeletons. The computer came up with twenty-six LML numbers spanning the past ten years.

Using that list, I asked for all cases lacking a

131

skull. That worked for remains received since I'd been at the LML. Prior to that, complete bone inventories hadn't been done. Skeletal cases were simply designated partial or complete. I highlighted the cases recorded as partial.

Next, using the list of incomplete skeletons analyzed during my tenure, I requested those lacking femora.

No go. The data had been entered as skull present or absent, postcranial remains present or absent, but specific bones had not been recorded. I would have to request the actual files.

Wasting no time, I walked down the hall to the records department. A slim woman in black jeans and a peasant blouse occupied the front desk. She was almost monochromatic, with bleached hair, pale skin, and eyes the shade of old dishwater. Her only signs of color were cherry red streaks around her temples, and a sprinkling of freckles across her nose. I was unable to count the number of studs and rings displayed in each of her ears. I'd never seen her before.

'*Bonjour. Je m'appelle Tempe Brennan.*' I held out my hand, introducing myself.

She nodded, but offered neither a hand nor name.

'Are you new?'

'I'm a temp.'

'I'm sorry, but I don't think we've met.'

'Name's Jocelyn Dion.' One shoulder shrugged.

O.K. I dropped my hand.

'Jocelyn, this is a list of files I need to review.'

I handed her the printout and indicated the highlighted numbers. When she reached for the paper I could see definition through the gauzy

132

sleeve. Jocelyn spent time at the gym.

'I know there are quite a few, but could you find out where the files are stored and pull them for me as quickly as possible?'

'No problem.'

'I need the full jacket on each one, not just the anthropology report.'

Something crossed her face, just a flicker of change and then it was gone.

'Where would you like them?' she asked, dropping her eyes to the list.

I gave her my office number, then left. Two strides down the corridor I remembered that I hadn't mentioned pictures. When I turned back I could see Jocelyn's head bent low over the printout. Her lips moved as a lacquered finger worked its way down each side of the paper. She seemed to be reading every word.

When I mentioned the photos, she started at my voice.

'I'm on it,' she said, sliding from her stool.

Weird one, I thought as I headed back to work on the Gately and Martineau reports.

Jocelyn brought me the dossiers within an hour, and I spent the next three going through them. In all, I'd worked on six headless women. Only two had lacked both thigh bones, and neither was young enough to be the girl in the pit.

From the years before I'd arrived in Montreal, seven female skeletons without crania remained unidentified. Two were young enough, but the descriptions of the remains were vague, and without skeletal inventories there was no way to know what bones had been recovered. Neither folder contained photographs.

133

I went back to the computer and checked the disposition of the earliest case. The bones had been held five years, rephotographed, then released for burial or destruction.

But the file contained no pictures. That was odd.

I asked for site of recovery. The bones had come in from Salluit, a village around twelve hundred miles north on the tip of the Ungava Peninsula.

I entered the more recent LML number and asked for site of recovery.

Ste-Julie. My pulse quickened. That was not twelve miles from St-Basile-le-Grand.

Back to the folder. Again, no photos.

I checked on the disposition and found nothing to indicate the case had been cleared.

Could I be that lucky?

When I began at the LML, I inherited a collection of skeletal cases. While I'd disposed of some, much of this material remained in my storeroom.

I unlocked the door and dragged a chair to the far end of the small room. Brown cardboard boxes lined both walls, arranged chronologically by LML number. I went to the section containing the oldest codes.

The case was on the top shelf. I climbed onto the chair, lifted it down, and carried it out to my worktable. Brushing off dust, I raised the lid.

To the left lay a mound of vertebrae and ribs, to the right a stack of long bones. Though most joint surfaces had been gnawed by animals, it was clear that both femora were there.

Damn.

I took everything out and checked for inconsistencies, but nothing seemed amiss.

Disappointed, I replaced the bones and reshelved the box. After washing my hands I crossed to my office, planning to regroup over a tuna sandwich and carton of Jell-O pudding.

Swiveling my chair, I crossed my feet on the window ledge and peeled the cover from the pudding container. A colleague at UNC-Charlotte had a sticker on her door that read: *Life is uncertain. Eat dessert first.* I'd always considered that good advice.

Gazing at the river, I slurped butterscotch, my thoughts adrift. Sometimes my mind works better that way, mingling associations freely rather than herding them into the center of my consciousness.

The skull and leg bones we'd found in St-Basile were not the missing parts of a body recovered earlier. That was clear. At least not a body recovered in Quebec.

O.K.

Unless Claudel came up with a name, the next step would be CPIC.

Easy enough.

If that failed, we'd go to NCIC. There was nothing to suggest that the girl was local. She could have traveled north from the States.

Ally McBeal's therapist was right. I needed a theme song for times when I felt stressed.

Runnin' down the road tryin' to loosen my load
Got a world of trouble on my mind . . .

Maybe.

Slow down, you move too fast.
Got to make the morning last . . .

135

As I reached for the sandwich an image of Saturday night's grotesque offering flashed across my mind. Again my skin went cold and prickly.

Forget it. It could be a pig's eye. Your picture was in the paper, and any moron could have stuck it on the car for laughs. If anyone is out there watching, it's some twisted nitwit without a life.

I am woman watch me—

Definitely no.

It's a beautiful day in the neighborhood . . .

Oh boy.

Game plan. Finish the reports on Gately and Martineau, finalize those on the Vaillancourt twins. Talk to Claudel. Based on his report, CPIC, then NCIC.

Life is under control. This is my job. There is no reason to feel stressed.

That thought had hardly materialized when the phone rang, destroying the calm I had worked so hard to achieve.

CHAPTER SIXTEEN

A female voice said, 'I have a call from Mr. Crease. Hold, please.'

Before I could stop her he was on the line.

'I hope you don't mind my calling you at work.'

I did, but held my tongue.

'I just wanted to say that I really enjoyed Saturday night, and hoped the two of us might get together.'

Original.

'Would you be free to have supper some night this week?'

'I'm sorry, but that's not possible right now. I'm really swamped.'

I could be free until the end of the next millennium and I wouldn't dine with Lyle Crease. The man was too glib for my taste.

'Next week?'

'No, I don't think so.'

'I understand. Can I have your nephew as a consolation prize?'

'What?'

'Kit. He's a fabulous kid.'

Fabulous?

'I have a friend who owns a motorcycle shop. He must stock five thousand items of Harley-Davidson paraphernalia. I think Kit would find it interesting.'

The last thing I wanted was my impressionable young nephew under the influence of a media smoothie. But I had to agree, Kit would enjoy it.

'I'm sure he would.'

'Then it's cool with you if I give him a call?'

'Sure.' Cool as dysentery.

Five minutes after I hung up Quickwater appeared at my door. He gave me his usual stony stare, then flipped a folder onto my desk.

I really needed to settle on a theme song.

'What are these?'

'Forms.'

'For me to fill out?'

Quickwater was preparing to ignore my question

when his partner joined us.

'I take it this means you came up empty.'

'As Al Capone's vault,' Claudel replied. 'Not a single match. Not even close.'

He gestured at the packet on my desk.

'If you get the papers filled out, I can access CPIC while Martin does NCIC. Bergeron's working on the dental descriptors.'

CPIC is the acronym for the Canadian Police Information Centre, NCIC for the National Crime Information Center operated by the FBI. Each is a national electronic database providing quick access to information crucial to law enforcement. Though I'd used CPIC a few times, I was much more familiar with the American system.

NCIC first went on line in 1967 with data on stolen autos, license plates, guns, and property, and on wanted persons and fugitives. Over the years more files were added, and the original ten databases expanded to seventeen, including the interstate identification index, the U.S. Secret Service protective files, the foreign fugitive file, the violent gangs/terrorist file, and files on missing and unidentified persons.

The NCIC computer is located in Clarksburg, West Virginia, with connecting terminals in police departments and sheriffs' offices throughout the United States, Canada, Puerto Rico, and the U.S. Virgin Islands. Entries can be made only by law enforcement personnel. And they definitely make them. In its first year NCIC recorded two million transactions. It currently handles that many each day.

The NCIC missing persons file, created in 1975, is used to locate individuals who are not 'wanted,' but whose whereabouts are unknown. A record can be entered for missing juveniles, and for people who are disabled or endangered. Victims of abduction and those who have disappeared following a disaster also qualify. A form is completed by the missing person's parent or guardian, physician, dentist, and optician, and entered by a local department.

The unidentified persons file was added in 1983 to provide a way to cross-reference recovered remains against missing persons records. Entry into the system is permitted for unidentified bodies and body parts, for living persons, and for catastrophe victims.

It was this packet that Quickwater had tossed onto my desk.

'If you'll fill out the NCIC form we can work both networks. It's basically the same data, just different coding systems. How long will you need?'

'Give me an hour.' With only three bones I'd have little to say.

As soon as they left I began working my way through the form, periodically checking the data collection entry guide for codes.

I checked the box for EUD for unidentified deceased.

I placed an 'S' in boxes 1, 9, and 10 of the body parts diagram, indicating that a skeletonized head and right and left upper leg bones had been recovered. All others boxes got an 'N' for not recovered.

I marked 'F' for female, 'W' for white, and wrote in the approximate height range. I left empty the space for estimated year of birth and estimated date of death.

139

In the personal descriptors section I wrote SHUNT CERB, for cerebral ventricular shunt, and checked that item on the supplemental form. That was it. No fractures, deformities, tattoos, moles, or scars.

Since I hadn't any clothing, jewelry, eyeglasses, fingerprints, blood type, or information as to cause of death, the rest of the document remained blank. All I could add were a few comments about where the body was found.

I was completing the sections on agency name and case number when Quickwater reappeared. I handed him the form. He took it, nodded, and left without a word.

What was it with this guy?

An image flicked through my mind and was gone. A bloated eyeball in a jelly jar.

Quickwater?

No way. Nevertheless, I decided to make no mention of the incident to Claudel or his Carcajou partner. I might have asked Ryan, might have turned to him for advice, but Ryan was gone and I was on my own.

*   *   *

I completed the Gately and Martineau reports and walked them to the secretarial office. When I returned, Claudel was seated in my office, a computer printout in his hand.

'You were right with the age but a bit off on the date of death. Ten years wasn't enough.'

I waited for him to go on.

'Her name was Savannah Claire Osprey.'

In French it came out Oh-spree, with the accent

140

on the second syllable. Nevertheless, the name told me that the girl was probably Southern, or at least had been born Southern. Not many people outside the Southeast named their daughters Savannah. I lowered myself into my chair, relieved but curious.

'From?'

'Shallotte, North Carolina. Isn't that your hometown?'

'I'm from Charlotte.'

Canadians have difficulty with Charlotte, Charlottesville, and the two Charlestons. So do many Americans. I'd given up explaining. But Shallotte was a small coastal town that didn't qualify to be part of the confusion.

Claudel read from the printout. 'She was reported missing in May of 1984, two weeks after her sixteenth birthday.'

'That was a quick turnaround,' I said, digesting the information.

'*Oui.*'

I waited, but he did not go on. I kept the annoyance from my voice.

'Monsieur Claudel, any information you have will help me confirm this ID.'

A pause. Then, 'The shunt and the dentals were unique so the computer spit the name right out. I called the Shalotte PD and actually talked to the reporting officer. According to her, the mother got the case entered, then dropped it cold. There was the usual media frenzy at first, then things died down. The investigation went on for months, but nothing ever turned up.'

'Troubled kid?'

A longer pause.

'There is no history of drug or discipline

141

problems. The hydrocephaly caused some learning disabilities and affected her eyesight, but she wasn't retarded. She went to a normal high school and did well. She was never considered a potential runaway.

'But the child was hospitalized frequently because of problems with the shunt. Apparently the apparatus would get blocked and they'd have to go in and fix it. These episodes were preceded by periods of lethargy, headache, sometimes mental confusion. One theory is that she became disoriented and wandered off.'

'Off what, the planet? What's the other theory?'

'The father.'

Claudel flipped open a small spiral notebook.

'Dwayne Allen Osprey. A real charmer with an arrest record longer than the Trans-Siberian Railway. Back then Dwayne's domestic routine revolved around drinking Jim Beam and beating up his family. According to the mother's original statement, which she later retracted, her husband always disliked Savannah, and things got worse as the child grew older. It wasn't beyond him to slam her into a wall. Seems Dwayne found his daughter a disappointment. Called her Water Brain.'

'They think he murdered his own daughter?'

'It's a possibility. Whiskey and rage are a deadly cocktail. The theory was that things got out of hand, he killed her, then disposed of the body.'

'How did she end up in Quebec?'

'An insightful question, Dr. Brennan.'

With that he rose and shot the cuffs on the crispest, whitest shirt I'd seen in decades. I gave him a drop-dead-peckerhead look, but he was already out the door.

142

I sighed and leaned back in my chair.

You bet your prim little ass it's an insightful question, Monsieur Claudel.

And I'm going to answer it.

CHAPTER SEVENTEEN

I took a deep breath. As usual, Claudel had made me furious.

When I felt calmer, I looked at my watch. Four-forty. It was late, but maybe I could catch her.

Checking my Rolodex, I dialed SBI Headquarters in Raleigh. Kate Brophy picked up on the first ring.

'Hi, Kate. It's Tempe.'

'Hey, girl, are you back in Dixie?'

'No. I'm in Montreal.'

'When are you going to get your skinny tail down here so we can tip a few?'

'My tipping days are over, Kate.'

'Oops. Sorry. I know that.'

Kate and I had met at a time when I was as committed to alcohol as a college freshman on spring break. Only I wasn't eighteen and I wasn't at the beach. Past thirty, I was then a wife and mother, and a university professor with exhausting teaching and research responsibilities.

I never noticed when I joined the rank of brothers and sisters in denial, but somewhere along the way I became a champion rationalizer. A glass of Merlot at home in the evening. A beer after classes. A weekend party. I didn't need the booze. I never drank alone. I never missed work. It wasn't a problem.

But then the glass became a bottle, and the late-night binges required no company. That's the beguiling thing about Bacchus. He has no entrance fee. No minimum drink order. Before you know it you're in bed on a sunny Saturday afternoon while your daughter plays soccer and other parents cheer.

That show had closed down, and I wasn't about to re-raise the curtain.

'It's funny you called,' said Kate. 'I was just talking to one of our investigators about the biker boys you glued together back in the eighties.'

I remembered those cases. Two entrepreneurs had made the mistake of dealing drugs on turf claimed by the Hells Angels. Their body parts were found in plastic bags, and I'd been asked to sort dealer A from dealer B.

That foray into fresh forensics had been a catalyst for me. Until then I'd worked with skeletons unearthed at archaeological sites, examining bones to identify disease patterns and estimate life expectancies in prehistoric times. Fascinating, but minimally pertinent to current events.

When I began consulting to the North Carolina medical examiner, I felt an excitement not present in my early work. Kate's bikers, like the cases that followed, had an urgency that ancient deaths did not. I could give a name to the nameless. I could provide a family with closure. I could contribute to law enforcement's efforts to reduce the slaughter on America's streets, and to identify and prosecute perpetrators. I'd shifted my professional focus, gone dry in my personal life, and never looked back on either front.

'How did you end up in Tulio's case review session?' I asked.

'I drove a couple of my analysts up to Quantico for a VICAP training session. Since I was there, I decided to sit in to see what's new.'

'What was?'

'Other than the fact that your biker boys are knocking each other off with greater alacrity than most social clubs, looks like the same old.'

'I don't think I've worked a Carolina biker case in years. Who's down home these days?'

'We've still got three of the big four.'

'Hells Angels, Outlaws, and Pagans.'

'Yes, ma'am. No Banditos yet. And it's been quiet for some time, but you never know. Things could heat up next month when the Angels hold their run at Myrtle Beach.'

'It's still pretty wild up here, but that's not why I'm calling.'

'Oh?'

'Ever hear of a young girl named Savannah Claire Osprey?'

There was a long silence. Across the miles the connection sounded like the ocean in a seashell.

'Is this a joke?'

'Absolutely not.'

I heard her take a deep breath.

'The Osprey disappearance was one of the very first cases I worked for the bureau. It was years ago. Savannah Osprey was a sixteen-year-old kid with a lot of medical problems. Didn't hang with a wild crowd, didn't do drugs. One afternoon she left her house and was never seen again. At least that was the story.'

145

'You don't believe she ran away?'

'The local police suspected the father, but no one could find a thing to prove it.'

'Do you think he was involved?'

'It's possible. She was a timid kid, wore thick glasses, rarely went out, didn't date. And it was common knowledge the old man used her for a punching bag.' Her voice was filled with contempt. 'The guy should have been locked up. Actually he was, but not until later. Got busted on a drug charge, I think. Died about five years after his daughter disappeared.'

What she said next hit me like a blow to the chest.

'He was such a peckerwood shit and she was such a pathetic little thing that the case really bothered me. I've kept her bones all these years.'

'What did you say?' I gripped the phone, barely breathing.

'The parents never accepted it, but I know they're hers. I still have them stored at the ME office. Doc calls every now and then, but I always ask him to hang on to the stuff.'

'Her remains were found?'

'Nine months after Savannah disappeared a female skeleton turned up near Myrtle Beach. That was the thing that shined the light on Dwayne Osprey. While he was never what you'd call a steady worker, around the time she went missing he was making deliveries for a local cheesecake company. The day of his daughter's disappearance Daddy made a trip to Myrtle Beach.'

I was so shocked I could hardly formulate a question.

'But did you ever get a positive on the remains?'

146

'No. There was too much missing and what was recovered was too damaged. And of course we weren't doing DNA back then. Why are you asking about Savannah Osprey?'

'Did you recover a skull?'

'No. That was the main problem. The victim had been dumped in the woods then covered by a sheet of corrugated tin. Animals pulled parts of the body out and scattered them all over creation. The skull and jaw were never found, and we figured they'd dragged them off. The bones left under the tin were intact but weren't very useful, and the rest of the skeleton was so badly chewed that it was hard to tell much except gender. Some pathologist was doing the anthropology back then. His report stated that nothing remained to indicate age, height, or race.'

A pathologist would not have known about microscopic aging, or about calculation of stature from partial long bones. Not a good job, Doc.

'Why do you think it's Savannah?' I asked.

'We found a small silver charm in the vicinity of the bones. It was a bird of some sort. Though she denied it, I could tell from the mother's reaction that she recognized the thing. Later I did some research. The charm was an exact replica of a fish hawk.'

I waited.

'The fish hawk is also known as the osprey.'

I told her about the skull and leg bones in Montreal.

'Holy shit.'

'Is the mother still around?'

'Anything's possible since they cloned that sheep. I'll find out.'

147

'Do you still have the file?'

'You bet.'

'Antemortem X rays?'

'Zillions.'

I made a quick decision.

'Get those bones, Kate. I'm coming down.'

*   *   *

Patineau authorized the trip, and I booked a morning flight to Raleigh. Kit and I had a late dinner that night, both of us avoiding mention of the bundle in the entrance hall that I had brought from the lab and would be taking with me. He was looking forward to tomorrow's outing with Crease and had no problem with my absence.

The plane was crowded with the usual assortment of students, businessmen, and weekend golfers. I stared out the window as attendants served coffee and soft drinks, wishing I, too, were off to a course—Pinehurst, Marsh Harbor, Oyster Bay, anything but the grim analysis of a teenage girl's bones.

My eyes dropped to the athletic bag under the seat in front of me. It looked innocuous enough, but I wondered what my fellow passengers would think if they knew the nature of its contents. I have flown out of Dorval often enough that the X-ray machine operators no longer ask for an explanation. I wondered how it would be leaving Raleigh.

Outside, the morning sun was painting the clouds a luminescent pink. When we broke through I could see a tiny shadow plane paralleling the one in which I rode.

Yes, that was it, I thought. That's how I saw the girl at my feet. Though I now had a name, in my mind's eye she remained a shadowy ghost on a formless landscape. I hoped this trip would change that image into a firm identification.

CHAPTER EIGHTEEN

Kate met me at the Raleigh-Durham airport and we drove directly to the SBI lab. She'd already brought the remains from the medical examiner's office in Chapel Hill, and secured a room where we could work. If samples were to be taken for DNA analysis, all parties agreed that this arrangement was the most efficient.

I gloved my hands and unwrapped my parcel as Kate retrieved hers from a locked closet. She placed a long white box on the table and stepped away. I could feel the familiar tension in my chest as I unwound the string and folded back the cardboard flaps.

One by one I arranged the bones, placing each in its correct anatomical position. Ribs. Vertebrae. Pelvis. Long bones.

The pathologist had been right in his assessment of animal damage. Scavengers had gnawed away so much that not a border, crest, or joint remained on any but the smallest bones. The pubic symphyses and iliac crests were completely gone, and only fragments of clavicle had survived. But one fact was immediately clear.

Both femora were missing.

I added the bones from St-Basile to those that

lay on the table. While they did not complete the skeleton, neither did they duplicate any element.

Kate spoke first.

'Looks like a match for size and muscular development. She must have been a tiny thing.'

'Using a femur I calculated a height of five foot two, plus or minus. Let's see what your tibia gives us.' I indicated two landmarks on the shaft. 'There's a regression formula that allows the use of just this segment.'

I took the measurement then did the math. The error range was large but bracketed the estimate I'd gotten with the femur. When I showed her the figure, Kate went to the side counter and riffled through a file that was thicker than a Manhattan phone book.

'Here it is. Savannah was five-one and three-quarter inches.'

She riffled some more, then withdrew a five-by-seven envelope and shook free several pictures. She spoke as she studied an image.

'It was so sad. Most of Savannah's classmates had no idea who she was. And Shallotte is *not* that big a place. The kids that did recognize her name or photo couldn't tell us a thing about her. She was one of those people that no one remembers. Born 1968. Died 1984.'

Kate held out a snapshot.

'The kid got a really bum deal. Miserable family. No friends. Anyway, you can tell she wasn't very big.'

I looked at the photo and felt a surge of pity.

The girl sat on a blanket, one scarecrow arm clutching her middle, the other held palm out to fend off the picture taker. She wore a one-piece bathing suit that showed skin so pale it was almost blue. She'd been hiding her face, but the camera caught her looking up, eyes enormous behind thick lenses. In the distance I could make out the horizontal slash of waves meeting shore.

As I stared at the wan little face, I ached inside. What could have prompted an attack on someone so fragile? Did a stranger force her at knifepoint, then strangle and leave her to the dogs? When did she realize she was going to die? Did she scream in terror, knowing no one would hear her cries? Had she died in her own home, to be hauled off and dumped? As her eyes closed for the last time did she feel terror or resignation or hatred or numbness, or merely bewilderment? Had she felt pain?

'—compare cranial features.'

Kate was pulling X rays from a large brown envelope and popping them onto a wall illuminator.

'This is a cranial series taken just four months before Savannah disappeared.'

I got my X rays from the athletic bag and clipped them next to the hospital films. Starting with the facial views, I compared the shape of the frontal sinuses. Varying from small and simple to large and multichambered, these hollow spaces above the orbits are as unique to an individual as his or her fingerprints.

Savannah's sinuses rose into her forehead like a crest on the head of a cockatoo, the configuration on her hospital X rays matching exactly the one in the skull on my film. And the surgical burr hole was clearly visible in every view, the shape and position identical on the antemortem and postmortem films.

There was no doubt that the skull unearthed in St-Basile was Savannah Claire Osprey. But could we link the skull and femora to the partial skeleton found near Myrtle Beach?

Before leaving Montreal I'd removed a sliver of bone from the shaft of one of the femora and extracted a molar from the upper jaw in the skull, thinking that if relatives could be located, or antemortem samples of the victim's tissue or blood could be recovered, DNA sequencing might confirm the suspected identity. While the dental and radiographic evidence now rendered DNA testing unnecessary for purposes of identifying the bones from Montreal, I had another goal in mind.

Using a bone saw, I cut a one-inch chunk from all of the tibiae and fibulae that Kate had been saving all these years. She watched in silence as the circular blade buzzed through the dry bone, sending up a powdery white spray.

'It's not likely the hospital will come up with samples after all this time.'

'No,' I agreed. 'But it happens.'

It was true. Gallstones. Pap smears. Blood spots. Old DNA had been found in all sorts of strange places.

'What if there are no relatives?'

'By comparing the sequencing from the Myrtle Beach bones to that found in the St-Basile-le-Grand bones we'll at least know if all the remains come from the same individual. If they do we have essentially identified the Myrtle Beach bones because we have a firm ID on the Montreal skull. But I would like to get a DNA.'

'What if there's no DNA?'

'I've already had microscope slides made from

152

one of the St-Basile thigh bones. When I get back I'll do the same with these samples, then I'll examine everything under high-powered magnification.'

'What will that tell you?'

'Age, for one thing. I'll see if that's consistent between the two sets of remains. I'll also look for details in microstructure that might be useful.'

It was almost one when we'd labeled and numbered the four specimens and Kate had done the paperwork necessary to release them to me. We decided to grab a quick lunch before tackling the case file. Over cheeseburgers and fries at the local Wendy's she related what was known of Savannah Osprey's last hours.

According to the parents, Savannah had had a routine week. Her health was good and she was looking forward to an event at her school, though they couldn't remember what it was. On the day of her disappearance she spent the early afternoon studying for a math exam, but didn't appear particularly anxious about it. Around two she said she needed something at the drugstore, and left the house on foot. They never saw her again.

'At least that was Daddy's version,' Kate concluded.

'He was at home that day?'

'Until around three-thirty, when he made a pickup in Wilmington, then set out for Myrtle Beach. The departure time was confirmed by his employer. He showed up a little late with the delivery, but blamed the delay on traffic.'

'Were you able to search the house or truck?'

'Nope. We had nothing on him, so we could never get a warrant.'

153

'And the mother?'

'Brenda. She's another piece of work.'

Kate took a bite of burger then wiped her mouth with a paper napkin.

'Brenda was working that day. I think she cleaned motel rooms. According to her statement, when she returned at five the house was empty. She didn't begin to worry until it got dark and Savannah didn't call or show up. By midnight Mama was panicked and reported her daughter missing.'

She drained her Coke.

'Brenda was cooperative for about two days, then did a complete reversal and decided her daughter had taken off with friends. From then on it was like talking to a frozen pork roast. It was the Shallotte PD that contacted us and eventually got the NCIC info from Savannah's doctors and dentist. That's normally the job of the parent or guardian.'

'Why the about-face?'

'Dwayne probably threatened her.'

'What happened to him?'

'About five years after Savannah disappeared Dwayne must have developed a yearning for the mountains. He drove all the way up to Chimney Rock to celebrate July Fourth by camping and drinking with his buddies. On his second night there he made a beer run into town and Yankee Doodle Dandied himself right off the highway and into Hickory Nut Gorge. He was thrown out and the car rolled over him. I understand that when they found him the diameter of Dwayne's head exceeded that of the spare tire.'

Kate bunched up her wrappers, centered them

on her tray, and pushed back from the table.

'The investigation pretty much died with Dwayne,' she said as she slid everything into a waste container.

We emerged from the restaurant and onto a small patio where an ancient black man in a Yankees cap greeted us with the standard 'Hey.' He was watering flowers with a garden hose, and the scent of wet earth and petunias mingled with the odor of cooking grease.

Afternoon sun glared off cement and warmed my head and shoulders as we crossed the parking lot to Kate's car. When we were buckled in I asked, 'Do you think he did it?'

There was a silence before she answered.

'I don't know, Tempe. Some things didn't add up.'

I waited as she sorted through her thoughts.

'Dwayne Osprey had a drinking problem and was mean as a snake, but the fact that he lived in Shallotte meant some village was deprived of its rightful idiot. I mean this guy was stupid. I never thought he could kill his child and transport her body to another city, then cover his tracks completely. He just didn't have the neurons. Besides, a lot was going on that week.'

'Such as?'

'Every year in mid-May there's a huge motorcycle rally in Myrtle Beach. It's a mandatory run for Hells Angels chapters in the South, and a lot of Pagans usually show up, as well. The place was crawling with bikers that week, everything from outlaw to Rubbie.'

'Rubbie?' She couldn't mean it in the Montreal sense, where the term was slang for wino.

155

'Rich Urban Bikers. Anyway, that's how I ended up on the case. My boss thought there might be a gang connection.'

'Was there?'

'We never found one.'

'What do you think?'

'Hell, Tempe, I don't know. Shallotte is right on Highway 17 en route to Myrtle Beach and there are dozens of motels and fast-food joints along there. With all the traffic heading to and from South Carolina that week she could have just bumped into some psychopath pulling off the highway for chicken and biscuits.'

'But why murder her?' I knew it was stupid as soon as I asked it.

'People are shot for driving too close, for wearing red where the blue gang hangs, for getting product from the wrong supplier. Maybe someone killed her just for wearing glasses.'

Or for no reason at all, like Emily Anne Toussaint.

*　　　*　　　*

Back at the SBI lab we spread out the dossier and began examining documents. Medical records. Dental records. Phone records. Arrest records. Transcripts of interviews. Reports of neighborhood canvassing. Handwritten notes taken on stakeouts.

The SBI and Shallotte investigators had pursued every lead. Even the neighbors had pitched in. Parties searched ponds, rivers, and woods. All to no avail. Savannah Osprey had left her house and disappeared.

Nine months after Savannah's disappearance,

remains were found in Myrtle Beach. Suspecting a link to the Osprey case the Horry County coroner contacted North Carolina authorities and sent the bones to Chapel Hill. The medical examiner's report noted consistency, but concluded that positive identification of the skeleton was not possible. Officially, no trace of Savannah was ever found.

The last entry in the file was dated July 10, 1989. Following Dwayne Osprey's death his wife had again been questioned. Brenda held to the story that her daughter had run away.

We finished with the file after seven. My eyes burned and my back screamed from hours of bending over small print and bad handwriting. I was tired, discouraged, and I'd missed my flight. And I'd learned almost nothing. A sigh from Kate told me she was on the same page.

'Now what?' I asked.

'Now let's get you a place to stay, have a nice dinner, and figure where to go from here.'

Seemed like a plan.

I reserved a room at a Red Roof Inn on I-40 and booked a morning flight. Then I tried Kit but got no answer. Surprised, I left a message and the number for my cell phone. When I'd finished, Kate and I packed our respective bones and drove up Garner Road to her office.

The structure housing the SBI stood in stark contrast to its ultramodern crime laboratory. While the latter is high-rise cement, all sterile and efficient, the headquarters building is only two stories, a genteel redbrick affair with cream-colored trim. Surrounded by manicured grounds and approached by an entrance lane of stately

157

oaks, the complex blends better with the tiny antiques store it faces than with the megalith down the road.

We parked on the main avenue, retrieved our packages, and headed toward the building. To the right lay a circular hedge with border plantings of marigolds and pansies. Three poles rose from the garden's center, like the masts on a square rigger. I could hear the flap of fabric and the clink of metal as a uniformed officer lowered the last of the flags. He was backlit by a partial sun dropping below the roof of the Highway Patrol Training Center.

We passed through the glass door with its North Carolina Department of Justice, State Bureau of Investigation crest, cleared security, and climbed to the second floor. Once again we secured the bones, this time in a locked cabinet in Kate's small office.

'What would you like to eat?'

'Meat,' I said without hesitating. 'Red meat marbled with real fat.'

'We had cheeseburgers for lunch.'

'True. But I just read a theory about the evolution of Neanderthals into modern human beings. Seems the key to the transition was increased fat in the diet. Maybe a pair of big prime ribs will help our thought processes.'

'I'm convinced.'

The beef turned out to be a good idea. Or maybe it was just the break from blurry print on photocopied documents. By the time our cobbler arrived we'd focused on the central question.

The bones in Montreal were without a doubt Savannah's. For the bones found here the jury was still out. Did a sickly sixteen-year-old girl with bad eyesight and a timid personality travel fifteen hundred miles north of her home to another country and die there? Or did some, but not all, of the bones belonging to a dead girl get taken from the Carolinas to Montreal and buried there?

If death occurred in Montreal, the Myrtle Beach bones *were not* Savannah's.

Though Kate didn't buy this theory, she did admit to its possibility.

If the Myrtle Beach bones *were* Savannah's, part of the skeleton had been moved.

I'd studied the scene photos and found nothing disturbing. The decomposition appeared consistent with a period of nine months, and a postmortem interval that tallied with the date of Savannah's disappearance. Unlike the pit at the Vipers' clubhouse, this scene gave no indication of a secondary burial.

This assumption presented several possibilities.

Savannah died in Myrtle Beach.

Savannah died elsewhere, then her body was brought to Myrtle Beach.

Savannah's body was dismembered, parts either brought to or left in Myrtle Beach, then the skull and leg bones separated and transported to Canada.

But if the body had been deliberately separated, why were there no cut marks on any of the bones?

The key question remained: How did Savannah, either in whole or part, alive or dead, end up in Quebec?

'Do you think they'll reopen the case?' I asked as we waited for the bill.

'It's doubtful. Everyone was pretty well convinced Dwayne did it. The investigation had stalled long before his accident, but his death really capped it.'

I handed the waiter my Visa card, ignoring Kate's protests.

'What now?'

'Here's my thinking,' she said. 'First of all, that was a sneak play on the check.'

Yeah. Yeah. I urged her on with a hand gesture.

'Savannah's skull was found on biker property in Quebec.'

She enumerated points by raising fingers.

'The Vipers are a puppet club for the Hells Angels, correct?'

I nodded.

'The Angels were gathering just down the highway from Savannah's hometown the week she disappeared.'

A third finger joined the other two.

'Her skeleton turned up in Myrtle Beach State Park, a stone's throw from the party venue.'

Her eyes met mine.

'Seems worth looking into.'

'But you did that.'

'We didn't have the Quebec link.'

'What do you propose?'

'The early eighties were a wild ride for Carolina bikers. Let's pull out my gang files and see what we can see.'

'They go back that far?'

'The gathering of historic information is one of my mandates. Predicate acts are often important in RICO investigations, especially old homicides.'

She referred to the Racketeering Influenced and Corrupt Organizations Act signed by Nixon in 1970. The statute was often used in the prosecution of organized crime.

160

'Also, gang members often shift between chapters and it's helpful to know who was at what location at what time when you're looking for witnesses. I have tons of information, including photos and videos.'

'I've got all night,' I said, spreading my hands.

'Let's go look at bikers.'

And that's what we did until my cell phone rang at 5:23 A.M. The call was from Montreal.

CHAPTER NINETEEN

Les Appartements du Soleil were anything *but* sunny, contrary to their name. But naming the place after its actual attributes would have been bad marketing. The building was dark and cheerless, its windows clouded by grime and painted shut by decades of careless maintenance. The tiny balconies jutting from each of its three floors were wrapped in turquoise siding and packed with rusted grills and cheap lawn chairs, plastic garbage cans, and assorted types of athletic equipment. One or two had flowerpots, the contents brown and withered from seasons past.

But no one could fault the heating system. In the day I'd been gone in North Carolina spring had finally made it to Quebec, and I touched down to a report of sixty-eight degrees Fahrenheit. It was above that now, but the Soleil's radiators soldiered on, raising the temperature inside to well over eighty. The heat and the odor of putrefaction combined to make one queasy and inclined toward shallow breathing.

161

From where I stood I could see into each of the rooms that made up the squalid little flat. The kitchen lay to my left, the living room to my right, the bedroom and bath straight ahead. The place looked as if its occupant had been holding a garage sale, though the filth and stench would have discouraged even the most ardent bargain hunter.

Every elevated surface was heaped with tools, magazines, paperback books, bottles and broken appliances, and the floor was crammed with camping equipment, automobile and motorcycle parts, tires, cardboard boxes, hockey sticks, and plastic bags tied with metal twisters. A pyramid of beer cans rose almost to the ceiling at the far end of the living room, with torn and curling posters tacked to the wall on either side. The poster on the right advertised a Grateful Dead concert. July 17, 1983. Below it a White Power fist advocated Aryan purity.

On the top left a poster entitled *Le Hot Rod* showed a penis in Ray-Bans, a smoking cigarette tucked between it and its companion genitalia. The image below featured an upright phallus, the words *Astro-Cock* in bold letters across the top. The organ was circled by the symbols of the Zodiac, a message of wisdom under each. I took a pass on consulting my sign.

As far as I could see, the only furniture available for practical use consisted of a Formica table and single chair in the kitchen, a twin bed in the bedroom, and an armchair in the living room. A body now occupied the armchair, its head a distorted red mass above a blackened torso and limbs. Embedded in the flesh I could see a shattered skull and facial bones, a partial nostril

162

with mustache skirt, and one complete eye. The lower jaw hung slack but intact, showing a purpled tongue and rotten teeth stained brown.

Someone had collected shards of bone and brain pudding and sealed them in a Ziploc bag. The plastic sack lay in the man's lap, as though he'd been put in charge of watching over his own brain. A large flap of skin clung to the edge of the chair, smooth and shiny as the belly of a perch.

The deceased sat opposite a small TV on which a coat hanger had been rigged to replace the broken antenna. One twisted end projected toward his head, like the finger of an eyewitness pointing to its find. No one had bothered to turn the set off and I could hear Montel talking with women whose mothers had stolen their lovers. I wondered what the discussants would think of their grisly viewer.

A member of the Ident section dusted the bedroom for latent prints, while another did the same in the kitchen. A third worked a camcorder, slowly sweeping each room, then zooming in for close-ups of the jumbles of junk. Before I'd gotten there, she'd shot dozens of stills of the victim and his gloomy surroundings.

LaManche had been and gone. Since the body wasn't badly burned and decomposition was only moderate I wasn't really needed, but that hadn't been clear in the early stages. Initial reports described a body and a fire, so I'd been called and transport arrangements had been made. By the time the scene was assessed, I was in transit from Raleigh and the simplest thing was to follow through with the original plan. Quickwater had picked me up at the airport and brought me here.

Les Appartements du Soleil were located

southwest of Centre-ville, on a small street running east from rue Charlevoix. The neighborhood, known as Pointe-St-Charles, was on the island of Montreal, so the murder fell to the CUM.

Michel Charbonneau stood across the room, his face the color of Pepto-Bismol, his hair projecting in clammy spikes. He was jacketless, his collar soaked with sweat, his tie hanging below the open top button of his shirt. Even loosened it was much too short. I watched him pull a hankie from his pocket and wipe it across his forehead.

Charbonneau once told me that as a teen he'd worked in the Texas oil fields. Though he loved the cowboy life, the heat won out and he'd returned to his home in Chicoutimi, eventually drifting to Montreal, where he joined the city police force.

At that moment Quickwater emerged from the kitchen. The victim was known to have gang connections, so Carcajou would also be involved.

The constable joined Charbonneau and the two stood watching a team examine bloodstains in a corner behind the victim. Ronald Gilbert held a gray-and-white L-shaped ruler against the wall while a younger man shot videos and prints. They repeated the shots with a plumb line, then Gilbert switched to sliding calipers and took a series of measurements. He entered the data into a laptop computer, then went back to the ABFO ruler and plumb line. More video footage. More photos. More measurements. Blood was everywhere, speckling the ceiling and walls and mottling objects stacked against the baseboards. The two looked like they'd be at their task a long time.

I took a deep breath and approached the detectives.

'Bonjour. Comment ça va?'

'Eh, Doc. How's tricks?' Charbonneau's English was an odd blend of québécois and Texas slang, most of the latter out-of-date.

'Bonjour, Monsieur Quickwater.'

Quickwater rotated slightly, looking annoyed at having to acknowledge my presence, then returned his attention to the blood-spatter team. They were filming an acoustic guitar propped upright on a rusted birdcage. Behind the cage I could see an athletic cap jammed against the wall, the letters '-cock-' visible in the center of a wine-colored blotch. I thought of the posters and wondered what lewd macho message we'd been spared by the gore.

'Where's Claudel?' I asked Charbonneau.

'Checking out a suspect, but he'll be here soon. These guys are really something, aren't they?' Charbonneau's voice filled with disgust. 'Got the moral qualities of dung beetles.'

'This is definitely gang-related?'

'Yeah. The guy that's not looking too good over there is Yves Desjardins, street name 'Cherokee.' He was a Predator.'

'Where do they fit in?'

'The Predators are another Hells Angels puppet club.'

'Like the Vipers.'

'You got it.'

'So this was a Rock Machine hit?'

'Probably. Though I understand Cherokee hadn't been active in years. He had a bad liver. No. Colon cancer. That was it. Not surprising given the shit these guys usually have on board.'

'What had he done to anger the opposition?'

'Cherokee ran some kind of spare-parts

165

business.' When Charbonneau made a sweeping gesture I could see a dark crescent under his armpit. 'But apparently sprockets and carburetors weren't profitable enough. We found about two kilos of coke hidden in the big brave's underwear drawer. No doubt a safe spot since the guy looks like he never changed his shorts. Anyway, that's probably what inspired the surprise visit. But who knows? Maybe it was retaliation for the Marcotte hit.'

'Spider.'

Charbonneau nodded.

'Were there signs of forced entry?'

'There's a broken window in the bedroom, but that's not how they got in.'

'It's not?'

'Most of the fragments are in the alley. Looks like the window was popped from inside.'

'By whom?'

He gave a palms-up gesture.

'So how did the killer get in?'

'He must have let them in.'

'Why would he do that?'

'Cherokee was wily as a pit bull and just a little less friendly. But he'd outlived the stats and was probably starting to feel immortal.'

'Except for the cancer.'

'Right. Let me show you something.'

Charbonneau crossed to the body and I followed. Close up the smell was stronger, a nauseating blend of charred wool, gasoline, excrement, and putrefying flesh. He pulled out his hankie and held it across his nose.

'Check out the tattoos.' Muffled.

Cherokee's right hand was in his lap, his left

166

flung at an odd angle across the arm of the chair, fingers hanging toward the carpet. Despite a thick layer of soot, a cluster of skulls was clearly visible on his right wrist. There were fifteen in all, arranged in a pyramid like the mysterious offerings found in European caves. But these trophies showed a distinction our Neanderthal ancestors had failed to make. Thirteen of the skulls had black eyes, two had red.

'They're like notches on a gun.' Charbonneau took the cloth from his mouth just long enough to speak. 'Black means he killed a male, red a female.'

'Pretty stupid to advertise.'

'Yeah, but our boy here was old school. Today they're listening more to their lawyers.'

From the amount of bloating and skin slippage I guessed the victim had been dead a couple of days.

'How was he found?'

'The usual. A neighbor complained about a foul odor. Amazing anyone would notice in this shithole.'

I looked at the body again. Other than the bad teeth and mustache it was impossible to tell what the man had looked like. What was left of his head rested against the back of the chair, a dark blossom staining the upholstery around it. I could see shotgun pellets in the flesh that had been his face.

'Like the special effects?'

Charbonneau pointed at the small braided carpet below the victim's feet. It was badly charred, as was the underside of the chair. Cherokee himself was smoke-blackened, and his dangling left hand, jean cuffs, and boots were singed. But beyond that there was little damage due to burning.

A fire had been set in front of the chair, and the

167

lingering smell of gasoline suggested the use of an accelerant. Flames had probably engulfed the body, but then, lacking fuel, petered out. By then the killers were long gone.

Charbonneau lifted the hankie again.

'Typical biker shit. Blast the target then torch the body. Only this team must have failed Arson 101.'

'Why would this guy open the door if he was dealing coke in someone else's backyard?'

'Maybe his colon backed up into his brain. Maybe he was smacked on drugs. Maybe he suffered from delusions of normalcy. Hell, who knows how they think? Or if they think.'

'Could it have been his own club?'

'Ain't without precedent.'

Claudel arrived at that moment and Charbonneau excused himself to join his colleagues. While I was curious about the suspect he'd been interrogating, I didn't want to take on a Claudel-Quickwater tag team, so I moved to the far side of the room and resumed observation of the blood-spatter analysts. By now they'd finished the west wall and were rounding the corner onto the north.

Though I'd positioned myself as far from the body as I could get, the smell in the room was becoming unbearable. And Charbonneau was right. The corpse was only one element in the sickening cocktail of mildew, motor oil, stale beer, perspiration, and years of bad cooking. It was hard to imagine how anyone could have lived in such a putrid atmosphere.

I looked at my watch. Two-fifteen. Starting to think about a taxi, I turned to the window at my back.

Cherokee lived on the first floor, his balcony not six feet above the sidewalk. Through the filthy glass I could see the usual armada of cruisers, vans, and unmarked cars. Neighbors stood in clumps or observed from the stoops of neighboring buildings. Press cars and minivans added to the confusion on the small street.

The morgue vehicle pulled up as I was surveying the assemblage, and two attendants hopped out, released the rear doors, and withdrew a gurney. They snapped the wheels into place and pushed the cart up the short front walk to the building's entrance, passing between rutted patches of mud, each furrow filled with standing water. An iridescent slick shone atop the surface of each. Nice. The front yard du Soleil.

In seconds the transport team knocked on the door. Claudel admitted them, then rejoined the group. Steeling myself, I crossed to the detectives. Claudel did not interrupt his account of the interview with the prime suspect.

'You think that wall is a mess?' Claudel gestured toward the northwest corner where the recovery team was still measuring and filming bloodstains. 'This guy's jacket looks like he wore it in the slaughtering house at a stockyard. Of course the little roach hasn't the brains to pull the wings off a moth.'

'Why did he hang on to it?' Charbonneau.

'He was probably too cheap to part with the leather. And he figured we'd never link him. But he'd taken the time to wipe it off and stash it under the bed, just in case.'

'He was spotted here Monday night?'

169

'Just after midnight.'

'That squares with LaManche's estimated time of death. What's his story?'

'He's having a little trouble remembering. It seems George drinks a bit.'

'Any ties to the vic?'

'George has been a Heathens hang-around for years. They let him drive and deal a little grass, so he thinks he's hot stuff. But he's so low in the hierarchy he needs a snorkel just to breathe.'

A transporter called to Claudel, and the detective gave a go-ahead gesture. One of the men unfolded a body bag and laid it on the gurney, while the other placed a brown paper bag on Cherokee's left hand.

Watching Claudel, I was struck by how out of place he appeared. His brow was sweat free, his hair perfect, the creases on his trousers sharp as razor blades. A spot of Armani in the midst of a nightmare.

'Maybe he saw the hit as his big chance for upward mobility,' said Charbonneau.

'Undoubtedly. But George Dorsey isn't going to be mobile for a long time.' Claudel.

'Is there enough to hold him?' Quickwater.

'I'll hold him on suspicion of spitting if I have to. My sources tell me Dorsey recently sent out word he was looking for work, and that no job was off-limits. We've got him pegged for another hit, so I showed his picture around. A witness put Dorsey right here when the shoot went down, and when I dropped in to discuss this fact, I found Dorsey's outerwear covered with blood. Does that sound dirty to you?'

At that moment Claudel's radio erupted in

170

static. He stepped toward the door, listened, spoke into the mouthpiece, then gestured to Quickwater. The two men exchanged words, then Quickwater turned to Charbonneau, pointed at me then at the door. When Charbonneau gave a thumbs-up Quickwater waved and exited into the hall, and Claudel rejoined us.

Great. I'd been passed off like someone's kid sister.

There are two emotions that cause me agitation: feeling trapped and feeling useless. I was experiencing both, and it was making me restless.

And something about the scene bothered me. I knew I was out of my element, but I kept remembering the slides I'd seen at Carcajou headquarters. What I was seeing didn't ring true.

What the hell. I hadn't asked to come here.

'Isn't this a little different from their normal method of dispatch?'

Claudel turned in my direction, his face pinched into its usual chilly expression.

'Excuse me?'

'Isn't the shotgun off from the MO for a biker hit? And the botched fire?'

Charbonneau cocked an eyebrow and shrugged both shoulders. Claudel said nothing.

'This seems so messy,' I pressed on, determined to make a contribution. 'In the cases I've reviewed the hits were pretty efficient.'

'Things happen,' said Charbonneau. 'Maybe the perp was interrupted.'

'I guess that's my point. Don't bikers research their victims and pick settings where they know they won't be interrupted?'

'With a dead biker who was freelancing in the

drug trade, we do not need to search the membership roster at the Unitarian church to find our hit man.' Claudel's voice was cool.

'Nor should we slam our brains shut after the first theory drifts into them,' I said caustically.

Claudel gave me a look implying infinitely strained patience.

'You may be very good at digging up bodies and measuring bones, Ms. Brennan. But those skills are not at the heart of this homicide investigation.'

'It's hard to find a hit man if you don't know who's been hit, Monsieur Claudel. Are *you* going to put his face back together?' Anger made my face burn.

'That will not be a problem here. Fingerprints should suffice.'

I knew that, but Claudel's arrogance was bringing out the worst in me.

Charbonneau crossed his arms and blew out a deep breath.

Claudel checked his watch and I saw the flash of a gold cuff link. Then the arm dropped to his side.

'Sergent-détective Charbonneau and I will drop you off.' His voice indicated he would not be discussing the case further on this occasion.

'Thank you.'

We crossed the room and I took one last look at the chair where Yves 'Cherokee' Desjardins had died. It was empty now, but a port-colored cloud marked the place where his head had rested. Dark rivulets curved from each lobe, like the talons on a raptor greedy for a kill.

Claudel held the door and I exited to the corridor, gripping my bags so tightly my nails bit into the heels of my hands. Still annoyed with

Claudel's superior attitude, as I swept past him I couldn't resist one last gibe.

'As you know, Monsieur Claudel, I am the lab's liaison to Carcajou. You have a professional obligation to share ideas and information with me, like it or not, and I expect nothing less.'

With that I strode down the hall and descended into sunlight.

CHAPTER TWENTY

Though we drove through bright sunshine, my thoughts were dark. When I had volunteered for the Carcajou unit it had been to help solve the Emily Anne shooting, not to join the murder-of-the-day club. I rode in back, my mind shifting between Yves 'Cherokee' Desjardins and Savannah Claire Osprey, victims as different as Charlie Manson and the Sugarplum Fairy.

But Savannah hadn't danced off with Ariel or Puck, and I couldn't shake the image of the spider-legged girl in the baggy swimsuit. I kept wondering about the poisonous web into which she'd been drawn.

I was also haunted by the horror we'd just left. Though the dynamic duo in the front seat were convinced Cherokee's killing was a biker hit, something about the scene seemed out of sync. It was not my call, but my uneasiness remained, prickling my brain.

Savannah and Cherokee. Cherokee and Savannah. And Ronald and Donald Vaillancourt, Robert Gately and Félix Martineau. And Emily

Anne Toussaint, the little girl who danced, and skated, and loved waffles. These lives seemed unconnected, the only tie a posthumous one, created by homicide files.

No one spoke. Now and then the radio sputtered as it scanned channels, diligent in its attention to police matters.

In the Ville-Marie Tunnel we were snared briefly by the clog of traffic exiting onto Berri. I looked at the flow of cars heading toward the old city and experienced a return to melancholy. Why was I trapped with Señor Surly and his partner, the bones of a dead girl at my feet and visions of mutilated bikers in my head? Why wasn't I heading for Place Jacques Cartier, thinking about dinner, dancing, or drinks with a lover?

But I couldn't handle the pleasure of drink.

And I had no lover.

Ryan.

Put it away, Brennan. That line of thought will take you from melancholy to depression. The simple fact is you chose this life. You could be limiting your bone analysis to archaeological digs and your professional commentaries to textbooks or classrooms in which you talk and they listen. You asked for this and you got it, so stop brooding and do your work.

When Charbonneau pulled up at the SQ building I said a terse thank you, slammed the door, and headed up the block toward the main entrance. Before I got to the end of the wrought-iron fence my cell phone rang, so I set the athletic bag on the sidewalk and dug the phone out of my purse.

'Aunt Tempe?'

174

'Hey, Kit.'

I was relieved and annoyed to hear his voice. Though I'd called several times since leaving for Raleigh, Kit hadn't once picked up.

'Did you get my messages?'

'Yeah. Bad timing. I was out, then when I got in I hit the sack. Figured you wouldn't want me to call that late.'

I waited.

'I was with Lyle.'

'For two days?'

'The guy's O.K.'

O.K.?

'We went to that cycle shop. Man, he wasn't exaggerating. They've got more shit than the Harley factory. Oops, sorry.'

'Hm.'

I placed the briefcase next to the athletic bag and rotated my shoulder to work out a kink. Hip-hop music pounded from a Caravan on the opposite side of Parthenais. The driver sat sideways, one arm draped around the wheel, the other drumming the back of the seat.

'I'll be home by six,' I told Kit. 'Tell me what you'd like and I'll throw something together for dinner.'

'That's why I'm calling. Lyle said he'd take me to the TV studio so I can watch them do the show tonight.'

A man emerged from an apartment building across the street and did a slow crawl down the steps, a cigarette dangling from his mouth. His hair looked as if he'd gotten his head too close to an explosion. Some of it stuck out in clumps, some strands lay in knots against his head. He wore a

175

sleeveless denim jacket that showed arms so fully tattooed that from where I stood they looked blue.

The man took a deep drag as he scanned the street. His eyes locked onto me then narrowed, like those of a terrier sighting on a rat. Two smoke streams shot from his nose, then he flicked the butt, crossed the sidewalk, and climbed into the van with the music lover. As the pair drove off I felt a chill, despite the warmth of the afternoon sun.

'. . . ever seen it in person?'

'What?'

'The news. Have you ever been at the station when they actually do it?'

'Yes. It's very interesting.'

'So if you don't mind, I'd really like to go.'

'Sure. That sounds like fun. I'm pretty beat anyway.'

'Did you find out who she is?'

The switch left me behind.

'The girl. Did she turn out to be who you thought she was?'

'Yes.'

'That's cool. Can I tell Lyle?'

'It's not official yet. Better wait until the coroner releases her name.'

'No sweat. So, I'll see you later.'

'O.K.'

'You're sure?'

'Kit, it's fine. I've been ditched by tougher men than you.'

'Ooh. Hit me where I bleed.'

'Bye.'

Lyle Crease. Was that bastard going to use my nephew to wheedle information that he couldn't get directly from me?

*   *   *

Upstairs, I secured Savannah's remains in my evidence locker, and gave one set of bone samples to Denis, the histology technician. He would use a microtome to cut slices less than a hundred microns thick, then stain them and mount them on slides for analysis.

I took the other set to the DNA section. While there I asked about the eyeball. As I waited I felt a band of tension move slowly up the back of my head, and I began to rub my neck.

'Headache?' asked the technician when she returned.

'A little.'

The results were not yet in.

Next I reported to LaManche. He didn't interrupt as I told him of my meeting with Kate, and showed him photos and copies of hospital records.

When I'd finished he removed his glasses and kneaded two red ovals on the bridge of his nose. Then he leaned back, his face devoid of the emotions normally created by death.

'I will call the coroner's office.'

'Thank you.'

'Have you discussed this with the people at Carcajou?'

'I mentioned it to Quickwater, but right now everyone is focused on the Cherokee Desjardins murder.'

That was an understatement. When I'd told him in the car, Quickwater had hardly listened.

'I'll talk to Roy tomorrow,' I added.

'The agent in North Carolina believes this child was killed by gang members?'

'Kate Brophy. She believes it's a good possibility.'

'Does she know of any ties between Quebec and Myrtle Beach gangs?'

'No.'

LaManche inhaled deeply, exhaled.

'Nineteen eighty-four is a long time ago.'

Sitting across from my boss, listening to his precise French and seeing him backlit by the St. Lawrence River, I had to admit the Carolina theory sounded bizarre even to me. What had seemed so right in Raleigh now felt like a remembered dream in which I couldn't sort reality from fantasy.

'We had to cut it short when I got the call about Cherokee's body in the fire, but Agent Brophy lent me a great deal of material from the SBI files, including old photos. Tomorrow I'll take everything over to Carcajou and we'll see what falls out.'

LaManche replaced his glasses.

'This Carolina skeleton may be unrelated.'

'I know.'

'How soon will they have the DNA results?'

I avoided the impulse to roll my eyes, but I'm sure the frustration showed in my voice.

'They're backed up because of the bomber twin case, and wouldn't give me an estimate.' I remembered the look I'd gotten when the technician spotted Savannah's DOD. 'And, as you said, it's not exactly a recent death.'

LaManche nodded.

'But it is an unexplained death, and the remains were found in Quebec, so we will treat it as a

178

homicide. Hopefully the SQ will do the same,' he said.

At that moment his phone rang. I gathered papers as he spoke. When he'd hung up I said, 'The Cherokee case doesn't fit the recent pattern here, but who knows why people kill.'

He answered as he scribbled something on a small yellow pad, his mind still on the phone conversation. Or perhaps he thought I was talking about something else.

'Occasionally Monsieur Claudel can be abrupt, but in the end he will get it right.'

What the hell did that mean?

Before I could ask, the phone rang again. LaManche reached for the receiver, listened, then held it to his chest.

'Was there anything else?'

A polite dismissal.

I was so preoccupied by LaManche's comment about Claudel that I almost collided with Jocelyn the temp as I left his office and headed toward my own. She wore large beaded loops in her ears, and the hair streaks were now the color of purple African violets.

As we circled each other, readjusting our armloads of papers, I again was struck by the whiteness of her skin. Under the harsh fluorescent light, her lower lids looked plum, her skin as pale as the underbelly of a lemon peel. It crossed my mind Jocelyn might be albino.

For some reason, I felt compelled to speak to her.

'How are you getting along, Jocelyn?'

She stared at me with a look I couldn't interpret.

'I hope you're not finding the lab too

overwhelming.'

'I can do the job.'

'Yes, of course you can. I just meant it's hard to be the new kid on the block.'

As she opened her mouth to say something, a secretary emerged from an adjacent office. Jocelyn hurried off down the hall.

Jesus, I thought. This one could use a bit of charm school. Maybe she could get a two-for-the-price-of-one deal for her and Quickwater.

I spent the rest of the afternoon clearing my desk of message slips. Calls from the media I threw away, those from law enforcement I returned.

I scanned a request from Pelletier, the oldest of the lab pathologists. Bones had been found by a homeowner in Outremont when he dug a hole in his cellar floor. The remains were old and brittle, but Pelletier was unsure if they were human.

Nothing urgent.

My desk reasonably clear, I drove home and spent another glamorous evening in the oldest French city in North America.

Pizza. Bath. Baseball.

Birdie stayed through the eighth inning, then curled into a ball on the guest room bed. When I turned in at eleven-fifteen he stretched and relocated to my bedroom chair.

I fell asleep almost immediately and dreamed piecemeal scenarios that made no sense. Kit waved from a boat, Andrew Ryan by his side. Isabelle served dinner. A headless Cherokee Desjardins tweezered pieces of flesh and dropped them into a plastic sack.

When Kit came in I floated to the surface, but was too groggy to call out. He was still fumbling in

180

the kitchen when I sank back into oblivion.

*   *   *

The next morning I was going through Pelletier's bones when Denis came into my lab.

'*C'est la vedette!*'

The star?

Oh no.

He opened a copy of *Le Journal de Montréal* and showed me a picture of myself at the Vipers' clubhouse. Beside it was a short story recounting the recovery of Gately and Martineau, and identifying the mysterious third skeleton as that of sixteen-year-old Savannah Claire Osprey, according to the coroner, an American missing since 1984. The caption described me as a member of the Carcajou unit.

'*C'est une promotion ou une réduction?*'

I smiled, wondering if Quickwater and Claudel would see the error as a promotion or demotion, then resumed sorting. So far I was up to two lamb dinners, a pot roast, and more grilled chicken than I planned to count.

By ten I'd finished with the bones and written a detailed narrative saying that the remains were not human.

I took the report to the secretarial pool, then returned to my office and dialed Carcajou headquarters. Jacques Roy was in a meeting and wouldn't be free until late afternoon. I left my name and number. I tried Claudel, left the same message. Charbonneau. Same name, same number. Please call. I thought of using pagers, decided the situation was not that urgent.

181

Frustrated, I swiveled my chair and surveyed the river.

I couldn't examine the microstructure of the Myrtle Beach bones because the slides weren't ready. God knew when I'd have DNA results, or if there would be anything there to sequence.

I thought of calling Kate Brophy, but didn't want to pressure her. Besides, she was as concerned about the Osprey case as I was. More so. If she discovered anything she'd let me know.

Now what?

LaManche was downstairs performing an autopsy on Cherokee. I could drop in, maybe assuage my doubts about the killing.

Pass. I was not enthused at the thought of studying another biker spread out on a table.

I decided to organize the material Kate had given me. I'd left in such a rush that I hadn't gone through it. We'd done a quick triage, packed everything into my briefcase, signed for possession, and raced to catch a flight.

I emptied the case onto my desk and stacked the photos to my left, the folders to my right. I picked a brown envelope, shook several five-by-sevens onto the blotter, and flipped one over. It was labeled on the back with a date, location, event, name, and several reference numbers.

I reversed the photo and stared into the face of Martin 'Deluxe' DeLuccio, immortalized on July 23, 1992, during a run to Wilmington, North Carolina.

The subject's eyes were hidden by dark lenses the size of quarters, and a twisted bandanna circled his head. His sleeveless denim jacket bore the grinning skull and crossed pistons of the Outlaws motorcycle club. The bottom rocker identified its owner as a member of the Lexington chapter.

The biker's flesh appeared puffy, his jawline slack, and a large gut bulged below the jacket. The camera had caught him straddling a powerful hog, a Michelob in his left hand, a vacuous expression on his face. Deluxe looked as if he'd need instructions to use toilet paper.

I was moving on when the telephone rang. I laid Eli 'Robin' Hood next to Deluxe and picked up, hoping it was Roy.

It wasn't.

A gravelly voice asked for me, dropping the final long 'e' from my first name, but correctly pronouncing the second. The man was a stranger, and obviously an Anglophone. I answered in English.

'This is Dr. Brennan.'

There was a long pause during which I could hear clanging, and what sounded like a public address system.

'This is Dr. Brennan,' I repeated.

I heard a throat cleared, then breathing. Finally a voice said, 'This is George Dorsey.'

'Yes?' My mind scanned, but got no hits.

'You're the one dug up those stiffs?'

The air had gone hollow, as if George Dorsey had cupped his hand around the mouthpiece.

'Yes.' Here we go.

'I saw your name in today's pap—'

'Mr. Dorsey, if you have information about those individuals you should speak with one of the investigating officers.'

Let Claudel or Quickwater deal with the postmedia circus parade.

'Ain't you with Carcajou?'

'Not in the sense you mean. The investigating officer—'

'That fuck has his head so far up his ass he's going to need sonar just to find it.'

That got my attention.

'Have you spoken with Constable Quickwater?'

'I can't speak with fuck-all while this moron Claudel is squeezing my nuts.'

'Excuse me?'

'This ass wipe has aspirations to higher rank, so I sit here sucking shit.'

For a moment no one spoke. The call sounded like it was coming from a bathysphere.

'He's probably putting something together for CNN.'

I was growing impatient, but didn't want to risk losing information that might be useful.

'Are you calling about the skeletons unearthed in St-Basile?'

I heard choking noises, then, 'Shit, no.'

It was then that my brain locked on to the name. George Dorsey was the suspect Claudel had locked up.

'Have you been charged, Mr. Dorsey?'

'Fuck, no.'

'Why are they holding you?'

'When they popped me I was holding six bumps of meth.'

'Why are you calling me?'

'Because none of these other fucks will listen. I didn't whack Cherokee. That was unskilled labor.'

I felt my pulse increase.

'What do you mean?'

'That ain't how brothers take care of business.'

184

'Are you saying Cherokee's murder wasn't gang-related?'

'Fuckin' A.'

'Then who killed him?'

'Get your ass over here and I'll lay it all out.'

I said nothing. Dorsey's breath was loud in the silence.

'But this ain't going to be a one-sided shuck.'

'I've got no reason to trust you.'

'And you ain't my choice for Woman of the Year, but none of these jag-offs will listen. They've launched the D-Day of police fuck-ups and parked me right on Omaha Beach.'

'I'm impressed with your knowledge of history, Mr. Dorsey, but why should I believe you?'

'Got a better lead?'

I let the question dangle a moment. Loser though he was, George Dorsey had a point. And no one else appeared inclined to talk to me today.

I looked at my watch. Eleven-twenty.

'I'll be there in an hour.'

CHAPTER TWENTY-ONE

For policing purposes, the Communauté Urbaine de Montréal is divided into four sections, each with a headquarters housing intervention, analysis and investigation divisions, and a detention center. Suspects arrested for murder or sexual assault are held at a facility near place Versailles, in the far eastern end of the city. All others await arraignment at one of the four sectional jails. For possession of methamphetamine, Dorsey went to his local facility, Op South.

The Op South headquarters is located at rue Guy and boulevard René Lévesque, on the outskirts of Centre-ville. This section is predominantly French and English, but it is also Mandarin, Estonian, Arabic, and Greek. It is separatist and federalist. It holds the vagrant and the affluent, the student and the stockbroker, the immigrant and the *'pur laine'* québécois.

The Op South is churches and bars, boutiques and sex shops, sprawling homes and walk-up flats. The murders of Emily Anne Toussaint and Yves Cherokee Desjardins had taken place within its borders.

As I turned off Guy into the lot, I passed through a group carrying placards and wearing signs. They'd spread down the sidewalk from the building next door, blue-collar workers picketing for higher pay. Good luck, I thought. Perhaps it was the political instability, perhaps the Canadian economy in general, but Quebec Province was in a financial squeeze. Budgets were being cut, services curtailed. I hadn't had a raise in seven years.

I entered at the main door and stepped to a counter to my right.

'I'm here to see George Dorsey,' I said to the guard on duty. She put down her snack cake and eyed me with boredom.

'Are you on the list?'

'Temperance Brennan. The prisoner asked to see me.'

She brushed chubby hands together, checked for crumbs, then entered something into a keyboard. Light reflected off her glasses as she leaned forward to read the monitor. Text scrolled down each lens, froze, then she spoke again without raising her eyes.

'Carcajou?' Ralph Nader couldn't have sounded more dubious.

'Mm.' *Le Journal* thought so.

'Got an ID?'

She looked up and I showed her my security pass for the SQ building.

'No badge?'

'This was handy.'

'You'll have to sign in and leave your things here.'

She flipped pages in a ledger, wrote something, then handed me the pen. I scribbled the time and my name. Then I slipped my purse off my shoulder and handed it across the counter.

'It'll be a minute.'

Ms. Cupcake secured my bag in a metal locker, then picked up a phone and spoke a few words. Ten minutes later a key turned in a green metal door to my left, then it opened and a guard waved me in. He was skeletal, his uniform drooping from his bones like clothes on a hanger.

Guard number two swept me with a handheld metal detector, then indicated I should follow. Keys jangled on his belt as we turned right and headed down a corridor lighted by fluorescents and surveilled by wall and ceiling cameras. Straight ahead I could see a large holding cell, with a window facing the hall I was in, green bars facing the other. Inside, a half-dozen men lounged on wooden benches, sat or slept on the floor, or clung to the bars like captive primates.

Beyond the drunk tank was another green metal door, the words *Bloc Cellulaire* in bold white to its right, beside that another counter. A guard was placing a bundle in one of a grid of cubicles, this one marked XYZ. I suspected a Mr. Xavier was arriving. He would not see his belt, shoelaces, jewelry, glasses, or other personal possessions until checkout.

'Man's in here,' said the guard, thrusting his chin toward a door marked *Entrevue avocat,* the door attorneys used. I knew Dorsey would pass through an identical door marked *Entrevue détenu,* for the prisoners.

I thanked him and brushed past into a small room not designed to lift prisoner or visitor morale. The walls were yellow, the trim green, the only furnishings a red vinyl counter, a wooden stool fixed to the floor, and a wall phone.

George Dorsey sat on the opposite side of a large rectangular window, back rounded, hands dangling between his knees.

'Push the button when you're done,' said the guard.

With that he closed the door and we were alone.

Dorsey didn't move but his eyes locked on me as I crossed to the counter and picked up the handset.

I flashed on Gran's painting. Jesus, skull circled with thorns, forehead covered with droplets of blood. No matter where I went the gaze followed. Look, the eyes were open. Blink, they were closed. The picture was so unnerving I avoided my grandmother's bedroom my entire childhood. Dorsey had the same eyes.

Inwardly trembling, I sat and folded my hands on the countertop. The man across from me was thin and wiry, with a hump nose and razor-blade lips. A scar started at his left temple, looped his

188

cheek, and disappeared into a circle of plumage around his mouth. His head was shaved, his only hair a dark bolt of lightning that touched down just above the scar's terminus.

I waited for him to pick up the phone and break the silence. Outside our little room I heard voices and the clang of steel against steel. Despite the intensity of his stare, Dorsey looked as though he hadn't slept in a while.

After several birthdays Dorsey smiled. The lips disappeared and small, yellow teeth took their place. But there was no mirth in his eyes. With a jerky motion he yanked the receiver from its cradle and placed it to his ear.

'You've got balls coming here, lady.'

I shrugged.

'Got cigarettes?'

'Don't smoke.'

He drew both feet in, flexed his toes, and jiggled one leg up and down on the ball of his foot. Again he went mute. Then, 'I had nothing to do with that piece of work in Pointe-St-Charles.'

'So you said.' I pictured the gruesome scene at Les Appartements du Soleil.

'This asshole Claudel is trying to cut my dick off. Figures if he sweats me hard enough I'll cop to burning Cherokee.'

The jiggling intensified.

'Sergeant-Detective Claudel is simply doing his job.'

'Sergeant-Detective Claudel couldn't blow a fart and get it right.'

There were times I agreed with that assessment.

'Did you know Cherokee Desjardins?'

'I've heard of him.'

189

He ran a finger back and forth along a groove on the countertop.

'Did you know he was dealing?'

Now Dorsey shrugged.

I waited.

'Maybe the stuff was for personal use. You know, medicinal. I heard he had health problems.'

He ran the finger through the hair on his chin, then went back to working the groove.

'You were seen at Desjardins' building around the time he was shot. They found a bloody jacket in your apartment.'

'The jacket ain't mine.'

'And O.J. never owned the gloves.'

'What kind of moron is gonna keep souvenirs after a hit?'

He had a point.

'Why were you in that neighborhood?'

'That's my business.'

He shot forward and spread his elbows on the counter. My heart did a hop, but I didn't flinch.

'And it had nothing to do with wasting Cherokee.'

I noticed a tightening around his eyes, and wondered what scenario he was constructing for my consumption.

More silence.

'Do you know who killed him, George?'

Mistake.

'Ohh, whee!' He curled his fingers and rested his chin on the back of one hand. 'And can I call you Tempe?'

'This isn't a social call. You asked to meet.'

Dorsey turned sideways and stretched a leg toward the wall. One hand played with the phone cord as he kicked at the baseboard with a laceless boot. Outside the door a man's voice called to someone named Marc. I waited. Finally, 'Look, I'm telling you. That hit was *Amateur Hour.* The only thing missing was Ted Mack.'

Dorsey swiveled back and tried to stare me down. Then his gaze dropped and he opened and closed his fingers several times. I watched the letters F.T.W. change shape across his knuckles.

'And?'

'That show was not four star, that's all I'll give up right now.'

'Then I can't help you. We've already determined it was a sloppy hit.'

Dorsey lunged forward again and spread his forearms on the counter.

'Your boy Claudel may think I'm just some Heathens coolie ass wipe, but he's got one thing wrong. I'm not stupid. And neither are they.'

I didn't point out that he'd listed two points of error.

'He likes you for this one.'

Dorsey leaned so close to the glass I could see dirt in the pores on his nose.

'It's a goddam lie. I didn't kill Cherokee.'

I looked into the face that was inches from mine, and for one heartbeat the mask slipped. In that fraction of an instant I saw fear and uncertainty. And something else in those bitter, dark eyes. I saw candor.

Then the lids narrowed and the bravado was back.

'I'm going to cut right to it. You don't like the way my friends and me do business. Fair enough. I don't like your righteous bullshit. But know this.

191

Keep grinding me and whoever did Cherokee is going to walk.'

'Is that all you can tell me, Mr. Dorsey?'

The eyes bored into mine and I could almost smell his hatred.

'I might be privy to additional knowledge,' he said, inspecting his fingernails with feigned nonchalance.

'About what?'

'I'm not telling you nothing. But Cherokee's not the only stiff in the news lately.'

My mind raced. Was he talking about Spider Marcotte? Did he know the identity of Emily Toussaint's killers?

Before I could ask, Dorsey slumped back again, an amused expression curling the corners of his mouth.

'Is there something funny you'd like to share?'

Dorsey ran a hand under his chin and the goatee curled around his fingers. He shifted the receiver to the other ear.

'Tell pus butt to ease off my case.'

I stood to leave, but his next words froze me in place.

'Work with me and I'll give you the girl.'

'What girl?' I asked, forcing calm into my voice.

'That sweet little thing you dug up.'

I stared at him, so angry my heart pounded.

'Tell me what you know,' I hissed.

'Are we dealing?' Though the little rat teeth were out, the eyes were dark as Dante's ninth ring.

'You're lying.'

He raised his eyebrows and the palm of his free hand.

'But truth is the cornerstone of my life.'

192

'Peddle it elsewhere, Dorsey.'

Trembling with anger, I slammed home the phone, whirled and hit the button. I couldn't hear Dorsey's last mocking addendum, but I saw his face as I stormed past the guard. His lips were clear.

He'd be in touch.

*   *   *

The drive back took almost an hour. An accident had closed all but one of the eastbound lanes of 720, and traffic in the Ville-Marie Tunnel was backed up for miles. By the time I realized the situation, reversing up the ramp was not an option, and there was nothing to do but creep along with the other frustrated motorists. The concrete tunnel blocked radio reception so there were no diversions. Dorsey had the floor in my head.

He'd been jumpy as cold water on a hot griddle, but could the man be innocent?

I remembered the eyes, and that moment the veil dropped.

I palmed the gearshift, inched forward, dropped back to neutral.

Was Claudel on the wrong track?

Wouldn't be the first time.

I watched an ambulance squeeze past along the right shoulder, its light pulsing red against the tunnel walls.

What would Claudel say when he learned I'd been to the jail?

That one was easy.

I drummed my fingers on the wheel.

Did Dorsey really know something about Savannah Osprey?

193

I shifted and advanced a car length.

Was he just another con scamming a deal to save his ass?

No answer.

I saw Dorsey's face, a study in macho contempt and antisocial scorn.

The man was repulsive. Yet, in that single nanosecond, I was certain I saw truth. Could I believe him? Did I need to believe him? If he would provide verifiable information on Savannah Osprey in return for the police casting a wider investigative net around the Cherokee murder, what was lost? But could that be done? Certainly not through Claudel.

After forty minutes I drew abreast of the accident. One car lay on its side, another rested against the tunnel wall, headlights pointed in the wrong direction. The pavement glistened with shattered glass, and police and rescue vehicles had circled the wreckage like a wagon train. As I watched workers position the jaws of life over the upturned car I wondered if its occupant would be heading for the same place as I.

I finally broke free, raced down the tunnel, exited at de Lorimier, and drove the last few blocks to the lab. When I got off the elevator on the twelfth floor I knew something was wrong.

The front desk was unattended, the phone clamoring for attention. I counted as I crossed the lobby. Five. A pause, then the ringing started again.

I inserted my security pass and the glass doors opened. Inside, the receptionist stood near the women's lavatory, eyes red, Kleenex bunched into a tight ball. A secretary comforted her, one arm draped around her shoulders.

194

Along the hall people in clumps spoke to one another, voices muted, faces tense. The scene was like a surgical waiting area.

Another flashback.

Fifteen years ago. I'd left Katy in the care of my sister while I ran errands. Rounding the corner to my street, the same hair-trigger fear, the same adrenaline rush.

Fragmented memory bytes. Harry and the neighbors standing on the drive. So wrong together. They didn't know each other. My sister's face, mascara running down blanched cheeks. Hands twisting.

Where was Katy?

Bargaining.

Dear God. Not Katy. Anything. Not my baby.

The neighbors' eyes, wide with sympathy, watching as I climbed from the car.

McDuff had bolted and run in front of a Buick. The dog was dead. Relief, later sorrow. Bad, but I'll take it. My poodle was dead but my daughter was not.

I felt that same dread as I looked at my colleagues.

What had happened here?

Through the second set of glass doors I could see Marcel Morin in conversation with Jean Pelletier. I keyed in and hurried down the hall.

At the sound of my footsteps they fell silent and looked in my direction.

'What is it?' I asked.

'Dr. LaManche.' Morin's eyes shone with emotion. 'He collapsed while doing the Cherokee Desjardins autopsy.'

'When?'

195

'He was working alone during the lunch hour. When Lisa returned she found him on the floor. He was unconscious and barely breathing.'

'Is it bad?'

Pelletier made a sound in his throat.

Morin shook his head.

'It is in God's hands.'

CHAPTER TWENTY-TWO

First thing Friday I called the hospital. LaManche had stabilized, but remained in intensive care, with no visitors allowed. The nurse would say nothing more about his condition.

Feeling helpless, I ordered flowers, then showered and dressed.

Kit's door was closed. I hadn't spoken to him since Wednesday, and wasn't sure where he'd been the night before. On arriving home I had found a note on the fridge. He'd be out late. I shouldn't wait up.

I didn't.

As I made coffee I reminded myself to call Harry. While my nephew was nineteen and past the age for active shepherding, I wanted to be clear on how much parenting was expected. And for how long.

Kit was slowly spreading. The refrigerator was crammed with frozen pizzas and pita-pocket sandwiches, hot dogs, jars of baked beans, and cans of Mellow Yellow. Cheese doodles, nacho chips, doughnuts, Lucky Charms, and Cocoa Puffs lined the counter.

In the living room my TV had been converted to a Sony PlayStation, and wires crisscrossed the floor like tangled spaghetti. CD's were stacked on the sideboard and scattered across the hearth. A heap of crumpled jeans, socks, and jockey shorts filled one chair, a Stetson hung from the wing of another. In the hall, two pairs of cowboy boots lay where they'd been kicked.

The place looked like I was living with Garth Brooks.

I replaced Kit's note with a reply, stating that I'd be home by five and requesting the pleasure of his company at dinner. Then I went to work.

The atmosphere at the lab was as somber as before. Morin announced in the morning meeting that he had spoken with LaManche's wife. Her husband was still comatose, but his vital signs were stable. They were attributing his state to cardiogenic shock. She would call if there was any change. The day's cases were discussed quickly and quietly, without the usual banter.

A tree had fallen on a man in Dollard-des-Ormeaux, crushing him. A couple was found dead in bed in Pointe-aux-Trembles, victims of an apparent murder-suicide. A woman's body had washed ashore near Rivière-des-Prairies.

Nothing for the anthropologist. Perfect. That would leave me free to go through the material Kate Brophy had loaned me. If Jacques Roy was available I'd drive over to Carcajou headquarters and see what he thought.

When the meeting ended I got my mug and went for coffee. Ronald Gilbert was at the counter, talking with one of the new technicians from his section. Though I didn't know the younger man's name I recognized him from the Cherokee murder scene. He'd assisted Gilbert with the blood spatter.

As I waited my turn at the coffee machine I heard snatches of their conversation and realized they were discussing Cherokee's case. I lowered my breathing, straining to hear.

'No, thank God. They're not all this complicated. You pulled a real pot of soup for your first time out.'

'Beginner's luck, I guess.'

'I'd like to have a heart-to-heart with LaManche before I write this up, but I guess that's not going to happen.'

'How's he doing?'

Gilbert shrugged, stirred his coffee, then arced the little wooden stick into the trash.

As I watched them leave I thought of Cherokee's apartment and again sensed uneasiness. None of the others had felt the murder was atypical. Why was I suspicious? What was it that didn't seem right? I had no answers to my questions.

I filled my cup, added cream, and returned to my office, where I sipped and pondered, feet on the sill, eyes fixed on a barge moving slowly up the river.

What was not right about the Cherokee scene? No forced entry? So the victim had grown complacent. So what? It happens. The bungled fire? Charbonneau was probably right. Something went haywire and the perp fled. Even good plans can fail from faulty execution. Look at Watergate.

I took a sip.

What did Gilbert mean by 'a real pot of soup'?

I took another sip.

What was so complicated?

198

Sip.

What did he want to discuss with LaManche?

Never hurts to ask.

Look at Watergate.

*   *   *

I found Gilbert in front of a computer screen. When I knocked he swiveled and looked at me over wire-rimmed glasses. His head, cheeks, and chin were covered with curly brown hair, giving him the look of a hero from Greek mythology.

'Got a minute?'

'As many as you like.'

He waved me in and pulled a chair next to his.

'It's about the Cherokee Desjardins case.'

'Yes. I saw you at the scene. Why are you working that one?'

'I'm not, exactly. I was there because initial reports described a burned body. As it turned out the victim was not in bad shape.'

'Not in bad shape? He looked like a still life in brain tissue.'

'Well, yes. Actually, that's what I'd like to talk to you about. I was going to ask Dr. LaManche but, of course, that's not possible right now.'

He looked puzzled.

'The investigators working the Cherokee case are convinced it's a biker hit.' I hesitated, unsure how to put my reservations into words. 'I can't nail it down, but something about the scene struck me as being off.'

'Off?'

I explained my assignment with Opération Carcajou, and what I'd seen at the briefing session.

199

'I realize I'm a novice, but maybe that's it. Maybe I'm seeing things through different eyes.'

'And what do your eyes tell you?'

'That the Cherokee murder was sloppy.'

'Anything else?'

'That the victim was sloppy. Apparently Cherokee admitted his killer. Does that sound like a former member freelancing drugs on gang turf?'

I didn't mention Dorsey, or his claims of innocence. I figured the less said about my prison visit the better.

Gilbert looked at me a long time, then smiled.

'Claudel thinks you're an interfering pain in the ass.'

'I think highly of him, as well.'

He threw back his head and laughed, then his face grew serious.

'How much do you know about blood-spatter analysis?'

'Not much,' I admitted.

'Ready for a crash course?'

I nodded.

'O.K. Here goes.'

He leaned back and raised his eyes to the ceiling, no doubt deciding where to begin and how to condense years of training into a brief lecture. I could picture him doing the same for a jury.

'A free-falling drop of blood is spherical due to the effects of gravity and surface tension. Think about when you prick your finger. Blood builds up on the down side until the drop is able to break free and fall. Seems simple, right?'

'Yes.'

'It's not. All kinds of opposing forces are at work. Gravity and the increasing weight of the blood are 'pulling' the drop downward. At the same time the surface tension of the blood is trying to reduce the exposed surface of the drop and is 'pushing' it upward.'

He gestured quotation signs around the verbs.

'Only when the 'pulling' forces exceed the 'pushing' forces will the drop break free. Initially it's elongated, but as it falls the drop flattens due to air resistance. The attractive forces of surface tension within the drop cause it to assume a shape with the least amount of surface area. Thus, drops of blood are shaped like spheres, not like teardrops as they're usually drawn. And shape is one of the things we consider in spatter-pattern analysis.

'A blood spatter is produced as a result of a force striking static blood. It could be in a pool on the sidewalk, or inside a victim's head. When hit, the blood breaks into drops, called spatter, which travel through the air as spheres.'

I nodded.

'When these spheres strike a surface they leave predictable types of trails. Bloodstain-pattern interpretation is concerned with examining stains produced by drops of blood that are *not* typical. The stains and trails have been altered in some way, usually by violent activity.

'The goal of bloodstain-pattern interpretation is to work backward from a crime scene and reconstruct the events that took place. What happened? In what sequence? Who was where? What weapon was used? What objects have been moved? To answer these questions we look at what has altered the drops of blood present.

'And it's very complex.' He began ticking points off on his fingers. 'For example, we have to take

201

into account the properties of the target. Blood will act differently when striking a smooth versus a textured surface.'

Tick.

'Shape. Since the ratio of a stain's width and length accurately reflects its angle of impact, regardless of striking surface, we look carefully at the shape of the stains.'

Tick.

'Spatter size. Smaller or slower-moving forces produce large spatters, while larger or faster-moving forces produce smaller spatters.'

He stopped, thumb pressed to his fourth finger.

'Still with me?'

'Yep.'

'We talk about low-, medium-, and high-velocity-impact spattering, although these terms are really relative.'

'Give me examples.'

'I'll do better than that. Come with me.'

He led me down the hall to a stainless steel refrigerator and withdrew a one-liter bottle labeled *Sang du boeuf.*

'Beef blood,' he explained.

I followed him along a narrow side corridor to an unmarked door, and we entered a windowless room where large sheets of white paper were taped to most surfaces.

The small chamber looked like a massacre site. Blood was pooled along one baseboard, streaked and splattered on the walls, and dripping from various-sized spots at knee level in the far corner. Above each stain I could see pencil notations.

'This is our blood-spatter experiment room,' said Gilbert, placing the bottle on the floor. 'Watch.'

202

He removed the cap, dipped a wooden rod into the blood, then allowed it to drop onto the paper under his feet.

'Low-velocity-impact spatters are associated with drops passively falling onto a surface. Dripping blood, for example. The characteristic spatter size is greater than three millimeters in diameter. In these situations the blood is moving slowly, from normal gravitational pull to up to five feet per second.'

I examined the small round stains he'd created.

'Medium-velocity blood spatter results from activities such as beatings, blunt trauma injuries, or stabbings. The blood is moving faster, with a force velocity between five feet and twenty-five feet per second.'

As he said this he poured a small amount of blood into a dish, signaled me to step back, then swung the rod into it. The blood flew up and struck the wall. Gilbert gestured me over and pointed to several of the stains. They were smaller than the ones at his feet.

'See these spatters? The size range for medium-velocity spatter is typically less, averaging between one and four millimeters in diameter.'

He lay down the rod.

'But the spots aren't as fine as with high-impact spatters. Come look at this.'

We moved to the far wall, where he indicated an area that looked as if it had been spray-painted.

'High-velocity-impact spattering means a force velocity greater than one hundred feet per second and results from gunshots, explosions, and mechanical accidents. It's more like a mist, with individual spatters averaging less than one millimeter in diameter.

'But don't get me wrong. Not every spatter falls neatly into one of these categories. Blood that is splashed, cast off, or projected can really complicate a picture.'

'How so?'

'These are actually forms of low- to medium-velocity spatter, but they differ from the ones I just described. For example, splashed blood results from someone stepping into already-pooled blood. This leaves long, narrow spatters surrounding a central stain, with very few round stains present.

'Projected blood results from someone running through, stamping into, or slapping a pool of blood. Or from arterial gushing, or beating a head on the floor. Again there are long, spiny spatters radiating from a central stain. But in this case the borders of the central stain are also distorted.

'Blood cast off from a weapon leaves yet another pattern. Let me show you.'

He went back to the rod, dipped, and swung it in an arc. Blood flew from the tip and struck the wall to his right. I drew close and studied the stain.

'Cast-off drops are smaller than those in typical low-velocity spatter, and the greater the force the smaller the drops. Also, since the blood is being thrown from a moving object, cast-off spatter occurs in straight or slightly curved trails, and the drops are fairly uniform throughout.'

'So you can determine the nature of an assault based on the size and shape of the spatter?'

'Yes. And in most cases we can pinpoint where the attack took place. Let's go back to my office and I'll show you something else.'

When we were once again in front of the

computer he placed his hands on the keyboard and entered a command.

'You saw us taking videos of the bloodstains in the victim's apartment, right?'

'Yes.'

'We used a simple video camera, but you can also use digital. We recorded each area of spatter using a scale and a plumb line.'

'Why a plumb line?'

'The program uses that to determine the vertical direction of the stain.'

Gilbert hit a key and a cluster of elliptical brown forms came up on the monitor.

'The images on the videotape are entered into the computer and can be played back on the monitor. Single frames are grabbed and recorded on the hard disk as bitmaps. A program then displays the image of each stain so we can take measurements. The measurements are used to calculate two angles: the angle of directionality, and the angle of impact.'

More keystrokes, and an oval-shaped white outline appeared superimposed over the stain at center screen. Gilbert pointed at it.

'The direction of the main axis of the ellipse with respect to the plumb line defines the directionality angle, or gamma of a stain. That can range from zero to three-sixty.

'The impact angle, or alpha, can range from zero to ninety degrees. That's calculated from the shape of the ellipse.'

'Why is that?'

'Remember, when a drop of blood travels through space it's spherical. But when it strikes a target it flattens and leaves a trail. That's because the bottom of the drop is actually wiping across the surface.'

He made a swiping gesture with his hand.

'The trail is small at first as the drop strikes, then widens, with the widest point of the trail corresponding to the center, or widest part of the drop. The trail then narrows and eventually tapers off. See this one here?'

He pointed to an elongated oval with a small dot at one end. It looked like many I'd seen in the blood-spatter room.

'It looks like an exclamation point.'

'That's exactly what it's called. Sometimes a small dot of blood detaches from the original drop and hops to the head of the trail. So looking at a spatter from above, it resembles either a tadpole or an exclamation point, depending on whether the far end is merely elongated, or a small portion detached completely. In either case the direction of travel is clear.'

'The dot points toward the direction the drop was moving.'

'Exactly. The program produces a file containing the values of the angles for each stain analyzed. It's from that data that point of origin is calculated. And believe me, using the computer is a lot quicker than the old string method.'

'Back up.'

'Sorry. With the string method one end of a string is fastened to the surface at the position of the stain, then stretched in the estimated direction of motion. This is repeated for a number of bloodstains around the scene. The result is a pattern of strings extending away from the spatter toward the source of the blood. Home plate is the point where all the strings converge. The procedure is time consuming and leaves a lot of room for error. Instead of doing it by hand the computer draws virtual strings computed from the data.'

His fingers flew over the keys and a new image appeared. X and Y coordinates ran down the left side and across the bottom of the screen. A dozen lines formed an X-shaped pattern, crossing each other in a geometric bow.

'This is a bird's-eye view of a set of virtual strings based on twelve spatters. It's hard to get this point of view with real strings, yet it's the most useful one.'

More key clicking and a new image appeared. The lines now plunged together from upper left to lower right, converging at a point two thirds of the distance from the bottom of the screen, then spreading slightly, like stems on a bunch of dried flowers.

'The program can also produce a side view, which is necessary to estimate the height of the source of blood. By combining the two views you have a pretty accurate idea of point of convergence and, therefore, of victim position.'

Gilbert leaned back and looked at me.

'So what do you want to know about the Cherokee scene?'

'Anything you can tell me.'

For the next forty minutes I listened and watched, interrupting only for clarification. Gilbert was patient and thorough as he walked me through the bloodbath in the apartment.

What he said increased my conviction that Claudel was leading us in a dangerously wrong direction.

CHAPTER TWENTY-THREE

The screen was filled with hundreds of tiny dots, like the spray-paint mist in Gilbert's test room. Scattered among them were small bits of flesh and bone.

'You're looking at a section of the north wall, right behind the victim's chair. That's forward spatter.'

'Forward spatter?'

'From the pellets exiting Cherokee's head. Blood from an entrance wound is called back spatter. Look at this.'

Gilbert hit the keys and a new image filled the screen. It was a similar spray of aerosolized blood, though less densely packed, and lacking the larger globs of tissue.

'That's from the TV. When the pellets struck Cherokee, blood flew backward.'

'He was shot sitting in the chair?'

'Yes.'

He entered several more keystrokes and the image was replaced by a view of the chair where the body had been found. Lines ran diagonally from the wall and the TV, and crossed at a point head-high above the seat.

'But the gunshot was icing on the cake. If he wasn't dead already, he was well on his way. Look at this.'

More keystrokes. Another image, this one with larger spots and more variation in their size.

'That's medium-velocity spatter. It was all over the northwest corner of the apartment.'

'But—'

'Just wait.'

He brought up another frame. This one showed spots slightly larger than those in the previous image, but of roughly uniform size. They varied in shape from round to ovoid.

When Gilbert hit a key and zoomed out I could see that most of this spatter was distributed in a long curving line, with some drops lying to either side of the arc.

'That's from the ceiling.'

'The ceiling?'

'It's what we call a cast-off pattern. It results from blood being thrown from a moving object, like my stick. When swinging a weapon, the attacker terminates his backstroke abruptly, then reverses direction to deliver the next blow. Most blood flies off on the backstroke, at least if there's enough force, but some can be thrown on the downward stroke, too.'

He pointed to drops in the center of the trail.

'These spatters are due to the backswing.'

He indicated several drops lying along the edge of the arc.

'And these are downswing trails.'

I took a moment to digest that.

'So you're saying that he was beaten before he was shot?'

'This trail is one of five we were able to identify. Generally, assuming the blunt injury trauma is the only source of blood, or at least the first, the number of trails equates to the number of blows plus two.'

'Why plus two?'

'There wouldn't have been any blood on the first blow. On the second blow blood is picked up by the weapon and thrown off as the attacker makes the backswing for the third blow.'

'Right.'

'This medium-velocity spatter was found down low on the walls, and on the crap stacked in the corner.'

He worked the keys again and more strings appeared, these converging on a point less than two feet above the floor.

'My opinion is that he was struck near the corner of the room, fell to the floor, and was then hit repeatedly. After that he was placed in the chair and shot.'

'Struck with what?'

Gilbert pooched out his lips. 'Pfff. Not my call.'

'Why bludgeon him then shoot him?'

'Definitely not my call.'

'If he was dragged, wouldn't that have left a trail?'

'The assailant may have wiped it up. Besides, there was so much blood everywhere, and so many people on the scene the floor was useless.'

'And the burning may have disguised some of it.'

'At least on the carpet. We may go in with Luminol, but it's not going to change what the spatters tell me.'

I was thinking about that when he spoke again.

'There's something else.'

'There's more?'

Again he worked the keys. Again a mist of high-velocity blood spatter filled the screen. But a portion of the cloud was missing, like a stencil with

210

a cut-out pattern.

'This is another shot of the wall behind the victim's head.'

'It looks like someone took a cookie cutter to it.'

'This is called a void pattern. It's produced when an object blocks the path of blood and is then removed.'

'What object?'

'I don't know.'

'Who removed it?'

'I don't know.'

*   *   *

As I hurried back to my office, Dorsey's words provided voice-over for Gilbert's images.

Amateur Hour. Whoever did Cherokee is going to walk.

I grabbed my phone and punched in a number. A secretary told me Jacques Roy had flown to Val-d'Or and would be unavailable until Monday. Impatient, I asked for Claudel. Neither he nor his Carcajou partner was in. I thought of pagers, again decided the situation was not sufficiently urgent, and left messages for everyone.

I had just replaced the receiver when the phone rang.

'Should I be sending the world's biggest fruit basket?'

'Hi, Harry.'

As usual my sister sounded as though she'd just completed some event requiring intense exertion.

'Why are you out of breath?'

'Akido.'

I didn't ask.

211

'Is my baby boy driving you back to the solace of drink?'

'He's fine, Harry.'

'Are you always this cheerful on Fridays?'

'I just heard something disturbing. What's up?'

'I suppose you know that Kit and Howard went at it again.'

'Oh?' I suspected as much, but hadn't pressed my nephew.

'It's the golf cart all over again.'

I remembered that episode. When Kit was fifteen he'd stolen a cart from the pro shop at Howard's country club. It was found the next morning, half-submerged in a water hazard on the fifteenth hole, with half a bottle of tequila in the back compartment. Daddy went ballistic and son lit out. A week later Kit showed up in Charlotte. The last leg of hitchhiking had not gone well, and he owed ninety-six dollars to a taxi driver. Katy and Kit bonded immediately, and my nephew stayed the summer.

'What was the fight about?'

'I'm not sure, but it involved fishing gear. Is he behaving himself?'

'Actually, I haven't seen that much of him. I think he's made friends here.'

'You know Kit. Well, if you could let the little buckaroo stay just a little while I'd appreciate it. I think he and his daddy need some distance and some time.'

'Doesn't Howard live near Austin?'

'Yes.'

'And Kit's in Houston with you?'

That seemed like distance to me.

'See, that's the problem, Tempe. I've had this

212

trip to Mexico planned for a long time, and I'm supposed to leave tomorrow. If I cancel I'll lose my deposit, and Antonio will be really torqued. Of course, say the word and that's what I'll do.'

'Uh. Hm.'

I wondered if Antonio was the akido link. With Harry, a new man usually meant a new interest.

'I would hate to leave Kit unsupervised and in my home for a week, and at the moment I can't send him to his daddy. And as long as he's with you anyway, and you say he's no problem . . .'

She let the sentence dangle.

'You know I love having Kit.' But not necessarily this week, I thought.

'Tempe, if this is just the least little tiny bit inconvenient you just say so and I'll cancel this trip quicker than—'

'I do want to know how much parental control is expected.'

'Parental control?' She sounded completely at a loss.

'Guidance? Parenting? It's a lonely job, but does someone have to do it?'

'Get real, Tempe. Kit's nineteen. You can parent until Tinkerbell bites the Pope, but that boy's born to boogie and that's what he's gonna do. I just need to have him check in daily and verify that he is physically fit and not wanted by the authorities. And that he is not using my home as a convention center for underage boozers. He didn't grow up in the Partridge family, you know.'

The Partridge family had not entered my mind.

'But that doesn't mean you shouldn't make him chop cotton. Make sure he keeps his belongings orderly and does the dishes now and again.'

213

I pictured the clothing heaped in my living room.

'In fact, I'm gonna call him myself and make sure he understands that your home is not a port of entry for any old thing he wants to drag in.'

'How long will you be in Mexico?'

'Ten days.'

'What if he wants to head home before you get back?'

'No problemo. Howie's given him about eleven hundred credit cards. Just make him understand that an early return means Austin, not Houston, and don't let him go off all depressed. You're good at that, big sister. And you know how crazy he is about you.'

Sweet-talkin' Harry.

'I'll keep that in mind when he pawns Gran's silver. Have a good time. And leave a number where you can be reached.'

As I was hanging up Claudel appeared in the doorway, his face so taut the bones seemed to push out on the tissue. I watched him cross to the chair opposite my desk.

Great.

'Bonjour, Monsieur Claudel.'

I didn't expect a greeting. I didn't get one.

'You made an unauthorized visit to the jail.'

'Did Mr. Dorsey tell you about our conversation?' I asked innocently.

'You interrogated my prisoner.'

'He's your personal property?'

'You are not homicide, you are not even a detective.' Claudel fought to keep his voice even. 'You have no business involving yourself in my case.'

'Dorsey called me.'

214

'You should have referred him.'

'He called me because he felt you would not listen.'

'He is just using you to interfere with my investigation.'

'Why won't you even consider that you may be on the wrong track, Claudel?'

'You are out of your league and I don't have to explain to you.'

'This thing with Dorsey is a very weak bust.'

'But it is *my* weak bust, madam, and not yours.'

'You are convinced Cherokee was murdered by bikers,' I said evenly. 'And I am on temporary assignment to Carcajou.'

'I am doing what I can to alter that,' said Claudel, his outrage barely concealed.

'Really.' I felt blood rise to my cheeks.

'I'm not going to argue the point, Ms. Brennan. Stay out of my investigation.'

'I do not take my orders from you!'

'We will see.'

'We worked together once, with good success.'

'That does not make you a detective, or entitle you to act directly in a case assigned to me.'

'You cannot overestimate how much you underestimate me, Monsieur Claudel.'

He straightened, dropped his chin, and took a deep breath. When he spoke again his voice was calm.

'Any further exchange is pointless.'

I agreed.

He walked toward the door, his back stiff as a dressage rider's. Before leaving, he turned, raised his chin, and spoke down his nose.

'There is one other thing that I should tell you,

215

Ms. Brennan.'

I waited.

'George Dorsey was charged with first-degree murder this morning.'

Though his words were ice, I could feel the heat all the way across the room. Then he was gone.

I took a long breath that caught several times on the way up. Then I uncurled my fingers, sat, and stared at children playing in the school yard twelve floors down.

I was angry for Dorsey. I was frustrated by Claudel's pigheaded refusal to listen. I was mortified that the man had taken steps to annul my appointment to Carcajou.

I was furious with Claudel, but I was equally angry with myself. I detest losing my temper, but seemed unable to control it in arguments with Claudel. But it was more than that.

While I hated to admit it, Claudel still intimidated me. And I still sought his approval. Though I thought I'd gained ground in the past, the man obviously continued to regard me with disdain. And it mattered. And that irked me. Also, I knew it had been wrong not to at least notify him of the Dorsey interview. Investigative teams demand that all information be contributed to the common pool, and rightly so. Because I knew Claudel would not include me in the loop, I had elected not to inform him. Only, he was one of the chief investigators on the Cherokee case. By my actions, I had handed him a weapon to use against me.

'The hell with him.'

I turned my gaze from the kick ball below and surveyed the contents of my office. Articles to be

216

filed. Forms to be signed for destruction of remains. Phone messages. A briefcase filled with biker info.

My scanning stopped at a pile of photocopies stacked on a corner cabinet. Perfect. I'd been putting it off for months. I decided to distance myself from the current quagmire of bones and bikers and surly detectives by updating my database on old cases.

And that's what I did until it was time to go.

On the way home I swung by the Métro store on Papineau and picked up the ingredients for puttanesca sauce. I wondered if Kit would like anchovies, bought them anyway. I'd proceed as I had when serving Katy a foreign dish. I wouldn't tell him.

The evening's cuisine was a moot point. When I arrived at the apartment no one greeted me but Birdie. The boots and clothing had been cleared, and a floral arrangement the size of Rhode Island filled the dining room table. A note had been placed on the refrigerator door.

My nephew was so, so sorry. He'd made plans that couldn't be changed. Sad face. He promised me the entire day on Saturday. Smiley face.

I slammed the bags on the kitchen counter, stomped to the bedroom, and kicked off my pumps.

Hell. What kind of life is this? Another Friday with the cat and the tube.

Maybe Claudel would like dinner. That would make my day.

I pulled off my work clothes, threw them on the chair, and slipped into jeans and a sweatshirt.

It's your own fault, Brennan. You're not exactly

Miss Congeniality.

I dug around on my closet floor, located my Top-Siders, and broke a nail yanking them on.

I couldn't remember when I'd felt so down. And so very alone.

The idea popped up without warning.

Call Ryan.

No.

I went to the kitchen and began emptying groceries, Ryan's face filling my mind.

Call.

That's past.

I remembered a spot just below his left collarbone, a hollowed-out muscle that cradled my cheek perfectly. Such a safe spot. So quiet. So protected.

Call him.

I did that.

Talk to him.

I don't want to listen to lame excuses. Or lies.

Maybe he's innocent.

Jean Bertrand said the evidence is overwhelming.

My resolve crumbled with the canned tomatoes, but I finished emptying the bags, balled and stuffed them under the sink, and filled Birdie's dish. Then I went to the living room phone.

When I saw the light my stomach did a mini-flip.

I pushed the button.

Isabelle.

The landing was like that of a gymnast after a bad vault.

The machine told me I had two entries that had not been erased.

I pushed again, hoping Kit had played them and

218

forgotten.

The first was Harry, looking for her son.

The second message was also for Kit. As I listened, the small hairs rose at the back of my neck, and my breath froze in my throat.

CHAPTER TWENTY-FOUR

After unsuccessfully attempting to decode the garbled message for Kit from a person named Preacher about a meet, I concluded that this probably involved Harleys, and not those owned by a suburban motorcycle club. I thought of waiting up, decided against it.

Impulsively, I dialed Ryan's number. The answering machine replied. My despondency complete, I went to bed.

I slept fitfully, my thoughts like colored chips in a kaleidoscope, congealing to form clear images, then drifting apart into meaningless patterns. Most of the tableaux involved my nephew.

Kit, driving his pickup through a tunnel of trees. Kit, arms overflowing with flowers. Kit on a Harley, Savannah Osprey riding the back, bookend bikers to either side.

At one point I heard the beep of the security system. Later, vomiting, then the sound of a toilet.

In between cameos of my nephew, my unconscious presented theme song suggestions. *Lord of the Dance* kept repeating. The music was like fleas in the carpet: Once in, it was impossible to dislodge.

Dance, dance, wherever you may be . . .

219

I awoke to pale gray lighting the edges of the window shade. Slamming a pillow across my head, I threw an arm over it and pulled my knees to my chest.

I am the lord of the dance, said he . . .

At eight I gave up. Why be annoyed? I reasoned. It isn't rising early that's a pain. It's *having* to rise early. I didn't *have* to get up, I was choosing to do so.

I threw back the covers and slipped on the same outfit I'd featured for my Friday evening with Bird. A Brennanism: When in doubt as to where the day will take you, underdress.

While the Krups pot brewed my 100 percent Kona I peeked out the French doors. Rain fell steadily, turning trunks and branches shiny, jiggling leaves and shrubs, and puddling in low spots on the courtyard brick. Only the crocus sprouts looked happy.

Who was I kidding? This was a morning to sleep.

Well, you're not. So do something else.

I threw on a jacket and sprinted to the corner for a *Gazette*. When I got back, Birdie was curled on a dining room chair, ready for our Saturday ritual.

I poured myself some Quaker Harvest Crunch, added milk, and set the bowl next to the paper. Then I got coffee and settled in for a long read. Birdie watched, secure in the knowledge that all cereal leavings would be his.

A United Nations human rights panel had blasted Canada for its treatment of aboriginals.

Dance, dance . . .

The Equality Party was celebrating its tenth birthday.

What's to celebrate? I wondered. They hadn't

220

won a single National Assembly seat in the last election. Equality had been born of a language crisis, but the issue had been relatively quiet over the past decade, and the party was hanging on by suction cups. They needed another linguistic flare-up.

The Lachine Canal would be undergoing a multimillion-dollar face lift. That was good news.

As I refilled my cup and gave Bird his milk, I pictured the place where Kit and I had skated last Sunday. The bike path ran along the canal, a nine-mile waterway filled with toxins and industrial sludge. But it had not always been a sewer.

Built in 1821 to bypass the Lachine rapids and allow ships direct passage from Europe to the Great Lakes, the canal was once an integral part of the city's economy. That changed when the St. Lawrence Seaway opened in 1959. The canal's mouth and several basins were filled with earth displaced by construction of the métro system, and it was eventually closed to navigation. The surrounding neighborhoods were neglected and, save for the creation of the bicycle path, the canal was ignored, tainted by a century of industrial dumping.

Now plans were afoot to revitalize the city's southwest side. Like Mont-Royal Park, designed by Frederick Law Olmsted one hundred and twenty-five years ago, the canal was to be the centerpiece for a renaissance of the entire sector.

Maybe it's time to buy a new condo.

I resettled at the table and opened to another section.

The RCMP had to squeeze more than twenty-one million dollars from its budget to cover salary

221

raises. The federal government would cough up only a portion.

I thought of the blue-collar workers picketing on Guy.

Bonne chance.

The Expos lost to the Mets, 10–3.

Ouch. Maybe Piazza *was* worth the ninety-one million the Big Apple had forked out.

Dorsey's rearraignment on new charges was on page five, next to a story about Internet crime. The only thing I learned was that he'd been arraigned late Friday afternoon, then transferred from Op South to the provincial prison at Rivière-des-Prairies.

At ten I phoned the hospital. Madame LaManche reported that her husband was stable, but still uncommunicative. Thanking me politely, she refused my offer of help. She sounded exhausted, and I hoped her daughters were there for support.

I sorted clothes and ran a load of whites. Then I changed to basketball shorts and a T and laced up my cross-trainers. I walked to McKay and Ste-Catherine, and took an elevator to the top-floor gym.

I ran the treadmill for twenty minutes, finished with another ten on the StairMaster. Then I lifted weights for half an hour and left. My usual routine. In. Exercise. Out. That's why I liked Stones Gym. No high-tech glitz. No personal trainers. A minimum of spandex.

When I emerged, the rain had stopped and the cloud cover was losing its hold. An especially promising patch of blue had appeared over the mountain.

I arrived home to the same quiet I'd left. Birdie was sleeping off the cereal milk, my nephew was sleeping off something I didn't want to contemplate.

Dance, dance . . .

I checked the answering machine, but the message light was dark. No response from Ryan. As with all recent calls to his number, his machine was not calling back.

O.K., Ryan. Message received loud and clear.

I showered and changed, then arranged myself at the dining room table. I sorted everything Kate had loaned me. Photos to the left, documents to the right. Again I began with the photos.

I glanced briefly at Martin 'Deluxe' Deluccio and Eli 'Robin' Hood, then at a dozen members of the same species, bearded, mustached, goateed, and stubbled. I moved on to the next envelope.

Color prints fell to the table. In most the focus was blurry, the subjects badly framed, as though each was shot quickly and covertly. I sifted through them.

The settings were predictable. Parking lots. Motel pools. Barbecue joints. Yet the amateur quality made these scenes somehow more compelling, gave them a vitality lacking in the police surveillance photos.

Going from picture to picture, I noted accidental events captured by tourists, salesmen, passing motorists. Each told the story of a chance encounter, a random intersection of the ordinary and the dark. Kodak moments of fascination and fear. Heart racing, palms sweaty, reaching for the camera before the wife and kids returned from the toilet.

I picked one up and studied it closely. An Esso station. Six men on chopped-down Harleys, twenty yards from the lens yet a universe away. I could feel the shooter's awe, his seduction-repulsion by the aura of the motorcycle outlaw.

For the next hour I worked my way through the stack of envelopes. From Sturgis, South Dakota, to Daytona Beach, Florida, whether shot by police or Joe Citizen, the events and participants were tediously similar. Runs. Campgrounds. Swap meets. Bars. By one o'clock I'd seen enough.

It was time to talk to Kit.

Bracing myself for the conversation, I went to the guest room door and knocked.

Nothing.

I knocked harder.

'Kit?'

'Yo.'

'It's after one. I'd like to talk to you.'

'Mmmm.'

'Are you up?'

'Uhm. Hum.'

'Don't go back to sleep.'

'Give me five.'

'Breakfast or lunch?'

'Yeah.'

Taking that as an affirmative for the latter, which was my preference, I made ham and cheese sandwiches and added deli dills. As I was consolidating Kate's material to make space at the table, I heard the bedroom door open, then activity in the bathroom.

When my nephew appeared I almost lost my resolve. His eyes were red-rimmed, his face the color of cooked oatmeal. His hair was doing Jim

Carrey.

'Mornin', Aunt T.'

When he raised both hands and rubbed them up and down over his face, the border of a tattoo peeked from the hem of his T-shirt sleeve.

'It's afternoon.'

'Sorry. I got in kind of late.'

'Yes. Ham sandwich?'

'Sure. Got any Coke?' he asked in a thick voice.

'Diet.'

'That's cool.'

I got two sodas and joined him at the table. He was regarding the sandwich as one might a squashed cockroach.

'You'll feel better if you eat,' I encouraged.

'I just need to wake up a little. I'm fine.'

He looked as fine as a smallpox victim. Up close I could see tiny veins threading through the whites of his eyes, and smell the smoke that clung to his hair.

'This is me, Kit. I've been there.'

I had, and I knew what he was going through. I could remember the feel of residual booze slugging through my bloodstream, churning my stomach and pounding the dilated vessels in my brain. The dry mouth. The shaky hands. The sense that someone had poured lead shot in the space below my sternum.

Kit rubbed his eyes, then reached over and stroked Bird's head. I knew he was wishing he were someplace else.

'Food will help.'

'I'm fine.'

'Try the sandwich.'

He raised his eyes to me and smiled. But as soon

225

as he relaxed the corners of his mouth hooked downward, unable to sustain the effort without conscious direction. He took a bite the size of a dime.

'Umm.' He popped open the Diet Coke, tipped back his head, and gulped.

It was obvious that he didn't want to travel in the direction I was headed. Well, neither did I. Perhaps there was no issue. He was nineteen. He'd had a big night. He was hungover. We'd all been there.

Then I remembered the phone message. And the new tattoo.

There were issues, and we needed to discuss them.

I knew what I said would make little difference. Probably none. He was young. Invulnerable. And 'born to boogie,' according to Harry. But I owed it to him to try.

'Who's the Preacher?' I asked.

He looked at me as he rotated his Diet Coke can on the table.

'Just a guy I met.'

'Met where?'

'At the Harley shop. When I went with Lyle.'

'What kind of guy?'

He shrugged the question off.

'No one special. Just a guy.'

'He left you a message.'

'Oh?'

'You listen. I can't translate it.'

'Yeah. The Preacher's kind of a head case.'

That was an understatement.

'How so?'

'I don't know. He's just out there. But he rides this chopped '64 panhead that is truly righteous.'

He took a long swig of Diet Coke. 'I'm sorry I stood you up last night. Did you find my note?' He was looking for a new topic.

'Yes. What was this event that was so important?'

'A boxing match,' he said without expression. His face had the consistency of bread dough. And about as much color.

'Do you follow boxing?'

'Not really. These guys do, so I went along.'

'What guys?'

'Just these guys I met.'

'At the Harley shop.'

He shrugged.

'And the tattoo?'

'Pretty cool, eh?'

He raised his sleeve. A scorpion wearing some sort of helmet spread its legs across his left biceps.

'What is it supposed to mean?'

'It doesn't mean anything. It just looks kick-ass.'

I had to agree.

'Your mother is going to kill me.'

'Harry has a tattoo on her left buttock.' He pronounced the last with a British inflection.

I am the lord of the dance, said he . . .

For a while neither of us spoke. I ate my sandwich while Kit picked at his, nibbling off a gram at a time then washing each down with Diet Coke.

'Do you want another?' he asked, pushing back his chair and wiggling his empty can.

'No thanks.'

When he returned I plunged in again.

'How much did you drink last night?'

'Too much.' He scratched his head roughly with

both hands and the hair went from Carrey to Alfalfa. 'But it was just beer, Aunt T. Nothin' hard. And I'm legal here.'

'Just beer?'

He lowered his hands and looked at me, making sure he understood my meaning.

'If there's one thing you can count on with this boy, it's a negatory on pharmaceuticals. This body ain't much, but I'm keeping it a drug-free zone.'

'I'm very glad to hear that.' I was. 'What about the Preacher and his flock?'

'Hey. Live and let.'

'It doesn't always work that way, Kit.'

Go ahead. Ask.

'Are these guys bikers?'

'Sure. That's why it's Disneyland for me. They all ride Harleys.'

Try again.

'Are they affiliated with a club?'

'Aunt T, I don't ask them a lot of questions. If you mean do they wear colors, the answer is no. Do they hang with guys that do? Yeah, probably. But I'm not going to sell my boat and strike for the Hells Angels, if that's what worries you.'

'Kit. Outlaw bikers don't draw lines between gawkers and those wanting charter memberships. If they perceive you as even the most minor of threats, or even a slight inconvenience, they'll chew you up and spit you into tomorrow. I don't want that to happen to you.'

'Do I look like an idiot?'

'You look like a nineteen-year-old kid from Houston with a fascination for Harleys and a romanticized image of the *Wild Ones*.'

'What?'

228

'The Stanley Kramer movie?'
A blank look.
'Marlon Brando?'
'I've heard of Brando.'
'Never mind.'
'I'm just feeling free. Having some fun.'
'So is a dog with its head out the car window. Until it leaves its brains on a utility pole.'
'They're not that bad.'
'Bikers are moral cretins, and they not only are that bad, they're worse.'
'Some of what they say makes sense. Anyway, I know what I'm doing.'
'No, you don't. I've learned more about these guys in the past two weeks than I ever wanted to know, and none of it is good. Sure, they give toys to tots once a year, but bikers are hoodlums with a contempt for the law and a predisposition for violence.'
'What do they do that's so bad?'
'They're reckless and treacherous and they prey on the weak.'
'What do they do? Abort babies with coat hangers? Rape nuns? Machine-gun seniors in fast-food joints?'
'For one thing, they sell drugs.'
'So does Eli Lilly.'
'They set bombs that butcher women and children. They lock men into trunks, drive them to remote areas, and blow their brains out. They chainsaw rivals, pack what's left into garbage bags, and toss them off ferry docks.'
'Jesus. We had a few beers.'
'You don't belong in that world.'
'I went to a bloody boxing match!'

229

The deep, green eyes bore into mine. Then a lower lid twitched and he squeezed them shut, dropped his chin, and rotated two fingers on each temple. I figured the blood was doing double-time behind his sockets.

'I love you as much as my own child, Kit. You know that.'

Though he refused to meet my gaze I could sense discomfort in the curve of his spine.

'I trust you. You know that, too,' I went on. 'But I want you to be aware of who these people are. They will feed your interest in Harleys, get you to trust them, then ask for some small favor that will be part of some illegal transaction, only you won't even know it.'

For a very long time neither of us spoke. Outside, sparrows battled over a seed bell I'd hung in the courtyard. Finally, without looking up, 'And what are you walking into, Aunt Tempe?'

'I'm sorry?'

'You're on some kind of ride these days.'

I had no idea where he was going.

'Hello from the cesspool. Welcome on in.'

'What are you talking about?'

'You play me like the old shell game. Allow me to see this. Hide that.'

'What am I hiding?'

He was staring straight at me now, the whites of his eyes like bloody water.

'I followed that conversation at dinner last week. I saw the eyeball. I saw your mysterious little package, watched you slip off on your secret trip. You said it yourself. You've seen more of this shit in the past few weeks than most people see in a lifetime.'

He turned away, went back to twirling the Diet Coke can.

'You want to know all about me, but when I ask what you're doing you shut me down.'

'Kit, I—'

'And it's more than that. Something's going on with this guy Ryan that's got you jumpier than an evangelist at tax time.'

I felt my lips part, but nothing came out.

'You put *me* in the crosshairs 'cause you think I'm shooting chemicals into my veins, but you don't let me ask *you* jack shit.'

I was too stunned to speak. Kit dropped his eyes and clamped his upper teeth on his lower lip, embarrassed by the emotion he'd allowed to surface. The sun shone through the muslin behind him, silhouetting his head against the brightness.

'I'm not complaining, but when I was growing up, you were the only one who listened. Harry was'—he turned his palms up and curled his fingers, as if groping for the proper words—'well, Harry was Harry. But you listened. And you talked to me. You were the only one who did. Now you're treating me like some kind of dimwit.'

He had a point. When Kit had shown interest, I'd been evasive and distant, avoiding disclosure of any meaningful information. I live alone and don't discuss casework with anyone not part of the lab. I automatically deflect questions that may arise in a social setting. Then this morning, out of the blue, I'd asked for an accounting of his activities.

'What you say is both fair and unfair. I have put off answers I could have given, but I also am obligated not to discuss open cases or ongoing investigations. That is a requirement of my job and

231

not a matter of personal discretion. Do you really want to know what I've been doing?'

Shrug. 'Whatever.'

I looked at my watch.

'Why don't you shower while I clean up here. Then we'll take a walk on the mountain and I'll lay some things out. All right?'

'All right.' Barely audible.

But my decision was far from all right.

CHAPTER TWENTY-FIVE

Locals call it 'the mountain,' but the small elevation is a far cry from the craggy spires of the Rockies, or the lush peaks of my Carolina Smokies. Mont-Royal is the vestige of an ancient volcano, smoothed by aeons to gentle curves. It lies at the heart of the city like the body of a giant slumbering bear.

Though lacking in height and geologic drama, the mountain gives more than its name to Montreal. It is the spinal cord on which the city is strung. McGill University lies on its eastern slope, with the predominantly English-speaking suburb of Westmount directly opposite. L'Université de Montréal and the largely French neighborhood of Outremont claim the northern flanks. Directly below lies Centre-ville, a polyglot fusion of the industrial, financial, residential, and frivolous.

The mountain is promontories, parks, and cemeteries. It is wooded trails and old mossy rocks. It is tourists, lovers, joggers, and picnickers during the precious summer months; snowshoers, skaters, and tobogganers in winter. For me, as for every Montrealer, the mountain is sanctuary from the urban tumult at its feet.

By early afternoon the temperature was windbreaker warm, the sky immaculate. Kit and I walked across de Maisonneuve, and turned uphill on Drummond. To the right of a tall round building with a sweeping curvilinear base that looks like the prow on a cement frigate, we ascended a wooden staircase to avenue des Pins. Pine Avenue.

'What is that building?' asked Kit.

'McIntyre Medical. It's part of McGill.'

'Looks like the Capitol Records Building in L.A.'

'Hmm.'

Halfway up the stairs, the air grew thick with the sharp, musky smell of skunk.

'*Une mouffette,*' I explained.

'Sounds good in French, but it stinks like plain old Texas varmint,' said Kit, wrinkling his nose. 'How 'bout we pick up the pace.'

'Right.' I was already panting from the steep climb.

At the top we crossed Pine, followed a serpentine dirt road to a cement staircase, climbed, took a hard right, more road, then another set of wooden stairs that shot straight up the escarpment.

By the time we arrived at the summit I was seriously thinking about defibrillation. While I paused to catch my breath Kit charged to the overlook. I waited for my heartbeat to descend from the troposphere, then I joined him at the balustrade.

'This is awesome,' said Kit, squinting down a pair of brass pointers lined up on the McTavish

Reservoir.

He was right. The view from the top is pure spectacle, a theater-in-the-round of a city in progress. In the foreground rise the skyscrapers and flats and smokestacks and church spires of downtown, beyond that the docks of the port and the city's main artery, the St. Lawrence River. In the far distance loom the peaks of St-Bruno and St-Hilaire, with the Eastern Townships at their feet.

Kit sighted down each indicator, and I pointed out landmarks I thought would interest him. Place Ville-Marie. The McGill football field. The Royal Victoria Hospital. The Montreal Neurological Institute and Hospital.

The complex reminded me of Carolyn Russell and our conversation concerning the shunt. Thinking of Savannah Osprey brought the familiar twinge of sadness.

'Come on, Kit. I'll tell you what I've been up to.'

We strolled up broad stone steps, wending between bicycles lying on their sides, and settled on one of the wooden benches flanking the entrance to the chalet. Above us pigeons cooed softly in the heavy wooden beams.

'Where should I start?'

'At the beginning.'

'O.K., wise one.'

What was the beginning?

'Quebec Province has the dubious distinction of hosting the only active biker war in the world right now.'

'That Hells Angels thing you talked about at Isabelle's dinner.'

'Exactly. These gangs are fighting over control of

234

the drug trade.'

'What drugs?'

'Mostly cocaine, some pot and hash.'

A busload of Japanese tourists appeared from the parking lot, worked its way toward the railing, then began photographing itself in varying combinations.

'I became involved about two weeks ago. Two members of the Heathens, that's a puppet club to the Rock Machine, were blown up while trying to bomb a Vipers clubhouse on the southwest side of the city.'

'Who were the bombed-out bombers?'

'Twin brothers, Le Clic and Le Clac Vaillancourt.'

'The Vipers are with the Hells Angels?'

'Yes. The sniper who took them out was arrested—'

'A Viper sniper. I like that.'

'The sniper investigation led to the recovery of two of the bodies we discussed at dinner.'

'The guys buried near the Vipers' clubhouse?'

'Yes.'

'Where is this clubhouse?'

'St-Basile-le-Grand.' An odd look crossed his face, but he said nothing.

'The two skeletons were later identified as members of an OMC called the Tarantulas, defunct now, but active in the seventies and eighties.'

'What about the girl's bones you found out there?'

'She has since been identified as Savannah Claire Osprey, from Shallotte, North Carolina. That's why I went to Raleigh. Savannah was sixteen when she disappeared in 1984.'

'Who killed her?'

'I wish I knew.'

'How did she end up here?'

'Same answer. Let me backtrack a minute. Before the discoveries at St-Basile-le-Grand, there was another murder. The sergeant at arms for the Vipers, a gentleman named Richard 'Spider' Marcotte, was shot in a drive-by outside his home. It may have been a Heathens hit in retaliation for Clic and Clac.'

'That saved the taxpayers some money.'

'Yes, but remember there was a toll exacted on the public. A child got caught in the cross fire.'

'That's right. She was nine years old.' His eyes were focused on my face. 'She died, didn't she?'

I nodded.

'Emily Anne Toussaint was killed the day you and Howard dropped off Bird.'

'Holy crap.'

'Since that time I have been pursuing forensic evidence pertaining to these biker crimes. So you can understand my lack of enthusiasm for your newly acquired friends.'

'And tattoo. You've seen some rough shit.'

'There's more.'

I glanced at his face. Though shadowed by the eaves, his eyes were bright as a songbird's.

'This past week another biker was killed. Yves 'Cherokee' Desjardins.'

'Which side?'

'He was a Predator. That's the Angels.'

'So the Heathens were still evening the score for the twins?'

'Maybe. The problem is Cherokee was an older

236

guy who hadn't been active for a while. Also, it seems he was running his own coke concession.'

'So he might have been snuffed by his own side?'

'It's possible. We don't have all the evidence. We just don't know. Right now our investigation has slowed.'

I told him about LaManche.

'Holy shit. Maybe they got to him, too.'

'Who?'

'The Angels. Maybe he was going to find something in that body they didn't want found.'

'I don't think so, Kit.'

'Maybe they slipped him something. You know, one of those poisons that leave no trace.'

'He was in the autopsy room. That's a secure area.'

'There could be a mole at your lab. They do that, you know. Position their people on the inside.'

'Whoa.' I laughed. 'Let's not get carried away.'

He turned and looked past the Japanese tourists to the misty peaks in the far distance. Someone opened a door behind us and pigeons startled from the steps.

'Jesus, Aunt Tempe, I feel like a real lowlife. Your boss is sick, and you're trying to juggle a zillion separate murders all at once. And what do I do? I show up, dump a dead fish on your counter, then run around town having fun.'

The Japanese were moving our way.

'And I was too distracted to follow what you were doing. Anyway, ready to hike?'

'I live to ramble.'

We circled the chalet and set off on one of the many dirt trails that honeycomb the mountain. We walked in silence for a while, watching squirrels

237

scuttle among last year's leaves, excited by the arrival of spring. The trees overhead were loud with chirps and trills and warbles and shrieks. At one point we stopped to listen to an old man perform a recorder adaptation of 'Ode to Joy.' Wearing a long overcoat and ear-flapped beret, he played with all the concentration of a symphonic virtuoso.

As we strolled west, the dome of l'Oratoire St-Joseph appeared on the horizon. I told Kit the story of Frère André's heart. Stolen from its altar crypt, the organ became the focus of a massive manhunt. Eventually it showed up at our lab, and was now ensconced in safer quarters deep within the church.

To the south rose the pale yellow tower of l'École Polytechnique at l'Université de Montréal, site of the 1990 slaughter of thirteen women. The day was too lovely to share that story.

We were heading downhill when Kit broached an equally unpleasant topic.

'So who's this guy Ryan?'

'Just a friend,' I hedged.

'Harry talked about him. He's a detective, right?'

'Yes. With the provincial police.'

I'd introduced my sister to Ryan during her stay in Montreal. Sparks had flown, but I'd left town almost immediately and didn't learn if there was liftoff. I'd avoided Ryan for a long time after that, but I'd never asked.

'So what's the deal?'

'He's gotten into some trouble.'

'What kind of trouble?'

A *calèche* passed on the road above, moving in the direction from which we'd come. I heard the driver cluck, then the slap of reins on the horse's neck.

'He may have gotten involved in drugs.'

'Using?'

'Selling.' Though I was trying hard, my voice sounded wavery.

'Oh.'

The clop of hooves receded, grew quiet.

'You care about this guy, don't you?'

'Yes.'

'More than Uncle Pete?'

'That's not a fair question, Kit.'

'Sorry.'

'Whatever happened to that fish?' I said, changing the subject.

'It's in the freezer.'

'Here's a plan. We zap Mr. Trout, then peruse *les motards* while he finishes defrosting. Tonight we throw him on the grill, then slide over to Hurley's for a few beers.'

'It's a salmon. Otherwise the plan is sound.'

We descended the rest of the way, cut through the Montreal General, and continued downhill on Côte-des-Neiges. At the bottom I turned and looked back up at the peak.

'Did you ever notice the cross at night?'

'Sure. It's pretty.'

'From down here, yes. From nearby it's just a pile of steel mesh and bare bulbs. I think Andrew Ryan's like that. Nice at a distance, but up close he's a tangled mess.'

CHAPTER TWENTY-SIX

The Berawan are a horticultural people living in longhouse villages on the island of Borneo. When I taught introductory anthropology, I used them as an illustration of the absurdity of Western funerary practices.

According to Berawan beliefs, the souls of the dead are released to the afterlife only when the flesh has decomposed. Until that point, the deceased hover in limbo, no longer part of the living, but unable to join the dead. And there's a hitch. Their bodies can be reanimated by malevolent spirits roaming the world in search of housing. Once revived, these living-dead cannot be killed. Needless to say, the villagers are not wild about having them around.

The Berawan were repulsed and horrified when their ethnographer responded to questions about American customs. In their view, embalming, treatment with cosmetics and waxes, and burial in watertight coffins and vaults are actions of pure folly. Not only are we prolonging the transition of our loved ones, but our cemeteries provide vast storehouses for potential zombies.

I wondered how the Berawan would react to Bernard Silvestre, centerpiece of the photo in my hand. The fish was taking forever to defrost, and in the interim Kit and I were working our way through Kate's collection.

Silvestre lay in his coffin, mustache and sideburns spread symmetrically on each cheek, hands folded piously on his black leather jacket.

Ten men crouched in a semicircle below, denimed and booted, while four stood flanking the open casket. Except for the dress and mangy appearance, they looked like a fraternity at a Paddy Murphy party.

Elaborate bouquets stretched from one side of the photo to the other, a mini Rose Bowl of floral condolences. One said 'Slick' in blue on yellow, another 'Good-bye BS,' in shades of red and pink. Carnations forming the number '13' rose directly behind the coffin, flaunting 'Slick's' connection to pot or meth.

But best of show was the rectangle on the upper right, a petal mosaic of cycle and rider, complete with whiskers, shades, and angel's wings. I tried, but was unable to read the banners above the helmet and below the front tire.

'Know anything about Slick?' asked Kit.

'He doesn't look like the pick of the litter.'

'Yeah, even from that motley litter.' He flipped the picture. 'Heck, this guy croaked when I was three years old.'

There were two more photos of Slick's funeral, both taken from a distance, one at the cemetery, the other on the church steps. Many of the mourners wore caps riding their eyebrows, and bandannas stretched to cover their mouths.

'The one you've got must be from a private collection.' I handed Kit the other pictures. 'I think these two are police surveillance photos. Seems the bereaved weren't anxious to show their faces.'

'Man, this chopper is one statement in chrome and steel. No wonder the dude rode it right up to the grave.'

I walked around the table and peered over his

241

shoulder.

'It looks pretty stark to me.'

'That's the point. Raw power. The guy probably started with a garbage wagon and—'

'Garbage wagon?'

'An old police cycle, probably an FLH touring model. He stripped away all the nonessential crap like the windshield, roll bars, and fiberglass luggage bags, and replaced the stock items with streamlined custom parts.'

'Such as?' It looked like a cycle without any of the good stuff.

Kit pointed out items on the graveside bike.

'A thin front wheel, coffin-shaped gas tank, bobbed rear fender, and tapered soda seat. Those are the coolest. Makes it look like you're straddling the motor.'

He pointed at the front wheel.

'And he extended the front end and added ape hangers.'

I assumed those were the long, backward-projecting handlebars.

'And check out the molding and custom paint job! Man, I wish I could see that up close. This machine is a work of art. All it needs to achieve perfection is a sissy bar.'

'From which to serve beer and mixed drinks?'

'It's a backrest.'

The bike *was* bizarre, but no more so than its owner. He had leather wristbands, a denim vest with assorted Harley-Davidson pins and patches, riding chaps, and more hair than a Wookie. He looked like a walking threat display.

'I'm going to poke Mr. Salmon again. If he's still cryogenic, we'll nuke him.'

He was and we did, then laid him on the grill for a charcoal finish. Then I buttered green beans and tossed a salad while Kit carved and served the fish.

We'd just opened our napkins when the phone rang. I answered, and a rough male voice asked for my nephew. Wordlessly, I handed him the phone.

'Hey, man, what's up?'

Kit stared at a spot on the glass tabletop.

'No go. Can't do.'

Pause.

'No way.' He shifted position, and worked at the spot with his thumbnail.

'Not this time.'

Though muted by my nephew's ear, I could hear the voice on the other end. It sounded harsh, like an angry dog locked in a cellar. The nerves in my stomach tightened.

'Well, that's how it is.'

The muffled response rose and fell in agitation.

Keeping his eyes averted, my nephew left the table and moved down the hall out of earshot.

I speared a green bean, chewed, swallowed. Mechanically, I repeated the action, but my appetite had evaporated. After five forkfuls he was back.

The look on his face brought a feeling like physical pain to my chest. I wanted to put my arms around him, to brush back his hair and comfort him the way I had when he was a little boy. But whatever had happened was not a skinned knee, and I couldn't do that now. Even if he allowed it, I knew the gesture would only discomfort him. I sensed his distress, but was helpless to ease it.

He gave me a big smile, shrugged palms and shoulders, then sat and dived into his fish.

I stared at the top of his head. Finally, he looked up.

'This is great.' He swallowed and reached for his iced tea. 'Yes, that was one of them. And no, I'm not going.'

I was suddenly ravenous.

The next call came as we were finishing cleanup. Kit answered, but I could hear nothing over the chugging and sloshing of the dishwasher. In a few minutes he reappeared at the kitchen door.

'It's Lyle. I guess I told him I like swap meets, so he's inviting us to an estate sale tomorrow.'

'An estate sale?'

'Well, it's a flea market in some place called Hudson. He thought if I called it an estate sale you might be more inclined to go.'

The doublespeak had little impact on my response. While I would have enjoyed a trek to Hudson, it was not worth the price of an afternoon with Crease.

'You go ahead, Kit. It's really very pretty out there. Horse country. I should stay and finish some things I've been putting off.'

'Like what?'

'Actually, I think I'm having my hair cut tomorrow.'

'Uh-huh.'

He returned to the living room and I finished wiping the counters. I couldn't believe I was feeling relief that my nephew would be with Lyle Crease. The guy was as smarmy as a snake-oil salesman from Matamoros.

And what was Crease's interest in a nineteen-year-old kid? I had no doubt that Kit could handle the little twerp, but I vowed to call Isabelle and ask

244

a few questions.

Easy does it, I told myself. Brush your hair and go see the fiddlers.

Hurley's is the closest thing to an Irish pub that Montreal has to offer. Though I don't imbibe, my Gaelic genes still enjoy the atmosphere.

The place was as big a hit with Kit as it had been with his mother. But then, it's hard to be gloomy with a fiddle and mandolin belting out reels, and dancers jigging up and down like Nijinsky with a neurological disorder. We stayed until well past midnight.

*   *   *

When Lyle Crease showed up the next morning I was idly flipping through the photos Kit and I had left on the table the night before.

'How's it going?' Crease asked, as I let him into the entrance hall. He wore khakis, a long-sleeved white shirt, and a windbreaker with *CTV News* printed on the left breast. His hair looked like molded plastic.

'Good. And yourself?' We spoke English.

'Can't complain.'

'Kit said he'd be just a minute. He overslept a bit.'

'No problem.' Crease chuckled, then gave me a knowing grin.

I did not return it.

'Can I offer you some coffee?'

'Oh no, thanks. I've already had three cups this morning.' He showed miles of capped teeth. 'It's a gorgeous day out there. Sure you won't change your mind?'

'No, no. I have things I have to do. But thanks. Really.'

'Maybe next time.'

When Moses does another bush, I thought.

We stood for a moment, unsure where to go from there. Crease's eyes roamed the hall, then came to rest on a framed photo of Katy.

'Your daughter?'

'Yes.'

He walked over and picked it up.

'She's lovely. Is she a student?'

'Yes.'

He replaced the portrait and his eyes moved on to the dining room.

'That's quite a bouquet. You must have a serious admirer.'

Nice try.

'May I?'

I nodded, though Crease was as welcome in my home as the *Exorcist* demon. He crossed to the flowers and sniffed.

'I love daisies.' His eyes drifted to Kate's photos. 'I see you're doing some research.'

'Would you like to sit down?' I indicated the living room sofa.

Crease helped himself to a picture, replaced it, chose another.

'I understand you're involved in the Cherokee Desjardins investigation,' he said without looking up.

'Only peripherally,' I said, and moved quickly to stack the photos.

He gave a deep sigh. 'The whole world's going crazy.'

'Perhaps,' I noted, reaching out my hand for him

246

to surrender the picture of the Silvestre funeral.

'Please,' I said, gesturing toward the sofa. 'Make yourself comfortable.'

Crease sat and crossed his legs.

'I understand Dorsey's been charged and moved to Rivière-des-Prairies?'

'So I've heard.'

'Think he did it?'

This guy never gave up.

'I'm really not involved in the investigation.'

'How about the Osprey girl. Anything breaking on that front?'

How about your face, I thought.

At that moment my nephew appeared, looking pure urban cowboy in his Levis, boots, and ninety-gallon hat. I popped to my feet.

'I'm sure you two want to get there early before the good stuff's gone.'

'What good stuff?' asked Kit.

'The bass fishing lures and Elvis T-shirts.'

'I'm actually looking for a plastic Madonna.'

'Try the cathedral.'

'The other Madonna.'

'Be careful,' I said, pointing a finger at him.

'Careful is my middle name. Christopher Careful Howard, C.C. to my close friends.' He tapped two fingers to the brim of his hat.

'Right.'

As Crease said good-bye he placed a hand on my shoulder, ran it down my arm, and squeezed just above my elbow.

'You take care,' he said with a meaningful look.

What I took was a long shower.

Later, scrubbed and smelling of sandalwood, I checked my e-mail. There was nothing earth-shattering. I offered suggestions for problems submitted by students, sent an opinion to a pathologist inquiring about an oddly shaped skull, and replied to my three nieces in Chicago. Daughters of Pete's sisters, the teenagers were avid computer buffs, and kept me informed of happenings within my estranged husband's extended Latvian family.

Finally, I thanked a colleague at the Armed Forces Institute of Pathology who'd forwarded a particularly amusing photo. The case involved a pig and a high-rise building.

At one-thirty I logged off and tried Isabelle. Predictably, she was not in.

Looking for an excuse to be outside, I set out to buy jumbo shrimp at the *poissonnerie.* I'd gone less than a block when I was stopped dead, distracted by photos at *Coiffure Simone.*

I stared at the woman in the black and white. She looked good. Stylish, but neat. Professional, but jaunty.

Jesus, Brennan. You sound like copy for a shampoo ad. Next you'll be telling yourself you're worth it.

I *had* told Kit I'd scheduled a haircut.

I studied the poster, estimating the amount of maintenance the style would require. I thought it could pass my ten-minute rule.

I started to move on, caught my reflection in the glass. What I saw was light-years from poster lady.

How long had it been since I'd tried a new do?

Years.

And the salon was offering a special Sunday discount.

Five dollars off. Right. You'll save about three-fifty U.S.

A new haircut could boost your spirits.

It could be a disaster.

Hair grows back.

That last came straight from my mother.

I pushed open the door and went in.

*   *   *

Hours later I was eating dinner with the Discovery channel. On the screen, male kangaroos kickboxed over control of the mob. On the hearth, Birdie eyed me silently, curious, but keeping his distance.

'Hair grows back, Bird.'

I dipped a shrimp and popped it into my mouth, wishing it would happen before Kit got home.

'And I could use your support,' I informed him.

If the new look was to have buoyed my spirits, the experiment had been a catastrophe. Since returning home I'd been thinking of ways to avoid public contact. Thanks to developments in telecommunication I had many options. I'd use telephone, fax, and e-mail. And lots of hats.

By ten I was feeling as low as I had on Friday evening. I was overworked, underappreciated, and my never-was lover turned out to prefer the robbers over the cops. My boss had collapsed, my nephew was out with the sleaze of the year, and I now looked like I'd been attacked by a Weed Eater.

Then the phone rang and things got terribly, terribly worse.

'*Claudel ici.*'

'Yes,' I answered, too surprised to switch to French.

'I thought you should know. George Dorsey was

249

attacked about two hours ago.'

'Attacked by whom?'

'He's dead, Ms. Brennan. Murdered because of your meddling.'

'Me?'

I was speaking to a dial tone.

The rest of the evening I was too distracted to focus on coherent thought. I barely acknowledged Kit's return and report that he had had a really good time.

'Murdered because of your meddling.' That was unfair. Dorsey had asked to see me. What if he had asked for Claudel or Charbonneau or Quickwater? This was a prison murder of someone who was a threat to others. Those things happen. I didn't cause it. Claudel was unfair. I tossed and turned all night and repeated 'unfair.'

CHAPTER TWENTY-SEVEN

The next morning I was at work by seven-thirty. Others wouldn't arrive for an hour, and the building was graveyard quiet. I cherished the calm and planned to take full advantage of it.

I let myself into my office, slipped on a lab coat, and crossed to the anthropology lab. Unlocking the door to the storage room, I pulled out the box containing Savannah's remains. I intended to get straight to work and let the Claudel matter arise in whatever manner he chose to raise it.

I laid the skull and femora on the table, and began the painstaking process of reinspecting every millimeter of bone under magnification and strong

250

light. Though doubtful, I hoped to find something I'd missed. Perhaps a tiny nick or scrape that would tell me how the bones had been separated from the rest of the body.

I was still at it when someone knocked at the door. When I looked up Claudel stood framed in the glass. As usual his spine was ramrod straight, his hair as perfect as a studio shot of Douglas Fairbanks.

'Nice tie,' I said, opening the door.

It was. Pale violet, probably designer silk. A good choice with the tweed jacket.

'*Merci,*' he mumbled with all the warmth of a pit bull.

I laid down the femur, clicked off the fiber-optic light, and stepped to the sink.

'What happened to Dorsey?' I asked as I washed my hands.

'A Philips screwdriver happened to him,' he replied. 'The guard was outside reading while Dorsey showered. Probably catching up on his professional journals.'

I pictured the man with the little rat teeth.

'The guard heard a change in the noise of the water, so he took a look-see. Dorsey was facedown in the drain with twenty-eight holes in his upper body.'

'Jesus.'

'But Dorsey didn't die right away,' Claudel continued. 'He shared a few thoughts on the ride to the hospital. That's why I felt I should come by.'

I reached for a paper towel, surprised that Claudel was being so open.

'The paramedic didn't get it all, but he caught one thing.'

Claudel lifted his chin a little.

'Brennan.'

My hands froze.

'That's it?'

'He said he was busy keeping Dorsey alive. But he noticed the name because of his dog.'

'His dog?'

'He's got an Irish setter named Brennan.'

'It's a common name.'

'Maybe in Galway, but not here. You did talk to Dorsey about Cherokee Desjardins, did you not?'

'Yes, but nobody knows that.'

'Except everyone at Op South.'

'We were in a private interrogation room.'

Claudel was silent. I pictured the corridor, with the holding tank just ten feet away.

'I suppose I could have been spotted.'

'Yes. These things have a way of getting back.'

'Getting back to whom?'

'Dorsey was a Heathens hang-around. The boys wouldn't be happy if they thought he was launching a self-preservation movement.'

I felt tension rise up my neck at the thought I might have triggered the attack.

'I don't think Dorsey killed Cherokee,' I said, bunching up the towel and tossing it into the trash.

'You don't.'

'No.'

'I suppose Dorsey claimed he was innocent as the Easter Bunny.'

'Yes. But there's more.'

He gave me an uncertain look, then folded his arms across his chest.

'All right. Let's hear it.'

I told him about the blood spatter.

'Does that sound like a biker hit?'

252

'Things go wrong.'

'Bludgeoning? Don't hit men usually come in shooting?'

'The last biker pulled from the river was hammered to death. So was his bodyguard.'

'I've been thinking about that void pattern behind Cherokee's head. What if he was killed for whatever was removed?'

'There were a lot of people milling around that scene. Someone could have knocked the thing out of position. Or maybe the neighbor snatched it.'

'It was covered with blood.'

'I'll talk to her anyway.' Finite at the best of times, Claudel's patience was clearly evaporating.

'And why would Cherokee let someone in?' I pressed on.

'Maybe the hit man was a buddy from the old days.'

That made sense.

'Has ballistics gotten anything?'

He shook his head.

'Who's heading the Spider Marcotte investigation?'

'That and the little girl fell to Kuricek.'

Sipowicz.

'Any progress?'

Claudel raised both palms.

'Dorsey hinted he had something he'd trade on that.'

'These degenerates will say anything to save themselves.'

He dropped his eyes and picked a nonexistent fleck from his sleeve.

'There's something I need to discuss with you.'

'Oh?'

At that moment we heard the door open in the adjacent lab, announcing the arrival of the technicians.

'May we . . . ?' He tipped his head toward my office.

Curious, I led him across the hall and slipped behind my desk. When he'd settled across from me Claudel withdrew a picture from his inside pocket and placed it on the blotter.

It differed little from Kate's biker photos. The vintage was more recent, the quality better. And one other thing.

Kit stood among the group of leather-jacketed men centered in the image.

I looked a question at Claudel.

'That was taken last week at an establishment called La Taverne des Rapides.' He looked away. 'That's your nephew, right?'

'So? I don't see any patches,' I said curtly.

'They're Rock Machine.'

He placed a second photo in front of me. I was getting very tired of celluloid bikers.

Again I saw Kit, this time straddling a Harley, engaged in conversation with two other cyclists. His companions were clean-cut but wore the standard bandannas, boots, and sleeveless denim jackets. On each back I could see a heavily armed figure in a large sombrero. The upper rockers said *Bandidos,* the lower, *Houston.*

'That was taken at a swap meet at the Galveston County fairgrounds.'

'What are you suggesting?' My voice came out high and stretched.

'I'm not suggesting anything. I'm just showing you pictures.'

'I see.'

Claudel frowned, then crossed his ankles and regarded me intently.

I folded my hands to disguise the shaking.

'My nephew lives in Texas. Recently his father bought him a Harley-Davidson motorcycle, and he's become enamored with the two-wheeled culture. That's it.'

'Riding in the wind is not what bikers live for these days.'

'I know that. I'm sure these were chance encounters, but I will speak to him.'

I handed back the photos.

'The Houston PD has a jacket on Christopher Howard.'

If I could have laid hands on Harry at that moment I would have committed a felony.

'He's been arrested?'

'Four months ago. Possession.'

No wonder his father had hauled him up to the north woods.

'I know what advice is worth on the open market,' Claudel went on. 'But be careful.'

'Be careful of what?'

He looked at me a long moment, no doubt deciding whether to confide.

'The paramedic actually picked out two words.'

The phone rang but I ignored it.

'Brennan's kid.'

I felt someone light a match in my chest. Could they know about Katy? Kit? I looked away, not wanting Claudel to see my fear.

'Meaning?'

Claudel shrugged.

'Was it a threat? A warning?'

255

'The paramedic says he doesn't listen to patients while he's working on them.'

I studied the wall.

'So what are you suggesting?'

'I don't want to alarm you, but Constable Quickwater and I think—'

'Oh, yeah. Quickwater. He's a lot of laughs.' I cut him off, my sarcasm triggered by anger and fear.

'He's a good investigator.'

'He's an asshole. Every time I talk to him he acts like he's deaf.'

'He is.'

'What?'

'Quickwater is deaf.'

I searched for a response, but couldn't come up with a single word.

'Actually, he's deafened. There's a difference.'

'Deafened how?'

'He took a cast-iron pipe in the back of the head while breaking up an alley fight. Then they shot him with a stun gun until the batteries died.'

'When?'

'About two years ago.'

'That destroyed his hearing?'

'So far.'

'Will it come back?'

'He hopes so.'

'How does he function?'

'Extremely well.'

'I mean, how does he communicate?'

'Quickwater is one of the quickest studies I've ever met. I'm told that he learned to lip-read in no time, and he's crackerjack. For distance communication he uses e-mail, fax, and TTY.'

256

'TTY?'

'It's an acronym for teletypewriter. Essentially, it's a keyboard and acoustic coupler built into one device. At home he has a special modem in his PC that communicates at the same band Baudot code as a regular TTY. He's got his fax and TTY on the same phone line and uses a switching device that recognizes an incoming fax tone. It sends faxes to the fax machine and all other calls to the TTY. We've got the same setup and software at headquarters, so calling back and forth is no problem.'

'What about when he's out?'

'He has a portable TTY. Battery-operated.'

'How does he talk to someone without a TTY, or to you if you're not at headquarters?'

'There's a relay service that acts as intermediary. The service takes the call, then types what the hearing person says. For someone who's also mute, they read aloud what the deaf person types. Quickwater speaks fine, so he doesn't need to type his words.'

My mind was struggling to take this in. I pictured Quickwater at the Vipers' clubhouse, then in the conference room at Quantico.

'But part of his assignment in Quantico was to report back on what he'd learned. How can he take notes and lip-read at the same time? And how does he know what's being said when the lights are dimmed, or when he can't see the speaker?'

'Quickwater explains this a lot better than I. He uses something called CARTT, Computer Assisted Real Time Translation. A reporter transcribes what's being said into a stenotype machine, then a computerized translation is performed and the words are displayed on a video monitor in real time. It's the same system used for closed-captioning of live television. The FBI has someone down there that can do it, but a hookup can be made from anywhere, with the reporter in one location and Quickwater in another.'

'By phone and PC?'

'Exactly.'

'But what about his other duties?'

I didn't voice what I was really thinking. Reporting on a conference or meeting is one thing, but how does a deaf officer cover himself when someone goes for the jugular?

'Constable Quickwater is a skilled and dedicated officer. He was injured in the line of duty and no one can say if the hearing loss is permanent or not. Obviously he can't do everything he used to do, but for now, the force is working with it.'

I was about to circle back to Dorsey when Claudel stood and placed a paper on my desk. I braced myself for more bad news.

'This is the DNA report on the blood found on Dorsey's jacket,' he said.

I didn't have to look. The expression on his face told me what the form would say.

CHAPTER TWENTY-EIGHT

When Claudel left I just sat there, my thoughts slipstreaming in and out of the conversation just concluded.

DNA doesn't lie. The victim's blood was all over the jacket, meaning Dorsey had killed Cherokee

258

just as Claudel suspected. Or had he? Dorsey had said the jacket was not his.

The man knew nothing about Savannah Osprey. He'd been scamming me to save himself, and I had fallen for it.

And my visit to the jail had gotten Dorsey killed. Or had it? Was he killed because he was the killer or because he was not the killer? Either way, he was dead because someone feared what he would tell me.

I felt burning behind my eyelids.

Don't cry. Don't you dare cry. I swallowed hard.

And there was Quickwater. He hadn't been glaring, he'd been reading my lips. Who had treated whom badly? But how was I to know?

And Kit. Were the surveillance shots truly chance encounters as I'd said, or was Kit involved with the Bandidos? Did that explain the Preacher? Was the real reason he'd come here something other than anger with his father? Or fondness for his dim-witted aunt?

And the eyeball. *Did* Kit find it on the windshield?

Claudel had gotten his report. Dammit, where was mine?

I slammed my palms on the blotter and shot to my feet. Weaving through clerical staff carrying papers and folders and technicians pushing specimen carts, I strode down the hall, took the stairs to the thirteenth floor, and went straight to the DNA section. I spotted my target bending over a test tube at the far end of the lab, and closed in.

'*Bonjour, Tempe. Comment ça va?*' Robert Gagné greeted me.

'*Ça va.*'

'Your hair is different.' His own was dark and curly, though graying at the temples. He kept it short and carefully combed.

'Yes.'

'Are you going to let it grow?'

'It's difficult to stop it,' I replied.

'It looks good, of course,' he mumbled, laying down a glass pipette. 'So, I guess that jacket will nail this Dorsey character. Claudel actually smiled when I gave him the news. Well, almost. He twitched.'

'I'm wondering if you've had time to do the comparison I requested.'

'Unnumbered, right?'

I nodded.

'Eyeball?'

I nodded again.

'To be compared with sequencing from LML 37729.'

'Yes.' His memory for case numbers always impressed me.

'Hold on.'

Gagné walked over to a honeycomb of folders, riffled through those in a middle cell, and pulled one out. I waited as he scanned the contents.

'The comparison is done, but the report isn't written.'

'And?'

'It's a match.'

'Without question?'

'*Mais, oui.*' His eyebrows shot up. 'The eye and the tissue sample come from the same person.'

Or persons, I thought, if they happen to be twins. I thanked him and hurried back to my office.

My suspicion had been right. The eyeball

belonged to one of the Vaillancourts. A member of the Vipers had probably found it at the scene and kept it for some macabre reason. But who had placed it on my car?

I heard the phone before I reached my door, and bolted the last few steps. Marcel Morin was calling from downstairs.

'We missed you at the morning meeting.'

'Sorry.'

He went straight to the point. In the background I could hear voices and the sound of a Stryker saw.

'A ship arrived at the port two weeks ago and several cargo containers were off-loaded for repair.'

'The big ones that go onto eighteen-wheelers?'

'*C'est ça.* Yesterday workers opened the last of the containers and found a body. The captain thinks the deceased is probably a stowaway, but has no explanation beyond that.'

'Where is the ship registered?'

'Malaysia. I've begun the autopsy, but the remains are so badly decomposed I'm not going to be able to do much. I'd like you to take a look at them.'

'I'll be down shortly.'

When I hung up and crossed to the lab I found Jocelyn the temp bending over my worktable. Ms. Charm School wore fishnets and a leather skirt that rode high enough to show dark at the top of each stocking. At the sound of the door she straightened and turned.

'Dr. Morin asked me to give you this.'

She extended an arm, and her earrings oscillated like tiny school-yard swings. Each hoop was large enough to perch a finch.

261

I crossed to her and took the request form, wondering why Morin hadn't left it on my desk.

'Killer haircut.' She spoke in a low, monotone voice, and I couldn't tell if she was being sarcastic. Her face looked more pallid than normal, her eyes red-rimmed and underlined by dark commas.

'Thank you, Jocelyn.' I hesitated, not wanting to pry. 'Are you all right?'

She reacted as though the question totally confused her. Then she hitched a shoulder and mumbled, 'Allergies kick me around in the spring. I'm fine.'

With one last puzzled look, she scurried out of the lab.

I reboxed the Osprey remains and spent the rest of the morning with the Malaysian stowaway. Morin had not exaggerated. The bulk of the soft tissue in the body bag belonged to maggots.

*   *   *

At noon I went back upstairs to find Kit seated in my chair, boots crossed on the windowsill, a Frank Sinatra fedora on the back of his head.

'How'd you get onto this floor?' I asked, trying to hide my surprise. I'd totally forgotten the lunch date we'd arranged via the refrigerator door.

'I left my driver's license with the guard and he let me come up.' He flipped the blue visitor's pass that was clipped to his collar. 'I was sitting in the lobby, then a lady took pity and brought me here.'

He swung his feet down and swiveled toward me.

'Whooaa! Let me get a bead on that.'

He must have seen something in my face.

'Don't take me wrong. That is one rad haircut.'

262

He leveled two index fingers at me. 'Makes you look younger.'

'Let's go,' I said, retrieving a sweater from the hall tree. I'd had more than enough comments on my hair.

Over brasserie subs and fries my nephew described his Sunday with Lyle Crease, the highlight of which had been the purchase of the fedora. No Madonna or fishing lures. After returning to Montreal, they'd dined on smoked meat at Ben's, then Crease took him to the newsroom.

'What do you two talk about?'

'The dude's really heads-up.' Muffled through cold cuts and cheese. 'It's awesome how much he knows about broadcasting. And he's pretty tight on cycles, too.'

'Does he ask you a lot of questions?'

I wondered how much Crease was using Kit to get information about my cases. The biker war was hot news just now.

'Some.'

Kit yanked a paper napkin from a metal box at the end of the table and wiped grease from his chin.

'About what?'

He bunched up the napkin and reached for another.

'All kinds of stuff. Lyle's amazing. He's interested in everything.'

Something in his voice told me my nephew had begun to worship Lyle Crease. O.K., I thought. I can live with that. Oily as the guy is, he beats the Preacher sight unseen.

After lunch Kit insisted on returning with me to

the lab. Though anxious to get back to my skeletal autopsy, I obliged him with a short tour. I could be heads-up, too.

During our rounds Kit made only two comments. I would recall them later, and chastise myself for taking no notice.

'Who's the freak show?' he asked, after passing Jocelyn at the Xerox machine.

'She works in records.'

'Bet that's a head full of slash and burn.'

'She has allergy problems.'

'Right. Nasal spray.'

The other remark was made in the ballistics section. He called their collection of firearms 'sweet.'

When Kit had gone I went back to the stowaway. By four-thirty I'd finished my preliminary examination, concluding that the remains were those of a male in his late twenties. I'd dissected out the bones and sent them upstairs for boiling. Then I'd washed up, changed, and returned to my office.

I was reaching for my sweater when I noticed a color print centered squarely on my blotter.

Oh, great, I thought. Here's something new. I haven't scoped a photo in at least two hours.

I reached for the picture, thinking that perhaps it belonged to Claudel.

It didn't.

Though the snapshot was old, and a network of cracks marred its surface, the color and focus were relatively good. It was a group shot, taken in a camping or picnic area. In the foreground a crowd of men and women milled around wooden tables jammed together to form a U. The earth was littered with empty cans and bottles, the tables heaped with backpacks, coolers, bundles, and paper bags. Loblolly pines rose in the background, truncated by the picture's upper border.

One large bag lay upright against a table leg, its print square to the camera lens. The logo caught my attention.

'—ggly Wiggly.'

I flipped to the back of the print. Nothing.

I rehung the sweater, dug out a magnifying glass, and sat down to examine the image. Within seconds I found confirmation on a gorilloid oaf in denim vest and fingerless leather gloves. An arm wider than a state highway reached across his chest, displaying swastika, lightning bolts, and the poetic acronym 'F.T.W.' While Kong's upper limb obliterated part of his T-shirt, the bottom words were fully legible.

'Myrtle Beach.'

Barely breathing, I began a close inspection of the persons pictured. Slowly, I worked the lens across the image, checking each face as it took form.

Within seconds I found her. Half hidden in a sea of caps and bushy heads, a frail figure leaned against a tree, little twig arms wrapped around her waist. Her head was tipped, and a ray of sunlight flashed off one of the huge lenses dwarfing her features.

Savannah Claire Osprey.

While I couldn't read her expression I could sense the tension in her body. From what, I wondered. Excitement? Fear? Self-consciousness?

I moved on.

265

The man to Savannah's right looked like a character from *The Life and Death of Cormac the Skald*. He had shoulder-length hair and a beard that hung to mid-chest. Cormac was caught with chin raised, a can of Miller pressed to his lips.

The companion on her other side was very tall, with short hair and scraggly beard and mustache. His face was obscured in shadow, making his belly the most conspicuous trait. It had the tone of a used Ace bandage, hanging in fleshy rolls over a large, oval belt buckle. On it I could see letters. I raised and lowered the lens trying to make out the message, but too much was obscured by paunch.

Frustrated, I slid the lens up the torso and studied the face, hoping something would click. No go. I dropped back to the buckle and brought my face close to the glass.

A random synaptic firing, and there it was. Back to the face. Could it be?

No. This man was much larger.

But maybe. I couldn't tell. I'd gotten there too late. Too much damage.

Yet, there was a resemblance.

Had George Dorsey known something after all?

Heart pounding, I reached for the phone.

CHAPTER TWENTY-NINE

When Claudel answered I identified myself and dived right in.

'There's something I didn't tell you. Spider Marcotte wasn't the only one Dorsey mentioned. He claimed to have information about Savannah

Osprey.'

'The young girl we found in St-Basile-le-Grand?'

'Yes. I think he may have been telling the truth.'

'Dorsey's trademark.'

I ignored the sarcasm.

'Did you leave a picture on my desk?'

'No.'

'Someone did. It's an old snapshsot taken at a biker gathering.'

'Probably a prayer meeting.'

'It looks like a picnic or camp-out.'

'Uh-huh.'

I took a deep breath to steady my voice.

'Savannah Osprey is there.'

'She is?' His tone told me he didn't believe it.

'Absolutely.'

'What does that have to do with Dor—'

'The picture was taken in Myrtle Beach.'

'How do you know?'

'At least one of the believers is wearing a Myrtle Beach T-shirt.'

'My son has a Kansas City Chiefs' shirt.'

'I know honeysuckle and kudzu when I see it. And I recognized a Piggly Wiggly logo on one of the grocery bags.'

'What's a Piggly Wiggly?'

'It's a chain of supermarkets, with several in the Myrtle Beach area.'

'Why would anyone call a supermarket Piggl—'

'And one of the picnickers may be Cherokee Desjardins.'

There was a moment of dead air.

'What makes you think that?'

'He's wearing a belt buckle that says "Cherokee."'

'What does the man look like?'

267

'Something Jack Hanna would keep on a chain and pacify with small chunks of meat,' I spat. His skepticism was irritating me.

'I mean does the man in the buckle resemble Cherokee Desjardins?'

'His features aren't clear. Besides, I never got a look at Desjardins when he was wearing a face.'

There was another moment of silence, then the sound of an exhaled breath.

'I'll get photos of Desjardins and come by in the morning.'

'We can try enhancing the image.'

'Set it up. But it will have to be quick. We're expecting difficulties because of the Dorsey murder, and the whole squad is on alert.'

*   *   *

I drove home plagued by feelings of self-doubt.

I'd been fooled by Dorsey, and my naiveté had gotten him killed.

What if the man in the photo wasn't Cherokee? Claudel obviously had reservations. If I was wrong he'd be even more convinced I was an idiot.

As I had been with regard to his Carcajou partner. I'd entirely misread Quickwater. Had I also misjudged Ryan? My nephew?

Where had the picture on my desk come from? Why no note, no phone call? It had to be one of the detectives or lab people. No one else would have an opportunity to leave it there.

I steered and shifted robotically, barely noticing the traffic around me.

Should I make a surprise call on Ryan? Would he answer the door? Probably not. Ryan had cut himself off because he preferred it that way. But how could it be true? I still couldn't believe the man was a criminal.

Was Kit involved with the Bandidos? With drugs? Was he in danger? What had Dorsey been trying to say to the paramedic?

Was it possible Katy was in danger from the biker gangs thousands of miles away on a ship? Her last letter had come from Penang.

Who was I kidding? Dorsey had been killed while under armed guard in a provincial prison. If *les motards* wanted you to be in danger, you were there.

'Dammit!' I slapped the steering wheel with the heel of my hand.

Ryan and Katy were out of my reach, but I could do something about my nephew. I vowed to have it out with Kit before the sun set.

Or rose, I thought, turning onto the ramp that led under my building. I had no idea how late he'd get in, but resolved to wait up.

It wasn't necessary.

'Hey, Auntie T,' he greeted me when I entered the condo, as did the aroma of cumin and turmeric.

'Something smells good,' I said, dropping my briefcase in the entrance hall.

My nephew and cat were sprawled on the sofa, surrounded by remnants of that morning's *Gazette*. The Sony PlayStation had been reattached to the TV and wires squiggled across the floor.

'I stopped by La Maison du Cari. Figured it was my turn to cook.'

He'd removed his earphones and draped them around his neck. I could hear the tinny sounds of the Grateful Dead.

'Great. What did you get?'

'*Uno momento.*'

He swung his feet to the floor and tossed the headset onto the couch. Bird bolted at the sudden proximity to Jerry Garcia. Kit retrieved a receipt from the kitchen and read off nine items.

'Are you expecting your state legislature?'

'No, ma'am. I wasn't sure what you like, so I got a cross section of regional cuisines.'

He pronounced the last in an accent that mimicked perfectly that of the restaurant's owner.

'Don't you worry. We'll graze right through it,' he added, reverting to Texan.

'Let me change and then we'll eat.'

'Wait. First you gotta see this.'

He dug through the scattered *Gazette* and came up with the front section. Opening to a middle page, he folded the paper in half and handed it to me, indicating a headline.

PRISONER SLAIN IN GANG ASSASSINATION

The article summarized the facts surrounding the Dorsey murder, referring to him as a prime suspect in the execution-style killing of Yves 'Cherokee' Desjardins. It described Dorsey as a Heathens associate, Cherokee as a member of the Predators, though inactive in recent years.

The story went on to speculate that Dorsey's death may have been ordered in retaliation for the Desjardins killing, and recounted the murders of the Vaillancourt twins, Richard 'Spider' Marcotte, and Emily Anne Toussaint. It reported that Dorsey's funeral would be held as soon as the coroner released the body.

The piece concluded by stating that the authorities were concerned that an escalation in violence was on the horizon, and that the Dorsey funeral might be used as an opportunity for revenge by Heathens sympathizers. Police would be taking extra precautions in the coming weeks.

I looked up to see Kit regarding me intently.

'It would be rockin' to go to that funeral.'

'No way.'

'The cops will have these guys so boxed in they'll be like altar boys heading to Mass.'

'No.'

'The bikes will be solid Harley.'

'You're not going anywhere near that funeral.'

'All that juice pounding along in formation.' He mimicked steering handlebars. 'Rolling thunder.'

'Kit.'

'Yeah?' His eyes were bright as a Pentecostal zealot's.

'I don't want you there.'

'Aunt Tempe, you worry too much.'

How many times had Katy said that?

'I'll throw on jeans, then let's have dinner. I want to ask you about something.'

I broached the subject during dessert.

'A Carcajou investigator came to see me today.'

'Yeah?' Kit scraped the top off then scooped a spoonful of rice pudding.

'You're supposed to eat the frosting.'

'It looks like silver.'

'It is.'

I was stalling.

'He brought a set of police surveillance photos.'

A quizzical look. More pudding.

'Of you.'

271

My nephew lowered his chin and raised his brows.

'The pictures were taken at the Galveston County fairgrounds. You're with members of the Bandidos motorcycle club.'

'Uh-oh,' he said, giving a goofy grin. 'Hanging out with bad companions.'

'Do you?'

'Do I what?'

'Hang out with the Bandidos?'

'Just that once. But the big kids made me do it.'

'This isn't funny, Kit! You were caught on film with drug dealers!'

He lay down his spoon and gave me another brilliant smile. I did not return it.

'Aunt Tempe. I go to flea markets. Bikers go to flea markets. Sometimes we go to the same flea markets. We talk about Harleys. That's all it is.'

'The detective said you'd been arrested on a drug charge.' I forced myself to speak calmly.

He slumped back and threw out his legs.

'Oh, great. That shit again.'

'What shit?'

'Jesus. You'd think I was supplying a preschool.' His voice was hard, the humor gone.

I waited.

'I bought a ten-dollar bag for a friend because she left her wallet at home. Before I could give her the weed a cop pulled me over for an illegal left and found the stuff in my pocket. How's that for a seasoned dope dealer?'

'Why did the cop search you?'

'I'd had a little beer.'

He scuffed at the rug with one big toe. A long thin toe, knobby at the joints, oblong under the

272

nail. My father's big toe. As I looked at him my heart ached. Every cell in his body reminded me of Daddy.

'All right, I'd had a lot of beer. But I don't do drugs. I told you that. Christ, you're acting just like my father.'

'Or any concerned parent.' Love and anger battled for control of my voice.

'Look, I did my community service and went to their lame substance abuse program. Aren't you people ever going to ease up?'

With that he lurched from the chair and slouched out of the room. In seconds I heard the slam of the guest room door.

Well-done, Brennan. Take a gold star for effective parenting.

I cleared the table, repackaged the uneaten portions of food, loaded the dishwasher, and tried Howard's number.

No answer.

Damn you, Harry, for not telling me about this. And damn you for being in Mexico.

I tried Isabelle, hoping to ask about Lyle Crease. Machine.

I spent the rest of the evening with the Pat Conroy book I'd laid down a week earlier. Nothin' could be finer than to be in Carolina.

*   *   *

Predictably, Kit was sleeping when I left for work. This day, I attended the morning meeting.

When I returned to my office, Claudel was there.

'Figure out who killed Dorsey?' I asked as I threw the morning's case log on the desk.

273

He gave me a look that could freeze molten lava, then held out an envelope.

I sat, unlocked my desk drawer, and handed him the Myrtle Beach photo.

'Where did you say this came from?'

'I didn't.' I gave him the lens. 'Because I don't know.'

'It just appeared?'

'Yes.'

His eyes roved the print.

'I noticed it yesterday. I can't say for certain when it arrived on my desk.'

After several seconds the lens froze and he drew closer to it. Then, 'You're talking about the man next to Z. Z. Top?'

'Show me,' I said, surprised at the musical reference. I would have pegged Claudel as strictly classical.

He turned the photo and pointed.

'Yes. The girl next to him is Savannah Osprey.'

Back to the lens.

'You're sure?'

I dug out the yearbook portrait Kate had given me. He studied it, then the picnic shot, going back and forth like a fan at Wimbledon.

'You're right.'

'What about Buckle Boy?'

He indicated the envelope in my hand. 'Desjardins was a large man before his illness.'

I shook out the photos and Claudel circled the desk so we could view them together.

Large was an understatement. The partially headless form I'd seen in the chair was a feeble reminder of the body that once had housed Cherokee Desjardins. Before cancer had parched

274

his innards, and drugs and chemo had done their magic, the man had been massive, though in a spongy, gut-bulging sort of way.

The file photos spanned a period of years. Beards came and went and the hairline crept backward, but the belly and facial features changed little.

Until the cancer struck.

Six months before his death Cherokee was a shadow of his former self, bald and death-camp thin. Had the picture been unlabeled, I would not have recognized the subject as the same man.

As I studied the face from shot to shot I remembered an old Brando quote. I have eyes like those of dead pig, the aging actor had said of himself.

Not to worry, Marlon. They served you well. This guy looked merely baleful, and mean as a pack dog with a stolen flank steak.

But try as we might we could not determine for sure if our late but unlamented Cherokee was the one wearing the buckle at Myrtle Beach.

CHAPTER THIRTY

I gathered the Cherokee photos, and we moved down the hall to a section labeled Imagerie. We'd decided that I would manipulate the image using Adobe Photoshop, since I was familiar with the program. Should that prove inadequate, a technician would help us with more sophisticated graphics software.

We were expected, and the equipment was

275

immediately available. The technician clicked on the scanner, keyed the computer to the proper program, then left us to our task.

I placed the snapshot on the flatbed scanner, cropped to include the full scene, then digitized the image and saved it to the hard drive. Then I opened the file to the Myrtle Beach picnic.

I clicked on Buckle Boy's face and zoomed in until his features filled the screen. Then I cleaned up the 'noise' of dust and cracks, modified the curves that control the contribution of red, green, and blue tones, adjusted the brightness and contrast, and sharpened the edges of the image.

Claudel watched as I worked the keys, silent at first, then making suggestions as his interest grew, despite his initial cynicism. Each correction morphed the highlights, shadows, and midtones, mutating the curves and planes of the face, and bringing out detail invisible in the original shot.

In less than an hour we sat back and studied our work. There could be no doubt. Buckle Boy was, in fact, Yves 'Cherokee' Desjardins.

But what did that mean?

Claudel spoke first.

'So Cherokee knew the Osprey girl.'

'Looks that way,' I agreed.

'And Dorsey killed him.' Claudel was thinking aloud. 'What do you suppose Dorsey had to trade?'

'Maybe Cherokee killed Savannah and Dorsey knew that.'

'Could she have traveled up here with him?' Again, it was verbalized thought, not conversation.

I pictured the puzzled little face, the wide eyes taking in the world through clock-face lenses. I shook my head.

'Not voluntarily.'

'He could have killed her in Myrtle Beach then displaced the body to Quebec.' This time he was addressing me.

'Why transport it all that way?'

'Less chance of discovery.'

'Does that sound typical of these guys?'

'No.' Behind his eyes I could see confusion. And anger.

'And where's the rest of her?' I pressed.

'Perhaps he cut off her head.'

'And legs?'

'This is not a question for me.' He flicked at an invisible speck on his sleeve, then straightened his tie.

'And how did she end up buried near Gately and Martineau?'

Claudel did not answer.

'And whose skeleton did they find in Myrtle Beach?'

'That's one for your SBI friends.'

Since Claudel seemed willing to talk for once, I decided to up the ante. I switched direction.

'Maybe Cherokee's murder wasn't a revenge killing at all.'

'I'm not clear where you're going.'

'Maybe it was connected to the discovery of Savannah's grave.'

'Maybe.' He checked his watch, then stood. 'And maybe I'll be invited to join the Dixie Chicks. But until then I had better collar some bad guys.'

What was it with the pop music references?

When he'd gone I saved the original and modified versions of the Myrtle Beach snapshot to a compact disc. Then I scanned and added selections from Kate's collection, thinking maybe I'd play with the images at home.

Back in my office I called the DNA section, knowing the answer but unable to bear the thought of another stroll through a biker-happy album.

I was right. Gagné was sorry, but the tests I'd requested had not been completed. An '84 case could not be given high priority, but they hoped to get to it soon.

Fair enough. You jumped the eyeball to the front of the line.

I hung up and reached for my lab coat. At least the slides should be ready.

I found Denis logging cases into the computer in the histology lab. I waited as he read the label on a plastic jar in which chunks of heart, kidney, spleen, lung, and other organs floated in formaldehyde. He made a few keystrokes, then returned the container to the collection on the cart.

When I made my request he went to his desk and brought me a small white plastic box. I thanked him and took it to the microscope in my lab.

Denis had prepared slides from the bone samples I'd brought from Raleigh. I placed a tibial section under the lens, adjusted the light, and squinted through the eyepiece. Two hours later I had my answer.

The samples I'd taken from the tibiae and fibulae in Kate's unidentified skeleton were indistinguishable histologically from those I'd cut from Savannah's femora. And each thin section yielded an estimate consistent with Savannah's age at the time of her disappearance.

Consistent. The favorite word of the expert witness.

Can you state with a reasonable degree of scientific certainty that the bones recovered in Myrtle Beach belong to Savannah Claire Osprey?

No, I cannot.

I see. Can you state that the bones recovered in Myrtle Beach come from an individual of exactly the same age as Savannah Claire Osprey?

No, I cannot.

I see. What can you tell this court, Dr. Brennan?

The bones recovered in Myrtle Beach are consistent in histological age and microstructure with other bones identified as belonging to Savannah Claire Osprey.

I clicked off the light and placed the plastic hood over the scope.

It was a start.

*   *   *

After a lunch of vegetarian pizza and a Mr. Big ice cream bar, I reported to Carcajou headquarters. Morin had completed his autopsy and was releasing Dorsey's body. Jacques Roy had called a meeting to discuss security measures for the funeral, and had requested my presence.

Dorsey's roots were in a neighborhood just southeast of Centre-ville, an area of narrow streets and narrower alleys, of crowded flats trimmed with steep stairs and tiny balconies. To the west lies the Main, to the east Hochelaga-Maisonneuve, site of some of the fiercest battles in the current gang war. The district boasts the highest rate of car theft in the city. Unlike most in Montreal, it has no name.

But it has notoriety. The quarter is the heartland of the Rock Machine, and it is home to the Sûreté

279

du Québec. I often gaze onto its streets, its playgrounds, its riverfront, its bridge, for the Laboratoire de Sciences Judiciaires et de Médecine Légale sits at its core.

Dorsey's funeral was to take place not six blocks from our door. Given that, and the fact that the streets would be crawling with local hoods, the police were taking no chances.

Roy used a map of the island to explain the deployment of personnel. The service was to begin at 8 A.M. Friday at the family parish at Fullum and Larivière. Following Mass, the cortege would move north on Fullum to avenue Mont-Royal, then proceed west and up the mountain to the Cimetière de Notre-Dame-des-Neiges.

Roy outlined the positioning of barricades, cruisers, foot patrolmen, and surveillance personnel, and described the procedures to be followed for the event. The area around the church would be under tight security, side streets blocked at their intersections with Mont-Royal during the funeral procession. The entourage would be limited to the eastbound lanes of Mont-Royal and surrounded by a police escort. Security at the cemetery would also be maximal.

All leaves were canceled. Everyone would report for work on Friday.

The slide show opened to a chorus of 'Sacré bleu!' and 'Tabernac!' but the complaints petered out as the screen filled with scenes of funerals past. Frame by frame we observed the cast of characters, smoking on church steps, riding in columns behind flower-laden hearses, clustered at gravesides.

The faces around me shifted from rose to blue to yellow as each new slide dropped into place. The projector hummed and Roy droned on, giving the date and location of each event, and pointing out the relevant players.

The room was warm, and a good portion of my blood had deserted my brain to work on the Mr. Big. After a while I felt myself yielding to the monotony. My upper lids reached for my lower, and the weight of my head approached the carrying capacity of my neck muscles. I began to nod off.

Then the projector clicked again and I was wide awake.

The screen showed bikers at a police road check. Some straddled Harleys, others had dismounted and were milling about. Though all wore the skull and winged helmet of the Hells Angels, I could read only two bottom rockers. One said *Durham,* the other *Lexington.* The words *Metro Police* were visible on a yellow van in the background, but the rest of the identifier was blocked by a bearded figure photographing the photographer. At his side, Cherokee Desjardins stared insolently into the lens.

'Where was that taken?' I asked Roy.

'South Carolina.'

'That's Cherokee Desjardins.'

'The big chief spent time down South in the early eighties.'

My eyes roved over the pictured group, then came to rest on a bike and rider on the outer edge. His back was turned, his face obscured, but the cycle was visible in full profile. It looked familiar.

'Who's the guy on the far left?' I asked.

'On the chop job?'

'Yes.'

'Don't know.'

281

'I've seen that guy in a couple of old photos,' Kuricek offered. 'Nothing recent, though. He's ancient history.'

'What about the bike?'

'A work of art.'

Thanks.

A discussion of Friday's operation followed the slides. When the investigators had gone I approached Roy.

'Could I borrow that shot of Cherokee Desjardins?'

'Would you prefer a print?'

'Sure.'

'Spot something interesting?'

'I just thought the bike looked familiar.'

'It's a hummer.'

'Yeah.'

We went to his office and he pulled a file from a metal cabinet, then leafed through until he located the picture.

'They sure as hell don't all look like this anymore,' he said, handing it to me. 'Now some of them wear Versace and own fast-food franchises. Made our job easier when they were drunk and filthy.'

'Did you leave another South Carolina print on my desk in the last couple of days?'

'Not I. Is it something I should see?'

'It's like the one you just gave me, but it includes the Osprey girl. I've shown it to Claudel.'

'Now that's interesting. I'll be curious to hear what he says.'

I thanked him and left, promising to return the print.

When I got to the lab I went directly to Imagerie

and added the photo to my compact disc. It was just a hunch, probably a dead end, but I wanted to make a comparison.

I left work at four-thirty and swung by the Hôte-Dieu Hospital, hoping LaManche had improved enough to receive visitors. No go. He was still unresponsive, and his doctors were keeping him in cardiac intensive care, with no visitors except immediate family. Feeling helpless, I ordered a small bouquet in the hospital gift shop, and headed for the parking lot.

In the car I turned on the radio and hit scan. The channel selector ran the band, pausing briefly on a local talk show. Today's topic was the biker war and the upcoming funeral for its latest victim. The host was soliciting comments on police performance. I clicked in to listen.

While opinions varied as to police handling of the gang situation, one thing was clear. Callers were nervous. Whole neighborhoods were being avoided. Mothers were walking their kids to school. Late-night carousers were changing watering holes, looking over their shoulders as they scurried to their cars.

And the callers were angry. They wanted their town released from the threat of these modern-day Mongols.

When I got home Kit was on the phone. He held the mouthpiece to his chest, and informed me that Harry had called from Puerto Vallarta.

'What did she say?'

'*Buenos días.*'

'Did you get a number?'

'She said she was moving around. But she'll call again later in the week.'

Then he resumed his conversation, disappearing into his room.

Good going, Harry.

Wasting no time worrying about my sister, I pulled out the print Roy had loaned me and laid it on the table. Then I sorted through Kate's photos for the shots of Bernard 'Slick' Silvestre's biker funeral down South. I was particularly interested in the graveside scene Kit and I had studied.

I went through the stack three times and came up empty. I checked everything in my briefcase. Then the desk in my bedroom. The papers around my computer. Every folder Kate had given me.

The photos were nowhere to be found.

Puzzled, I stuck my head into Kit's room to ask if he'd borrowed them.

He hadn't.

O.K., Brennan. Play the remembering game. When did you last see them?

Saturday night with Kit?

No.

Sunday morning.

In the hands of Lyle Crease.

The anger hit me like a sucker punch, sending heat up my neck, and curling my fingers into fists.

'Goddammit! Sonovabitch!'

I was furious with Crease and more furious with myself. Living alone, I had gotten into the habit of working investigative material at home, a practice discouraged by the lab. Now I was missing a piece of potential evidence.

Slowly, I calmed down. And I recalled something a detective once told me while working a homicide in Charlotte. Media vans surrounded the charred suburban colonial where we were bagging what

284

remained of a family of four.

'Our free press is like a sewer system,' he said, 'sucking in everyone and grinding them to shit. Especially those who ain't paying attention.'

I hadn't paid attention, and now I would have to retrieve those photos.

CHAPTER THIRTY-ONE

To work off my anger at Crease, my disgust with myself, and my fear for LaManche, I pounded out three miles on the treadmill at the gym. Then I lifted for thirty minutes, and sat in the steam room for another ten.

Walking home along Ste-Catherine I felt physically tired, but still mentally anxious. I forced my thoughts to innocuous things.

The weather had turned heavy and humid. Seagulls screamed at the dark clouds that hung low over the city, trapping the smell of the St. Lawrence and bringing on a premature dusk.

I thought about city gulls. Why fight pigeons for urban scraps when a world-class river flows a mile away? Are gulls and pigeons variations of the same bird?

I thought about dinner. I thought about the pain in my left knee. I thought about a tooth in which I suspected a cavity. I thought about ways to conceal my hair.

Mostly I thought about Lyle Crease. And I understood the rage of Islamic fundamentalists and postal workers. I would call him and demand the return of the photos. Then, if the little reptile crossed my path again I would probably get my name in the papers.

As I rounded the corner onto my street I saw a figure moving toward me, a leather-vested white-trash redneck who looked like a hyena pack of one.

Had he come from my building?

Kit!

I felt a constriction in my chest.

I quickened my pace and kept to the center of the sidewalk. The man held his path, banging into me as we passed. His bulk was such that the impact knocked me off balance. Stumbling, I looked up into dark eyes, made darker by the brim of a baseball cap. I stared into them.

Look at me, asshole. Remember my face. I'll remember yours.

He met my gaze, then puckered his lips in an exaggerated kiss.

I offered a digit.

Heart pounding, I raced to the complex and into the vestibule, taking the steps two at a time. With shaking hands I unlocked the front door, hurried down the hall, and inserted the key to my condo.

Kit was in the kitchen adding pasta to boiling water. There was an empty beer bottle by the sink, a half-full one at his elbow.

'Kit.'

His hand jumped at the sound of my voice.

'Hey. What's up?'

He poked the noodles with a wooden spoon, and took a swig of beer. Though the greeting was casual, his jerky movements belied tension.

I was silent, waiting for him to go on.

'I found some store-bought sauce. Roasted garlic and black olive. It ain't gourmet, but I thought you'd like a home-cooked.'

He gave a brilliant Kit smile, then tossed back another mouthful of Molson.

'What's going on?'

'NBA play-off game tonight.'

'You know what I mean.'

'I do?'

'Kit.' I did not disguise my annoyance.

'What? Just ask, ma'am.'

'Was someone here while I was gone?'

He swirled the linguine, tapped the spoon on the edge of the pot, and looked straight at me. For several moments the steam rose between us. Then the corners of his eyes pinched, and he tapped again.

'No.'

He dropped his gaze, stirred, flicked back to me.

'What's the deal?'

'I saw someone on the sidewalk and thought he might have been coming from here.'

'Can't help you.' Another shit-eating grin. 'You like your linguine *al dente,* madam?'

'Kit—'

'You worry too much, Aunt Tempe.'

It was becoming a familiar refrain.

'Are you still seeing those men from the bike shop?'

He extended his hands, wrists pressed together.

'O.K. I give up. Arrest me on suspicion of involvement with organized pasta.'

'Are you?'

His voice grew stern. 'Who hired you to ask these questions, ma'am?'

It was clear he would tell me nothing. I pushed the fear to a corner of my mind, knowing that it wouldn't stay there, and went to my room to change. But I'd made a decision.

Kit was going back to Houston.

*   *   *

After dinner Kit settled in front of the TV and I went to my computer. I'd just pulled up the jpg files that contained Kate's photos and the one I'd borrowed from Jacques Roy, when the phone rang.

Kit answered, and I heard laughter and banter through the wall, then the tone changed. Though I could make out no words, it was clear Kit was upset. His voice grew loud and angry, and at one point I heard something slammed.

In a moment Kit appeared at my door, his agitation apparent.

'I'm going out for a little bit, Auntie T.'

'Out?'

'Yep.'

'With?'

'Just some guys.' Only his mouth smiled.

'That's not good enough, Kit.'

'Oh hell, don't you start in.'

With that he stormed down the hall.

'Shit!'

I leaped to my feet, but Kit was already out the door when I rounded the corner into the living room.

'Shit!' I repeated for emphasis.

I was about to go after him when the phone rang. Thinking it was Kit's earlier caller, I grabbed the handset.

'Yes!' I seethed.

'Jesus, Tempe. Maybe you need to get into some

288

kind of exercise program. You are becoming consistently rude.'

'Where the hell are you, Harry?'

'The great state of Jalisco. *Buenos noch*—'

'Why didn't you tell me about Kit's trouble in Houston?'

'Trouble?'

'The tiny matter of the drug bust!' I was almost shouting.

'Oh, that.'

'That.'

'I really don't believe that was Kit's fault. If it weren't for the pasty-faced little pricks he was hanging out with, he'd never have gotten involved with that stuff.'

'But he did, Harry. And now he has a police record.'

'But he didn't have to do any jail time. Howard's lawyer got him off with probation and some community service. Tempe, that boy worked at a homeless shelter for five nights, ate there and slept there and everything. I think it gave him a real good understanding of how the less fortun—'

'Did you get him into counseling?'

'It was just wild oats. Kit's fine.'

'He could have a serious problem.'

'He just took to runnin' with the wrong crowd.'

I wanted to explode from sheer exasperation. Then another thought occurred to me.

'Kit is on probation?'

'Yes, that's all. So it didn't seem worth mentioning.'

'What are the terms of his probation?'

'What?'

'Are there restrictions on what Kit is allowed to

do?'

'He can't drive after midnight. That's been a real pisser. Oh, yeah. And he can't associate with criminals.' She said the last with exaggerated drama, then snorted. 'As if he roams with Bonnie and Clyde.'

Harry's inability to grasp the obvious never ceased to amaze me. She talked to houseplants, but had no inkling of how to communicate with her son.

'Are you supervising what he does, whom he sees?'

'Tempe, it's not like the boy's gonna rob a bank.'

'That's not the point.'

'I really don't want to discuss this anymore.'

Harry was a grand master at 'I really don't want to discuss this.'

'I've got to run, Harry.' The conversation was degenerating into an argument, and I had no desire to go there.

'Okeydokey. Just wanted to make sure y'all are doing fine. I'll keep in touch.'

'Do that.'

I disconnected and stood for a full five minutes, considering my options. None was appealing, but I finally settled on a plan.

After checking the phone book for an address, I grabbed my keys and headed out.

*   *   *

Traffic was light, and within twenty minutes I pulled to the curb on rue Ontario. I cut the engine and looked around, while butterflies took flight in my stomach. I'd have preferred a decade of laser resurfacing to the enterprise I was about to undertake.

La Taverne des Rapides was directly across from me, sandwiched between a tattoo parlor and a motorcycle atelier. The place looked as seedy as I remembered from the photos of Kit that Claudel had brought to my office. Neon signs promised Budweiser and Molson through window glass last washed in the Age of Aquarius.

Zipping a can of Mace inside my jacket pocket, I got out, locked the car, and crossed the street. From the sidewalk I could feel the throb of music vibrating the tavern. Opening the door, I was blasted by the smell of smoke and sweat and stale beer.

Inside, a bouncer looked me up and down. He wore a black T-shirt with the words *Born to Die* emblazoned across a screaming skull.

'Sweet darling,' he said with an oily purr, leering at my chest. 'I think I'm in love.'

The man was missing several teeth, and looked like a member of Thugs Anonymous. I did not return his greeting.

'You come back to Rémi when you're ready for something special, honey.'

He ran a hairy hand down my arm, then signaled me to proceed.

I moved past, wanting to reduce Rémi's dentition by another two or three incisors.

The place had the feel of an Appalachian hooch house, complete with pool table, jukebox, and TV's bolted to corner shelves. A bar occupied one wall, booths another. The rest of the room was filled with tables. It was dark except for Christmas lights framing the bar and front windows.

When my eyes adjusted, I did a sweep. The clientele were alpha male, scruffy and longhaired, looking like Visigoth extras from central casting. The women had swirled their hair into styling-gel do's, and stuffed their breasts into halters with rock-my-world cleavage.

I did not see Kit.

I was threading my way toward the back of the room when I heard shouts and the sound of scuffling feet. Lowering my head, I plowed a course through a sea of beer bellies and flattened myself against a wall.

Near the bar, a goon with Rasputin brows and concave cheeks bellowed and shot to his feet. Blood streamed down his face, staining his sweatshirt and darkening the chains around his neck. A puffy-faced man glared at him from the opposite side of a small table. He was holding a Molson bottle by the wrong end, jabbing it forward to keep his opponent at bay. With a yell, Rasputin grabbed a chair and slammed it into his rival. I heard glass shatter as man and bottle hit the cement.

Tables and bar stools emptied as patrons surged forward, eager to join in whatever was happening. Rémi the bouncer appeared with a baseball bat, and boosted himself onto the bar.

That was enough for me. I decided to wait for Kit outside.

I was halfway to the door when a pair of hands clamped my upper arms. I tried to wrench free but the grip tightened, squeezing my flesh hard against my bones.

Furious, I twisted, and looked into a face strikingly like that of a swamp gator. It sat atop a thick neck, with protruding beady eyes, jaw long and narrow and slung forward at an obtuse angle.

My captor curled his lips and split the air with a piercing whistle. Rasputin froze, and there was a moment of surprised silence as he and his spectators located the source of the whistle. George Strait crooned in the sudden quiet.

'Hey, cut the shit, I got some show-and-tell.' The man's voice was surprisingly high. 'Rémi, get the goddam bottle from Tank.'

Rémi dropped from the bar and stepped between the combatants, the bat resting lightly on his shoulder. He placed a foot on Tank's wrist, applied weight, and what remained of the bottle rolled free. Rémi kicked it away, then pulled Tank to his feet. Tank started to sputter but the man holding me cut him off.

'Shut the fuck up and listen.'

'You talking to me, JJ?' Tank swayed, then spread his feet for better balance.

'You fucking bet your ass I am.'

Again Tank opened his mouth. Again JJ ignored him.

'Look what we have here, gents.'

A few listened, faces vacant from booze or boredom, most turned away. George finished his song and the Rolling Stones took over. The bartender went back to pouring drinks. The hubbub began to swell.

'Big fuckin' deal,' yelled a man at the bar. 'You found a broad who don't puke when she looks at you.'

Laughter.

'Take a good look, dick brain,' JJ replied in an adenoidal whine. 'Ever hear of the bone lady?'

293

'Who the fuck cares?'

'The one what did a little yard work for the Vipers?' He was shouting now, the tendons in his neck taut as guy wires.

A handful of customers turned back to us, confusion floating across their faces.

'Don't any of you assholes read the papers?' JJ's voice cracked with the effort to be heard.

While others went back to their drinks and conversation, Tank picked his way toward us, moving with the exaggerated care of the very drunk. Breathing heavily, he planted himself in front of me, and ran a hand down my cheek.

I turned away, but he cupped my chin and twisted my face to his. His beery breath made my stomach lurch.

'She don't look like such a ball buster to me.'

I said nothing.

'You out slummin', *plotte*?'

Ignoring the whore reference, I looked him straight in the eyes.

With his free hand Tank fumbled with the zipper of his jacket. When it opened I could see the butt of a .38 tucked into his waistband. Fear slithered along my nerves.

On the edge of my vision, I saw a man slide from a bar stool and move in our direction. He stepped close and gave Tank a shoulder-jab greeting.

'*Tabernouche*, I could definitely get a bone on for this.'

The man wore baggy black trousers, gold neck chains, and an open vest showing skin that was fish-belly white. Jailhouse art decorated his chest and arms, and wraparound shades covered his eyes. His muscles were swollen with steroids, and he spoke in

294

heavily accented French.

Tank released my chin and stepped back, staggering slightly.

'She's the bitch dug up Gately and Martineau.'

Stay calm, I told myself.

'You dig Pascal, sugar, you come up with something really big.'

When Pascal removed his shades my fear escalated. His eyes had the bright, glazed look of omnipotence only meth or crack can bestow.

Pascal reached toward me, and I yanked an arm free and parried his move.

'What the fuck?' He glared at me, all pupil.

'Somebody put this guy on his leash.' I said it with much more bravado than I felt.

Pascal's flush deepened and the muscles in his neck and arms corded.

'Who the fuck is this bitch?'

Again he reached for me. Again I knocked his hand away. I was almost numb with fear, but I couldn't let them see it.

'You probably come from a dysfunctional home where no one can spell the word polite, so the lack of manners may not be your fault. But don't ever touch me again,' I hissed.

'*Sacré bl*—' Pascal's fingers balled into fists.

'Want me to shoot her ass?' asked Tank, reaching for the .38.

'Be cool, bitch, or these guys'll leave your brains on a wall.' JJ giggled, shoved me forward, then melted into the crowd.

I started to bolt, but Pascal grabbed and spun me, angling my arm up hard against my back. Pain shot to my shoulder, and tears blurred my vision.

'Not in here, Pascal.' Rémi spoke in a low,

bloodless voice. He'd positioned himself behind my assailant, the bat still on his shoulder. 'Take it somewhere else.'

'No problem.' Pascal wrapped an arm around my throat and pressed his body into mine. I felt something cold and hard against my neck.

I flailed and twisted as best I could, but I was no match for the drugs pumping through his veins.

'Allons-y,' Pascal snarled, half-pushing, half-dragging me toward the back of the bar. 'This bitch is going to the opera.'

CHAPTER THIRTY-TWO

'No!' I protested, terror overcoming my resolve to stay cool.

One arm compressing my trachea, the other bending my elbow at an excruciating angle, Pascal drove me through the crowd. His blade jumped with each step, and I felt blood ooze down the side of my neck.

Rage and fear rocketed my adrenaline, and my mind screamed conflicting orders.

Do as he tells you!

Don't go with him!

Frantic, I looked around for sources of help. The bartender just watched our progress, smoke curling across his face. Rockabilly music pounded from the jukebox. I heard catcalls and hoots, but the faces we passed were passive, carvings in apathy. No one showed interest in what happened to me.

Don't let him take you outside!

I struggled and twisted, but my efforts were

useless against Pascal's strength. Increasing the pressure on my throat, he forced me out a back door and down a set of metal steps. Bootfalls told me Tank was right behind.

When my feet hit gravel, I took a deep breath, ducked and twisted, but Pascal only tightened his choke hold. Desperate, I dipped my chin and bit his hand with all the strength my jaws could muster.

Pascal bellowed and threw me to the ground. I scrabbled through soggy wrappers, condoms, beer caps, and cigarette butts, my stomach curdling at the smell of sludge and urine, trying to unzip the pocket that held the Mace.

'No such fucking luck,' Pascal snarled, coming down hard with a boot to my back.

My chest slammed into gravel. Air burst from my lungs, and white light exploded in my brain.

Scream!

My thorax was on fire. I couldn't make a sound.

The boot withdrew, then I heard footsteps, and a car door opening. Gasping for air, I started hitching forward, elbows and knees sliding in the reeking mud.

'Is today the day, cunt?'

Feeling a gun barrel against my temple, I froze. Tank's face was so close I could smell his breath again.

I heard boots on gravel.

'Your limo's here, bitch. Tank, get her fuckin' feet.'

Rough hands lifted me like a rolled carpet. I squirmed and bucked as best I could, but it did no good. Panicked now, I cast desperate looks up and down the alley. There was no one in sight.

Stars and rooftops wheeled out of sight as I was

turned and thrown into a car. Tank climbed in back, placed a boot across my shoulders, and forced my face into the carpet. Smells of dust, dried wine, stale smoke, and vomit sent a wave of nausea through my body.

Doors slammed, tires spun, and the car sped down the alley.

I was trapped! I was suffocating!

I maneuvered my hands to shoulder level and raised my head. The boot lifted, and a heel struck my back.

'Make a sound and you get a bullet up your ass.' Tank's voice had grown hard, less slurry than in the bar.

With the booze and pills to stoke their ordinarily malevolent dispositions, I had no doubt these men would kill me without a hitch in their thoughts. Don't provoke them while there's no opportunity for escape, I thought. Look for an opening. I lowered my head and waited.

Pascal drove erratically, hitting the gas and brake pedals with quick, jerky movements. The car rolled and lurched, intensifying my nausea. Unable to see out, I counted the stops and turns, trying to memorize the route.

When we stopped, Tank's boot withdrew, and doors opened and slammed. I heard voices, then the back door opened again. Pascal grabbed my arms and dragged me from the car.

As I struggled for balance my gaze fell on Tank, and a wave of terror traveled up my spine. He held the .38 aimed directly at my head. His eyes gleamed black in the pale pink of the streetlight, feral with anticipation. I resisted the impulse to beg, knowing my pleas would only fuel his blood

298

lust.

Pascal shoved me up a short walk toward a building with a green roof and brick exterior wall. When he withdrew a key, unlocked the gate, and pushed me through, my painfully constructed calm crumbled.

Run! Don't go inside!

'No!'

'Move your ass, bitch.'

'Please no!' My pulse beat at a ferocious pace.

I tried to plant my feet against the advance, but Pascal forced me across the courtyard toward the house. Tank followed closely. I could feel his gun on the back of my head, and knew escape was impossible.

'What do you want from me?' I was almost sobbing.

'All you got and then some, bitch,' Pascal snarled. 'Shit you ain't even dreamed of.'

He spoke into an intercom. I heard a metallic voice followed by a click, then he shouldered open the steel-reinforced door and pushed me inside.

There are moments in life when it seems clear the wrap-up is at hand. Your heart pounds and your blood pressure rises, but you know the blood will soon be spilled, never to flow again. Your mind flip-flops between an urge to launch one last desperate effort and a sense of resignation, a desire to just give in.

I've had this feeling a time or two, but never as vividly as at that moment. As Pascal shoved me down the hall, I knew with certainty I would not leave that house alive. My brain opted for furious action.

I turned and drove my fist as hard as I could into

299

Pascal's face. I felt something crunch, but swung back with my elbow and brought it up under his chin. Pascal's head flew back and I slipped below his arm and bolted through a doorway on my left.

I found myself in a game room similar to that at the Vipers' clubhouse in St-Basile-le-Grand. Same bar. Same neon art. Same video monitors. The only difference was that these were working, throwing a cool blue light over the bar and its occupants.

I ran to the far side of the pool table, grabbed a cue in one hand, and fumbled for the Mace with my other, my eyes searching for any door or window.

Two men sat at the bar, another stood behind it. All three had turned at the sound of Pascal's roar. They watched me tear across the room, then shifted their attention back to the door when Pascal burst through it.

'I'll kill that little bucket of shit! Where the fuck is she?'

Light from the neon sign angled obliquely across Pascal's face, deepening the furrows and casting shadows across his eyes and cheeks.

'Hold it right there.'

The voice was low and hard as quartz, and stopped Pascal dead. The sound of the outer door suggested Tank had opted out of further involvement. I stole a look at the man who had spoken.

He wore a double-breasted tan suit with a pale peach shirt and matching tie. His skin was tanning-booth bronze, and he probably paid his hairstylist eighty dollars per visit. Large rings adorned each of his hands.

It was the man beside him who caused my heart

300

to stop.

Andrew Ryan wore black jeans, boots, and a gray sweatshirt with the arms razored off. The muscles in his face looked hard and tense, and stubble roughened his cheeks and chin.

Ryan's eyes met mine and the flesh underneath tensed slightly, then he looked away.

I felt heat rise up my neck and spread across my cheeks. My legs trembled, and I leaned into the pool table to steady myself.

After several seconds Ryan swiveled on his bar stool and stretched his legs in my direction. A smirk spread across his face.

'Well, if it ain't shit for brains.'

'You know this fuckin' cunt?' Pascal's voice trembled with rage. Blood trickled from his nose, and he wiped it on his sleeve.

'It's Dr. Too Goddam Many Degrees,' Ryan said, drawing a pack from his pocket and tapping out a Marlboro.

The others watched as Ryan placed the cigarette between his lips, drew a wooden match from under the cellophane, lit up, and exhaled.

So did I. Ryan's hands looked so familiar on the match and cigarette I felt tears behind my lids. My chest gave a small heave.

Why is he here?

Ryan took his cigarette between thumb and forefinger, upended the matchstick between his teeth, then arched and sent it winging across the room toward me. I watched the match drop onto green felt, and fury exploded inside me.

'You turncoat bastard! You contemptible son of a bitch! Read my lips, Ryan. Drop dead!'

'See what I mean.' Pascal wiped his nose again.

301

'We're gonna teach this cunt some manners.'

'Bad idea,' said Ryan, taking a long drag.

The man in the gabardine suit stared at the side of Ryan's face. Several long seconds passed. The tension in the room was enough to launch arrows. Then, 'Why do you say that?' he asked quietly.

'She's a cop.' Another drag. 'And the cops already have a two-by-four up Pascal's ass for exactly this kind of shit.'

'So? You got no balls?' Pascal challenged.

Ryan blew smoke out both nostrils.

'Here's the news flash, asshole. You've already screwed up big time messing up one of your tramps, and now you drag a cop in here. You mess up a cop, particularly a dame, and the whole force comes screaming up your butt. Now, you may not mind taking the bounce for Goldilocks here, but the rest of us sure as hell will. All the shit we have in the works goes into the deep freeze while the cops dissect us top to bottom.'

Pascal looked at Ryan, his eyes blazing with fury and speed.

'The fucking bitch hit me! I'm gonna tear her a new asshole.' The muscles in his face jumped and his eye and mouth twitched.

The man in the suit continued to study Ryan, his face devoid of expression. Then he turned to Pascal.

'No,' he said calmly. 'You are not.'

Pascal started to bluster, but Ryan held up a hand.

'You want to bloody her up? Watch this.'

Walking to the end of the bar, Ryan snatched a red plastic bottle, circled the pool table, and held it over me. Then he squeezed, making circular movements with his hand. I didn't budge.

'Read *that*, Shakespeare.' He slammed the bottle onto the table.

I looked down. Ketchup swirled across my shirt. As my eyes crawled back to Ryan's face, words eddied in my head I knew I wouldn't use.

The smirk was gone, and for a long moment the Viking blues held mine. Then Ryan's gaze left me and slid back to Pascal.

'This party's over.'

'The party's over when I say it is.' Pascal's pupils were wider than a sewer main. He appealed to Ryan's companion.

'This puke can't talk to me like that. He's not ev—'

'But I can. This party's over. Now get the fuck out of here.' Barely above a whisper.

Pascal's brow furrowed, and a vein bulged along his temple. With one last 'Sonovabitch!' he turned and exited the room.

The man in the gabardine suit watched in silence as Ryan swung back to me.

'You keep your sorry ass, slut, but don't get any wrong ideas. This wasn't for you.' He emphasized each word with a jab to my chest. 'For all I care you could be upstairs doing the dirty boogie on all fours with Pascal. And take note.'

He stood so close I could smell his perspiration, a scent as familiar as my own body.

'Tonight's adventure is one big black hole in your memory bank. It didn't happen.' He grabbed my hair and pulled my face to his. 'You talk, and I'll personally lead Pascal to you.'

He released me with a shove to the chest, and I staggered backward.

'We'll buzz the gate. Now disappear.'

Ryan rejoined the man at the bar, sucked once on his cigarette, then flipped the butt against the stainless steel below the counter.

As I watched the spray of sparks, I felt something inside me curl into a cold, hard ball.

Without a word I lay down the pool cue, and fled on shaking legs. Outside the gate, I finally got the Mace out of my pocket and in a venting of frustration, humiliation, relief, and rage, I turned and sprayed the house. Sobbing, teeth chattering, I clutched the cylinder to my chest and bolted into the dark.

*   *   *

The clubhouse was less than six blocks from La Taverne des Rapides, and, after half-stumbling, half-running that distance, it did not take long to find my car. Once inside, I locked the doors, then sat a moment, legs trembling, hands shaking uncontrollably, my mind numb. I took a deep breath and forced myself to move with slow, deliberate motions. Belt. Ignition. Shift. Gas.

Though lightning flickered, and raindrops battered the windshield, I broke all speed laws getting home. My thoughts were chaos.

Ryan had given his companion sound advice. An outlaw enterprise needs a strong reason to mess up even an adjunct cop like me. Retribution would be powerful and the organization would be out of business for an extended time. Unless the cop was wreaking major havoc, it made no sense and the man in the suit had understood that. But what about Ryan? Had sound *consigliere* advice been his sole motive?

What had just taken place? Had I stumbled onto Ryan in his new life? Was he there as a member of the pack, or did he have other motives? What did his actions mean? Had he humiliated me as a message that his past life was done and he now belonged to the other side, or had he done it as part of a scene designed to get me out of there safely? Had he put himself at risk?

I knew I should report the incident. But what would be gained? Carcajou knew of the clubhouse, no doubt had files on Pascal and Tank.

Carcajou. Claudel and Quickwater. My stomach knotted. What would they say when they learned how I'd literally thrown myself in jeopardy? Would the incident reinforce Claudel's desire to have me removed as liaison to the unit?

What if Ryan was undercover? Could a police report threaten his cover?

I didn't have answers, but I made a choice. Regardless of the man's motives, I would do nothing to hurt Andrew Ryan. If the slightest chance existed that an incident report could harm him, I would make no report. Tomorrow I would decide, I thought.

When I got home Kit's door was closed, but I could hear music through the wall.

Good call, Auntie. This is why you're not a cop.

I threw my clothes on a chair and dropped into bed. As I did so, the thought hit me. What if Pascal had taken me someplace else? Sleep came much, much later.

CHAPTER THIRTY-THREE

The next morning I slept late, finally waking around ten, sore and achy. I spent the morning nursing myself with aspirin, tea, and hot baths, fighting off flashbacks to the night before. Though I had bruises on my legs and back, and a small cut on my neck, my face had escaped largely unmarked. After a late lunch I applied extra makeup, chose a turtleneck sweater, then went into the lab and spent the day on routine matters. I made no report.

When I got home Kit and I had a quiet dinner. He had no questions about my previous night's outing, and I assumed he was unaware that I'd been gone. I did not bring up his storming out, and he offered no explanation.

After dinner I decided to do laundry. Pulling the basket from the bedroom closet, I added the clothing I'd worn the night before. I sorted, then loaded the washer, holding back items requiring special treatment. My stomach tightened when I lifted the shirt with the ketchup blotch, the scene still vivid in my mind.

I spread the shirt and began spraying the stain, the product jingle for the spot remover bouncing through my head.

I'll Shout *you* out, you sonovabitch. I squeezed the handle. Phhht!

I pictured the smirk on Ryan's face, remembered his finger jabbing my chest.

I squeezed again. Phhht!

Read that, Shakespeare! Phhht!

My hand froze and I stared at the pattern. The squiggles were not random, but formed two perfect sixes.

Read that, Shakespeare. Shakespeare. The sonnets were a passion with Ryan.

I recalled something from a long time ago. High school. Mr. Tomlinson. Senior Honors English.

Was it possible?

I raced to the bedroom bookshelf and pulled out a volume. *The Complete Works of William Shakespeare.* Hardly breathing, I opened to the sonnets and flipped to number sixty-six.

Come on, Bill, let it be there.

Tears welled when I read the line.

And right perfection wrongly disgraced . . .

Wrongly disgraced.

It was a message. Ryan was saying that all was not as it seemed.

Right perfection.

Ryan was not a point man for the dark side! He had not gone over!

What then?

Undercover?

But why hadn't he contacted me?

He couldn't, Brennan. You know that.

It didn't matter. Suddenly I was certain that whatever Ryan was doing, the man I knew remained beneath. In time I would know the full story.

And I was equally certain I would never report the previous night's events. I would do nothing to compromise Ryan's cover.

I closed the book and went back to the laundry.

Though I understood that covert operations could last months, or even years, at least now I knew.

A smile spread across my face as I bunched the shirt and tossed it into the washer. I can wait, Andrew Ryan. I can wait.

Feeling happier than I had in weeks, I shook off the vision of Pascal and Tank and went back to the photos I'd abandoned the night before. I'd just booted up the disc when Kit appeared in the doorway.

'I forgot to tell you that Isabelle phoned. She's going out of town and wanted to return your call before she left.'

'Where is she going?'

'I forget. Something to do with an award.'

'When is she leaving?'

'I forget.'

'Thanks.'

His eyes shifted to the screen.

'What are you doing?'

'I'm trying to clean up some old photographs so I can view the faces.'

'Whose?'

'Savannah Osprey is in one shot. And the man who was killed last week.'

'The guy who was stabbed in jail?'

'No. The person the police think was his victim.'

'Awesome.'

He moved into the room.

'Can I see?'

'Well, I guess there's nothing in the way of sensitive information here. As long as you promise not to discuss these things with anyone but me, you can pull up a chair.'

I brought up the Myrtle Beach photo and

indicated Savannah and Cherokee Desjardins.

'Man. That dude looks like a reject from the W.W.F.'

'World Wrestling Federation?'

'World Wildlife Fund.' He pointed at Savannah. 'She's sure no ole lady.'

'No. But it's not uncommon for bikers to drug young girls and hold them against their will.'

'And she's no beach bunny. Man, her skin's the color of a bedsheet.'

I had a thought.

'I want you to take a look at something.'

I closed the picnic photo and opened the police-check photo.

Kit leaned in and studied the scene.

'Is that the same dude?' He indicated Cherokee.

'Yes.'

'We still in Dixie?'

'South Carolina.'

'Looks like a road bust.'

His eyes moved across the group, then locked onto the cycle at the periphery.

'Holy shit. Sorry. When was this taken?'

'That's unclear. Why?'

'That's the same chopped hog we saw in the funeral picture.'

My pulse stepped up.

'Are you sure?'

'Auntie T, that is the sweetest piece of Milwaukee iron I have ever seen. You could really ride the edge on those wheels.'

'That's why I was asking about the other picture.'

'Did you find it?'

'No.'

'Doesn't matter. That's the same bike.'

'How can you be sure?'

'Can you zoom it up?'

I magnified that part of the photo.

'Jesus. That is five hundred pounds of thunder.'

'Tell me how you know it's the same bike.'

'Like I said before, it's an old FLH, a police touring cycle that's been stripped and customized. That's no big deal. But it's the way he did the chop that's so bitching.'

One by one he again pointed out the bike's wonders. 'This dude wanted a truly raw machine, so he changed the power-to-weight ratio.'

His finger touched the front of the bike.

'He lengthened the wheel base and raised the front end by installing longer front forks. Man, those puppies must be twenty inches over stock. He probably cut out a section of the neck of the frame. You've really got to know your shit to pull that off.'

'Why?'

'If you screw it up the bike will split and you'll find yourself eating cement at high speed.'

He indicated the handlebars.

'He used dog bones, steel struts to raise the handlebars.'

'Mm.'

'The guy that did this was definitely not interested in comfort. He's riding a springer front end, that's one with external springs, not hydraulic shock absorbers, and a 'hard tail' frame.'

'A hard tail?'

'It's a rigid frame with no rear shock absorbers. It's called a 'hard tail' because your ass really takes a beating.'

He pointed to a set of pins at the front of the

bike.

'Check out the highway pegs.'

I must have looked blank.

'He's got extra foot pegs up front, and a forward-positioned custom-shift-and-brake assembly so he can stretch out his feet. This guy is into serious puttin'.'

'And you're sure this is the same bike we saw at Silvestre's grave?'

'Same righteous hog. But that's not my only clue.'

I knew I was in over my depth, and said nothing.

'Look at this.' He pointed at the gas tank. 'He's sculpted the tank with some kind of molding material. What does that look like to you?'

I bent close. The front end did look odd, but the shape brought nothing to mind. I peered at it, forcing my brain cells to draw meaning from the tapered form.

Then I saw it.

'Is that unusual?' I asked.

'It's the only one I've ever seen. The guy's a regular Rodin with bondo.'

He stared at the screen, mesmerized. Then, 'Yeah! Jammin' in the wind sitting on a snake's head. Hee ha—'

He stopped short and an odd look crossed his face. Then he leaned in, back, then in again, like a bird sighting on a curious insect.

'Can you bring that guy's face up?'

'The one on the bike?'

'Yeah.'

'It will blur as I enlarge it.'

'Try.'

I did, then went through the same manipulations

I'd performed with Claudel. As lines and shadows shifted, congealing pixels into recognizable features, then reordering them into meaningless patterns of color and shape, I gradually realized what my nephew had spotted.

In twenty minutes I'd done what I could do. During that time we had not spoken. I broke the silence.

'What made you recognize him?'

'I'm not sure. Maybe the jaw. Maybe the nose. It grabbed me as I was pointing out the snake's head. Before that I hadn't even noticed the rider.'

We stared at the man on the marvelous hog. And he looked into space, intent on a happening long since past.

'Did he ever mention riding with the Angels?'

'He's not wearing colors.'

'Did he, Kit?'

My nephew sighed.

'No.'

'Does he hang with them now?'

'Oh, please. You've seen the guy.'

Yes. I'd seen the guy. On a country road in St-Basile-le-Grand. Across a dinner table. On the late-night news. And in my own home.

The man on the bike was Lyle Crease.

CHAPTER THIRTY-FOUR

Words and images flashed in my brain. Pascal's face in neon and shadow. George Dorsey mumbling my name to a paramedic. A glossy eyeball.

'. . . are you going to do?' Kit asked.

312

'Call Isabelle, then go to bed.' I closed down the program and slid the CD into its holder.

'That's it?'

'That's it.'

Sometimes when thoughts are ricocheting inside my head, the best strategy is to lay back and let them find their own patterns.

'Aren't you curious?'

'Very. And I *will* find out if Crease has ties to the Hells Angels. But not tonight.'

'I could ask around.'

'That is precisely what you will *not* do,' I snapped. 'He could be a dangerous man with dangerous friends.'

Kit's face froze. Then his eyes dropped and he turned away.

'Whatever.' He shrugged.

I waited for the click of his bedroom door, then dialed Isabelle's number. She answered after four rings, sounding slightly out of breath.

'*Mon Dieu,* I was buried in the back of the closet. I've misplaced my Vuitton overnighter and can't imagine where it is. And, really, nothing else will do.'

'Isabelle, I need some information.'

My tone suggested I was not in the mood for a luggage discussion.

'*Oui?*'

'I'd like to know about Lyle Crease.'

'Ahhh, Tempe, you little pixie. I knew you would change your mind.'

Like hell. 'Tell me about him.'

'He's cute, eh?'

As a mealworm, I thought, but said nothing.

'And you know he is an investigative reporter

with CTV. Very glamorous.'

'How long has he done that?'

'How long?'

'Yes. How long?'

'Mon Dieu, forever.'

'How many years?'

'Well, I'm not sure. But he's been on the air as long as I can remember.'

'What did he do before that?'

'Before that?'

'Yes. Before CTV.' This was harder than questioning George Dorsey.

'Let me think.' I heard a soft ticking, and pictured lacquered nails tapping the handset. 'I know the answer to this, Tempe, because Véronique told me. Véronique hosts a talk show on Radio-Canada now, interviews celebrities, but she started out doing the weather at CTV. Do you know her?'

'No.' My left eye was beginning to throb.

'She dated Lyle briefl—'

'I'm sure I've seen her.'

'I think she told me Lyle was hired away from an American newspaper. No. Wait, this is coming back to me.' Tick. Tick. Tick. 'It was a paper somewhere out west. Alberta, I think. But originally he comes from the States. Or maybe he went to school down there.'

'Do you know which state?'

'Somewhere in the South, I think. You should like that.'

'When did he come to Canada?'

'Oh my goodness, I have no idea.'

'Where does he live?'

'Off the island, I think. Or maybe downtown.'

'Does he have family here?'

'Sorry.'

'How well do you know Lyle Crease?'

'I am not his confidante, Tempe.' Her tone was becoming defensive.

'But you tried to pair me up with him!' I tried to keep my voice neutral but the irritation curled around the edges.

'You needn't put it like that. The gentleman asked to meet you, and I saw no reason to refuse. It's not as though your love life has been bountiful this year.'

'Hold it. Back up. It was Crease's idea that we meet?'

'Yes.' Guarded.

'When was this?'

'I don't know, Tempe. I ran into him at *L'Express,* you know, that bistro on rue St-Denis th—'

'Yes.'

'Lyle saw your picture in the paper and was absolutely smitten. Or so he said, though not in those exact words. Anyway, we were talking, and one thing led to another, and before I could help myself I'd invited him to dinner.'

Tick. Tick.

'And really, he wasn't so bad. In fact, he was quite charming.'

'Um.' So was Ted Bundy.

For a few moments no one spoke.

'Are you angry with me, Tempe?'

'No, I'm not angry.'

'I'll see what I can find out. I'll phone Véronique an—'

'No. Never mind. It's not important.'

The last thing I needed was an alert to Lyle Crease.

'I was just curious. Have a good trip, Isabelle.'

'*Merci*. Where do you suppose that overnighter has gone?'

'Try your storage locker.'

'*Bonne idée. Bonsoir, Tempe.*'

When we disconnected, I realized I hadn't asked where she was going.

*   *   *

An hour later the mental commingling began. As I lay in bed, trying to block out Kit's music, images, facts, and questions floated to the surface then sank into the deep, like tropical fish in a subliminal tank.

Image. Lyle Crease pouring wine.

Fact. Crease had finagled the introduction. He was at St-Basile-le-Grand and knew about the skeletons, and had seen the article in the *Gazette*, before Isabelle's dinner party.

Questions. Why did he want to meet me? Was his request linked to the discovery of the burials? Was he simply looking for an inside scoop, or did he have other reasons for wanting information?

Image. A young Lyle Crease on a chopped hog.

Fact. Crease had ties to the Southern states.

Questions. What was Crease doing with the homeboys? Had he stolen the Silvestre funeral photo from me? If so, why? Could his past somehow endanger him now? Whom did he fear?

Image. A hyena redneck lumbering up my block.

Fact. Besides initial fear, the man had triggered something in my psyche.

316

Questions. Had Kit been lying when I asked about visitors? Why? Who was the goon in the baseball cap? Why did the man provoke such a strong reaction in me?

Image. LaManche on tubes and life support.

Fact. The pathologist was in his sixties and had never taken time for exercise or a proper diet.

Questions. Would he survive? Would he ever return to work?

Image. Ryan slouching on a barroom stool.

Fact. He was undercover, and hadn't gone over.

Questions. Had his actions on my behalf jeopardized his cover? Was he in danger? Had I contributed to that?

These musings mingled with more mundane considerations. How to relocate Kit to Houston. Birdie's overdue vaccinations. The cavity. Hair growth.

But underlying all my thoughts was the nagging signal from my subconscious, unrelenting, yet out of reach. The redneck in the baseball cap. I tossed and turned, frustrated that my psyche was beaming a message I could not decipher.

I was sleeping fitfully when the phone shrilled.

'Hello.' Groggy.

'Oh, were you in bed?'

The digits on my clock glowed one-fifteen.

'Mm.'

'It was the University of South Carolina,' Isabelle chirped.

'What?'

'Lyle is from London, Ontario, but he went to school in South Carolina.' Her voice beamed with satisfaction. 'And don't worry about my source. I was *très* discreet.'

317

Oh boy.

'Thank you, Isabelle.' Mumbled.

'Now, go back to sleep. Oh, and I found the suitcase in the bathroom closet. Silly me. *Bonsoir.*'

Dial tone.

I clicked off and flopped back on the pillow, noticing that the bedroom wall no longer vibrated. Had Kit gone out?

As I began to drift off my id made one more try at sending up images. The hyena took form with his leather vest and grungy long hair. Boots. Cap.

Cap.

My eyes flew open and I shot to a sitting position, searching my stored memories for another image.

Could it be?

*   *   *

The next morning I was up before the alarm. A peek told me Kit was asleep in his bed. I showered, dressed, and puttered until it was time to go to the lab.

I went directly to Ronald Gilbert's office and made my request. Without a word he crossed to a shelf, selected a videotape, and handed it to me. I thanked him and hurried to the conference room.

Nervously, I inserted the plastic box into a VCR and clicked on the monitor. Not knowing at what point I'd find the scene, I started at the beginning and hit fast-forward.

Views of the Cherokee Desjardins apartment jerked across the screen. The living room, the kitchen, the faceless corpse. Then the tape focused on bloody walls.

318

The camera swept across a corner, zooming in, then drawing back. I hit play and the pace slowed to normal.

Two minutes later I spotted the object wedged between the wall and a rusted birdcage supporting a guitar. I hit freeze and read four letters peeking from a wine-colored stain.

'—cock—'

I studied the cap closely. It was red and white, and I could see portions of a familiar logo that hadn't registered while I was at the scene. My mind completed the letters obliterated by Cherokee's blood.

G-a-m-e----s.

Yes.

Gamecocks.

The cap hadn't proclaimed some macho obscenity. It had broadcast the name of an athletic team. The Gamecocks.

The University of South Carolina Gamecocks.

The hyena's cap had nudged my id. Isabelle's call had allowed my brain's summons to assemble and organize to breakthrough.

Just then the door opened and Michel Charbonneau stuck his spiky head into the room. He held up a brown envelope.

'Claudel asked me to give you this. It's the official game plan for tomorrow, and Roy wanted you to have it.'

'I guess Monsieur Claudel is too busy.'

Charbonneau gave one of his shrugs. 'He's working these homicides for both agencies.'

His eyes drifted to the monitor.

'Desjardins?'

'Yes. Look at this.'

He circled the table and stood behind me. I pointed at the cap.

'It's from the University of South Carolina.'

'You can't lick our Cocks.'

'You've heard of the team.'

'With a motto like that, who hasn't?'

'That's not the official slogan.'

'Cherokee's decor suggested he was an athletic supporter.'

I ignored that.

'In all the photos you've seen of him, was Cherokee ever wearing headgear?'

Charbonneau thought a moment.

'No. So what?'

'Maybe the cap isn't his. Maybe it belongs to his killer.'

'Dorsey?'

I told him about the pictures of Lyle Crease.

'So the guy spent some time in South Carolina. Big deal. Half the population of Quebec vacations down there.'

'Why would Crease take a sudden interest in me after I dug up those bodies?'

'Aside from the fact that you're cute as a sea monkey?'

'Aside from that.'

'O.K., when things quiet down we might reel Crease in and query him on Gately and Martineau. But there's nothing to tie him to the Cherokee hit.'

I told him about the Myrtle Beach photo.

'Crease and Cherokee knew each other, and that photo was not of a Boy Scout camporee.'

'A trip through Dixie back in the Ice Age. Crease is a journalist. He might have been covering a story.'

320

Charbonneau flipped the envelope onto the table.

'Look, Cherokee had chemo. He probably got the cap when comb-overs were no longer an option. But if it makes you feel better, I'll check Crease out.'

When he'd gone, I turned back to the tape, my mind zigzagging through a labyrinth of explanations. The cap could belong to Dorsey. He claimed to have knowledge of Savannah Osprey. Maybe he'd been to South Carolina.

When the camera moved off along the wall I hit rewind and did another sweep through the corner. Bloodstains. Guitar. Birdcage. Cap.

Then the lens drew very close, and I felt movement in the tiny hairs at the back of my neck. I leaned in and squinted at the screen, hoping to make sense of what I'd spotted. It was fuzzy, but definitely there.

I rewound the tape, switched off the VCR, and hurried from the room. If what I saw was real, Claudel and Charbonneau would have to find another theory.

*   *   *

I took the stairs to the thirteenth floor and went to a large window opening onto a room filled with shelves and lined by storage lockers. A small blue sign identified it as the *Salle des Exhibits*. The property room.

A uniform from the SQ was sliding a deer rifle across the counter. I waited while the clerk filled out forms, handed the officer a receipt, then tagged the gun and carried it to the storage area. When

321

she returned I showed her the Cherokee case numbers.

'Could you check to see if the evidence inventory includes an athletic cap?'

'There was a long list for that case,' she said, entering the number into a computer. 'This may take a moment.'

Her eyes scanned the screen.

'Yes, here it is. There was a cap.' She read the text. 'It went to biology for testing on a bloodstain, but it's back.'

She disappeared into the shelves and returned after several minutes with a Ziploc plastic bag. In it I could see the red cap.

'Do you need to sign it out?'

'If it's all right I'll just take a look at it here.'

'Sure.'

I zipped open the seal and slid the cap onto the counter. Gently raising the brim, I studied the hat's interior.

There it was. Dandruff.

I resealed the cap and thanked the technician. Then I flew to my office and snatched up the phone.

CHAPTER THIRTY-FIVE

Claudel and Quickwater were not at Carcajou headquarters. Neither Claudel nor Charbonneau was at CUM headquarters. I left messages, and returned to Ronald Gilbert's office.

'Thanks for the tape.'

'Did it help?'

'May I ask you about something?'

'Please.'

'Do you remember the corner of the room with the guitar and birdcage stacked against the wall?'

'Yes.'

'There was a cap there.'

'I remember it.'

'Did you make observations on the bloodstaining?'

'Certainly.'

'I'm interested in the cap's position at the time of the murder. Would your notes have anything on that?'

'I don't need my notes. I recall perfectly. The stain and spatter on the cap came from the blunt object attack near that corner.'

'Not the gunshot.'

'No. That would look quite different. And the orientation of the spatter was consistent with the type of assault we discussed.'

'With Cherokee lying on the floor.'

'Yes.'

'Was he wearing the cap?'

'Oh my, no. That's impossible. The cap was behind the birdcage when struck by most of the spatter.'

'How did it get there?'

'It was probably flung there during the struggle.'

'How do you know that?'

'There was blood under as well as on the cap. The assailant probably lost it in the frenzy of the attack.'

'Cherokee was not wearing it?'

'I'd bet my life on it.'

'Thanks.'

Back in my office I looked at the clock. Ten-thirty. I had no message slips. I had no case requests.

I drummed my fingers and stared at the phone, willing it to ring. It didn't. Not optimistic, I dialed Harry's number in Houston, then listened to a recording in very bad Spanish. I tried Kit, got my own voice.

Damn. Where was everybody?

I called Claudel again, this time leaving my cell number. Ditto Charbonneau. Then I grabbed my purse and bolted, unable to bear the waiting.

*   *   *

When I stepped outside I was blinded for a moment. Sunlight bathed the day and sparrows twittered in the branches overhead. Lab and SQ staff chatted along the drive and relaxed at picnic tables on the lawn, enjoying a midmorning smoke or coffee.

I inhaled deeply, and started up Parthenais, wondering how I could have lost track of spring. For a moment I had an odd fantasy. The Dorsey funeral would take place in less than twenty-four hours. If I could freeze time I could hold it at bay, keep the birds singing, the sun shining, and the ladies on the lawn with their shoes kicked off.

But I couldn't, and the tension was making me jumpier than a proton in a particle accelerator.

Jesus, Brennan. Upstairs you wanted things to move faster. Now you want a freeze-frame. Clear your neurons.

The situation called for a hot dog and fries.

I hung a left on Ontario, walked east a block,

and pushed open the door to Lafleur. At 11 A.M. there was no line, and I stepped directly to the counter.

Lafleur is Quebec's version of the fast-food joint, offering hot dogs, burgers, and poutine. The decor is chrome and plastic, the clientele largely blue collar.

'*Chien chaud, frites, et Coke Diète, s'il vous plaît,*' I told the man at the cash register. Why did the literal translation of hot dog in French still sound strange to me?

'*Steamé ou grillé?*'

I chose steamed, and in seconds a cardboard container was slapped in front of me. Grease from the fries already stained the left side.

I paid and carried my food to a table with an excellent view of the parking lot.

As I ate my eyes roved over the other patrons. To my left were four young women in nurse's white, students from the technical school across the street. Tags identified them as Manon, Lise, Brigitte, and Marie-José.

Two painters ate in silence beyond the students. They wore coveralls, and their arms, hair, and faces were speckled like the walls of Gilbert's spatter lab. The men worked on platters of fries topped with curd cheese and brown gravy. In a city renowned for its fine cuisine, I have never understood the appeal of poutine.

Across from the painters sat a young man trying his best to grow a goatee. His glasses were round and he was overweight.

I finished my fries and checked my cell. The phone was on, the signal strong, but there were no messages. Damn! Why wasn't anyone returning my call?

I needed release. Physical release.

I spent two hours running, lifting, rolling around on a large rubber ball, and taking a high-impact aerobics class. By the time I finished I could hardly drag myself to the showers. But the exercise was an effective antivenin. My anger had dissipated along with the toxins from the hot dog and fries.

*   *   *

When I returned to the lab two messages lay on my desk. Charbonneau had called. Morin wanted to talk about LaManche. That didn't sound good. Why hadn't Madame LaManche phoned?

I hurried down the hall, but Morin's door was already closed, indicating he'd left for the day. I went back to my office and dialed Charbonneau.

'There may be more to this Crease than I thought.'

'Such as?'

'Seems he and the Angels go back a ways. Crease is Canadian, but he did his undergraduate studies at South Carolina. Go Cocks.'

'You're really hung up on that.'

'Hey, beats the Redmen.'

'I'll pass on your opinion to the McGill board.'

'Politically it's more correct.'

I waited.

'Newsboy completed a B.A. in journalism in '83 and decided to go on for a master's degree, using outlaw bikers as his thesis topic. By the way, he was calling himself Robert then.'

'Why would anyone choose Lyle over Robert?'

'It's his middle name.

326

'Anyway, Robby got a hog and a nod from the brothers, and roared off with the pack.'

'Did he finish the degree?'

'He completely dropped from sight. He attended classes for a month or two, then his professors never heard from him again.'

'There's no record of where he was? Driver's license? Tax return? Credit card application? Blockbuster membership?'

'*Nada.* Then Crease resurfaced in Saskatchewan in '89, working the crime beat for a local paper and doing some on-air stories for the evening news. Eventually he was offered the job at CTV and relocated to Quebec.'

'So Crease was interested in bikers as a student. That was the Ice Age, remember?'

'Apparently Crease left Saskatchewan in a bit of a hurry.'

'Oh?'

'Ever hear of Operation CACUS?'

'Wasn't that an FBI sting using informants inside the Hells Angels?'

'Informant. Tony Tait joined the Alaska chapter in the early eighties then rose through the ranks to national prominence. He wore a wire for the bureau the whole time.'

'Angels Forever, Forever Angels.'

'I guess Tony preferred cash.'

'Where is he now?'

'In witness protection if he's smart.'

'What does this have to do with Crease?'

'It seems the Mounties had their own investigation going in the eighties.'

'Are you telling me Lyle Crease was an RCMP informant?'

'No one will talk and I've found nothing on paper, but I've always heard we had someone inside for a while. When I leaned on a couple of long-timers, they wouldn't confirm, but they didn't deny.'

He paused.

'And?' I prodded.

'This is just for us, Brennan.'

'But I share everything with my hairstylist.'

He ignored that.

'I run my own sources on the street. Shit, I can't believe I'm telling you this.'

I heard rattling as he switched the receiver to his other hand.

'Word is someone was definitely going to church with the Angels back then, and the guy was American. But it was a two-way street.'

'The snitch was working both sides?'

'That's the story my sources gave up.'

'Risky.'

'As a cerebral hemorrhage.'

'Do you think the plant was Lyle Crease?'

'How else does a guy completely bury six years of his life?'

I thought about that.

'But why would he reappear in such a public line of work?'

'Maybe he figures visibility confers protection.'

For a moment no one spoke.

'Does Claudel know this?'

'I'm about to give him a call.'

'Now what?'

'Now I dig deeper.'

'You'll question Crease?'

'Not yet. We don't want to spook him. And Roy owns Claudel's ass until this funeral is over. But

328

then I'll get him to help me take a run at the guy.'

'Do you think Crease was involved in the Cherokee murder?'

'There's no evidence of that, but he may know something.'

'That cap didn't belong to Cherokee or Dorsey.'

'How do you know that?'

'The inside is covered with dandruff.'

'So?'

'Dorsey shaved his head and Cherokee was bald from chemo.'

'Not bad, Brennan.'

'Gately and Martineau were killed during the time Crease was underground.'

'True.'

'And Savannah Osprey.'

Silence hummed across the wire.

'What about asking Rinaldi?'

'Frog?'

'Yeah, Frog. He was willing to spill his guts about the Gately and Martineau graves. Why not ask him about Cherokee? He might know something.'

'Claudel says they've questioned Frog until they're blue in the face. He was willing to trade the St-Basile-le-Grand bodies because they're old news. He doesn't think the brothers will take him out for that. On anything recent he turns into a potted palm.

'Look, I'll get Claudel to help me flush Crease once the circus is over tomorrow. And, by the way, Brennan, keep your head low. Bandidos patches have been spotted in town, and there are rumors the Angels may make a move. Don't—'

He hesitated.

'Yes?'

'Well, your nephew might want to check out the action.'

My cheeks burned. Claudel had discussed Kit with his CUM buddies.

'My nephew won't be anywhere near that funeral.'

'Good. A Bandidos presence could force a show of strength by the Angels. Might turn hairy.'

We'd hardly hung up when I started worrying. How could I keep Kit away if he was intent on going?

What did Morin want to say about LaManche? Had my old friend died?

Could Ryan be in immediate danger? Had helping me compromised his cover? Had I put him in peril as I had George Dorsey?

I laid my head on the fuzzy green surface of my desk blotter and slowly closed my eyes.

CHAPTER THIRTY-SIX

I was under water and Lyle Crease was speaking to me. Seaweed undulated from below, like strands of hair on a submerged corpse. Here and there a shaft of sunlight penetrated the murky gloom, illuminating tiny particles floating around us.

My neck hurt. I opened my eyes then lifted and rotated my head, gingerly working the kink from my cervical vertebrae. My office was dark except for a pale fluorescence oozing through the glass beside the door.

How long had I slept? I strained to see my watch.

330

When I noticed the figure outside my door an alarm went off in my head. I froze, watching and listening.

The floor was still, except for my heart drumming against my ribs.

The figure stood motionless, a silhouette framed by low-level light spilling from my lab.

My eyes dropped to the phone. Should I call security?

My hand was on the receiver when the door swung inward.

Jocelyn's face looked ghostly. She was dressed in black, and the pale oval head seemed to float, a disembodied jack-o'-lantern with dark holes for eyes and mouth.

'*Oui?*'

I stood, not wanting to give her the advantage of height.

She didn't answer.

'*Puis-je vous aider?*' I asked. May I help you?

Still, she said nothing.

'Please turn on the light, Jocelyn.'

The command brought forth a response where the questions had failed. Her arm rose, and the office was thrown into brightness.

Her hair clung damply to her neck and face, and her clothes were corrugated, as if she'd been sitting a long time in a hot, cramped space. She sniffed and ran the back of a hand under her nose.

'What is it, Jocelyn?'

'You're just letting them slide.' Her voice was hard with anger.

'Who?' I asked, confused.

'I thought you might be different.'

'Different from whom?'

331

'Nobody gives a shit. I hear cops joke about it. I hear them laugh. Another dead biker. Good riddance, they say. It's cheap trash removal.'

'What are you talking about?' My mouth felt dry.

'It's these cops who are a joke. Wolverines. Pfff.' She puffed air through her lips. 'Dickheads would be more like it.'

I was stunned by the hatred in her eyes.

'Tell me why you're upset.'

There was a long silence while she studied my face. Her gaze seemed to focus then withdraw, as if grabbing my image for testing in some mental equation.

'He didn't deserve what he got. No fuckin' way.' The obscenities sounded odd in French.

Quietly I said, 'If you don't explain I can't help you.'

She hesitated, taking a final tally, then the angry eyes fixed on mine.

'George Dorsey didn't kill that old man.'

'Cherokee Desjardins?'

She answered with a shrug.

'How do you know?'

She frowned, deciding if the question was a trap.

'Anyone with the IQ of celery would know that.'

'That's not terribly convincing.'

'A real mechanic would have done it right.'

'What does that mea—'

She cut me off. 'Do you want to hear this or not?'

I waited.

'I was there that night.'

She swallowed.

'I was hardly in the door when some guy showed up, so I went into the bedroom. He and Cherokee

332

started talking, friendly at first, but pretty soon I heard shouting, then slamming and banging. I knew something was coming down, so I hid in the closet.'

'Why were you there, Jocelyn?'

'Cherokee was gonna sponsor me in the Kiwanis,' she sneered.

'Go on.'

'I hunkered in until things quieted down, then when I thought the guy was gone, I started to split. That's when I heard the gunshot. Jesus.'

Her eyes slipped past me to a spot somewhere over my shoulder. I tried to imagine what for her was memory.

'Then I heard the guy banging drawers and flinging crap around. I figured he was a smackhead looking for Cherokee's rock, and I nearly shit my shorts, 'cause I knew the stuff was in the bedroom with me.

'When I smelled smoke it was time to haul ass, junkie or no junkie. I smashed the window, dropped to the alley, and ran to the corner. Now here's the weird part. When I cut around the building and looked up the block, the little roach was still outside Cherokee's pad, scratching at something in the mud. Then a car turned onto the street and he took off.'

'What was he looking for?'

'How the hell should I know?'

'Then what?'

'When I was sure he wasn't coming back I walked over and poked around.'

There was a long silence. Then she dropped a purse strap from her shoulder, dug inside, and withdrew a small, flat object.

'I found this where the guy was squatting.' She thrust it at me.

I unfolded a pharmacy sack and removed a photograph framed in cheap plastic. Two men smiled through a mist of spattered blood, inner arms entwined, outer arms raised, middle fingers pointing skyward. The one on the right was Cherokee Desjardins, robust and full of life.

When I recognized the man on the left my throat tightened and my breath came in short, quick spurts. Jocelyn went on speaking but I didn't hear her.

'. . . torn bag beside it. When the headlights hit him he bolted like a jackrabbit.'

My thoughts raced. Images flashed.

'. . . why the fuck he wanted it. But go figure what burns in a junked-out head.'

I saw a face.

'. . . wish I'd gotten a look at him.'

I saw a baseball cap.

'. . . this son of a bitch get away with it.'

I saw flecks of gold circling in a watery vortex.

'. . . didn't deserve a shiv up his ass.'

I pulled myself back to the present and willed my face neutral.

'Jocelyn, do you know a newscaster named Lyle Crease?'

'English?'

'Yes.'

'I don't watch English TV. Why are you asking me that? Look, I'm trying to tell you Dorsey didn't whack Cherokee.'

'No,' I agreed. 'He didn't.'

But I had a pretty good idea who did.

When Jocelyn left I phoned Claudel. He was not in, but this time I hung up and dialed his pager.

Urgent enough, I thought, as I entered my number.

When Claudel called back I relayed Jocelyn's story.

'Can she identify the man?'

'Never saw his face.'

'Fantastique.'

'It's Crease.'

'How can you be sure?'

'The cap found in Desjardins' apartment had a USC logo. Crease went to school there.'

'We've alread—'

'Did Charbonneau tell you about the dandruff?'

'Yes.'

'I had the pleasure of dining with Crease not too long ago. He has enough dandruff to open a ski hill.'

'Motive?'

I described what I'd seen in the photo.

'Holy Mother of Christ.'

Rarely had I heard Claudel blaspheme.

'What's this woman's relationship to Dorsey?'

'She was not receptive to personal inquiries.'

'Can she be trusted?' His breath sounded moist against the mouthpiece.

'She obviously has a habit, but I believe her.'

'If she was terrified, why hang around?'

'She probably thought the intruder dropped drugs and she had a shot at a free score.'

'Michel Charbonneau told me of your conversation.' More breathing. 'I think it's time to

335

net this Mr. Crease.'

When we disconnected I phoned for air reservations. Willing or not, Kit was on his way to Texas. Until then, I wasn't going to let him out of my sight.

*   *   *

I arrived home to find Kit in the shower.

'Have you eaten?' I shouted through the door when I heard the sound of the water stop.

'Not much.'

O.K, podna. I, too, can cook pasta.

I made a run to Le Faubourg for scallops and greens. Back home I sautéed the seafood with onions and mushrooms, then mixed and added a yogurt-mustard-lemon-dill sauce. I ladled the mollusk concoction over angel-hair pasta, and served it with a baguette and tossed salad.

Even Kit was impressed.

We talked as we ate, but said little.

'How was your day?' I asked.

'Pretty good.'

'What did you do?'

'Not much.'

'Did you stay here?'

'I rode the subway to some island and cruised around the parks.'

'Île-Ste-Hélène.'

'Yeah. There's a beach out there and lots of trails. It's pretty slick.'

That explained the skateboard in the entrance hall.

'How 'bout your day?' he asked, picking a crouton from the salad remains.

'Pretty good.'

A cokehead security risk in our own lab accused me of indifference to bikers, and I discovered one of your *Easy Rider* playmates may be a killer.

'Cool,' he said.

I took a deep breath.

'I made airline reservations today.'

'Off on another trip?'

'The flight is for you.'

'Uh-oh. The bum's rush.' He kept his eyes on the salad bowl.

'Kit, you know I love you, and I love having you here, but I think it's time you went home.'

'What is it they say about houseguests and old fish? Or is it relatives?'

'You know that isn't it. But you have been here almost two weeks. Aren't you bored? Don't you want to see your friends and check on the boat?'

He shrugged. 'They're not going anywhere.'

'I'm sure Harry and your father both miss you.'

'Oh, yeah. They've been burning up the phone wires.'

'Your mother's in Mexico. It's not eas—'

'She arrived in Houston yesterday.'

'What?'

'I didn't want to tell you.'

'Oh?'

'I knew you'd hustle me off when she got back.'

'Why would you think that?'

His hand dropped, fingers curling over the bowl's edge. Outside, a siren wailed, soft, loud, soft. When he answered he didn't look at me.

'When I was a little kid, you always stayed just out of reach, afraid Harry might feel jealous. Or angry. Or resentful. Or inadequate. Or, or—'

337

He picked a crouton, threw it back. Drops of oil jumped onto the table.

'Kit!'

'And, you know what? She *ought* to feel inadequate. The only thing I should thank Harry for is not burying me in a goddam shoe box when I was born.' He got to his feet. 'I'll pack my stuff.'

I stood and grabbed his arm. When I looked up his face was tight with anger.

'Harry has nothing to do with this. I'm sending you home because I'm frightened for you. I'm frightened over the people you've been seeing and what they may be doing, and I'm afraid you're involved with things that could place you in jeopardy.'

'That's bullshit. I'm not a baby anymore. I make my own decisions.'

I flashed on Frog Rinaldi, his shadow rippling across a grave. Gately and Martineau had made a decision. A deadly decision. So had Savannah Osprey. And George Dorsey. I would not permit Kit to do the same.

'If something happened to you I'd never forgive myself.'

'I'm not going to get hurt.'

'I can't take that chance. I think you've been putting yourself in dangerous circumstances.'

'I'm not six years old, Aunt Tempe. You can kick me out of here, but you can't tell me what to do anymore.' His jaw muscles bunched, then his Adam's apple rose and dropped.

We both fell silent, realizing our proximity to words that, once spoken, would wound. I released my grip, and Kit disappeared down the hall, bare feet swishing softly on the carpet.

I slept fitfully, then woke and lay in the dark, thinking about my nephew. The window shade changed from black to charcoal. I gave up on sleep, brewed tea, and took it to the patio.

Bundled in Gran's quilt, I watched stars fade overhead, and remembered evenings in Charlotte. When Katy and Kit were small we would identify constellations and christen patterns of our own. Katy would see a mouse, a puppy, a pair of skates. Kit would see a mother and child.

I tucked my feet and sipped the hot liquid.

How could I make Kit understand my reasons for sending him away? He was young, and vulnerable, and desperate for recognition and approval.

But recognition and approval from whom? Why does he want to stay with me? Do I provide a base from which he can pursue activities he won't disclose to me?

From the day of Kit's arrival his apathy had puzzled me. While Katy would have craved constant peer contact, my nephew seemed satisfied with limited sight-seeing, video games, and the company of an aging aunt and her aging cat. The current Kit was jarringly at odds with the youngster I remembered. Skinned knees. Stitches. Broken bones. Kit's perpetual motion had kept Harry on a first-name basis with her local paramedics for the duration of his childhood.

Had Kit been staying in, or had he been out and about with Lyle Crease? Or the Preacher? Or the hyena? Was he lethargic around me because he was tired?

More tea. Tepid now.

I pictured two men behind blood-spattered

plastic, and even the tea couldn't warm my chill.

Was I making a mistake? If Kit was going through a rough patch could I have some positive influence? If he was involved in something precarious would it be safer to keep him with me?

No. The overall situation made it too risky. I would stick to my plan. My nephew would be in Texas before George Dorsey's body was underground.

As dawn crawled up from the horizon, a gentle wash spread across my yard, tinting trees, hedges, and the old brownstones across the street. Edges softened, until the city resembled a Winslow Homer landscape. A gentle watercolor, a perfect backdrop for a gangland funeral.

I poured the last of my tea onto the lawn, and went to wake my nephew.

His room was empty.

CHAPTER THIRTY-SEVEN

A note was stuck to the refrigerator. I read it in place, afraid to trust my unsteady hands.

Thanks for everything. Don't worry. I'm with friends.

Friends?

My heart felt dead in my chest.

I looked at the clock. The Dorsey funeral would start in a little more than an hour.

I dialed Claudel's pager, then made coffee, dressed, and made the bed.

Seven-fifteen.

340

I sipped and picked at a cuticle.

The earth rotated. Tectonic plates shifted. Twelve acres of rain forest disappeared from the globe forever.

I went to the bathroom, combed my hair, dabbed on makeup, added blush, returned to the kitchen for a second cup.

Seven-thirty. Where the hell was Claudel?

Back to the bathroom, where I wet and recombed my hair. I was reaching for dental floss when the phone rang.

'I wouldn't have thought you an early riser.' Claudel.

'Kit's gone.'

'Cibole!'

I could hear traffic in the background.

'Where are you?'

'Outside the church.'

'How does it look?'

'Like a theme park of deadly sins. Sloth and gluttony are well represented.'

'I don't suppose you've seen him.'

'No, but I might not spot Fidel Castro in this crowd. Looks like every biker on the continent is here.'

'Crease?'

'No sign.'

I heard a hitch in his breathing.

'What?'

'Charbonneau and I did some more checking. From '83 to '89 Lyle Crease was playing foreign correspondent, not secret agent. But the only reports he was filing were with the guard on his cell block.'

'He did time?' I asked, unnerved.

'Six years, south of the border.'

'Mexico?'

'Juárez.'

My heart came back to life and thumped inside my chest.

'Crease is a killer and Kit may be with him. I've got to do something.'

Claudel's voice went cop cold.

'Don't even think about freelancing, Ms. Brennan. These bikers look like sharks smelling the water for blood, and it could get rough down here.'

'And Kit could get sucked into the feeding frenzy!' I heard my voice catch, and stopped to steady myself.

'I'll send a patrol car to pick Crease up.'

'Suppose he has funeral plans?'

'If he shows his face, we'll arrest him.'

'And if a nineteen-year-old kid gets nailed along the way?' I was almost yelling.

'All I'm saying is don't come down here.'

'Then find this bastard!'

I'd hardly disconnected when I heard my cell phone.

Kit!

I raced to the bedroom and pulled it from my purse.

The voice was quavery, like a child after a long cry.

'You need to know what they're doing.'

At first I felt confusion, then recognition, then apprehension.

'Who, Jocelyn?'

'Someone needs to know what these Heathen scum are doing.' She inhaled sharply through her nose.

'Tell me.'

'This town is turning into a slaughterhouse, and your kid is ambling right down the chute.'

My stomach went tight with fear.

'What do you mean?'

'I know what's coming down.'

'How does this involve my nephew?'

'I need money and I need cover.' Her voice was stronger now.

'Tell me what you know.'

'Not till we deal.'

'I don't have that kind of authority.'

'You know who does.'

'I will try to help you,' I said. 'But I need to know if my nephew is in danger.'

Silence. Then, 'Fuck, I'm dead anyway. Meet me in the Guy métro in twenty minutes. Westbound platform.'

Her voice was leaden with defeat.

'I'll wait ten minutes. If you're late, or bring a buddy, I'm gone, and the kid'll be a footnote when this whole thing is written up.'

Dead air.

I dialed Claudel's pager and left my number. Then I stared at the phone, ticking through options.

Claudel was unreachable. I couldn't wait for a return call.

Quickwater.

Ditto.

Claudel hadn't told me to avoid the underground. I'd meet with Jocelyn, then ring him when I had information.

I punched in the number at Carcajou

343

headquarters, but didn't hit send. Then I slid the phone into my purse, and bolted for the door.

*   *   *

Jocelyn was seated at the end of the tunnel, a canvas duffel in her lap, another at her feet. She had chosen a corner bench, as if concrete backing conferred protection from whatever menace she feared. Her teeth worked a thumbnail as she scanned the commuters standing to either side of the tracks.

She spotted me and followed my approach. I stayed to the middle of the platform, my pulse louder in my ears than any competing noise. The air was warm and stale, as though breathed and rebreathed by legions of subterranean travelers. I felt an acrid taste and swallowed hard.

Jocelyn watched in silence as I sat on the bench. Her chalky skin looked violet in the artificial light, the whites of her eyes yellow.

I started to speak but she stopped me with a hand movement.

'I'm going to say this once, then I'm taking off. I talk. You listen.'

I said nothing.

'I'm a junkie, we both know that. I'm also a whore and a liar.' Her eyes roved the faces lining the tracks, her movements ragged and jerky.

'Here's the mind-fuck. I come from a Girl Scout–summer camp–tuna casserole background just like you. Only somewhere along the way I joined a freak show I can't escape.'

Purple shadow turned her eyes cadaverous.

'Lately I've been doing some hard time with

344

hate. I hate everyone and everything on the planet. But mostly I hate myself.'

She backhanded a sheen of liquid from below her nostrils.

'You know it's closing time when you can't look in a pond or pass a mirror or storefront because you despise what you see looking back.'

She turned to me, the lobotomy eyes burning with rage and guilt.

'Talking to you may get me killed, but I want out. And I want these guys to pay.'

'What are you offering?'

'Spider Marcotte and the little girl.'

'I'm listening.'

'It was George Dorsey. He's dead now, so it don't matter.' She looked away, then focused again on my face.

'Marcotte was Heathen payback for the Vipers blowing up the Vaillancourts. George and a full-patcher named Sylvain Lecomte took him out. The kid was a mistake.'

She braced a booted foot against the duffel.

'George thought the hit was his ticket to stardom. But the Heathens burned George because they thought he was going to give up Lecomte.' She snorted and tipped her chin. 'George was actually waiting for me near the Cherokee hit scene. When he got busted by the Carcajou and then set up a meet with you, the Heathen brothers decided to do George before he could finger Lecomte. Big man, Lecomte. Wasted a little girl. Big turd,' she spat.

'Anything else?'

She shrugged.

'The St-Basile burials. I've been on the scene nine years. I've got plenty to trade.'

345

'Are you talking about witness protection?'

'Money and out.'

'Rehab?'

She shrugged.

'What about Cherokee?'

'He brought the girl's bones up North, but I've put his story on paper. I give it up when my ass is safe and a long way from here.'

She sounded like the thought was collapsing even as she voiced it.

'Why now?'

'They wasted Dorsey. He did their work, and they wasted him.'

She shook her head and turned back to her surveillance.

'And I've become them.' Her voice dripped with self-loathing. 'I set that reporter up.'

'What reporter?'

'Lyle Crease. I figured something was up when you asked about him, so I tuned into the news that night. Sure enough, he was the one I saw at Cherokee's place. I dropped his name to the Vipers for a bag of flake.'

'Jesus Christ.'

'I'm a goddam junkie, all right?' It was almost a shriek. 'When you're coming down and the world is closing in, you'll dime your mother for a score. Besides, I had other reasons.'

Her hands began to tremble, and she pressed her fingertips to her temples.

'Later, I phoned Crease to set up a meet at the cemetery.' Again the self-deprecating laugh. 'Back on big rock candy mountain.'

'Did they ask you to arrange a meeting?'

'Yeah. They plan to take Crease out, and some

Heathens, too.'

'What does this have to do with my nephew?' My mouth was so dry I could hardly speak.

'Crease said not to try anything funny because he would have the kid with him.'

I heard the rumble of a train far up the tunnel.

Again, the head shake. Her face looked hard in profile.

'This funeral's going to be one big snuff film, and your nephew could have a starring role.'

I felt a change in air pressure as the train grew louder. Passengers on the far side moved toward the platform's edge.

Jocelyn's gaze froze on something across the tracks. The hooded eyes grew puzzled a moment, then widened in recognition. Her mouth opened.

'Lecom—!' she screamed, and her hand shot to the duffel's zipper.

The train thundered in.

Jocelyn's head flew backward, and a dark cumulus spread around it on the wall. I threw myself to the concrete, and covered my head with both hands.

Brakes shrilled, whooshed.

I tried to scramble behind the bench, under it, anywhere. It was bolted to the wall! There was nowhere to go!

Doors opened. Commuters both boarded and left the train.

On our side, screams. Faces turning. Bewilderment. Horror.

The train barreled off.

Then the sounds changed. Panicked retreat. People running.

After a full minute with no more shots, I

cautiously rose to my feet, bone and brain matter on my jacket. My stomach lurched and I tasted bile.

Voices. English. French.

'*Attention!*'

'*Sacrifice!*'

'Call the police.'

'*Elle est morte?*'

'They're on the way.'

'*Mon Dieu!*'

Confusion. A rush for the escalators.

Jocelyn's body twitched, and a thread of saliva trailed from the corner of her mouth. I could smell urine and feces, and see blood pooling on the bench and floor.

I had a vision of Cherokee. Others, fast, like flashbulbs. Gately. Martineau. Savannah Osprey. Emily Anne Toussaint.

I could not have stopped those deaths, nor had I done anything to bring them about. And I could do nothing for Jocelyn. But I would not allow my nephew to be the next casualty. I would not permit that. Death dealt out by bikers would not happen. Not to Kit. Not to Harry. And not to me.

On rubbery legs I staggered to the escalators, rode to ground level, and was carried along by the crush of pedestrians distancing themselves from tragedy. Already two cruisers blocked the entrance, doors open, lights flashing. Sirens foretold the arrival of others.

I should have stayed, given my story, and let the police handle the rest. I felt sick, and repulsed by the carnage we seemed powerless to stop. Fear for Kit twisted in my gut like a physical pain, overriding judgment and sense of duty.

I broke from the crowd and ran.

CHAPTER THIRTY-EIGHT

My hands still trembled as I let myself into my silent condo. I called out, not expecting an answer.

From my briefcase, I dug out the envelope Charbonneau had delivered from Roy. I scanned the protocol, checked my watch, and raced to the garage.

Though rush hour was tapering off, Centre-ville remained clogged. I crawled along, engine idling, heart racing, hands sweaty on the wheel, until I finally broke free, shot up the mountain, and pulled into a car park opposite Lac aux Castors.

The cemeteries sprawled along the uphill side of Chemin Remembrance, cities of the dead flowing toward the horizon. According to Roy's map, the Dorsey plot was just inside the perimeter fence, twenty yards from the south gate. The cortege would arrive from the east and enter the cemetery opposite where I sat.

I wiped my hands on my jeans and checked the time.

Soon.

Normally, early morning meant few people on the mountain, but today mourners lined the shoulder and stood along the drive leading through the gate. Others wandered among the trees and headstones inside the cemetery grounds. The ritual hypocrisy struck me as surreal. Heathens and Rock Machine, burying with great ceremony the comrade they themselves had killed.

Manned cruisers were parked on both sides of Remembrance, lights flashing, radios sputtering. I locked the car and ran across the road, slipping on new grass beginning to green the median. Hurrying along the shoulder, I inspected those milling about. Most were male, young, and white. I saw Charbonneau leaning on a squad car, but there was no sign of Crease or Kit.

A uniformed officer stopped me at the gate.

'Whoa, there. Slow down, madam. I'm sorry, but there is a funeral expected shortly, and this entrance is closed. You'll have to move on.'

He held out both arms, as if physical restraint might be necessary.

'Dr. Temperance Brennan,' I identified myself. 'Carcajou.'

His face crimped with suspicion. He was about to speak when a sharp whistle split the air, like someone calling a dog. We both turned.

Claudel stood on a knoll a short distance back from the Dorsey grave site. When he had our attention he gave a crisp come-on signal with one hand. The guard pointed to me, and Claudel nodded. With a disapproving look, he passed me through the gate.

The Mont-Royal cemeteries are strange and beautiful places, acres of elegant landscaping and ornate funerary architecture rising and falling across the curves of the mountain. Mont-Royal. The Jewish. Notre-Dame-des-Neiges.

The latter is for the Catholic dead. Some are buried with elaborate tombs and monuments, others with simple plaques and ten-year leases. Since the mid-nineteenth century, over a million souls have been laid to rest within the cemetery's wrought-iron fence. The complex contains mausoleums, crematoria, columbaria, and

350

interment sites for the more traditional.

There are sections for the Polish. The Vietnamese. The Greek. The French. The English. Visitors can obtain maps pinpointing the graves of Montreal's famous. The Dorsey family lay in the Troie section, not far from Marie Travers, the thirties singer known as La Bolduc.

More relevant was the fact that today's burial would take place less than ten yards from Chemin Remembrance. Roy's advisers felt that if a hit was planned the cemetery was the most likely location. And the most difficult to secure.

I sprinted up the gravel path and scrambled uphill to join Claudel. His greeting was not warm.

'What the hell do you think you're doing?'

'Kit is with Crease and they're coming here,' I panted.

'You just don't listen, do you, Ms. Brennan?' His eyes swept the crowd as he spoke. 'There's already been one homicide today.'

My mind flashed to the métro. Jocelyn, searching. Jocelyn, in agonal spasm.

'I was with her.'

'What?' Claudel's eyes flew to my face, then dropped to the blood and brain matter on my jacket.

I told him.

'And you left the scene?'

'There was nothing I could do.'

'I'm not going to point out the obvious.'

'She was dead!' I snapped. Fear, anger, and guilt churned in my head, and his unfeeling attitude did nothing to calm me. A sob welled in my chest.

No. No tears!

At that moment his Carcajou partner appeared

over the edge of the hillock. Quickwater approached Claudel, spoke in a low voice, and left without acknowledging my presence. In seconds he reappeared below, wove through a grouping of ornamental headstones, and positioned himself behind a pink granite obelisk.

'If I say dive, you take cover. No questions. No heroics. Do you understand?'

'Fine.'

He did not resume our conversation.

That was fine, too. I recoiled from voicing my fear for Kit, afraid that shaping the threat into words might cause it to be realized. I would tell him later about Lecomte.

Five minutes passed. Ten. I scanned the bereaved. Business suits mixed with chains, swastikas, studs, and bandannas.

I heard the noise before I saw the procession. It started as a low rumble and grew to a roar as two police cruisers rounded the curve, then a hearse, limo, and a half-dozen cars. A phalanx of cycles followed, four abreast behind the cars, in twos and threes farther back. Soon the road was dense with bikes, and I could not see the end of the line.

Sun flashed off chrome as the cortege slowed and turned into the cemetery. The air filled with the sound of engines and shifting gears as bikers broke formation and massed around the entrance. Men in greasy Levis, beards, and shades began to dismount and move toward the gate.

Claudel's eyes narrowed as he watched the graveyard below become a human zoo.

'*Sacré bleu.* We should keep this outside the fence.'

'Roy says that's not possible.'

'Civil rights be damned. Bar the vermin, and let their lawyers sue.'

The cortege turned left and crept along the tree-lined road skirting the Troie section. When it pulled to a stop a suited man moved to the limo and opened the rear door. People emerged wearing the bewildered expressions of those unfamiliar with personal service.

I watched the funeral director lead the family to folding chairs beneath a bright green canopy. An old man in an old suit. Two matrons in black dresses, faux pearls around their necks. A young woman in a floral print. A boy in a jacket with sleeves that did not reach his wrists. An elderly priest.

As friends and relatives climbed from cars, Dorsey's other family drew together. Joking and calling, they formed a ragged horseshoe outside the canopy. Under it, the new grave lay draped like a patient awaiting surgery.

A detachment of eight slowly gathered at the hearse, all in denim and shades. At a sign from the director, an assistant offered gloves, which a behemoth in a do-rag batted aside. Barehanded, the pallbearers slid the casket free and carried it toward the canopy, struggling under the weight of the deceased and his packaging.

The branches above me lifted and fell, and I caught the scent of flowers and freshly turned earth. The bikes had gone still. A sob drifted from under the canopy, slipping free on the breeze to ride over the graves of the surrounding dead.

'Sacré bleu!'

When I turned, Claudel was staring at the gate. I followed his gaze, and fear shot through me.

Crease and Kit were making their way through those lingering at the entrance, moving past the semicircle of mourners, and stepping into the shadow of a life-sized bronze angel, its arms perpendicularly outstretched, as if treading water.

I started to speak but Claudel silenced me with a hand. Lifting his radio, he looked down at his partner. Quickwater made a subtle gesture, first to his right, then straight ahead.

I looked where Quickwater had indicated. Beyond the mourners, partially hidden among the tombstones and trees, were men whose attention was not on the service. Like Claudel and Quickwater their eyes never rested, and they carried handsets. Unlike the Carcajou investigators, these men were tattooed and booted.

I looked a question at Claudel.

'Rock Machine security.'

Under the canopy the priest stood and opened his prayer book. Hands rose and fell, crossing chests. Missal pages fluttered as the old priest began the rites for the dead, and he extended a gnarled finger to hold them still. The breeze played with his words, stealing some, sharing others.

'—who art in heaven, hallow—'

Beside me, Claudel tensed.

A man had appeared among a cluster of cement crypts sixty feet to the west. Head down, he walked toward the canopy.

'Thy kingdom— thy will—'

I looked down at Quickwater. His eyes were fixed on the Rock Machine sentries. One spoke into his walkie-talkie. Across the grounds, another listened. Quickwater stared at them, then raised his radio.

354

Claudel keyed his partner, eyes glued to the man closing in on the grave site.

'—*forgive— who trespass against us—*'

'Trouble?' I asked when the transmission ended.

'He's not Rock Machine. He could be Bandidos, but the lookouts aren't sure.'

'How—?'

'He reads lips.'

'Do you recognize the guy?'

'He's not a cop.'

My nerves prickled. As with many in the crowd, a bandanna covered the lower face of the approaching figure, and a cap shadowed his eyes. But this man looked wrong. His jacket was too heavy for the day, his arms held too tightly to his sides.

Suddenly a Jeep roared up Remembrance and veered toward the fence. At the same moment a motor flared and a Harley shot through the gate.

The next events seemed to continue forever, each unfolding in slow motion. They told me later that the entire episode lasted two minutes.

In the horseshoe of bikers a man spun sideways and flew into a canopy support pole. Screams. Gunfire. The tent collapsed. The crowd froze momentarily, then scattered.

'Down!'

Claudel pushed hard on my back, slamming me to the ground.

A bearded man crawled from the heap of canvas and ran toward a stone Jesus with outstretched arms. Halfway there his back arched, and he fell forward. He was dragging himself across the ground, when his body jerked again and collapsed.

I spit dirt from my mouth and tried to see. A

bullet whacked into the chestnut behind me.

When I looked again the jacketed man with the bandanna-covered face was behind a vault, bending toward the base of the crypt. He stood, and sun glinted off steel as he pulled back the slide on a semiautomatic. Then he dropped his hand straight to his side and walked toward the swimming angel.

Fear shot through me.

Without thinking, I began to crawl toward the path.

'Get back here, Brennan,' Claudel shouted.

Ignoring him, I pushed to my feet and scrabbled down the hill, keeping to the far side to avoid gunfire. Crouching low and darting from monument to monument, I worked my way toward the statue sheltering my nephew.

Pistols and semiautomatics barked around me. The Angels were reaping their vengeance, and the Machine were returning fire. Bullets sparked off tombs and headstones. A granite splinter struck my cheek, and something warm trickled down my face.

As I rounded the statue on one side, the jacketed man appeared on the other. Crease and Kit stood directly between us. The gunman raised his arm and aimed.

Crease swung Kit around to shield himself.

'Get down!' I screamed. Sweat trickled from my hairline, and the wind felt cold on my face.

It took Kit a moment to realize his situation. Then he spun and brought his knee up hard between the reporter's legs. Crease's hand flew up and his mouth opened in a perfect O, but one hand held tight to Kit's shirt.

Kit twisted to his right, but Crease yanked hard

356

just as the shooter squeezed the trigger. A deafening sound reverberated off the bronze torso and wings above us. My nephew fell to the ground and lay still.

'No!' My scream was drowned by the sound of engines and gunfire.

Another thunderous roar. I saw a hole open in Crease's chest, and a liquid river of red streamed down his front. He went rigid for a moment, then dropped next to Kit.

I sensed a figure moving around the monument, and threw myself forward to cover Kit. His hand moved feebly and a burgundy stain was spreading across his back.

The figure loomed larger and filled the gap between the angel and the neighboring tomb, feet spread, pistol extended in a two-handed grip toward the gunman above us. The muzzle flashed. Another deafening crack. The gunman's eye exploded, blood bubbled from his mouth, and he crumpled to the ground beside me.

My eyes met eyes bluer than a butane flame. Then Ryan whirled and was gone.

At that instant Quickwater flung himself under the angel and dragged and shoved Kit and me toward the base. Crouching in front of the supine bodies of Crease and his assassin, he swept his gun in wide arcs, using the monument for cover.

I tried to swallow, but my mouth was a desert. Bullets strafed the earth beside me, and again I was conscious of the smell of dirt and flowers. Outside our tiny cave I could see figures running in all directions.

Quickwater's eyes scanned, his body coiled and ready to spring. In the distance I heard sirens and

357

engines, then the sound of an explosion.

Adrenaline pumping, I pressed a hand to the hole in my nephew's back, and tried to stuff a hankie into the one in his chest. Time lost all meaning.

Then it was silent. Nothing appeared to move.

Beyond Quickwater I saw people crawl from under the canopy, disheveled and sobbing. Bikers emerged from hiding and coalesced into groups, faces furious, fists pistoning as if they were angry hip-hop artists. Others lay motionless on the ground. Ryan was nowhere to be seen.

Far down the mountain sirens wailed. I glanced at Quickwater, and our eyes locked. My lips trembled, but no words came.

Quickwater reached down and wiped blood from my cheek, then gently brushed the hair from my face. His eyes went deep into mine, acknowledging what we had just seen, the secret we shared. My chest heaved and tears burned my lids. I turned away, not wanting a witness to my frailty.

My gaze fell on a tiny portrait, encased in plastic and secured to the angel's pedestal. A solemn face stared out, separated by death and faded by years of rain and sun.

No, God. Please, no. Not Kit.

I looked down at the blood oozing through my fingers. Openly weeping, I applied more pressure, then closed my eyes and prayed.

CHAPTER THIRTY-NINE

'What the hell did you plan to do?' Charbonneau asked.

'I didn't plan. I acted on instinct.'

'You were unarmed.'

'I was armed with righteous fury.'

'Rarely wins against a semiautomatic.'

A week had passed since the shoot-out at Notre-Dame-des-Neiges, and we'd been over it a dozen times. Charbonneau was in my lab, watching me prepare Savannah Osprey's bones for shipment.

DNA sequencing had come back positive, linking the Myrtle Beach skeleton to the remains from St-Basile-le-Grand. Kate Brophy had established that Savannah's mother was dead, but had located a maternal aunt. Burial would take place in North Carolina.

I felt melancholy each time I pictured that lonely, little ceremony. My satisfaction at finding and identifying Savannah was tempered by sadness over her life. She was so young and frail, hampered by physical disability, lonely, loathed by her father, abandoned in death by her mother. I wondered if there was anyone left who would care for her grave.

'Do you think Savannah chose to go to Myrtle Beach that day?' I asked, changing the subject.

'According to Crease the kid went willingly.'

'Bad decision.' I pictured the pale little waif and wondered what had led her to it.

'Yeah. A deadly decision.'

I looked at Charbonneau, surprised at how closely his thought echoed mine. There had been so many fatal decisions. Gately and Martineau. Jocelyn Dion. George Dorsey. The Hells Angels responsible for the cemetery attack. And near-fatal decisions. Kit and Crease, both of whom had managed to survive.

A Hells Angels death squad had been sent from the States to blow away Crease because Jocelyn had fingered him as Cherokee Desjardins' killer. The Angels had intended to send a message that killing one of their own meant certain retribution, and had chosen a very public forum to deliver that message. The gunman assigned to Crease was to have escaped by cycle. The cycle did get away, but the shooter didn't. Ryan and Quickwater saw to that, though the public version would be different.

Unfamiliar with the local terrain, the shooters in the Jeep went off the mountain while speeding from police. The two in front were killed in the crash, the third hospitalized with multiple injuries. A routine check turned up a New York warrant for murder. The man was providing limited cooperation, preferring the non–death penalty attitude of our northern neighbors to the laws of his home state. His thinking was that a life sentence in Canada was preferable to a lethal injection in New York, even though the state hadn't executed anyone since 1963.

Six hours of surgery had pulled Crease through, but the reporter was still in intensive care. The story of his involvement was emerging piecemeal as his periods of lucidity lengthened.

Crease and Cherokee traveled with the Angels in the early eighties, the latter aspiring to brotherhood, the former a wannabe academic charmed by the biker lifestyle. The two were drawn

360

together by their shared Canadian roots.

According to Crease, he and Cherokee encountered Savannah Osprey on the Myrtle Beach run and invited her to ride along. Later, a party turned ugly and Savannah wanted to leave. Things got out of hand, the girl was strangled, and Cherokee hid the body in the woods.

'Has Crease admitted to a part in the murder?'

'He denies that, but admits to the return visit, when Cherokee decided to collect bones to decorate the clubhouse.'

'The bastards.'

I glanced at Savannah's remains and experienced the same anger and repulsion I'd felt on seeing the photo Jocelyn had taken from Cherokee's apartment. I'd recognized the cranium instantly by the tiny burr hole in its side. The skull was mounted on a wall, the leg bones crossed below like the symbol on a pirate flag. Crease and Cherokee were posed below the macabre Jolly Roger, hands raised in a one-finger salute.

'Where was that snapshot taken?' Until then, I hadn't asked.

'At the Vipers' clubhouse in St-Basile. Crease and Cherokee went back to Myrtle Beach the winter after Savannah was killed. They checked out the body, found the skull and leg bones still under the tin, the rest skeletonized and scattered by animals. Thinking a human skull would be a hit with the brothers, they decided to haul the undamaged parts back to Quebec.'

I was too disgusted to respond.

'Savannah's bones decorated the bar for several years before the Vipers, worried about heat from the police, buried them in the woods.'

'Why so close to Gately and Martineau?'

'The proximity of the graves was coincidental. Gately and Martineau were strictly business. Back in '87 the Angels wanted a bar that Gately owned. That was their way of getting it. Martineau was a friend of Gately's, and had taken a shot at an Angel who was hassling Gately about the bar.'

'Bad move.'

'Indeed.'

'If Crease is innocent of the Osprey murder, why was he so desperate to get that picture?'

'He figured that with the bones becoming front-page news, his past might come out and his career would be over.'

'So he killed Cherokee for it.'

'We haven't worked that out, but we will. And the blood on the thing is gonna put him away for the rest of his worthless life.'

'He'll deny any link to that photo, and your sole eyewitness won't be testifying.'

Jocelyn had arrived at the Montreal General DOA.

'Then the dandruff will nail him.'

'What if the DNA is inconclusive?'

'It won't matter. He's dirty and he'll give it up.'

So we believed, for another nine hours.

*   *   *

At the hospital the blinds were drawn, the room filled with slatted sunlight. Kit was staring at a talk show, the sound turned completely down, while Harry flipped through a fashion magazine. Though he'd been moved from intensive care four days earlier, his face was still white, and his eyes looked

362

as though they'd been underbrushed with violet paint. His chest was bandaged, and an IV needle ran into a vein in his left arm.

He brightened when he saw me.

'How's it going?' I rubbed the back of his arm.

'Acey, peachy.'

'I brought more flowers,' I chirped, holding out the selection I'd grabbed at the hospital florist. 'The Spring Daisies Bouquet. Guaranteed to freshen the most sagging spirit.'

'Pretty soon we're going to need some kind of permit with all the photosynthesis going on in here.'

Wriggling to sit higher, he reached for the orange juice on his tray, winced and pulled back.

'Let me help with that.'

I handed him the glass, and he settled into his pillows, closing his lips around the straw.

'How's the breathing?'

'O.K.' He rested the glass on his chest.

The bullet intended for Crease had caught Kit at a high angle. It fractured two ribs, nicked a lung, and exited through muscle. A complete recovery was expected.

'Have they busted these sons of bitches yet?'

I turned to my sister. She sat in a corner chair, her long legs braided like a Chinese contortionist's.

'The getaway cycle got away. The guy who survived the Jeep crash has been charged with attempted murder, among other things. He's cooperating with the police.'

'Tempe, if I get my h—'

'Harry, do you think you could ask the nurse for another vase?'

'I get it. Time for an auntie-nephie chat. I'll

363

scoot for a nicotine hit.' She gathered her purse, kissed her son on the top of the head, and stepped into the corridor, leaving behind a trail of Cristalle.

Perching on the side of the bed, I squeezed Kit's hand. It felt cool and pliant.

'Acey, peachy?'

'It's a drag, Aunt Tempe. Every five minutes some nurse sticks me with a needle or shoves a thermometer up my butt. And we're not talking 'Hot Lips' Houlihan here. These women feed on small furry things.'

'Uh-huh.'

'And they're saying I have to stay another two or three days.'

'The doctors want to be sure that lung won't collapse again.'

He hesitated, then, 'What was the count?'

'In addition to you and Crease, two family members were wounded, and three Heathens and Rock Machine bikers were killed. Of the attackers, one got away, one was killed, two died in a crash, and one was captured. It was a bloodbath the likes of which has seldom been seen in Canada.'

He dropped his eyes and picked at the blanket with his free hand.

'How's he doing?'

'He'll make it. But he's about to be charged with the Cherokee Desjardins murder.'

'I know Lyle didn't kill that guy. He couldn't.'

'He tried to sacrifice you to protect himself.'

Kit said nothing.

'And he was using you to get information.'

'He may have done that, but he would never murder anyone.'

I pictured the skull and crossbones, but said

nothing to contradict him.

'Why did he bring you to that funeral?'

'He didn't want to, but I was crazy to see the bikes. I told him I'd go on my own if he didn't take me. Hell, except for going to that cycle shop, Lyle didn't even hang around with those guys. When we went there he tried to look cool, but I could tell nobody really knew him.'

I remembered my conversation with Charbonneau, and our initial suspicion that Crease had been a double agent. In retrospect the idea seemed ludicrous. It was ironic, however, that my worry for Kit had been based on fear of his involvement with bikers. I should have worried about Lyle Crease.

Kit worked a thread loose with his finger.

'Look, Aunt Tempe, I'm sorry for all the grief I've caused you.'

He swallowed, doubled back on his finger with the thread.

'The Preacher and those other guys are losers who can't even get it together to buy their own wheels.'

I'd already learned this from Claudel, but let him go on.

'I let you think they were big-ass bikers to make myself look cool. Instead I almost got you killed.'

'Kit, who was the man outside my condo?'

'I really, honestly don't know. He was probably some goof just passing by.' A grin teased the corners of his mouth. 'Maybe he was applying for a job at the place that cut your hair.'

I gently punched his good shoulder. This time I believed him.

'Hey, careful with the rough stuff. I'm an

invalid.'

He took a sip of juice and handed me the glass.

'What about that eyeball?'

'The police think the Vipers put it on my car to discourage further interest in their history.'

A pause. On-screen, a man mouthed the news while stock prices ticked by below.

'I think I'm going to look into school when I get back home. Try a few courses. See how it goes.'

'I think that's a wonderful idea, Kit.'

'You must think I'm about as dumb as a largemouth bass.'

'Maybe a perch.'

'I hope you don't give up on me.'

'Never.'

Embarrassed, he changed the subject.

'How's your boss?'

'Much better. He's starting to give the nurses a hard time.'

'I'm with him there. And Ryan?'

'Don't push it, fish brain.'

'How long do you think he'll be moonin' around here, expecting flowers and caramel clusters?' Harry stood in the doorway, a smile on her lips, a vase in her hand. Both were the same geranium red.

*   *   *

Leaving the hospital, I drove home, had dinner with Birdie, and began a series of household tasks. A return to normalcy by immersion in the mundane. That was the plan and it was working.

Until the doorbell chirped.

Dumping an armload of dirty sweaters, I glanced

366

at my watch. Eight-fifteen. Too early for Harry.

Curious, I went to check the security screen.

What the hell?

Sergeant-Detective Luc Claudel stood in my vestibule, hands clasped behind his back, weight shifting from the heels to the balls of his feet.

'So much for normalcy,' I muttered as I buzzed him in.

'*Bonsoir, Monsieur Claudel.*'

'*Bonsoir.* I apologize for disturbing you at your home, but there has been a development.' His jaw tensed, as though what he had to say was pushing him to the limits of civility. 'I thought that you should know.'

Courtesy from Claudel? In English? What now?

Birdie did a figure eight around my ankles, but offered no conjecture.

I stepped back and gestured the detective inside. He entered and waited stiffly as I closed the door, then followed me to the living room sofa. Settling into the armchair opposite, I remembered my conversation with Ryan's partner, Jean Bertrand, and the thought of Ryan brought the usual stomach clutch.

God, please let him be safe!

I pushed the thought aside and waited for Claudel to speak.

He cleared his throat and looked away from me.

'You were right about George Dorsey. He did not kill Cherokee Desjardins.'

There was a revelation.

'Nor did Lyle Crease.'

I stared at him, too surprised to respond.

'Shortly before her death Jocelyn Dion mailed a letter to her mother giving information about a

367

number of illegal biker activities. Among the subjects discussed were the shooting of Emily Anne Toussaint and Richard 'Spider' Marcotte, and the murder of Cherokee Desjardins.'

'Why did she do that?'

'Her motives were complex. First and foremost, she feared for her own life and felt the letter might confer protection. In addition, she was angry over Dorsey's murder, which, by the way, was ordered by his own gang. Jocelyn Dion was living with George Dorsey at the time of his death.'

I felt heat climb the sides of my neck, but did not let on what Jocelyn had said about Dorsey's death.

'Was Dorsey killed because he spoke with me?'

Claudel ignored the question.

'Dion also felt remorse for certain of her own actions, including the killing of Cherokee Desjardins.'

'What?' I blurted in astonishment.

'That is correct. Jocelyn Dion killed Desjardins.'

'But Jocelyn told me she heard Crease bludgeon and shoot him.'

'It seems your clerk was somewhat economical with the truth.'

He tented his fingers under his chin.

'According to the young lady's letter, she'd gone to Desjardins for drugs when Crease showed up, wanting the infamous barroom photo. The men argued, Crease knocked Cherokee unconscious with a pipe, then began ransacking the apartment. Hearing noises in the bedroom, he panicked and fled.

'It seems your Jocelyn had a big habit and a short budget. She went over there high on drugs, and saw the situation as an opportunity to stock her

368

medicine chest. When Crease left, she battered Desjardins' unconscious body, dragged it to a chair, and used a shotgun to remove his face.'

'Why bother to shoot him?'

'She didn't want Desjardins coming after her. Also, she was stoned, but sober enough to realize that she had to cover her tracks, so she made it look like a biker hit.' Claudel dropped his hands. 'On that point you were correct.'

More throat clearing, then he went on.

'Thinking it contained more pharmaceuticals, Dion retrieved a package Crease had dropped. It contained an old photograph of Crease and Desjardins. Later, she cooked up a blackmail scheme, figuring that if Crease wanted the picture badly enough to fight for it, he might be willing to pay.'

'In the meantime, the Heathens heard about my meeting with Dorsey and ordered his death.' Again the tension in my neck.

'Yes. Fearing for her own safety, Dion cooked up and floated the story that Crease had murdered Desjardins. The Vipers got wind and decided payback was due. Desjardins had been an Angel, his killer was an Angel dropout, despised by the brothers, and his killer had to die. Also, they had not settled the Spider Marcotte account, as far as they were concerned. They phoned New York for outside help, persuaded Dion to lure Crease to Dorsey's funeral, and decided they would settle several Heathen scores at the same time.'

A pause.

'It must have been Jocelyn who left the picture on my desk.'

'To throw suspicion toward Crease.'

369

I thought of something else.

'That's why Cherokee's blood was on that jacket.'

'For once the little lizard was telling the truth. The jacket belonged to Jocelyn, but Dorsey couldn't admit that if he wanted to protect her.'

'And meeting with me got him killed.' I bit down on my lip.

'Dorsey was killed because his brothers feared he was about to turn on them. Had it not been you, he'd have contacted someone else.'

I felt myself swallow.

'Do you believe Dion's letter?'

'Largely, yes. We'd already had reason to suspect Lecomte in the Marcotte-Toussaint murders. We are keeping him under close surveillance. The prosecutor feels that what you heard Dion scream as she was shot is not enough to arrest him now, but in time, we will know.'

'Undoubtedly Jocelyn was the leak at our lab.'

'She got the position there to spy for the Heathens, but wasn't averse to an occasional chat with the press.'

'When approved by the home office.'

'Yes.'

Claudel drew air through his nose, exhaled.

'These biker gangs are the mafia of the new millennium, and have tremendous power over those attracted to them. Jocelyn Dion was among those who feed at the bottom of the chain, the hookers, the pimps, the strippers, the petty street dealers. She probably needed clearance to take her mother to Sunday Mass.

'One rung up are the more successful entrepreneurs, the chop shop operators, the fences, the bar owners, those who are allowed to hang around because they wash dirty money or perform some service useful to the club. Climb higher and one finds the full-patchers who run their own drug cells. At the very top are men with links to cartels in Mexico and Colombia, and to their counterparts in gangs worldwide.'

I'd never seen Claudel so animated.

'And who are these degenerates who make their living off the weak? Most have neither the moral nor intellectual ability to complete a traditional educational process or function in an open market. They use women because, deep down, they fear them. They are uneducated, self-deluded, and, in many cases, physically inadequate, so they have themselves tattooed, create nicknames, and band together to reinforce their shared nihilism.'

He took a deep breath and slowly shook his head.

'Sonny Barger is in retirement, probably writing his autobiography. Millions will buy the book, and Hollywood will make a film. *The Wild Ones* will be romanticized anew, and the myth will deceive another generation.'

Claudel rubbed his face in his hands.

'And the flow of drugs will continue to our school yards, and to the ghettos of the hopeless.'

He shot his sleeves, straightened each gold cuff link, and stood. When he spoke again, his voice was hard as tempered steel.

'It is ironic. As the Angels carried out their slaughter at the cemetery, their opponents were sending forth assassins of their own. I do not know which of these subhumans killed George Dorsey, and I do not have the evidence to prove that

371

Lecomte shot Jocelyn Dion, Spider Marcotte, and Emily Anne Toussaint, but I will. One day I will.'

He looked me dead in the eyes.

'And I will not rest until this evil is driven from my city.'

'Do you believe that can be done?'

He nodded, hesitated, then, 'We will be a team?'

Without hesitation, I nodded back.

'*Oui.*'

CHAPTER FORTY

The next morning I slept late, went to the gym, then brought coffee and doughnuts home and shared them with my sister. When Harry left for the hospital, I phoned the lab. There were no anthropology cases, so I was free to reactivate the plan interrupted by Claudel's visit.

I soaked the sweaters, then launched myself full speed at the refrigerator. Items older than one month, I threw away. Ditto for anything that could not be identified.

My mood was better than it had been in weeks. Claudel had come around once again to admitting my value as a colleague. I was confident that he, Charbonneau, and Quickwater would pursue the investigation until the Dorsey and Dion killers were behind bars.

I had apologized to Martin Quickwater, and the man seemed to hold no grudge. He'd even smiled in my direction.

LaManche was recovering.

Savannah Osprey's murder had been resolved,

and her bones were heading to her family.

Katy would be home in two weeks. My nephew was going to be fine, in every sense of the word.

And my hair was showing signs of growth.

The only shadow in my life was cast by worry over Ryan's safety. He had broken cover to save my life, and I prayed that action would not cost him his. I hoped fervently it had not been another deadly decision.

Right perfection wrongly disgraced.

The line still brought tears to my eyes.

I knew Ryan couldn't contact me, and had no idea when I would see him again.

It didn't matter. I could wait.

I tossed a lump of old Cheddar into the garbage bag.

But it might take time.

Two jars of congealed jelly. Out.

I would definitely need that theme song.

I've got sunshine on a cloudy day . . .